HAPPY
ever
AFTER

HAPPY

ever

AFTER

JOANNE TRACEY

First published in Australia in 2018

by Joanne Tracey

https://joannetracey.com

Copyright © Joanne Tracey 2018

Print ISBN 978-0-6484533-2-1 | Kindle ISBN 978-0-6484533-1-4 | Epub ISBN 978-0-6484533-0-7

Cover design Christa Moffit of Christabella Designs

A catalogue record for this book is available from the National Library of Australia

For Grant and Sarah ... always ...

One

It was a Sunday in late May – one of those perfect Autumn days that Sydney does well – and I sat on the deck with my daughter, Ash, my husband, Neil, and his girlfriend, Vanessa – although after the age of twenty-something no one really has boyfriends or girlfriends, do they? They have partners or, as my mother used to refer to them, 'friends'. She always said the word as if there were quotation marks around it, implying that a great deal more than friendship was going on – which there usually was. Besides, Neil, at almost fifty-five, was way too old to have a girlfriend. Men of fifty-five had mistresses or lovers – although that hinted at something furtive and exciting. It would also imply that Neil and I were still together – which we weren't.

Ash and her fiancé, Reece, had wanted to get both sets of parents together to talk about the final arrangements for their wedding. With just under a month to go until the big day, there were plenty of details to discuss. I'd offered to host lunch and it hadn't occurred to me not to involve Vanessa, even though I'd never really liked her.

Now Reece had taken his parents home, and it was just the four of us sitting together, nursing coffees.

'Is your hens' night and kitchen tea all sorted?' Vanessa asked Ash.

'We're having a weekend away,' Ash said. 'Us girls are off to the Hunter Valley for spa and bubbles, and Reece and his friends are playing golf.'

Neil smiled indulgently. 'So it's not a night any more, but a weekend?'

'Things have changed since you and Mum did it. Did you guys even have a bucks' night?'

'We certainly did,' said Neil. 'But we ended up going out together. The wedding was organised so quickly thanks to you,' he smiled at Ash, 'that we didn't have a lot of time to mess around with the details.'

Ash grinned back. 'Well, you should have kept your hands to yourself until after you were married then, shouldn't you?'

I'd been four months pregnant with Ash when I walked down the aisle, a filmy empire-line dress covering my tiny baby bump.

'Yes, well,' said Vanessa, seeming keen to change the subject. 'What about your kitchen tea?'

'The girls want to go to one of those places that specialise in high teas, but I want to have it here on the deck. We can make it look fabulous, and Mum can do one of her huge spreads.'

I groaned inwardly. This was the first I'd heard of these plans.

Vanessa wrinkled her nose. 'Carbs and sugar? Are you sure? Won't you still be on your bridal diet? And your friends will all want to fit into their dresses too.'

A look of hurt swept across Ash's face. Vanessa's approval was important to her. Vanessa must have noticed because she rushed to mend the situation.

'Don't listen to me. I'm only thinking about how I'm going to fit into my dress. Your metabolism is so much better than mine.' She smiled at Ash, and all was suddenly right in my daughter's world again.

'Besides,' I added, 'if you can't fit into your wedding dress two weeks out from the wedding you have bigger problems than a few scones.'

Ash giggled. 'That's so true, Mum.'

'What are you going to do when Ash gets married and leaves for good, Kate?' Vanessa asked me. 'You must get lonely rattling around in this big house as it is.' She looked down at her empty coffee cup, a small smile playing around her mouth. 'I know it's a big thing after all these years, but maybe it's time you started dating?'

I looked across at Neil, who was saying nothing.

'Oh, I don't know,' I replied. 'Work keeps me very busy.'

'But you only work three days a week,' said Vanessa, and added in a teasing tone, 'I think you're looking for excuses, and I understand that. It can be really daunting to put yourself out there again, but you've done it with work. Going into a legal aid role and helping all those women must have been tough after so many years of being a stay-at-home mum.' She smiled at me. 'If you like I can help you put together an online profile. I have a number of friends who are doing online dating at the moment – with, I must admit, varying degrees of success. But you've got to be in it to win it, right?'

Seriously? Vanessa wanted to give me dating advice? I faked a smile but said nothing.

She was probably thinking that if I had a man of my own I wouldn't need Neil to help me with the maintenance of the house and yard. Despite our break-up, Neil was still my best friend. He came over every Saturday afternoon to mow the lawn, see to the pool, and fix whatever needed fixing. Quite often he'd stay for lunch and we'd talk about anything and everything – including Vanessa – just like two old friends would. It was all very happy families.

'Online dating sounds a bit dodgy, Katie. Are you sure you want to go there?' Neil's face showed concern.

Vanessa waved it away. 'It's fine. You simply set up safety mechanisms with your friends and have some rules in place. As long as someone knows who you're meeting and where, it's perfectly safe.' She smiled encouragingly. 'I could tell you some of the get-out-quick messages my girlfriends have used.'

'Mum doesn't have time to date until after the

wedding,' Ash said with a grin. 'I've made sure of that. Until then, it's all about me. After that – maybe it is time, Mum. Even if it's not dating, you need some sort of challenge at least.'

'Perhaps I do need something to get my teeth stuck into,' I said. 'With you gone, and Nathan up in Far North Queensland doing amazing things with corals and turtles and nudibranches –'

Vanessa choked on the water she was sipping. 'Nudie whats?'

'Nudibranches. They're like sea slugs, but come in amazing colours. One of Nathan's diver friends is putting together a phone app to identify them. "Pick that Nudibranch". That sort of thing.'

My and Neil's son, Nathan, was a marine biologist, and one of the few people who had very little time for Vanessa. He didn't trust her, and said her niceness was an act she was putting on until she got what she wanted. If it was an act, she'd sustained it for over three years now.

Ash was frowning. 'I thought Nath was monitoring coral bleaching and ocean temperatures and counting whales, not mucking around with snails and phone apps.'

'He is, but he's also helping them keep an eye on the sea turtle population,' I said. 'Did you know that only one turtle in a thousand makes it through to adulthood? They return to the beach they were hatched on to lay their own eggs. The more we can learn about –'

'Yeah, okay, Mum, we get the idea.' Ash shook her head and laughed. 'Besides, Vanessa and I are bored already.'

Vanessa smiled slightly.

'I keep telling Nath that he needs to quit chasing turtles and corals and get a real job,' Ash went on. 'He's never going to make any money doing what he's doing. And if he never makes any money, he's never going to meet a decent girl. He's still a good-looking guy, but his looks won't last forever and then he'll be a dried-up old academic who ends up with some sun-baked hippie who doesn't even shave her armpits.'

'Ashleigh!' I said. 'That's enough. Your brother has made his choices in life, and just because he has different priorities to you is no reason for you to ridicule him. What he's doing is making a difference – not just to us, but to your children and maybe even your grandchildren. He happens to believe in what he's doing and I don't think there's many of us who can honestly say that.'

Ash scowled, but Neil was grinning. 'There's no guessing where Nathan got his tendencies from, is there? Your mother had an opinion on everything when she was younger.'

'Yes, so you've told me,' Ash said. 'And it might have been fashionable then, but now? Even this job – coordinating legal advice for women who can't afford to pay for it – well, I have no idea what Reece's parents think about it.'

'Ashleigh!' This time it was Neil chastising our daughter.

'It's okay,' I said, rising to take the rest of the plates into the kitchen. When Vanessa stood to help me I waved at her to keep her seat. 'No, you stay there and talk to Ash.'

'I'll help clean up,' said Neil. 'No, don't argue. Besides,' he grinned, 'I'll leave these two to talk weddings.'

He brought the plates I wasn't able to manage into the kitchen, and helped me load the dishwasher. One thing I'd never been able to fault Neil on – he'd always helped around the house.

'I'm glad that's over,' I said, referring to Reece's parents. 'Susan and Derek are nice enough, but I always feel as though they're looking down their noses at us, and they think Reece is marrying below his class.'

Ash and Reece had been together since their final year of high school when they'd met through swimming training. There was an unwritten custom that the boys from Reece's exclusive school looked to their sister school to find partners for the end-of-year formal but Reece had stepped outside tradition and taken Ash to his formal. They'd been together ever since, despite, I suspected, Reece's parents' hopes that he'd grow out of his fascination with our daughter. But here they were, blissfully happy and about to be married.

'This whole idea of a big wedding is ridiculous,' I added. 'It would be so much easier if she'd done what I suggested and had one of those island weddings where all anyone has to do is turn up. I would have liked a holiday. I can't remember the last time I had one – probably when Mari's Caitlin got married in Bali, and that was before you left.'

I looked across at Neil and caught his poor attempt at a smile. I waited for him to defend Ash the way he usually did, making a joke of how she'd always been dramatic and liked a production, but he said nothing, just carried on stacking the dishes into the dishwasher as if it was a game of Tetris. He had the ability to fit more into the dishwasher than I could ever have dreamed of fitting. It was a talent.

As he worked, I studied him – there were more lines under his eyes than I remembered seeing a month or so ago. He looked tired.

'What's going on?' I asked.

He smiled. 'Typical Katie, why beat about the bush when you can blurt out a question.'

I shrugged one shoulder. 'You know me. And I know you. I'll ask again – what's going on? And don't bother fobbing me off with a "nothing". That might work with Vanessa, but it won't work with me.'

Rather than answer he turned his attention to the leftover pork. 'Do you want this in freezer containers?'

'Yes, please. Is it work?'

He nodded. 'Yes.'

'Is it serious?'

He nodded again.

'I see. Are we talking redundancy?'

He shook his head. 'They've told me they won't pay me out, but they do intend to push me out. Apparently I no longer fit the bank's preferred demographic.' He shrugged. 'I'm a middle-aged man who is being paid more than my boss. Nothing I can do will change any of those factors.'

After thirty-odd years with the same bank, Neil's salary was a function of annual pay rises and consistent performance rather than a meteoric rise to the top.

'Please tell me you got that in writing?' I said. Neil's grimace gave me my answer. 'No, I don't suppose you could be that lucky. Have they put you on performance management?'

'Not yet, but I'm failing one of my targets so I suspect that's coming. Then they'll give me three months to turn it around.'

'Or what?'

'Or they'll dismiss me.'

I gasped. 'For failing one target out of how many? They can't do that!'

He shrugged. 'It would appear they can. It's happened already to a few of my friends – men I came up through the ranks with. We're all of a similar age and apparently past our use-by date.'

He filled the sink with water and began washing dishes. Automatically I picked up the tea-towel and began drying. Through the kitchen window I could see Vanessa and Ash talking, their heads bent over Ash's phone.

'Have you told Vanessa?' I asked.

He shook his head, just once, but it told me all I needed to know. That he was worried, anxious and embarrassed.

'Okay,' I said. 'Maybe it's best that you don't tell her just yet.' I thought for a second – I'd recently advised a client with a similar problem. 'What I want you to do is start keeping a file on everything. Everything your boss says, every one-on-one meeting, and also everyone else's performance against the targets you're being managed on.'

He nodded, but didn't say anything.

'I'm serious, Neil. We need to start to control this.'

He smiled at me, not seeming to notice the "we" that had slipped out. 'I feel better for having told you, Katie. It's one of the things I always loved about you – the way you'd take a problem and organise it away for me. I sometimes thought that you enjoyed fighting my battles as much as you used to enjoy fighting for your causes.'

'It's just that I know how important your job is to you – how important it's always been.'

He gave a short laugh. 'It's not only my job.

Remember all those times you marched up to that school if you felt they'd told the kids something you didn't believe in?'

I returned his smile. 'Ash was always so embarrassed. Her friends' mothers didn't do things like that.'

'I know, but you taught our kids that it's okay to stand up and fight for something you believe in. Why do you think Nathan is doing what he's doing?'

Suddenly embarrassed at the personal turn of the conversation, I snuck another look out the kitchen window and met Vanessa's curious gaze.

'I think Vanessa's wondering what we're doing in here,' I said.

'I'm glad we talked, Katie,' he said again. 'I feel so much better about things now. I always do once I talk to you.'

Ash made her excuses soon after we'd finished clearing up, and left to meet up with Reece and some other friends.

'Thanks for lunch, Mum. It was great.' She leaned in and kissed my cheek. 'You're fine with having the kitchen tea here, aren't you?'

I smiled. 'Of course I am.'

'You know what your mother's like,' Neil said, flashing a grin at me. 'Always happy to feed people.'

'I'll see you in a couple of weeks then, Ash,' said Vanessa, standing to hug her. 'If your theme is high tea, I'll bring along some of those raspberry and vanilla macaroons from that French patisserie near my house.'

'Oh, would you? They'd look perfect on the table. Thanks, Vanessa.'

Listening to Ash's gushing thanks, anyone would think that Vanessa had offered to cater the entire event. I pushed the uncharitable thought aside and wrapped my cardigan more tightly around me. Despite it having been mild for this time of the year, the temperature was dropping now.

'Perhaps we should head into the kitchen,' I suggested. 'Did you guys want another coffee?'

I held my breath as I waited for their answer. Surely now that Ash had gone, they would too? I'd been up early this morning to prepare lunch and really wanted to sit down with a glass of wine and a book and relax for what was left of my Sunday.

'Thanks, Katie, that would be great,' said Neil.

He and Vanessa sat at the kitchen table while I bustled around with the coffee machine. Neither of them spoke so I ended up chattering to fill the uncomfortable silence.

'I don't suppose Ash mentioned how many people she's inviting to this kitchen tea?'

'No, she didn't,' said Vanessa.

More silence. As I placed their coffee cups in front of them, I surprised a look passing from Vanessa to Neil.

I raised my eyebrows and focused my gaze on

him. 'What?'

'Just tell her, Neil,' urged Vanessa.

Neil, god love him, looked anywhere but at me. It was so typical of him. When we were together it was always me who had to have the difficult conversations with the kids, his mother, the builder that needed pulling into line, the police officer threatening to give him a ticket. Neil hated conflict, and it used to frustrate me beyond belief when he'd refuse to talk about anything even vaguely uncomfortable. If I was angry and spoiling for a fight, Neil would stay silent. At the very most he'd say something like, 'I don't want to fight, Katie.' And he truly didn't. All he ever wanted was to keep the peace.

The problem was, his idea of keeping the peace also meant avoiding whatever uncomfortable subject he didn't want to address. And his reluctance to fight made little difference to me. I'd bait, and pick, and rip at the bandaid of silence that he'd attempted to put over the gaping wound, until he'd throw his hands up and walk out of the room. Invariably I'd be left steaming and pacing and wishing he'd just argue back, tell me what he thought, stand up for something. Stand up for us.

I wondered whether Vanessa yelled at him the way that I did. Or whether she didn't need to. Maybe that was why he was attracted to her – aside from her youth and perfect body. Maybe he'd left me because he wanted some peace and quiet.

I watched now as he shifted in his seat and wouldn't look at me. My heart skipped a beat, and then another. Whatever he had to tell me was serious.

'Come on, Neil,' I said. 'You're starting to worry me.' He lowered his head and the knot in my stomach moved higher. 'You're not sick, are you? Oh god, you are! What is it?'

Surely he couldn't be sick. He was fit and supremely healthy. He ran and cycled and worked out. He had biceps that he'd never had when we were together, and he and Vanessa avoided pasta and drank kombucha. But he was in his mid-fifties and that's when the risk factors for everything seemed to increase. What was the point of exercising to exhaustion and activating your almonds if it wasn't going to keep you alive?

Vanessa sighed loudly and shook her head. 'Oh, for goodness sake, Neil. Just tell her or I will.'

'What is it?' I turned to Vanessa. 'What's wrong?'

She glanced at Neil and shook her head slightly. 'Nothing's wrong, Kate. It's just that Neil wants a divorce.'

The relief that he wasn't sick rose from my heart in a little burst at exactly the same time that the realisation of what Vanessa had just said hit my brain and sent my stomach dropping to the floor.

Dealing with both emotions at the same time helped me keep the surprise I was feeling from showing on my face. Or was it horror? I didn't know.

I sat down carefully, sipped at my coffee – burning my tongue in the process – and made an attempt to corral all my thoughts into one part of my brain.

'Why now?' I said, and was proud of how calm I sounded.

Neil raised his eyes slowly, as if afraid of what he'd see on my face. I couldn't blame him. He, Ash and Nathan always said I was at my most frightening when I sounded calm, because it usually preceded an almighty thunderous storm. But he didn't need to worry. There was no way I was losing my composure in front of Vanessa.

'I think it's time, Katie.' As he spoke he opened his hands, as if pleading with me to understand. 'We've been apart for so long that we really should formalise it now. We both need to move on. You need to move on.'

Next thing he'd be telling me he was doing this for me.

'Are you planning on getting married again?' I asked. 'Is that why you want to do this now?'

He looked at Vanessa, then back down to his coffee cup, then back at me. 'No. That's not what this is about. I've – we've – made no plans to get married.'

It was the way he held my eyes unflinchingly that told me he was lying. My heart fell down to join my tummy.

I forced myself to smile at them both. 'Well, if you've no plans to get married any time soon, there's no need for us to rush through the divorce, is there? I don't want anything to cast a shadow on Ash's and Reece's big day – and I'm sure that you don't either – so how about we wait until after the wedding to start the proceedings.' I looked straight at him. 'After all, we've waited four years. What's another four weeks or so?'

Neil nodded and a look of relief passed across his face. Had he thought I'd rant and rave and make trouble for him? Possibly. I had when he'd announced that he was leaving. But that was four years ago.

'I agree,' he said. 'Nothing should get in the way of Ash's wedding. We'll get things moving when that's over.' He smiled into my eyes as if it was all settled and all the unpleasantness was over and done with.

Vanessa, however, wasn't done. She looked at Neil with exasperation, then turned to me. 'Kate, it's all very well leaving the divorce until after the wedding.' Did she even realise how ridiculous that sounded? 'But we can still sit down in the meantime and talk about the financial split. I'm sure it's something we can all agree on without too many issues, don't you? I don't think you'll need it, but I can refer you to a good solicitor if you do – much better than any of those Legal Aid guys you use for your women's shelter, or whatever it is. Not that there's anything wrong with them, of course. It's just that my guy will have both of your interests at heart.'

She smiled sweetly at me when she was finished. My eyes widened, and I saw Neil's gaze drop down to the table again.

I swallowed down the bile that had risen in my throat, and swallowed again as I felt the storm clouds within me begin to thunder. I gripped my coffee cup tighter with one hand – so tightly I was surprised it didn't break. My other hand rested on my thigh under the table, where I could ball it into a fist without either of them noticing.

I took a deep breath before speaking. 'Thank you for the offer, Vanessa, however *Neil* and I will sit down together to talk this through when we're ready to.' I gave her the same falsely sweet smile she'd given me. 'If we're unable to agree and decide that we need some legal assistance, we'll deal with that hurdle when we come to it.'

'But –' she started.

Neil had been watching me carefully and knew what that look on my face meant. Before she could finish her sentence he placed a hand on Vanessa's arm. 'Katie's right,' he said gently. 'She and I will sit down together to talk through the settlement details. While we both appreciate your help, this one really is between us.' His smile was a plea for her to say no more.

He looked back at me. 'Thanks for lunch, Katie, but I think it's time that we left. I'll call you during the week, okay?'

My teeth were gritted together as I nodded and stood for the customary farewell peck on the cheek.

As I saw them out, Neil hesitated in the doorway. 'Are you okay with this?'

'Why wouldn't I be? As you say, it's been four years. It's time.'

Then I went back into the kitchen, calmly picked up the coffee mug Vanessa had been drinking from, and threw it as hard as I could onto the hardwood floor. As it smashed into pieces I collapsed back into the chair and buried my face in my hands.

Two

'He wants a divorce,' I wailed down the phone to Lachie, my brother. He was always the first person I called when I had no idea what to do.

'Hello, Kitty, how are you?' he said.

'Okay, sure. Hello, Lachie, how are you?'

'I'm very well, thank you for asking. Now, what's this about a divorce? And, more importantly, why now? I thought Neil was happy with things as they are.'

'So did I. But instead he asks me – sorry, she asks me – for a divorce. Just a few weeks before Ash's wedding. The timing couldn't be worse. How do you stand in a church and watch your daughter say her forever vows on the happiest day of her life knowing that you've broken yours and the formal conclusion of your marriage is with lawyers?'

'Surely you don't need lawyers?' Lachie said. 'You two have managed this far without them.'

'Yes, but now that he wants the divorce he also wants to agree the financial settlement. She even offered to help me with the legals. Surely she knows that if I need legal help I'll go straight to Mike.' Mike was Lachie's husband, and also a lawyer. 'Although maybe I should just ask Vanessa – she seems to be the one running this particular show and she says she has my best interests at heart.' I knew I sounded bitter, but I couldn't help it.

'Now, now, little cat, put those claws away. What did you tell him?'

'Well, first I had to make sure that none of the surprise showed on my face – no easy feat, let me tell you. Then I asked him why he wants to do it now. He said he felt that it's time, that I needed to move on. Like he's doing this for me? I don't think so. Naturally I asked if he wanted to get married again, and he said he had no plans to – which of course isn't saying that he isn't. I knew it was a lie, which was also when I knew it was really over.'

'You mean the years of separation and living with another woman didn't give you a hint?'

'Ha ha. No, it's the first time in our entire relationship that Neil's ever lied to me. The first time, Lachie. Besides, they're not living together.'

'Surely he's told the little white lies we all tell?'

'Nope, not Neil. He's the most steadfastly honest man that I know. But he sat there and lied to me. It was how he looked me straight in the eye that gave it away. Neil doesn't do that – especially not in a conflict situation.'

'What did you do?'

'I played along. I told him that if there's no reason for him to rush the divorce through, then surely we could wait another four weeks, and I didn't want anything casting a shadow on Ash's day. That's when Vanessa brought up the financial settlement and I nearly lost it. What right does she have to discuss any of this with me? None of it is her business.'

'Well, you have invited her into your house and played happy families with the two of them for the last few years,' Lachie pointed out.

'Thanks for that. Seriously though, that made me so mad!'

'What exactly did she say?'

'Kate, we'll need to sit down at some point over the next couple of weeks and talk about the financial split. I'm sure it's something we can agree without too many issues, don't you?'

'Oh my fucking god! She said that?' Lachie sounded as outraged as I felt.

'Yep. And I smiled and thanked her for her help and told her that Neil and I would sit down and talk about it, and whether or not we needed legal help would be up to us. Somehow I managed to keep a straight face, but Neil must have known I was pissed off because he stopped her from saying anything else and they left soon after.' I paused, the fight suddenly gone from me. 'Can you believe that all these years of love and friendship have come to this?'

'No, Kitty, I can't. But if Vanessa is already looking at property settlements, you need to make sure that all your financial ducks are in a row.'

'But Neil said –'

'Kitty, Vanessa is young and she's ambitious. If they want to get married, it's for one reason only – because her hormonal clock is going tickety-tock. You might think you can trust Neil, but can you really when he has a hot thirty-something in his bed pressuring him to make full financial allowance for her and any children they might have?'

Lachie was a similar age to Neil, and had often wondered how it was that a woman as young, lovely and intelligent as Vanessa could really fall for him. Even though Neil was fit and still quite attractive for a man of his age, he wasn't the rich, flashy type that you'd expect to attract someone like Vanessa. Aside from being physically perfect – five foot ten when she didn't have her heels on, with a size ten body and perfect breasts – she was also a physiotherapist. Gorgeous, smart and ambitious.

'Neil doesn't want any more children,' I said.

'He might not have any say in the matter. Your responsibility is to make sure your children's inheritance isn't impacted by this. As I said, you need to start getting your finances in order. Do you understand me?'

'I do, but I have no idea where to start.'

'Of course you do. What do you tell the women who come in to see you at the centre?'

I worked as a liaison officer for a community initiative specialising in women's issues. The service we offered was a valuable one – even if I was paid just the minimum wage. We were there to help women when they were at their most vulnerable and unable to think straight – when their marriage had broken down, or if they were single parents and having problems with workplace harassment, if they had no idea where to turn and no financial means of hiring someone to assist them. We had solicitors and accountants on the books who took the cases as part of their pro bono work. If the women needed emotional support to visit banks, we did that too. I'd started in the role not long after Neil began dating Vanessa, and it had given me a purpose that had been missing in my life until then, along with the satisfaction of knowing that the work I did was making a difference to someone's life.

'I tell them to get together all their bank statements,' I said, 'and to make sure they know what property and accounts they have, and we start from there.'

'And that's the same advice you need to give yourself,' Lachie said. 'It's fortunate that I can help with the finance part.'

'Thanks, Lachie. I know I couldn't be in better hands.'

'You're very welcome, my dear. We'll talk during

the week, hey?'

I'd no sooner poured yet another medicinal glass of red wine when my phone rang again. This time it was Neil.

'Hey, Katie, I'm sorry we threw that on you today. I just thought we should probably start talking about it.'

I took a deep breath and a swig of wine. The wine gave me courage to say what I needed to say.

'You're right, we should start talking about it – you and me, not you, me and Vanessa. I know she's part of your life, but this is between us. Her involvement in our property doesn't start until she's married to you.'

There was silence for a second. Then Neil said, 'I know, and I'm sorry. It won't happen again. I've told her that.'

I raised my eyebrows. He must have known I was angry to have risked that sort of confrontation with Vanessa. I wondered if he'd ever confronted her about anything before. No, Kate, that's unfair.

'Okay,' I conceded. 'We can talk about it later.'

'There's no rush you know. We – I – just thought we should probably get the ball rolling.'

'You're right, Neil. We should. After the wedding.'

'Yes, we'll do nothing until after the wedding.'

We hung up, and I drained my wine, reached for the bottle to pour another and quickly drained it too. It wasn't until I was midway through the third glass that I acknowledged what was at the base of my anger. Betrayal. The whole time that Neil and I had been talking in the kitchen about his job and what we could do to save it, working through his problem in the way we used to do when we were still together, there'd been no hint of what was to come, what he knew he had to tell me.

I supposed I'd thought that we'd remain the best of friends, getting on better than we had in our last few years together. Now, with divorce looming, I felt our relationship had been dragged back to how it was when he first left.

Three

When I turned forty and told Neil that I wanted us to travel, to see the world and have adventures together, he wasn't interested. His job was stressful, and now wasn't the right time to ask for annual leave, he said. He needed the downtime that home offered.

What about everything we'd talked about and dreamed of, I'd asked. There was plenty of time for all that, he'd replied. The adventures could wait until we retired. Until then, we had my parents' holiday house down the south coast that we could use.

Every so often I'd rant and rave and stomp around the house, waving my hands and complaining that we never did anything together.

'Why can't we go away like we used to?' I'd ask.

Neil would raise his head from his book and say, 'That was when we needed a break from the kids.'

'What about needing a break from our lives? Isn't there anything you want to do?'

'Not really. All I want is for you to be happy. If you're bored, why don't you go back to work now that the kids have finished school? Just two or three days a week – it'll give you something to do.'

So I did. I took a part-time job as a teacher's aide at the local primary school that Nath and Ash had gone to. It kept me busier, but it didn't quash the restlessness. The vague feeling that there was more to life than this. There had to be … didn't there?

I couldn't tell Neil any of that. Although we talked about almost everything else, we didn't talk about how we felt. I couldn't tell him that I thought I'd lost myself; that I'd compromised more than just the future I'd originally planned. I couldn't tell him that now the kids were grown-up I no longer had a purpose or a reason. The fire that used to burn in my belly had gone out and left a gaping hole of nothingness and a hunger that no amount of food or wine could quell. Neil was happy with the way things were. How could he be so satisfied when I was exactly the opposite? How could he not know how dissatisfied I was?

I couldn't tell him that I craved kisses like the ones we used to share – long, drugging moments of kissing just for the sake of kissing. I couldn't tell him that I wanted spontaneous sex, the sort of sex where he'd sneak up behind me and grind himself into me, where he couldn't keep his hands off me, where we'd have sex wherever and whenever just because our desire for each other was so strong. The sort of sex that we'd never seemed to have. There were the stolen moments when we were first together, but since then it had always been in the marital bed after the kids had gone to sleep, each of us knowing how to get the other off while making the least amount of noise and utilising the least amount of energy. Over the last few years even that had dwindled into nothingness. I didn't know whether Neil could no longer be bothered asking for it or whether he was no longer interested in me. What if that was it, the end of my sex life as I knew it? What if I never experienced that rush ever again?

But you don't leave a marriage out of boredom, or routine or non-existent sex, do you? You leave because of cruelty and neglect and affairs – and Neil had never been cruel or neglectful, and had never had an affair. He couldn't have said the same about me. I'd come a little too close for comfort to an affair – not that Neil knew about it. I'd very nearly stepped over the brink – no one would have known, and it would have been just sex – but the thought of the guilt afterwards, the history I'd be throwing away, the trust I'd be destroying, held me back. Besides, I loved Neil and he loved me. I couldn't do that to him.

When Neil announced that he was going to hike to Everest Base Camp, I didn't believe it at first. He'd just turned fifty and up until now his idea of exercise was mowing the lawns and coming inside complaining about having raised a sweat. He wasn't the type of man who went to the gym or jogged. He'd never really played any team sports and he didn't even watch sport on TV. Other than Brett, who he'd known since school, Neil's friends were the husbands of our friends. He wasn't into afternoons at the pub with the boys, or long weekends away doing whatever men did on those weekends. He was perfectly content to spend his weekends at home, and was at his happiest with his head in a book.

That's why I'd laughed when he'd said he was doing the hike because he wanted to push himself out of his comfort zone. I'd honestly thought he was joking. Next he'd be telling me that he needed to find himself. But he wasn't joking.

'I'm serious,' he said. 'I really feel like I need to challenge myself. Somewhere along the way I feel that I've got lost.'

'What about me?' I said. 'Can't I come too?'

A sad look had come over his face. 'I'm sorry, Katie, this is something I need to do on my own. Besides, we both know that climbing a mountain isn't your idea of a good time.'

He'd smiled when he said that, but it didn't make me feel any better.

'How do you know? It could be?'

He shook his head. 'This will be a good opportunity for us both to have some space, work out what we really want. You can go and visit Nathan in California if you want, or see Ash in London.'

Nathan was doing his postgraduate degree in Berkeley, which was apparently the place to study earth and marine sciences; and Ash was in London on a gap year from her arts degree, doing, from what I could understand, as little as possible.

'How long will you be away for?' I asked.

'Four weeks.'

'That's not really long enough to do anything in,' I said.

I knew I sounded like a petulant child, but I'd thought I had a right to feel resentful. I'd been the one pressing for the holiday and Neil was the one taking it.

'It's up to you, Katie,' he said. 'But I'm doing this.'

'When are you going?'

'April next year. That'll give me six months to train and make the preparations I need to make.'

'So it's a done deal then?'

'Yes, it is,' he said firmly. Once Neil had made a decision, there was no swaying him from it. 'This will be good for both of us,' he added.

I'd nodded and pretended I was okay about it, but I wasn't. Since when did he get to go off and find himself when I was the one who'd been feeling so incredibly empty inside?

Neil attacked his training with a passion I hadn't seen in him since our early days together. He was up at dawn each morning for a walk. The walk became a jog and then a run. On weekends he'd take himself off to one of the national parks around Sydney for a longer hike. He began shopping at outdoor stores and came home with hiking boots, water pouches, thermal underlayers and pants with pockets in the legs.

In November, when my parents died in a car accident on their way home from their holiday house on the south coast, Neil supported me through my grief, but it didn't interrupt his plans. He was still heading to the Himalayas in April.

When I dropped him at the airport and kissed him goodbye, I told myself that I didn't care, that I was looking forward to the time alone, but when he held me close and I breathed in his familiar scent, my throat closed up. I couldn't breezily send him on his way.

Instead I mumbled into his jacket, 'Please be safe, Neil. I love you.'

He pulled back so he could look into my eyes. His were glistening in the same way that mine were. 'I love you too, my Katie. I always have and I always will.'

And then he was gone.

I told myself I was looking forward to having the house to myself; the bed to myself with no snoring husband to disturb my already disturbed peri-menopausal sleep. For the first time in my adult life I had a whole four weeks where I could do whatever I wanted whenever I wanted. What could be wrong with that? I was going to relish this time, I truly was. It would be bliss. But after sleeping beside him every night for over twenty years, my foot automatically reached out to touch the back of his calf in bed. The house without him was too quiet, and despite our arguments over the remote control I found there was nothing on television that I wanted to watch.

I missed having him there each evening to talk through the day with. While we were preparing dinner, I'd pour myself a wine and he'd open a beer and we'd cook and talk and catch up. We'd talk some more when we were eating – always at the table, always with some music playing in the background, always with a glass of wine. There was a sameness and structure to our life that I'd taken for granted, and couldn't replicate when he wasn't there.

At first I cooked meals that I knew Neil hated, and sat on my own at the dining table to eat, playing my choice of music. By the end of the first week, I was balancing a bowl of soup on a tray in front of reality TV. The nights out with friends that I'd envisaged didn't happen – everyone was too tied up with work and family. I was the only one whose children had both flown the coop and whose husband had done the same. Invitations to dinner from our friends dried up. 'We'll get together when Neil's back,' they said. Nobody seemed to want to invite just Kate.

Neil had been right in one respect: the time apart did show me what it was that I wanted. Him.

Somehow I needed to push away the restless urges and be content with our life as it was. Aside from that insatiable restlessness and the vague feeling that there had to be something more, I had no real reason for even contemplating wanting out. What Neil and I had was so much more important than urgent can't-wait-to-tear-your-clothes-off sex against the back of a door. That sort of passion quickly burned out and what would I be left with then? Somebody I didn't really like.

Neil and I had a history together, a friendship; we had two wonderful children we were proud of. Nothing else mattered. Once he was back, I'd show him that. I'd put all the madness of my early forties into a box marked *Never to be opened again*, and I'd concentrate on being grateful for the wonderful life I had now.

The day before Neil was due home, I planned a special dinner. I'd do the tarragon chicken dish that he liked so much, but rather than making it casserole-style as usual, I'd pour the creamy mushroom and tarragon sauce over a roasted chicken breast. For dessert I'd bake his favourite little orange cakes, and serve them on custard with warm orange butter sauce spooned over the top. Even though I'd tell him I'd missed him, he'd know I really meant it as soon as he sat down at the table.

I couldn't stop the tears when I saw him walk into the arrivals hall, his backpack still on his back. He looked gaunt, his cheeks hollower than when he'd left, but when he saw me his smile smoothed out the lines on his face. He put down his backpack and hugged me hard and I knew that everything would be fine. Neil had come home to me.

'I've missed you so much,' I said into his chest.

'I've missed you too, Katie,' he said and held me more tightly. I felt him kiss the top of my head.

In the car he was quiet. I put it down to exhaustion and caught him up on the details of what had been happening at home and the conversations I'd had with each of the kids.

'Reece has turned up in London to be with Ash,' I said.

'I wonder what his parents think about that,' Neil said. 'I thought they'd agreed to no contact while Ash is in London.'

'I have no idea what his parents think, but there's not a whole lot they can do about it given that Reece and Ash are both twenty-three. Ash seemed very happy when we Skyped the other night. She's still staying the whole year, but Reece could only get four weeks off work so they're going to do some travelling while he's there.'

'That makes sense.'

'How was it?' I asked after we'd travelled another few minutes in silence. 'The hike, I mean?'

'Hard. Intense. So much better and worse than I expected it to be.'

We were travelling over the Harbour Bridge and he gazed out the window rather than looking at me.

'You made it though.'

'Yes. I made it.'

I took a quick sideways glance at his face. It was expressionless.

'Are you okay, Neil? You're not injured or anything? No altitude sickness?'

He turned to look at me then. 'No, I'm fine. I'm sorry, it was a long flight and it's been a long trek to get home. I'm just tired.' He smiled weakly. 'What I'm really interested in is what's for dinner. I feel like I haven't eaten properly since I left.'

'I thought that might be the case, so we're having tarragon chicken and little orange cakes.'

'With the orange butter sauce?'

'Of course.'

'Aaah,' he sighed. 'My favourite.'

'I know,' I said smugly.

He went straight upstairs for a rest when we got home, and I emptied his backpack into the washing machine – although I was sure that if I'd just left it on the laundry floor and opened the zip some of his clothes could have walked into the machine themselves.

He was quiet during dinner, but made all the right noises of appreciation. It wasn't until after we'd finished dessert and I'd made us both a coffee that he spoke about what was on his mind.

'I did a lot of thinking while I was away,' he started hesitantly.

'So did I. In fact –' I stopped mid-sentence when I saw the look on his face. His eyes were screwed shut and he rubbed absently at his forehead. 'Sorry, you continue,' I said.

He opened his eyes and met mine for a heartbeat before dropping them again and sighing. 'I don't know how to say this.'

My tummy dipped as if I'd driven over two hills quickly and it hadn't caught up. A feeling of pure dread rushed through me. 'Just say it then.'

He swallowed hard and took a deep breath. I could see a little pulse beating in his jaw.

'As I said, I've been doing a lot of thinking while I was away and I've decided that we need to take a break.'

'What?' Did he just say what I thought he'd said?

'I'm moving out.'

'But …' I shook my head as if it might jumble the words he'd said into a different order that made sense. 'Why? Is there someone else?'

He turned his coffee cup around and around on the coaster until I wanted to scream at him to stop it. 'No,' he finally said. 'There's no one else. It's just that we've grown apart. We've changed.'

I laughed, but it was harsh-sounding. 'Next you'll be telling me that we want different things. That even though you still love me, you're just not in love with me.'

He didn't smile, but he did look at me at last. 'It's true. We do want different things, and I do still love you. It's just that these last few years it's been like living with my best friend, not my wife.'

'You mean the best friend who washes your clothes, cleans your house and cooks your dinner? I don't have a best friend like that.' My voice was rising but I couldn't seem to help it.

He closed his eyes briefly as if to gather his thoughts. 'I didn't mean it like that. I just meant that we've grown stale. We've had some great years together, but I think we're done.' He reached for my hand and I pulled it away. 'You know I'm right, Katie. You can't tell me there haven't been times over the last few years when you haven't thought about it.'

I opened my mouth to argue with him, and shut it just as quickly. I couldn't lie. I had thought about it. I'd even got as far as fantasising what life would be like as a single woman. I'd travel to places Neil had no inclination to go to – like India and Morocco. I might even go back to university. I'd be able to fall in love again, to feel that rush of the new, the passion, the thrust. But then I'd woken up to myself and realised that what we had together was worth more than all the travel in the world. It hadn't occurred to me that the whole time I was trying to hide my cravings from Neil, he'd had the same concerns.

'I know you haven't been happy,' he said, 'and

nor have I. I didn't realise how stuck I'd been feeling until I went to Everest. That experience taught me that sometimes to find your true purpose you have to do something that scares you and makes you uncomfortable. I was scared every day up there. My body felt broken, I was sick from the bad food and no air, and I didn't see hot water and soap for days – but I felt as though I was free. I hadn't felt like that in years.'

'You're saying I trapped you?'

'No, I'm saying we trapped each other. We've been content and safe in our marriage, but we've also been holding each other back. I know you're not satisfied doing what you're doing. You always wanted more from life than that – and so do I.'

'Take a break then,' I cried. 'Take three months and go climb another mountain. I don't know – even sleep with someone else if this is about sex. Heaven knows you're not doing it with me! But don't break our marriage. We're good together, you know we are. We have plans. We're going to retire and move to the country and run a bookshop together. It's what we always dreamed of, remember? What about that and the other adventures we're going to have when you finally retire? Don't tell me now that all the sacrifices I made for your job – that we made for your job – were for nothing.'

He nodded sadly. 'We are good together and that's what makes this so hard. I do love you, Katie – I always have and I imagine I always will. That's not going to change when we separate. But love changes, and that's what's happened to us. We've grown in different directions. I know you so well, and these last few years it's felt like you're burying what you want under more and more layers. At some point that's going to blow, and when it does it could destroy us all. We have a chance to finish this before it ends badly, while we're still friends and still care about each other.'

Understanding the logic of what he was saying made no difference to the way I felt about it. How dare he take action when I'd discounted it for fear of hurting him? What gave him the right to make that decision now for me?

I screamed and cried and ranted at him, but he'd made up his mind and wasn't going to be swayed. That night he slept in the guest room, and I stared at the ceiling in our bedroom. He might have been just down the hall, but it felt as though he were a million miles away.

By the end of the week, he'd moved out – not far, just a couple of suburbs away to our investment apartment in Wollstonecraft near the city. We'd bought it just before he went away with the inheritance I'd received from Mum and Dad, and I hadn't even set foot in it. The idea was for it to provide us with an income when Neil finally retired. Now it was a symbol of our separation.

~

The first weekend after he moved out, he came back to mow the lawn and prune the camellia hedges. I stayed inside so I didn't have to speak to him. He waved when he saw me watching him from the kitchen window, but I didn't wave back.

On the fourth weekend, I left a cold drink on the table on the deck for when he'd finished. And on the fifth, I invited him inside.

'I'm sorry, Katie,' he said. 'I truly am.'

'I know. So am I.'

The tears I'd been holding in since he left rushed out of me in one strong burst. He held me as I cried. When I looked up into his face, his eyes were wet too.

After that we talked; really talked in a way that we hadn't in years. Of course I didn't tell him how close I'd come to ruining everything, but other than the almost-affair I shared how I'd been feeling too.

'What happens now?' I asked. 'Do we do the divorce thing?'

He shook his head. 'There's no reason why we need to, is there? I don't see the point unless one of us decides that we might want to marry again. I'll continue to pay the mortgage on the apartment, maintain this house and put money into the joint account for you. Nothing needs to change.'

He rang me most days, and called by every weekend to look after the house and the garden. He even fixed things that I'd been asking him to fix for years. We talked more than we had when we were together, but at the end of the conversation he hung up or went back to his apartment. It was all so deeply, heartbreakingly sad, but I told myself that in some ways the only difference was that I was cooking for one and sleeping alone.

Every so often the anger I'd felt when he left came back and I'd find myself yelling at him, demanding to know who she was, who he'd left me for.

He'd hold me until my shaking had stopped, then say gently, 'There's no one else, Katie. It just wasn't working any more, and we're both young enough to find something else that does.'

None of my friends understood it. 'He has someone else,' they said. 'You just don't know about it yet.'

My best friend, Mari, was particularly disbelieving. 'Women might leave a marriage for reasons other than sex, but men don't. They need to have a Plan B lined up. You just don't know who she is yet. Do you think he knew about …?'

'Of course not,' I snapped. 'Besides, nothing happened. And I'd know if he had someone else – he's never been able to lie to me.'

Mari made her sceptical face – her eyebrows went so high they almost disappeared into her proudly grey curls, and her mouth twisted sideways – but resisted the urge to say more.

To the rest of the world, we were being incredibly civilised. Neil's best friend, Brett, said, 'How can we pick sides if you guys are being so reasonable? Where are the court battles, the solicitor's costs, the recriminations?'

I did notice, however, that the invitations stopped coming. No one really believed that our separation was as amicable as we'd made it out to be, so they avoided asking us over for dinner together – presumably in case the evening deteriorated into a nasty slanging match – and seemed to feel uncomfortable inviting one without the other. Even then I didn't really feel lonely. Neil was always at the other end of the phone, or sitting at my kitchen table. We still had each other; we just weren't living together.

As much as the death of my parents had been a terrible shock, I was grateful that I didn't have to explain our separation to them. It was difficult enough attempting to talk to Neil's parents about it. We did it together, calling over one Sunday afternoon about six weeks after Neil had moved out. They were, quite simply, perplexed.

'But if you don't have anyone else, son, why upset the apple cart?' his father, Dave, asked, shaking his head. 'Mo and I don't know why you've done this.'

I smiled the pretend smile that I'd been practising. 'It's a little tough to understand, but we've decided that we're better apart at the moment.'

Neil's mother, Maureen, looked confused. 'I didn't know there was a problem between you. What do we tell people?'

It was at the tip of my tongue to say that it was no one else's business, but Neil placed a calming hand on my shoulder.

'You don't need to tell them anything, Mum,' he said. 'We're still friendly, and I'll still be at all the family things. It's just that we've decided to live apart.'

'Well, I don't understand it,' Maureen said.

Neil's sisters cornered him and demanded to know the name of the woman who had come between us.

'Why would you leave Kate for someone else?' Libby said. 'You two have loved each other forever. She's done nothing wrong and this isn't fair on her.'

'There isn't anyone else and I still love her. We've just grown apart.' I could hear the weariness in Neil's voice but had no sympathy.

'And what about Kate? Have you considered how she must be feeling?' Leanne said. 'It's not as if she's even looked at another man the whole time that you two have been together.'

'Of course I've thought about how Kate is feeling. I've thought about nothing else. You think this was a spur-of-the-minute thing? That one day I woke up and decided I didn't want to be married any more?'

Neil rarely lost his temper, but his voice was rising now – as was a sob that had lodged itself in my throat.

Libby noticed my discomfort and shot a warning look at her sister. 'You know, this is really none of our business. It's between Neil and Kate.'

'Of course it's our business,' Leanne said. 'Kate's part of our family.'

'And she'll continue to be part of our family,' said Libby softly. 'Just because our brother's decided to be a dick doesn't mean that we need to lose Kate. Does it, Neil?'

'No, of course not.' Neil looked desperately to me for support. 'This isn't something we've done lightly, is it, Katie?'

'No, it's not,' I said, even though I was tired of pretending it was a decision we'd come to jointly when it absolutely wasn't.

I said as much to Lachie when I broke the news to him and Mike.

'I don't get it,' Lachie said. 'How can Neil decide that he still loves you but he doesn't want to be married any more? Is this something that happens when you turn fifty? If so, I'd better warn Mike.'

Lachie would be fifty himself the following year. He looked at Mike, who smiled gently back at him.

'I think you and Mike are safe,' I said. 'It's only my life that's falling apart.' My voice caught on the last word.

Lachie put his arms around me and held me while I cried.

'Is there any chance of him changing his mind?' Mike asked. 'Do you think it's a phase? I've heard it can happen to some guys – like the male menopause.'

I smiled and shook my head. 'No. He's done. At first I thought it was one of those "I just need to find myself moments", so I offered him some time out in case he wanted to go and climb a mountain somewhere again.'

'Wasn't that what Everest was supposed to be about?' Lachie said. 'None of this sounds like the Neil I know.' My brother had known Neil almost as long as I had.

'I know. But he says Everest showed him that we both deserve to live with more passion in our lives. He told me I need to find my true purpose, and that isn't going to happen while I'm stuck in my comfort zone with him.'

'He blamed you for this?' Mike said, pausing in his decision about which wine bottle to open.

'Maybe it is my fault,' I said. 'Maybe he did know about that almost thing and this is payback.'

Lachie gripped my shoulders. 'No, Kitty, don't think like that. This is his decision. Get angry, sob uncontrollably, throw things, but don't blame yourself. You did nothing wrong. Okay?'

'Are you sure about that?'

'Yes, I am. This is all about Neil. This is Neil's decision. Do you understand?' His eyes bored into mine as if he was willing me to absorb what he'd said.

He didn't let go of my shoulders until I nodded. 'I understand.'

As for telling the kids? Neil and I made the Skype

calls together.

'Did you have an affair, Mum?' Ash demanded. She'd always been a daddy's girl.

'Ash, this is nobody's fault,' Neil said. 'We really have just grown apart.'

'People only say that when they're seeing somebody else and don't want to talk about it,' Ash said sulkily.

'There's no one else involved,' he said. 'I'm sorry, Ash, but this isn't about you or Nathan. It's about us. You guys have your own lives; now it's time for us to live ours.'

His tone was firm.

'But surely you don't have to split up?' she said. 'Can't you just go off and climb something else? Or can't Mum find some cause to absorb herself in? Surely Nathan has some turtles that need saving or something?'

'It's not as simple as that,' Neil said.

'What about you, Mum? Do you agree with this? Oh, don't tell me, this is your idea, isn't it, and Dad's just pretending to be okay about it?'

I felt my eyes welling again.

Neil saw and gripped my hand. 'Actually, Ash, your mum isn't completely used to the idea yet.'

'This is what you want?' she said. 'I don't believe that. I love you, Dad, but let's face it – other than Everest, you've never done anything that Mum hasn't organised.'

'Not this time,' Neil said.

Nathan's reaction was different. He listened to

what Neil had to say, then said to me, 'I'm sorry, Mum. Do you need me to come home? I can, you know, if you need me to.'

'Thanks, Nath, but I'm alright. Sad.' I looked at Neil and smiled weakly. 'Very sad. But when you think about it, we had a pretty good run. No one could say we didn't give it a good go.'

He nodded. 'I suppose.' Then added, 'There'd better not be anyone else, Dad. I get that there probably will be at some point, but for now show Mum a little respect, hey?'

'I've always shown your mother respect.' Neil sounded upset.

'I know, but especially now. It's not a free pass for you to go and shag anything that moves.'

'Nathan!' I chided.

'I know, I'm sorry, but it needed to be said. Dad also needs to understand that this means you're free to date too.'

'I do understand that, Nath,' Neil said. 'It will be hard to sit back and watch, but I'll understand.'

At the time, I wondered whether he would understand. I also wondered which of us would be the first one to replace the other.

I didn't have to wonder for long.

We'd been separated for about six months when Neil told me about Vanessa. It was a Saturday afternoon in November and he'd dropped around to mow the lawns for me. As he often did these days, he stayed for some lunch – a pot of Thai-style pumpkin soup that I'd shredded some leftover chicken into and served up with sourdough. He seemed distant, but I knew his work had been particularly difficult of late so I decided to let him eat and see if that prompted him to talk.

Neil had a habit of digging his head into the sand and pretending that whatever was wrong wasn't happening. Usually by the time he talked to me about it, it had become a real problem – and also my problem to solve so he could go back to pretending it didn't exist. Over the years I'd come to recognise the signs, which was one of the reasons why his leaving had taken me so much by surprise. I hadn't seen that one coming at all. He'd kept it to himself until he'd found the courage to talk to me – by which time it was already decided.

'Katie,' he said as he swirled the remains of his coffee around in its mug. 'I'm seeing someone.'

'What do you mean?' I knew what he meant but I needed him to spell it out.

'I'm dating.'

'I see.' The pain in my heart came from nowhere, and I struggled to stop it showing in my face. Instead I picked up our lunch plates and took them across to the sink. 'What's her name?'

'Vanessa. She's a physiotherapist.'

I spooned the leftover soup into plastic containers

for the freezer. It was full of such containers – easy dinners for one. I enjoyed cooking and saw no reason to let my standards slip just because I had no one else to eat with. It was one of the reasons I enjoyed Neil's visits on a weekend – it gave me someone else to feed. I supposed that would change now he had Vanessa.

'How did you meet her?'

I still couldn't look at him. If I did I'd cry, and I didn't want him to feel bad about me feeling bad. Although, I reminded myself, it was his fault that I was feeling bad.

He hesitated for just a second too long. Long enough for me to anticipate his answer.

'Neil, how long have you known her?' I asked.

'It's not like that,' he said.

That's when I knew. If he hadn't actually been having an affair with her when he left me, he'd definitely had it in mind.

'How long have you known her?' I asked again.

'I met her on the Everest hike, but it's not what you think.'

'And what exactly am I thinking?' I gripped the side of the sink to stop me from throwing something at him.

'You're thinking that's why I left you, and it isn't. You know it isn't.'

'I thought I knew,' I said.

'I met her at Base Camp, but nothing happened, not then. I met her again through the gym. She was giving a talk about easing back into marathon-running after injury.'

I'd taken comfort in the belief that Neil was different from every other husband who'd left his wife. He didn't have a Plan B, he wasn't having an affair, and he didn't have an affair in mind. I'd been prepared for another woman to come into his life eventually. What I wasn't prepared for was finding out the other woman had been in his life when we were still together.

Even if they hadn't slept together then, there was no doubt in my mind that Neil had wanted to. People bonded over experiences as intense as the Everest Base Camp hike. I imagined the two of them together at night after having hiked all day, possibly a little befuddled by the lack of fresh food and a touch of altitude sickness. Maybe it started with some idle conversation and moved into flirting. Maybe he spoke to her about our problems and she sympathised with him. Perhaps he saw something in her that he hadn't seen in me for a very long time – passion and purpose, a willingness to push herself out of her comfort zone. I wondered if they'd spoken about me, about our marriage, if he'd complained that I wasn't content and always pushing him, about how we hadn't made love in a very long time, how we'd both stopped asking for it, how we loved each other but were no longer in love with each other, that I was prickly and selfish and – I stopped myself there. None of those thoughts were helping.

Neil was sitting at the kitchen table looking miserably at where his bowl had been. I'd been kidding myself that this no-man's land of separation could continue in the way it had been. Our marriage was over. Neil had left; and now, it seemed, he had someone else in his life. What happened next – how we would communicate with each other at our children's weddings, the births of our grandchildren, and other family triumphs and disasters – would all come down to what I said now. I could give in to my pain. Or I could remember that, underneath it all, I still wanted him to be part of my life – of our lives.

I swallowed hard and got two mugs from the cupboard. 'Okay, I'll put the kettle on, and you can tell me all about her.'

Four

Ash called on Wednesday night to go through the arrangements for her high tea on the weekend. Luckily her vision and mine were aligned.

'I want it to feel like a woodland tea party,' she said. 'Everything pretty but nothing matching. You know what I mean, don't you?'

'I think so. It's lucky I have a cabinet full of china just waiting for an excuse like this.'

She laughed. 'That's what I was thinking. And when Vanessa said she'd bring those pink and white macaroons – well, that got me thinking that it would be great if all the food was in a similar colourway, like strawberries and cream. I'm thinking a sponge with strawberry jam and cream, scones with raspberries, maybe the louise cake you make with the meringue topping – that sort of thing. Perhaps some little choux buns with lemon curd filling. I don't suppose you know how to get that crackle top on the choux?'

Typical. Vanessa offered to drop by a shop for some macaroons and all of a sudden the whole tea party was designed around them. I gritted my teeth and told Ash it sounded mostly doable – with the exception of the crackle-topped choux.

'I'm sorry, darling, but I won't have time to muck about filling choux buns and making little red sable biscuits to melt over the top.'

She laughed. 'I know I've put a lot on you, so just choose what you think is right. I trust you, Mum.' She paused. 'Have you decided what you're wearing yet? To the wedding?'

My silence was all the answer she needed.

'Oh, Mum!' she wailed. 'It's three and a half weeks until my wedding and you have nothing to wear? I don't believe it! What were you intending to wear? One of those boxy suits you wear to work and some sensible shoes? They make you look *years* older than you are. There'll be photos and everything! How can you do this to me?'

I thought my work suits were alright – they were practical and served a purpose.

I sighed. 'Don't worry, Ash, it's all under control. I have some ideas – pictures that I've been, ummm … pinning.' I crossed my fingers behind my back. 'Mari and I are going shopping on Saturday. We won't come home until we've found something.'

'You've got a Pinterest board? You have to share it with me.'

I grimaced. 'Well, not a board as such. But I do

have ideas.'

'And Aunty Mari's going with you?'

'Yes.' I tapped out a message to Mari on my mobile as I talked to Ash: *Shopping Saturday. Don't even think of an excuse.*

'But you both hate shopping,' Ash said. 'You'll lead each other astray.'

'Which means we'll make sure we get something quickly so we can get out of there,' I said soothingly.

'That doesn't make me feel any better. Mother of the Bride is a big thing for most mothers. Reece's mum has had her dress for months.' Her tone was accusing; rightly so, I had to admit.

'I know, darling, but time got away from me. I promise I won't let you down.'

A text came back from Mari. *Not the dreaded mother of the bride?*

I tapped a reply. *Yep, there'll be wine in it for you.*

If there's wine I'm in, she sent back.

'Okay. Call me on Saturday afternoon,' Ash said. 'I expect to see pictures. If not, I'll be dragging you out on Sunday.'

'Yes, well, we don't want that, do we?' I said, making a face. Shopping trips with Ash were more like all-day expeditions into uncharted territory, and just as dangerous.

'Exactly,' she said smugly.

~

'Okay,' Mari said when Ross dropped her at my house. 'Let's get this over and done with.'

'Glad to see you've brought your enthusiasm with you.' I picked up my bag and locked the door behind me. 'But yes, let's get it over and done with.'

'I still don't understand why Ash has to do the great white toilet-roll-doll extravaganza. Haven't we taught her anything?'

'You know Ash – once she sets her mind on something, there's no swaying her.'

We went to all the boutiques that specialised in all things bridal and big event-y, and laughed ourselves silly at some of the dresses on offer, but didn't find anything that didn't make me look even older and lumpier than I felt. Most of the outfits were so highly structured they looked as though they could walk down the aisle under their own steam.

'Oh god, Mari. When did I get so short and fat?' I moaned, looking at myself in the mirror.

'I hate to break it to you, darl, but you've always been a tad on the vertically challenged side. And you're not fat, it's just this outfit makes you look that way. The colour is completely wrong for you.'

'Just remind me not to stand next to Vanessa in any photos,' I said, running my hands across the width of my tummy. I pictured Neil and Vanessa with Ash and Reece – all four of them tall and lean – and then me. The odd one out – in more ways than one.

'Don't worry, I'll make sure she's kept out of shot,' Mari said. 'Do you know what she's wearing?'

'No. But whatever it is, she'll look tall and slim and fabulous. It's no wonder –' I stopped, and looked at the woman in the mirror again before pulling wildly at the coral lace. 'I need to get out of this thing. It feels like a straitjacket.'

Mari gripped my shoulders. 'Okay, the dress is bad, but let's get it off you in one piece, hey?'

As I was back behind the curtain, getting changed, Mari asked, 'What were you about to say before?'

'When?' I stepped out of the dress and tossed it into the corner of the change room.

'When you said "It's no wonder", then stopped.'

I hesitated before answering. 'I was going to say that it's no wonder Neil is divorcing me.'

Mari ripped the curtain open.

I grabbed at it to try and cover my undies and bra. 'Mari!'

'Sorry,' she said, not at all apologetic. 'When were you going to tell me that particular gem?'

I shrugged and held the curtain tightly to my middle. 'Maybe over wine this afternoon.'

'Or maybe, knowing you, not at all.'

My face burned under her gaze. 'I'm sure I would have. Let's get the dress disaster finished and then I'll tell you. Okay?'

She let go of the change-room curtain. 'Okay.' To

the wide-eyed assistant she said, 'These rooms need more privacy.'

As it turned out, we found the perfect dress in the local department store. It was a deep forest green, knee-length and relatively simple – almost like a slip. The bodice dipped in a modest beaded vee, with more beads on the hips fastening a chiffon overskirt that fell softly in handkerchief style around my legs. It was sleeveless but had a little beaded chiffon top in the same colour that hid the flabby bits at the tops of my arms. The minute I tried it on I knew it was the one.

'That's it,' said Mari when I emerged from the change room. 'The style is perfect for you and the colour is too. It makes your eyes almost green, and adds little highlights to your hair. Yes, perfect.'

Mari was right; the green brought out some colour in my hazel eyes. I twirled around, loving the feel of the fabric as it floated around my legs. 'It is, isn't it? I'm thinking some strappy silver shoes to go with it.'

Mari looked on approvingly. 'Right. Just stand there a sec first so I can get a photo for Ash.'

A couple of hours and one excited phone call from Ash later – 'Oh, Mum! It's fabulous!' – Mari and I were sitting at my kitchen table with some much-needed wine.

'Are you going to tell me about the divorce now?' she asked once we'd toasted the dress and the shoes and our tenacity in braving the shops to tick that particular task off the long list of wedding things still to do.

'There's not a huge amount to tell. Just that he's decided it's time. Although,' I mused, 'I'm not sure whether it's him or her who's decided.' I relayed the conversation to Mari.

'Wow, she's a piece of work. I've always thought she was just biding her time and then the real Vanessa would come out.' Like Nathan, Mari had never trusted Vanessa. 'Has she still got Neil on that low-carb diet?'

I nodded. 'I've got to say though, whatever he's doing, it's working. He certainly wasn't in that sort of shape when he was with me.'

'Hmmm, well, she obviously wants to keep him alive then.'

'Mari!'

'What?' she said innocently. 'I'm just saying the bitch has an underlying motive. Maybe she's scheming on getting half of everything that's currently yours, popping out a baby or two, and then divorcing him. In this town it's the best road to real estate. Come to think of it, with house prices as they are, it's probably one of the only roads. Let's face it, the likelihood of that generation being able to get into the housing market under their own steam is slim at best.'

'I'm sure that's not what she has in mind.' Even to my ears, I didn't sound convinced.

'Perhaps not, but it's an added bonus,' Mari said.

'You should have sorted this all out when he first left. Now everything's complicated.'

'I know, but we've gotten on so well that neither of us saw the need up until now.'

'Sometimes it doesn't work in your favour for things to be friendly. I was talking to someone the other day who was telling me about her friend who split with her hubby and, like you, stayed friends with him. When he left, she was working in an office and he was the main income earner. After they separated she started her own business – I can't remember what – and it really took off. Suddenly she was worth a fortune. Anyway, ten years later he decides to get married again and asks for a divorce, and she ended up having to give him half of the business she'd built up after they separated. She thought they'd done the right thing by keeping it amicable all these years and it absolutely backfired.'

Mari saw my face and hurriedly added, 'Not that any of that story applies to you guys. He's still the main income earner and you're on a minimum wage. They take earning capacity into consideration when they decide these things, so I'm sure you'll be okay. Neil would make sure of that.'

'It won't need to go to court,' I said. 'Neil and I are mature adults and friends. We'll deal with this in the same way we've always dealt with everything. Mike is there if I need him for legal advice, and Lachie's just waiting to be called on to help with the financial side.

I'm sure it'll be fine. Besides, we're not even talking about it until after the wedding.'

Mari wore her sceptical expression. 'Well, I hope it works out like that. To be honest, I think it's a good thing to get it all wrapped up. It'll be good for you – you can finally date again, even though there's been nothing stopping you from dating now.'

'I know there's been nothing stopping me,' I said, 'but what would I need to date for? Neil's still around if something needs fixing, and I have you to talk to. What more do I need?'

'One word, darl – sex.'

'I've lived without that for a number of years and am quite used to it.' I got up from the kitchen table and rescued another bottle of wine from the fridge. 'Ross is picking you up, isn't he?'

Mari nodded. 'Yes, so pour away. But back to sex – surely you miss it?'

'I used to when we were together and nothing much was happening. But now I hardly think about it.'

I focused on my glass so she couldn't see my expression. Yes, I still thought about sex, and yes, I missed it. Sometimes I wondered whether it was the intimacy with another person that I missed, the contact of skin on skin, more than the act itself, but every so often I'd read a spicy paragraph in a romance novel, or wake panting from a dream where I was chasing an orgasm that was just out of reach.

'Are you sure?' Mari said.

'Okay, maybe I miss it just a little,' I conceded. 'But I don't have time to think about dating. I might only work a few days a week, but Ash makes sure that every other available minute is filled with arrangements for this wedding. Who would think that the big white wedding would still be a thing in this day and age? I really thought we'd be over all of that palaver by now.'

'I know. I was so glad my Caitlin did the barefoot-in-Bali thing. That kind of wedding has as much chance of lasting as an extravaganza costing ten times as much. But then Ash has always enjoyed some theatre,' Mari said with affection.

She was Ash's godmother and had always admired how Ash went after whatever it was that she wanted with every fibre of her being. My daughter was an absolute force of nature who wore her heart proudly on her sleeve. Nathan preferred to work in the background for what he believed in, but if Ash was passionate about anything, by goodness did you know about it.

'I have been thinking about what's next,' I said, holding my glass of wine in front of me and watching the way the light shone through the liquid. 'After this is all over, I mean. Neil and I had our dreams about what life would look like when the kids had both left home and he'd retired. If he marries Vanessa he'll be starting a whole new future, and I'll be stuck in my old one.'

'There's no reason why you can't still do those

things,' Mari pointed out. 'As long as they're your dreams and not just some way of holding on to the past.'

I stared at her. 'What are you implying?'

'I haven't said anything before because it's none of my business –'

'Since when has that ever stopped you?' I said, laughing.

'True,' she acknowledged with a smile. 'No, the reason I haven't said anything is because I didn't know how to. The thing is … Well, you know that I love Neil, right? I didn't always, but I do now.'

'Where are you going with this?'

'I've often thought that his heart wasn't really in this separation. At first I figured he was giving you some time to miss him and then everything would go back to the way it was. But then I realised that he actually wanted it all – you as the wife who would deal with anything that needed dealing with, and Vanessa in his bed.'

'That's unfair,' I said.

'Yes, it has been – to you. You've been stuck in this half marriage for the last four years. You haven't been able to move forward, and you can't go back.'

'I have moved forward. I took the job I have now – I would never have done that while I was still with Neil. I'm doing things that I believe in again.'

'I get that, and I know your work makes a

difference to those women, but you can only afford to do it because Neil is still helping you financially. Minimum wage doesn't get you far in this city unless you have another source of income.'

I thought about arguing with her and decided against it.

'And it's not just the money,' she went on. 'Neil's here whenever you need him to be, you still feed him at least once a week, you talk most days –'

'Not since he dropped the bombshell,' I clarified.

'Okay, up until last weekend you talked most days. There was never any need for you to strike out and find someone of your own because he was always around. In fact sometimes I wondered whether he did that so you wouldn't find anyone else.' She held up her hand when I would have interrupted. 'No, Kate, think about it. Why else are you so thrown by the idea of divorce? Because you still consider yourself married, that's why.'

'I don't.'

'Really? Neil's had you in exactly the position he's wanted you in.' She frowned and pursed her lips together. 'I wonder what's happened to make him upset that sweet arrangement. He must be terrified of losing you.'

'I already told you. Despite what he said about not having any plans, I think he must be doing it so they can get married. Besides, how can he lose me when he no longer has me?'

I reached over to pour her more wine.

'Doesn't he? You might think you're an independent single woman, but you don't do anything without telling him, and if he doesn't like it you make an excuse not to do it. If this goes the way I suspect Vanessa wants it to go, he'll lose you.'

'I'm not sure what you mean,' I said, although I knew exactly what she meant. Although Neil never stopped me from doing anything, he certainly was still able to influence me.

'Think about it. If you let Neil off lightly on the settlement, and he and Vanessa get married, that's money that will never make it to Nathan and Ash. With that age difference, the likelihood is that Vanessa will outlive him – meaning that his estate will go to her, not to your kids.'

'Lachie said something similar but I wasn't in the mood to listen.'

'You need to listen, darl. This is important. Up to half of what you two have worked for and sacrificed all these years will potentially go to her.' She sat back and raised her eyebrows. 'You might have told Neil you don't want to talk about it until after the wedding, but if I were you I'd phone that brother of yours and his wonderful husband and start getting together all the information you need. Don't wait until Neil decides he wants to begin negotiations. He'll be banking on you playing nice – the way you have ever since Vanessa came into this house. You've gritted your teeth and pretended for the sake of the family. Now you need to look after yourself – for the sake of the family. And you can't do that by being nice.' She watched my face closely. 'You know I'm right, don't you?'

I nodded and drained my glass, setting it back on the table with more force than it deserved. 'You know what I think I want to do?'

Mari grinned. 'No, but you said it with such decisiveness that I like it already.'

'I want to climb my own mountain,' I declared.

'Are we talking an actual or a figurative mountain?' She filled our glasses again. 'I really need to cut back on wine – maybe when I get back from Europe.'

She and Ross were off on an extended holiday soon after Ash's wedding.

'Don't rush into that decision,' I said. 'No, I'm talking about a real mountain. I want to do what Neil did. Well, not exactly what he did – I have no inclination to go to Everest Base Camp. I'm thinking somewhere closer to home – like New Zealand. I could do one of those multi-day hikes that has a mountain in the middle of it.' I struggled to remember the article in the magazine I'd read last night. 'Milford Track – that's what I'm going to do. Heaps of people do it every year so it can't be that hard. In fact they say it's very doable for anyone with an average level of fitness.'

'You're saying that you have average fitness?' Mari's smile had grown wider.

'Maybe not yet,' I conceded. 'But by November I will have.'

She raised her eyebrows. 'November? You have a date? When did you decide this?'

'Just now. But I think it's a good idea, and a great way to start my new life as a divorced woman. Who knows? Neil found a new love when he climbed his mountain, maybe I will too.'

'Maybe you will. You'll need to train for it though.'

'Yes, that's probably the most inconvenient part of my plan. I'll start after the wedding. I have the feeling I'll need the distraction.'

'So do I.' Mari raised her glass. 'Here's to mountains and getting to the other side of them.'

'I'll drink to that.'

That evening, after Mari had left, I thought some more about what she'd said. Was it true? Did I still consider myself married to Neil?

Sure, I hadn't dated since we'd separated, but that had absolutely nothing to do with hoping he would get over this thing with Vanessa and come back to me. Our marriage was done. We were done. We were better as friends – we all knew that. Neil would have been fine if I'd met somebody; just as fine as I was with Vanessa. I was sure of it.

I'd do as Mari suggested though – ask Mike and Lachie for help now. But not because I thought

Neil was planning to manipulate me in some way. He wouldn't do that – not to me.

I picked up the phone to call Lachie.

Five

I spent most of Monday afternoon with a new client at the bank, sorting through her accounts to ensure that she had money to feed herself and her children. And then introducing her to the solicitor who would be managing her divorce and settlement.

As a result I hadn't long stepped in my front door when I opened it again to Lachie and Mike.

'Hi, guys. Oh good – you've brought Chinese takeaway. Can you set up while I get out of these clothes and into something comfortable? You know where everything is.'

I waved them in the direction of the kitchen and wearily began climbing the stairs.

'Red or white?' called Mike.

'I'm not fussy – whatever's open,' I yelled back.

By the time I'd changed and was back downstairs, they'd set the food out on the table and poured each of us a large glass of wine. I took a sip and leaned back in my chair with a sigh. 'Oh, I needed that tonight.'

'Tough day?' asked Mike.

'Uh-huh. I didn't sleep well last night.' I watched the raised eyebrows that passed between Lachie and Mike. 'I know, surprise surprise, right? And I spent most of this afternoon at the bank with a new client. Someone should run financial education lessons for girls when they're still at school. These women aren't stupid, by any means; it's just that they've handed control for everything over to him, signed everything he's ever put in front of them, and don't have the knowledge to ask the questions they need to. It's all fine as long as the relationship lasts, but if I had a dollar for everyone who came into our office with the same or similar story, I'd be a wealthy woman.'

'Let me guess,' said Mike. 'He's self-employed, she gave up work to help him get the business off the ground and didn't take a proper salary for all of that time. Now he no longer earns enough – at least as far as the tax office is concerned – to pay decent maintenance for the kids, but surprisingly has the funds to take the new girlfriend on an all-expenses-paid trip to Europe.' He grinned at me over the top of his glass. 'Am I close?'

'Right on the money. Give the man a drink. Seriously though, we should be teaching our kids about money in schools. Who do you reckon I'd need to lobby for that?'

Lachie passed me a plate. 'I agree, but you, my dear, don't have the time for that right now. Your focus needs to be on yourself.'

'Can I at least eat first?' I said, reaching for the chicken with ginger and shallots.

Once we'd finished, Mike poured more wine and Lachie cleaned off the table.

'Sit there, Kitty, and let someone else do the work for a change,' he said. 'You need to concentrate.'

'Okay, let's talk about joint assets.' Mike's pen was poised above his notebook. 'What do you guys have? Is it just this house and the apartment at Wollstonecraft?'

'Yes. There's no debt on the house – we paid it off when Mum and Dad's money came through – but there is some debt on the apartment. Neil said we needed to borrow against it for negative gearing – although I have no idea how that works now he's living in it and it's not producing an income. That's one for you to take care of, Lachie.'

'Got it,' he said from the sink.

'Remind me, Kate, when did you buy the apartment?' Mike asked.

I looked at the ceiling as I took my mind back to those terrible months after my parents' accident. 'Let's see, Neil announced he was going to do the hike in October. Mum and Dad died in November, the money from the sale of their house and the rest of the estate came through in February – so we must have bought the apartment at the end of February or early March. I remember settlement was the week before Neil left the country, and we agreed we wouldn't do anything about tenants until he came back.'

By the look on Lachie's face, I figured he'd had the same idea I had.

'You think he was planning this before he went away, don't you?' I said.

Lachie shrugged one shoulder. 'I don't know, Kitty, but the thought did just cross my mind. Tell me, why did you put the apartment in joint names?'

I shook my head. 'It didn't occur to me not to. Besides, it made sense seeing as how we were taking a mortgage against it.'

'Fair enough.'

'Is that all? In assets?' Mike asked. 'Other than the usual joint accounts and superannuation accounts. Do you still have a joint account?'

'Yes, we do. Neil still deposits a reasonable amount of his salary into it, and I pay all the household bills and car expenses from it. I have the statements here – and the super fund stuff. I'll get it all together for you. Neil's super fund statements are here as well.'

Lachie and Mike looked at each other.

'Really?' Mike asked. 'How come?'

'He never got around to changing his address on any of that stuff.' I smiled at Lachie. 'You know Neil – unless I organised it, it didn't happen.'

'In this case, that's a good thing,' Mike said. 'If you can dig out the paperwork over the next few weeks, we'll be prepared.'

'No problems. Oh, there's one more thing – Mollymook. Will that come into consideration? It shouldn't, should it?'

When Lachie and I dissolved our parents' estate we'd decided to hold on to the holiday house at Mollymook on the south coast. Despite the fact that Mum and Dad had died on their way back from the house, we had fond memories of family holidays there. Neil and I had given Nath and Ash similar memories, and we'd all hoped that the next generation could enjoy it in the same way.

'I wouldn't think so – not unless Neil decides to play hardball,' Mike said.

'Don't you mean unless Vanessa does?'

'There is that,' he acknowledged.

I sighed. 'You don't think about things like this when you get married.'

'It's probably the best time to think about it,' Mike said. 'You couldn't talk Ash into doing a prenup?'

It was something we'd spoken about when Ash and Reece first got engaged, but Ash was firmly against it.

'No, but at least I know that she's got good financial common sense if the worst happens. Not that I think it will with them – she and Reece are made for each other.'

Lachie stood to put the remainder of the wine back in the fridge. 'We thought the same about you and Neil.'

'I guess. At least we've achieved the miraculous though – a truly amicable split.'

'Don't count your chickens too soon, Kitty. I suspect things are about to get real interesting.'

The rest of the week flew by and almost before I knew it, the Saturday of the kitchen tea was here. I'd been busy making slices, biscuits and scones over the past day or so, and got up early that morning to bake the centrepiece – a very pretty Victoria sponge cake. Then I dragged from the cupboards all the mismatched vintage china I could find, draped a white sheet over the long table on the deck, and set out the plates, cups and saucers.

Neil arrived at about eleven to help us set up, so I put him and Ash to work hanging flowers and herbs – mostly from the garden – in jam jars around the deck. I arranged more flowers into china jugs and old teapots and placed them along the table and on stools I'd grouped in the corners. We piled the food onto tiered cake stands, and placed glass bowls of whipped cream, strawberry jam and hulled strawberries along the table.

Vanessa called just as we were finishing dressing the deck to say she'd be later than expected. 'Sorry, I forgot I had a late hair appointment. Unfortunately it means I won't get to pick up the macaroons. I hope that won't inconvenience you too much.'

I gritted my teeth, resisted the urge to glare at the

phone while Neil was there, and told her it would be fine, we'd see her when she got here.

I glanced warily at Ash. 'Vanessa's running late and said she can't pick up the macaroons after all.'

Ash flew immediately into a panic. 'No way! She was the one who offered to bring them. She said the raspberry and vanilla ones would look so pretty. Now the whole theme is ruined!'

With the guests arriving in an hour it was too late for me to bake anything else, so I mentally went through the contents of the fridge and freezer. 'Okay, we'll do some cucumber sandwiches with lemon herb butter. They'll look pretty on the plate – in fact, they'll add to the whimsical woodland feel that you're going for. We'll also do a tray of fairy bread for a little bit of fun. What do you think?'

'Oh, Mum, that's the best idea.' She threw her arms around me, the picture of the radiant bride-to-be again. 'You know, come to think of it, with everything else being homemade the macaroons might have looked a bit try-hard. What can I do?'

'Can you pick some dill and some chives, please, and I think we have a couple of lemons on the tree. If not, there should be one in the vegetable crisper. Then you can go and get dressed – your father and I will do the rest.'

I was already pulling a loaf of bread from the freezer and separating the slices out to defrost. Neil lurked around waiting for instructions, knowing that as Vanessa had let us down he'd need to pick up her slack.

'Neil, you can get the cucumbers out of the fridge and start peeling the skin off them while I whip the butter up.'

Into some butter I grated lemon rind and scissored in dill and chives. Then I swapped places with Neil and got him buttering the slices of bread while I stripped the cucumber into thin ribbons for the sandwiches. Then it was simply a matter of cutting off the crusts, slicing the sandwiches into three fingers and piling them high onto a delicate china plate.

In the meantime I instructed Neil to sprinkle hundreds and thousands onto buttered bread before slicing it into little triangles.

'I don't think I've made fairy bread since Ash was a little girl,' he said, grinning at me. 'Thanks for letting me help.'

'I didn't have a lot of choice after your girlfriend let us down,' I snapped.

His face fell and I was immediately remorseful. 'I'm sorry, that was unfair,' I said, reaching out to touch his arm. 'I appreciate your help. We appreciate it.'

'Regardless of what's happened between us, Ash is my daughter too,' he reminded me.

'I know, and I'm sorry. It's been good to have you here today.'

His smile was warm and his eyes held mine for a

second longer than they should. I turned away before he could see the confusion on my face and busied myself arranging the fairy bread onto yet another china plate. Normally I cursed how much room the vintage china I'd inherited from Mum took up, but today I was grateful she'd collected so much over the years. The table looked delightful, like something from Alice in Wonderland without the strange creatures.

When Ash appeared in a jumpsuit made from some floaty fabric, she let out a little squeal of delight. 'Oh, Mum, this is exactly what I'd hoped for. If it wasn't on a deck on the north shore of Sydney, this could be in a magical forest somewhere. It's perfect.' She kissed me on the cheek. 'Thanks for your help too, Dad. I love it.'

Mari was the first to arrive, greeting Neil with more reserve than usual, which earned her a look of confusion from him and a warning frown from me.

When Ash saw her she threw her arms around her. 'I'm so glad you're here, Aunty Mari.'

Mari hugged her back. 'I mightn't agree with this big wedding palaver, and kitchen teas belong back in the fifties, but if it gives us an excuse to eat like this I'm prepared to overlook that – for one afternoon only.'

Ash laughed and hugged her again. 'That's what I love about you, Aunty Mari, always fighting the good fight.'

'At least after insisting on this white wedding rubbish you're not dragging the whole thing out into a two-year engagement like all the girls seem to be doing these days,' Mari said.

'You know what I'm like,' laughed Ash. 'I'm not great at waiting. Six months is long enough.'

Vanessa turned up soon after, full of apologies for the macaroons. 'I'm so sorry. You've probably got a massive hole in your catering now.'

'No, it's fine,' I said. 'Neil helped out and we whipped up some cucumber sandwiches and fairy bread.'

Her eyebrows raised slightly and her lips tightened. I wasn't sure whether it was the idea of Neil helping in the kitchen, or the idea of Neil helping me in the kitchen, that had annoyed her. For the first time I suspected that she'd intended to create a problem with the kitchen tea. She hadn't counted on our ability to work together to make it right.

'It was fun,' said Neil, taking off the apron he'd donned to make the sandwiches.

'Looking at all this, I'm not surprised you're not starting your training until after the wedding,' Mari said to me.

'Training?' asked Neil. 'What are you training for?'

I glared at Mari, who smiled sweetly back. 'I'm doing the Milford Track – in New Zealand.'

'I think that's a fabulous idea,' said Vanessa.

'You would,' muttered Mari.

Vanessa didn't appear to have heard her, but I bit

the inside of my cheek to keep a straight face.

'Everyone needs a challenge to aspire to,' Vanessa went on. 'I'm sure that once you get into it the walking will do you the world of good. Who knows, you could start off walking and end up running.'

I shook my head. 'That's never going to happen.'

'Never say never. This friend of my mother's decided that for her sixtieth birthday she was going to hike up to Everest Base Camp.' She looked at Neil. 'And remember how our yoga teacher is walking the Camino de Santiago next month? She'd have to be in her early sixties.'

Since when did Neil do yoga, I wondered. 'I'm only just fifty,' I reminded Vanessa.

'So you are.' She laughed. 'Sometimes I forget that Neil is that little bit older. Maybe because it rarely occurs to me that he's that much older than me.' She rubbed his arm, smiling up at him. 'After all, he's so fit and active.'

Mari coughed, and I felt a little bit of vomit rise into my mouth. What was that about? After the first couple of rather awkward meetings, Vanessa hadn't shied away from public displays of affection – PDAs as Ash called them – with Neil. It hadn't really worried me. Well, not once I got used to it. Yet today it annoyed me. Everything about her annoyed me.

'Are you serious about doing this, Mum?' Ash looked worried. Surely I wasn't that out of condition

… was I?

I nodded. 'I've been thinking for some time that I need to get fit. I might be healthy on the inside, but my outside needs a little work. Besides, I need a challenge.'

'Who are you doing it with?' Neil asked, his face showing concern.

I thought back to what Mari had said the other day about how I never did anything he didn't approve of. He didn't look as though he liked the idea of this.

'Nobody,' I said.

'Is that safe?' No, he wasn't happy about it.

'I imagine so. After all, it's New Zealand, not the Himalayas.' I raised my eyebrows, daring him to come back at that.

'It's just –' he started.

'What? What is it just?'

Neil looked away from me and down at his feet.

'I appreciate your concern,' I went on, 'but this is something I intend to do for myself. Let's just say it's my personal Everest Base Camp.'

I heard Mari clear her throat and realised just how close I was to telling Neil that what I chose to do was no longer any of his business. It also reminded me that this was Ash's party and we were making it about us. Mari caught my eye and waved her hand slightly in a signal to me to let it go. I sent her a look that I hoped translated to 'you started this'.

Neil also took a deep breath and came back to

practicalities. 'What does it entail?'

'You leave out of Queenstown, and it's a five-day walk with a mountain in the middle. I won't do it until the end of November, so there's plenty of time to train.'

Now that Mari had brought it out into the open and I'd defended it so publicly, I supposed I'd better do something about booking it.

He nodded slowly. 'Six months. That's a sensible time frame. A lot can happen in that time.' Was I imagining it or was there an edge to his voice? 'I can help you if you like. Go for a bush walk somewhere or a long walk with you once a week.'

I was about to say that I didn't need his help, but Vanessa got in first.

'I don't think that's necessary, babe. I'm sure this is something Kate would want to accomplish on her own.' She touched his arm again as if to remind him who he belonged to.

The devil inside me popped its head up. 'I think it's a fabulous idea. Thanks, Neil, I'll look forward to that.' I smiled at him and he smiled back.

'Well,' said Mari, 'now that's sorted, do I have to drink tea at this tea party, or are there bubbles on offer?'

'Of course there are bubbles,' said Ash. 'Dad, can you open a bottle for me?' She raced off to open the door to her future mother-in-law.

Neil popped the cork on a couple of bottles and

poured glasses for us all.

'Unless you need me for anything else, I'll leave you ladies to it.' He kissed Vanessa on the lips. 'Do you need me to come back later and help tidy up?' he asked me.

'Oh, I don't think that's necessary,' Vanessa said. 'I can hang around and help Kate – it shouldn't take too long. Plus, don't forget we've got that birthday party down at the Opera Bar tonight.'

Neil grimaced. 'I had forgotten.'

'Wishful thinking perhaps?' I said under my breath.

Neil grinned to let me know that he'd heard. 'I'll see you later,' he said, kissing me on the cheek. 'Phone if you need help, or you want me to drop around tomorrow. I'll call you regarding a training walk next weekend, and I've taken all of the following week off in case there's any last-minute running around that needs to be done for the wedding.'

Vanessa turned to Reece's mother. 'I did tell Neil that he probably should have insisted that Nathan fly in earlier, so Kate doesn't need to rely on him as much as she does. But apparently there are turtles to save or something.' She laughed and used her fingers to make little quotation marks. 'Nathan "works" for one of those environmental organisations, although I'm not sure he does much more than spend his days diving.'

Susan had the grace to look embarrassed.

I ignored Vanessa and smiled gratefully at Neil.

'Thanks. I think I'll need the help. Anyway, you get out of here – this is a girls-only event.'

He kissed Ash and left. I was sure I saw the leftover of a glare on Vanessa's face, but it was soon gone, leaving me wondering whether I'd imagined it.

Six

The kitchen tea was a huge success, with Ash's friends devouring the food – seemingly blissfully unconcerned about the carbs or the sugar. I packaged up the leftovers and sent some home with Susan and Mari, and put more to one side to take over to Neil's parents when I called in on them tomorrow. I liked to try and see them at least once a fortnight. Between me, Libby and Leanne, we managed to keep their freezer stocked with meals and their fridge with treats.

True to her word, Vanessa stayed to help with the clean-up. She'd returned to her usual pleasant self and I began to think I'd imagined her glare earlier. Perhaps she'd just been wishing that it was her kitchen tea we were at. Not that I imagined I'd be a guest. And I certainly wouldn't be volunteering to cater for it.

It wasn't until I was stacking away the last of the china that Vanessa strayed into controversial territory.

'Has Neil mentioned anything about the valuer to you yet?'

'A valuer? No, what on earth for?'

'To get an indicative value for this house and Wollstonecraft, of course. I suppose he'll need to arrange for someone to do Mollymook as well, but that can probably come later.' She rubbed thoughtfully at her chin. 'Although that property is jointly owned with your brother, isn't it? That could present a few complications.'

I managed to catch the saucer that slipped from my grasp before it hit the floor, and remained kneeling with my head in the china cupboard until I'd composed myself.

'Neil and I will no doubt discuss it when we get together to discuss the divorce – after the wedding.' I emphasised the last three words.

'I was just trying to be –'

'I'm sure you were.'

Ash chose that moment to come back into the kitchen. 'Oh good,' she said. 'I timed that really well – you've finished cleaning up.'

I forced a laugh and got to my feet. 'You've always had a perfect sense of timing. Vanessa, did you want to take any of these leftovers home for Neil?'

'You must take him some scones,' Ash said. 'Mum's scones have always been Dad's favourite. He says no one has as light a touch as she does.'

Vanessa smiled at Ash. 'He might have used to enjoy them, but he's very much carb-free these days, so I'm afraid they'll go to waste.'

'Oh?' Ash looked confused. 'But didn't I see –'
She noticed my expression. 'Nothing, I saw nothing.
Granny and Pops will love them.'

I turned away before Vanessa saw my grin. Neil
had eaten his fair share of scones before they'd even
hit the table, as well as a couple of the cucumber
sandwiches.

'Anyway, I'll leave you to it,' said Ash. 'I need to
get some photos of the table and the spread Mum
created up on Instagram. You should be doing this for
a living, Mum. I'll see you in a fortnight, Vanessa … at
my wedding!' She squealed and kissed Vanessa on the
cheek.

Once Ash had left the room, Vanessa went back
onto the attack. 'I've been meaning to talk to you about
Neil's parents. I'm not sure it's helpful for you to visit
them as often as you do. I think that's why they're not
as comfortable with me as they could be. They need
to understand that Neil and I are together now and
you're no longer part of his life.' She was smiling, but
her voice was pure steel.

Why had I never noticed this side of Vanessa?
Perhaps it was coming out now because she was so
sure of Neil and her position in his life? Well, if her
gloves were coming off, so were mine. If she thought
I'd upset Dave and Maureen by deliberately depriving
them of my company, she had another think coming.
Was she planning on helping out when they needed

transport to and from medical appointments? Was she going to spend hours making sure the garden was weeded and planted with the veggies they liked to grow every year? I didn't think so.

More importantly, I enjoyed my visits with Neil's parents, and with Libby and Leanne and their families. Not only was I still a part of their life, but they were a very large part of mine. I'd always be grateful for the way they'd welcomed me into Neil's life without hesitation; and how they'd stepped in to help and comfort Lachie and me when our parents died. I loved them like they were my own family.

'I hate to tell you, Vanessa, but even when this divorce you're so keen to get moving on goes through, I will still be a part of Neil's life, whether you like it or not. That means I'll be a part of his parents' life too, and they'll be part of mine. If Neil wants me to stop visiting his parents, he can tell me so – but just like the property settlement and the divorce, this is none of your business. And me being off the scene won't make them, as you put it, feel more "comfortable" with you. Here's an idea: instead of keeping an eye on your phone every time you're over there, how about you sit down and really talk to them? Take a walk with Dave through his garden. Ask Maureen to tell you what Libby's and Leanne's kids are up to. Take an interest. If you intend being part of Neil's life, you need to be part of theirs.'

'I was just trying to be helpful,' she said.

I shook my head in disbelief. 'No, you weren't. I don't know yet what you were trying to do – although I have my suspicions – but being helpful was not your motivation.'

'You do realise I can make this whole process a lot more unpleasant than it has been,' she said.

I was too angry to care what I said now. 'Yes, you've made that abundantly clear, so I'll make myself just as clear. I'm in no hurry to complete this divorce, and I can drag it out for a very long time.'

She stared at me for a few seconds longer, and I stared back. Finally her eyes dropped and she picked up her bag. 'I might as well go then. You really should see someone to help with your coping mechanisms. You're going to need it.'

I managed to wait until she was out of the driveway before calling Neil.

'Hey, Katie,' he said. 'Did everything go well? Is Ash happy?'

'Ash is ecstatic and everything went to plan. I have some leftovers to take over to your parents tomorrow, but that isn't why I'm calling.'

He picked up on the tone of my voice. 'What's wrong?'

I took a breath before speaking. 'I thought we'd agreed that we wouldn't do anything about the divorce until after the wedding.'

'Yes, that's right.'

'Then why the fuck was your girlfriend asking me about making arrangements to get this house and the apartment valued? She was even talking about Mollymook. What the hell's that about?'

It was all I could do to keep my voice at a reasonable level. The last thing I wanted was for Ash to hear me. There was silence on the other end of the phone.

'Neil?' I prompted. 'Aside from the fact that this is none of her business, doesn't she know that Mollymook was Mum and Dad's holiday house? Are you guys planning on taking that too?'

'No.' He said it quietly, so quietly I had to strain to hear him.

'Is that no, she doesn't know it's the family holiday house? Or no, you're not planning on taking it?'

'Both. Katie, I don't expect you to believe me, but I've never talked to Vanessa about the ownership of any of our property. She doesn't know that we bought Wollstonecraft with your share from the sale of your parents' house, and she doesn't know that you and Lachie decided to keep Mollymook for the family.'

'I think you'll find that she does. She even said she knew it's owned jointly with Lachie.'

'Well, I didn't tell her. Nor have I done anything about getting valuations. We have plenty of time to be doing things like that. I don't think we should rush into it.'

'We've been separated for four years. I think you

can safely say that we haven't rushed into anything.'

He laughed. 'True.'

'Neil, when you said you weren't planning on getting married were you lying to me? Is that what this is about?' When he hesitated I added, 'You can tell me the truth, you know. I'm a big girl.'

'I have told you the truth. We've talked about it – or rather she has, and I haven't stopped her. It didn't seem right to have her move into our apartment so I might have said that I didn't want us living together or getting engaged or anything until after you and I had formalised things between us.'

I shook my head at the phone. 'You "might have said"? Seriously, Neil – that's what this is all about. She wants to marry you. Her clock is ticking.'

Of course Vanessa wanted to marry him – he was a good man. I didn't know why I hadn't done more to hold on to him while I had the chance.

'Regardless of whatever you two might or might not have talked about,' I went on, 'this is between you and me. I might have welcomed her into this house and dealt with her being part of my life, but I won't have her interfering in this, Neil.' Although I tried my best to control it, my voice broke. 'This is about us and our family – and she's not part of that. Not yet, at least.'

'I understand, Katie, and I'm sorry. I'll talk to her about it.'

'Thanks.' Then, in an effort to try and lighten the moment, I said, 'If you don't, I'll tell her that you had three scones, a brownie and two cucumber sandwiches.'

'No! Not that! If you don't tell her about the fairy bread I'll be your servant forever.'

When he hung up, we were both laughing.

I believed Neil when he said he hadn't organised the valuations. I even believed that he wouldn't have talked about the inheritance from my parents. Neil had always been a very private person and it wouldn't have occurred to him to think that might have mattered to Vanessa. Now that he knew just how upset I was, I suspected he would confront Vanessa about it, which gave me a shameful amount of perverse pleasure.

The Vanessa we'd been exposed to for the last three years was turning out to be a very different version from the Vanessa who had decided that not only did she want my husband, she also wanted what had been ours. And I wasn't about to let my children's future be endangered.

Vanessa might be Neil's girlfriend, but he and I had a deal about protecting our family until after the wedding, and he had way too much personal integrity to go against that. Regardless of how young and gorgeous Vanessa was.

—

The following afternoon, Ash came with me to visit Neil's parents. Maureen was keen to hear about the kitchen tea and see the photos, so while Ash talked Maureen through it, I buttered some scones and boiled the kettle.

'It's all getting very close,' said Dave. 'Saturday after next.'

'I know.' I paused, knife held mid-air. 'It's hard to believe that this time in two weeks my little girl will be married.'

'Reece seems like a good sort of man.'

'He is, Pops. I think they'll be happy together.'

'I thought you and Neil would be too,' he said pointedly. 'Once you sorted yourselves out after that first upset.'

I smiled at Dave's turn of phrase. 'We were happy.'

'You're not seeing anyone else at the moment?'

'No. I don't have time for that. There's a lot of organising that goes into a wedding, you know.'

'Especially one that Ash is planning, I'd imagine,' he said wryly.

The screen door opened and closed.

'Just me, Dad,' came Neil's voice.

'Through here, son. In the kitchen. Kate is just buttering me some scones.'

Neil kissed my cheek in greeting. 'I hope there's enough for me too. I can never resist Katie's scones.'

I raised my eyebrows in mock surprise. 'I would

have sent some home last night with Vanessa, but she said you're carb-free.'

'Only when she's around.' He reached for a scone, a wicked grin on his face.

'I'll just go and get Mo and Ash,' said Dave, leaving Neil and me in the kitchen together.

'It's a surprise seeing you here today,' I said.

'I wanted to see you – to apologise again for Vanessa yesterday – and guessed you'd probably be here. I can't imagine what you must be thinking. Actually, I can imagine and that's why I'm sorry. I talked to her last night and told her she's not to involve herself in it again – that we'll deal with it together.'

I nodded slowly. 'I see. She's not going to be happy about that.'

'She wasn't.' His smile was rueful. 'But she also knows I'm serious about it.'

Neil mightn't enjoy conflict, but when he was pushed on something he didn't want to be pushed on, there was absolutely no moving him. I imagined that Vanessa was finding that out.

'Dad!' Ash greeted her father.

'We didn't expect to see you today, Neil,' Maureen said.

'I couldn't let you have all the leftovers to yourself,' he said, bending down to kiss his mother.

'I think there's plenty to go around,' said Ash.

A couple of hours later, I announced that Ash and

I had to be on our way.

'Okay,' said Ash. 'Can you give me five? I just need to talk to Dad about something.'

'Sure.'

Ash looped her arm into Neil's and took him down into the backyard. From where I was in the kitchen I saw him put his fingers to his lips, and then rub at the back of his neck the way he always did when he was thinking.

Ash and I were almost at the car when she announced that she'd left her phone in the house and rushed back to get it.

'Why didn't you tell me?' Neil said.

'Tell you what?'

'That Vanessa asked you not to come around here any more. Mum and Dad would be devastated if that happened.'

'How did Ash know?'

'She said she overheard Vanessa talking to you about it.'

My tummy flipped as I went through our conversation. Did we mention the divorce? Yes, I thought we had. That was all I needed – for Ash to be upset so close to the wedding. Maybe she hadn't heard that part?

'What else did she tell you?'

His eyes narrowed. 'What else should she have told me?'

'Nothing, it just surprises me. Ash has always really liked Vanessa. I suppose I thought it would be more likely that she'd run to you with stories of what I said to Vanessa rather than tell you what Vanessa said to me.'

He laughed at that. 'You'd be surprised. Our girl is very loyal. And for the record, she did tell me that you stood up to Vanessa, but I think only because she knew it had upset you.'

He watched me keenly. My eyes dropped from his and I concentrated on making indents in the lawn with the heel of my boot.

'I was more upset about the possible ramifications for your parents than I was for myself,' I said. 'I can see her point, I suppose. Your parents don't understand the situation, and Vanessa believes they won't until I'm completely off the scene.'

'Do you want to be completely off the scene?'

'Of course not! Dave and Maureen are part of my family. It's not their fault that –' I stopped.

'That I stuffed things up,' he finished.

'That things didn't work between us,' I corrected.

'Perhaps, but the reason they don't like Vanessa is because she's rarely here. And when she does come for a duty visit, I can see her counting down the minutes until she can leave.'

I felt my eyes widen. I'd never heard him speak about Vanessa in such a disparaging way before.

'She's got no right to deny them your company just because she's jealous,' he added.

'Jealous? Of me? She has nothing to be jealous about.'

'Of course she does. My parents love you, and are clear that they believe I fucked up – something I'm beginning to wonder about myself. Then there's you. I think she'd prefer it if I criticised you or hated you or couldn't wait to be rid of you.' He smiled and touched my shoulder. 'And that's not the case. In fact ...' he hesitated, 'we need to talk.'

'I know. We'll do it after the wedding, as we agreed.'

'Not just the divorce, Katie. I –'

'It was in my bag the whole time,' Ash said, looking between Neil and me. 'Wedding nerves are making me lose my mind.'

'Somehow I don't think that's the case,' said Neil, ruffling Ash's hair. 'I'll call you during the week, Katie. We need to start your training.'

'Do we? Really?' I asked.

'Yes Mum, you do.'

Seven

True to his word, Neil came over the following weekend to walk with me.

'I thought we might park down near Barangaroo Reserve and walk from there around through the finger wharves at Walsh Bay,' he suggested. 'It's not that far and quite flat. Besides, I've been wanting to see what they've done down there.'

'If you're sure. I'm happy just to stay local.'

'No, it's all good. I've got nothing else on this afternoon.'

In the car, he outlined the training plan he'd determined for me. 'You can start with a local walk for an hour a couple of times a week, and on the weekends we'll build up to longer. I have a few routes I use when I'm training for marathons that'll be good for distance walking, and we can do some of the bush tracks once you've got some basic fitness. The problem you have is that you'll need to mix up your training with hills or stairs and uneven ground. And you probably should do some of it with your pack on as well. Have you thought about what gear you need yet?'

'No, but it's New Zealand, not the Himalayas.'

'You'd be surprised. The weather in those alpine regions can change quickly, and late spring is unpredictable.'

I smiled to myself. Since when was Neil an expert on New Zealand's weather patterns?

'I've been doing some research online and you're definitely going to need some thermal base layers,' he said. 'Have you thought about boots yet?'

'No. I've got plenty of time.'

'Yes, but the sooner you get your boots, the sooner you can begin breaking them in. The last thing you want is blisters. You're doing a guided walk, aren't you?'

'I am.' After the announcement last weekend I figured that I'd probably better actually book the hike and selected a company that offered fully guided walks. Comfortable beds, hot showers, three course meals that I didn't need to cook myself, and a bar that sold wine.

'Good. That means you'll be sleeping in lodges. You can wash your clothes out each night and dry them in the drying rooms. It also means you won't have to carry your own food.'

'You have been busy,' I said, surprised that he'd done as much research as I had – if not more.

He smiled at me. 'I mightn't be able to talk you out of doing this on your own, but at least I know you'll be in good hands.'

Mari's comment about how Neil was still controlling me came into my head, but I chased it out. He was just taking an interest, that's all.

The day was cool, but clear and blue, and the harbour glistened in the sunshine. As we walked along the sandstone-lined path, the Harbour Bridge came into view.

'Remember that park under the bridge we used to go to all the time?' Neil asked. 'The one with the cannons?'

I nodded. 'We walked miles back in those days. I think we must have known every inch of lawn from the bridge through to the Botanical Gardens. Not here though. This area was all shipyards, I think.'

'It's like the Museum of Contemporary Art – to me it'll always be the Maritime Services Board building, and where we met.' I felt his eyes on me, but didn't turn to meet them. 'I can't believe that was nearly thirty-two years ago. Sometimes it feels like yesterday.'

He stopped walking and stood looking across the water, before turning back to me. The look on his face confused and concerned me at the same time. There was sadness, and something else I hadn't seen for a long time. I had no idea where this little trip down memory lane had come from, but rushed to find a subject that would bring us back into the present.

'Can you believe that this time next week you'll be walking Ash down the aisle?'

'No. When did she grow up? It seems like only yesterday I was comforting her because some mean boy had teased her.'

I laughed. 'You should have been comforting the boy – Ash always managed to get even.'

'She certainly did.'

After that, the time flew as we covered most subjects from work to the kids, Ash's wedding, books – pretty much anything and everything except Vanessa's and Neil's plans.

Neil was the one who brought up his continued issues at work.

'Is early retirement an option?' I asked. 'You can walk away from what's happening with all your retirement benefits in place, and maybe buy that bookshop we always talked of.'

He shook his head sadly. 'I don't think Vanessa would go for the retirement idea – it would remind her of my age. She has this idea that I'm still reaching for the next promotion, and is constantly at me to apply for other roles in other companies. Sometimes I think she's convinced herself that I'm as young and as hungry as she is. As for the bookshop? That was our dream – I couldn't contemplate doing that with anyone else.'

It had been our dream. We both loved books – it was the thing that first drew my attention to him. For a second I saw him sitting there on the grass in front of the Maritime Services Board, his head in a book. Until he decided to use his weekends to get fit, that was how he often spent them – with his head in a book. For him, the dream of owning a bookshop meant he could have access to anything he wanted to read and the time to read it. For me, it would be a place for people to meet and learn and discuss the issues of the day. I'd imagined getting people in to teach evening courses for those who still had an interest in learning but didn't want the expense or commitment of formal education, or those who'd missed out on that opportunity when they were younger. The bookshop would be the amalgamation of what was important to each of us; the perfect way to end our brilliant careers.

I couldn't help the little thrill that went through me at knowing I'd never have to see Neil share that dream with Vanessa instead. It was something of him that would always be mine.

'Are you going to marry her?' I asked.

He hesitated before answering. 'I don't want to marry again.'

'Have you told her that?' Knowing Neil as I did, I doubted it.

'Not in so many words.'

'In other words, you haven't. And children?'

He grimaced and shook his head. 'She says she doesn't want any, and I've certainly finished with that part of life. In fact, I've been thinking about things and it worries me that …' He paused, and I could see him playing with the words in his head, possibly deciding whether or not to tell me what was on his mind. 'What I'm trying to say is that I've been thinking that when we do the settlement I might put most of my share into a trust, so that if I do end up with Vanessa, Nathan's and Ash's inheritance isn't impacted. I think if I'm to start again with anyone, it should be from scratch – the way it was with us.'

'Have you talked to Vanessa about this?' I asked softly. Was Neil beginning to mistrust her motives too? I wondered what she'd said or done to prompt that.

'No. And I won't – not until it's done. I just want to make sure that what you and I have worked for together is preserved for our kids.' He smiled, and I found myself unable to look away from him.

'If you're not intending to get married again, and she doesn't want children, why the divorce?'

'So you can move ahead with your life, Katie. We can't continue like this – in this half-marriage – it's not fair to you. You can't start again until we're completely finished.' He paused before adding, 'I want you to be happy. It's all I've ever wanted.'

I didn't know how to respond to that. And even if I had, the lump that was suddenly in my throat would have stopped the words from coming out. Instead I smiled briefly and walked on.

~

Ash was home when we got back from our walk. She kissed Neil on the cheek. 'Hey, Dad. So Mum's serious about this hiking idea?'

'It would seem to be the case.' He grinned and ruffled her hair. 'A week to go, hey, Ashie?'

'I know. I keep thinking about what I haven't done yet, and then figure it'll be alright on the night – or Mum will fix it for me.' She hugged my arm to her. 'Won't you, Mum?'

She knew I'd move heaven and earth to make sure her day was perfect.

'I don't think there's anything that your mother can't fix – or at least make better,' Neil said, and his stare disarmed me. It was the same look he'd given me this afternoon while we were walking and I was no closer now to knowing what it meant.

'Oh, I'm sure that's an exaggeration,' I said. 'In any case, I think everything is under control. We have the running sheet of who needs to do what on Friday and Saturday morning, so as long as you and Nathan know your respective jobs, all will be fine.'

'What time does Nathan fly in on Thursday afternoon?' Neil asked.

'About three thirty.'

'Okay. I'll come by and we can go to the airport together to get him. Then I thought we might all go for dinner on Thursday night – just the four of us.'

'That sounds like a great idea.' I couldn't remember

the last time we'd done that.

'I'd really like that, Dad,' Ash said. 'And as the bride, I get to choose the venue.'

Neil grimaced. 'My wallet is groaning already, but it's a deal.'

'When I agreed that Ash could choose the venue, I wasn't expecting her to pick the Golden Rabbit,' said Neil, holding the menu in front of his mouth so she wouldn't hear.

I giggled and looked across at our children bantering good-naturedly just as they used to when they were young. 'It mightn't be her usual style, but the Rabbit is part of their childhood.'

Our neighbourhood Chinese restaurant had been the staple for Thursday night takeaways and Sunday morning yum cha. The kids loved its comfort, its kitschy decor and its Aussiefied Chinese menu. Mostly, though, they loved the wacky fortune cookies.

'I thought you should know,' Neil added, 'Nathan asked me tonight if it's true that we're getting divorced.'

'How did he –'

'Ash told him.'

I sighed. 'She overheard Vanessa and me after the kitchen tea?'

Neil nodded.

'Okay.' I reached for the wine bottle. 'I guess it was too much to expect we could keep it secret until after the wedding. Is it something we need to have a party line on?'

Neil shrugged. 'I just told him that after four years apart we thought we should finalise things. He told me that was bullshit, and I was only pushing for it now because I wanted to marry Vanessa.'

'I see.'

'Katie –'

I shook my head. 'No, we can't talk about it now. How about for tonight we pretend we're a normal family out for a meal together?'

'That sounds good to me.' He smiled warmly, and I returned it.

Maybe we could still be best friends after the divorce. I'd heard of plenty of examples where that had happened – where the couple had outgrown their marriage but not their friendship.

Before I could think too much about it, Neil had closed the menu and asked Nathan and Ash, 'Are we ordering the usual?'

'If by the usual you mean sweet and sour pork, chicken and cashew nuts, chicken in satay sauce and –'

'Beef and black bean sauce with a large special fried rice and spring rolls to start, then yes,' Nathan said, finishing Ash's sentence for her.

As we ate and talked, it was easy to pretend that we really were a normal family out for a meal, that this was something we did every Thursday night. I looked at Neil, talking and smiling with the kids. Despite what he said, Vanessa had marriage on her mind, and once that happened there'd be no more dinners like this. He'd be lost to me.

Who was I kidding? Neil had been lost to me since before he left – although as hard as I'd tried to pinpoint the exact moment when we fell out of love, I couldn't. More importantly, I couldn't pinpoint the exact moment when he gave up on us. Everest wasn't the catalyst; I knew now that he'd only done it because he knew we weren't working. It was a reaction, not the cause.

Or maybe it was me who had given up on us. Not for the first time I wondered whether Neil had known about that almost affair. Sure, I hadn't slept with Connor, but I'd been tempted to. He was a tradesman employed to build some sun shelters at the primary school where I worked. I became obsessed with him, and fantasised about how it would feel to have his rough builder hands against my skin, my breasts, between my legs. It wasn't just that it felt like years since anyone had paid me the sort of attention he was paying me, I wanted to feel the excitement of the new. I wanted to kiss someone and feel desire rip through me; to be held against a body that was hard for me. I was bored with comfortable sex; I wanted discovery sex, spontaneous sex, the sort of sex you have when you're getting to know each other and everything is wondrous.

It all came to a head at the Christmas party harbour

cruise. I'd told Neil it was a no-partners thing, and dressed carefully with Connor in mind. I'd been waxed and even ensured that my bra and undies matched. Neil commented that I'd gone to a lot of effort for a work thing, but I laughed it off.

He dropped me off at the Quay and asked what time the boat would be back.

'I'll be fine,' I said. 'I can get a train or a taxi. You don't need to pick me up.'

'I do. I'll be here by ten.'

I got angry and we argued. Or rather, I argued and his jaw and mind remained firm.

'I'm not a teenager,' I told him. 'I'm a grown woman.'

His grim 'I know' seemed to have an underlying meaning.

The argument triggered a rebellion within me and I approached the evening as if I were a spoilt teenager acting up against a parent. Neil had no right to tell me what to do and what time I'd be home. I was a forty-something-year-old woman and I'd been a responsible wife and mother for too long. Now I wanted to feel something other than responsible.

So when Connor appeared by my side and commented on my dress and my heels and how sexy I looked, I felt the fire of long ago stirring in my belly. Later in the evening when we were out on the deck, he pushed me into the shadows against a wall and kissed me, his tongue driving into my mouth and his hand grabbing at my breast. I kissed him back. It was only when he suggested we take it further that I came to my senses.

Images of Neil filled my head: his smile, the way he held me, the way he cared for me, the way he loved me, the family we'd made together. It all came rushing through in one overwhelming flood of memories. That's what I'd be throwing away if I went with Connor. And it would be easy to do. I'd just need to text Neil and tell him that a few of us were heading to a club or to the casino. He'd believe me – why wouldn't he? I'd never lied to him before. He trusted me.

I pushed Connor away and muttered something about being sorry. As I straightened my dress, I couldn't look at him. He said it was okay, that it was my loss, and went back to the party, leaving me out there in the dark.

I couldn't believe how close I'd come to betraying everything Neil and I had and were for some 'fun'. I didn't want fun; I wanted passion. What I really wanted was my husband's passion, yet that had been gone for some years, lost in the pressures of work and family. I reminded myself that a marriage was about more than sex, and vowed that from now on I'd stay on the straight and narrow. Neil need never know just how close I'd come to tearing everything apart for a quick, and probably unsatisfying, fumble in the dark.

I stayed outside on deck for the last half-hour of

the cruise, not wanting to face Connor again. When we docked, I faked some smiles and agreed with my colleagues that it had been a great night, that the prawns were fresher than they usually were, the salads seemed more interesting, and the turkey and ham were appropriately festive. When I climbed into the car and kissed Neil hello, I was a more subdued version of myself than when I'd kissed him goodbye four hours before.

'Good night?' he asked.

'The usual, you know what these things are like – average food, average company and probably dodgy prawns and salmonella in the salad.' I forced a laugh. 'Anyway, that's it for another year.' I rested my head against the seat back and closed my eyes.

Neither of us ever spoke of that night again. I didn't see Connor again either. By the time school started back, the sun shelters were finished.

I set about feeding my hunger in other ways, subconsciously creating barriers against future temptation, willing myself to be satisfied with contentment and stability when something very deep within me wanted more. I said nothing to Neil about it because he wouldn't understand. He didn't have those thoughts; he was happy with things as they were. At least I thought so – until he announced he was going to hike to Everest Base Camp.

I wondered what would have happened if Vanessa

hadn't been on that hike. If Neil hadn't met her, would he have come back and tried to start over with me? Not that any of the what-ifs mattered now. That was all yesterday.

But what if he and Vanessa didn't make it? I'd sensed a reticence in him towards her recently that hadn't been there a month ago. It wasn't just the occasional remark; he also didn't seem to involve her as often in the conversation. And whereas before he'd reach out to touch her, as if he needed to know she was still there, she was instigating that more than he was now.

When Neil had mentioned that he wanted to protect his assets for our kids, I couldn't help wondering if he was beginning to think that Vanessa was in this for the money. With the way she was pushing for valuations and solicitors, the thought had certainly crossed my mind. I hoped for his sake that I was wrong.

And Neil didn't like being forced into action. She'd mistaken his dislike for conflict as an inability to act, when in fact there were things he wanted someone else to take care of for him, and others that he'd get around to in his own sweet time. There was a very fine line between the two, and it took a practised eye and the experience of thirty or so years to know which issues to push and which to leave.

Neil turned to me and smiled, and it was all I could do not to cry. Looking at his dear, familiar face, I realised something that I should have understood all along. I'd taken what we had for granted and mistaken contentment for apathy. I'd brought all of what had happened over the last four years – and what was to come: the settlement and divorce – on myself. I vowed now that no matter what happened, I'd never forget what we once meant to each other.

Neil must have seen the moisture in my eyes and reached across to cover my hand with his. Ash saw the action and exchanged a glance with Nathan, who also smiled. I pulled my hand away and used the back of it to wipe at the stray tear.

'Yes, I know,' I said, 'I'm getting sentimental in my old age. I just can't believe we're all here together. That Nathan has taken some time away from counting whales and turtles –'

'Yes, thanks, Ash,' Nathan cut in, 'for scheduling your wedding conveniently between the turtle-hatching and the height of the whale-migration seasons. I would have hated to have to make a choice between them and you.'

She pulled a face at him.

'And,' I continued, 'I can't believe that Ash is getting married on Saturday. When did you grow so beautiful and so clever? Reece is a lucky man, and your dad and I couldn't have let you go to anyone else.'

Ash's eyes filled as well, and Nathan rolled his.

'What are you going to do, Mum, when you finally have the whole house to yourself?' he asked.

'I'm going to make like your father and climb a mountain to figure it out.' As his eyes grew wider, I clarified my statement. 'Don't worry, I'm not talking about Everest. I'm talking about Milford Track in New Zealand. You go for a long walk, and there's a mountain in the middle – and plenty of good scenery to keep your mind off the pain of the mountain.'

'You're serious about this?' he asked.

'I'm absolutely serious. I've even booked it. I'm doing the posh version where you stay in lodges overnight with drying rooms, three-course meals, flushing toilets and a bar.'

'Even if it is the posh version, there's still a mountain to climb – and from what I've read, it's a challenging hike. Are you sure?' Nathan sounded concerned.

'You think it's ridiculous, don't you?'

'Actually, no. I think it's a great idea. You've spent so much time thinking about us and organising us, you deserve to prove to yourself that you can achieve something that's just for you. I'm just worried, that's all.'

'You're going to need to train a lot more, Mum,' Ash added. 'This isn't one of those turn-up-and-it'll-be-alright-on-the-night things. You really do have to prepare. I know you went walking with Dad last weekend, but you've done nothing this week.'

'It's not until the end of November,' I said. 'Once

this wedding of yours is over I'll have plenty of time to train.'

'Maybe we can do a mid-week walk as well,' offered Neil.

'Thanks, but I don't think that would go down well with Vanessa.'

'Especially not the way she is at the moment,' said Ash. 'Nath, you should have heard the way she spoke to Mum the other night. It's the first time I've seen that side of her and I didn't like it at all. I tell you what, Dad, if you're thinking about marrying her when this ridiculous divorce of yours comes through, I'd think again.' She glared at Nathan. 'What was the kick under the table for? So I'm talking about the elephant in the room – so what? Obviously Mum and Dad didn't want to say anything in case it upset us before the wedding, but –'

'Ash,' said Neil gently, 'that's enough. I'm sorry you had to overhear about the divorce the way you did – and before you accuse us of keeping it from you, that isn't the case. Your mother and I have agreed not to discuss it until after the wedding. We're in no hurry to finalise things.'

'That wasn't how Vanessa made it sound,' Ash said. 'You should have heard her, Nath. It was like she couldn't wait for Mum to move out of the house so she could get her half.'

Neil rubbed his forehead with his hand. 'I know how Vanessa made it sound, but that's not how it is.

I've told her she's to stay out of it. As I said, we're in no rush to settle things, and the last thing I want is for your mother to have to move out of the house.'

All of a sudden it was all too much for me.

'Let's face it, Neil, what you want is probably not going to come into it, is it?' I said. 'The only way this is going to be settled to her satisfaction is if I'm forced to move out so you can sell up.' I held up my hand to stop him interrupting. 'This is why I didn't want it to get out before the wedding. Tonight was supposed to be special, just the four of us one last time. So, please, can we just not talk about it tonight?' I fought to get my words out past the lump in my throat. 'Can we have tonight, and tomorrow and the wedding?'

The tears streamed down my face now, and I scrambled in my bag for a tissue.

'Of course we can,' said Neil, reaching out an arm to pull me close.

'I'm sorry, Mum,' said Ash. 'You're right. Tonight is for us.' She flashed an overly bright smile. 'And then the next few days are all about me.'

'As they should be, little Ash-tray,' said Nathan.

Ash attempted to glare at him. 'You haven't called me that in years – you know I hate it.'

'Yep, I sure do, and once you're a responsible mature married woman I won't be able to call you it again.'

I watched the two of them arguing the way they had so many times before in this suburban restaurant.

Neil watched me watching them and reached for my hand.

'It will be okay, Katie.'

'Will it?'

'I promise – and have I ever broken any promise that I've made to you?' At my raised eyebrows he corrected himself. 'Okay, you probably think that I broke the biggest one of the lot?'

'The one where you promised to love, honour and cherish me?'

'You know I haven't really broken that one,' he said awkwardly. 'I still love, honour and cherish you. It's just that –'

'It's alright, Neil, I get it.'

'No, I don't think you do. I –'

'Ooh, fortune cookies!' Ash swooped on the plate. 'I'm the one getting married so I get to choose mine first.'

'Because it's all about you,' Nathan reminded her, grinning.

Ash smiled sweetly back. 'Yes, it is. I'll choose mine first, but open it last.' She passed the plate around the table.

Nathan unwrapped his first. '*A day without sunshine is like night,*' he read aloud.

Next up was Neil. '*Some days you are pigeon, some days you are statue. Today, bring umbrella.* I should have read that earlier today,' he added. 'Katie, it's your turn.

What's in your cookie?'

I opened it and smiled. '*In two days time, tomorrow will be yesterday*. Ash, you're up.'

She carefully unwrapped her cookie, snapped it in half and burst out laughing. 'Oh, this is the best yet!'

She passed it to Nathan, who read it and choked on his beer. Next it went to Neil, who tried to be serious but failed spectacularly.

'Well, what does it say?' I asked.

With a solemn face, Neil handed me the little slip of paper. On it was written just one word.

Run!

Eight

'Oh, Ash!' My hand came to my mouth as I gazed at the vision that was our daughter.

I turned to face Neil, who was also wiping tears from his eyes. He smiled and took my hand. 'We made this,' he whispered.

'I know,' I whispered back. 'We did good.'

Ash's dress was like a modern-day fairy tale – an organza bodice decorated with delicate white feathers, leading down to layers upon layers of filmy organza that floated to the floor. Her hair was in a soft up-do, her make-up neutral and soft. She looked like a fairy princess come to life. Her bridesmaids, dressed in sage green, were woodland nymphs.

'What do you think?' Ash asked, for once seeming self-conscious.

'You're beautiful, Ash. Radiant.' There was a tremble in my smile. 'I'd hug you but I'd mess everything up.'

She smiled. 'You would. No hugs until after all the photos. You look lovely too, Mum.'

'She does, doesn't she?' Neil said. 'Just beautiful. At this minute I think I'm the luckiest man alive.'

Nathan appeared behind us. 'Wow, you scrub up alright when you make an effort, little Ash-tray.'

'You should try it some time,' she retorted. 'Who knows, you might actually attract a keeper.'

He laughed. 'Mum, the car's waiting – time for us to go.' He turned to Neil. 'Dad … are you alright?'

Neil blinked and drew his eyes away from the vision that was our daughter. He patted Nathan's back. 'Yes, I'm fine.'

'Good.' Nathan steered me out the front door. 'Then let's get this show on the road before Reece wakes up to himself and changes his mind.'

The ceremony went off without a hiccup. My eyes filled when I saw Reece watch Ash float down the aisle on her father's arm. The complete adoration in his eyes took my breath away.

I remembered Neil looking at me like that on our wedding day all those years ago. As he came to sit beside me in the pew, he leaned in and whispered, 'I remember feeling like that when I saw you walk towards me. I'd never seen anything or anyone so perfect in my life.'

Our wedding had been very different to Ash's. We'd invited all our friends and family to a picnic in the Botanical Gardens to celebrate our engagement, and surprised them with a wedding under the Moreton Bay fig that we'd come to think of as our tree. We'd set up tables laden with cold chicken, bread rolls and salads, and eskies full of cold drinks. As Nathan and I walked across the grass to where Neil stood, Lachie – the only one in on the secret – played Jason Donovan and Kylie Minogue's 'Especially For You' on a portable cassette player. I remembered holding Nath's little hand in mine, the bump that was Ash hidden below the cut of my simple dress.

Now, watching our daughter twenty-seven years later, I swallowed and wiped away a tear. Neil smiled and reached for my hand, and I hoped that Vanessa, sitting a few rows behind us, wasn't able to see.

Outside the church, people congratulated us. 'How lovely was the service?' 'You and Neil must be so proud.' 'Didn't Ashleigh look a dream?' 'She and Reece look perfect together.'

Then there were the family photos, Neil at my side for all of them. If I didn't know that next week – or some week very soon – we'd be sitting down to negotiate a divorce, I could have convinced myself that we were as happy together as we had been on our own wedding day.

Vanessa was seated at our table for the reception, so with everyone else coupled up, I felt a bit like a third wheel, despite Neil's efforts to include me in conversations. Every time I looked at them, Vanessa was touching him – his arm, his thigh, a piece of imaginary fluff on his jacket sleeve.

Neil's speech was lovely. He spoke about the love he'd felt for Ash the minute he'd known she existed inside of me, the rush of feeling the second he set eyes on her, and how he hadn't thought those moments could ever be surpassed until he'd seen how happy she was tonight.

'Katie and I couldn't be prouder of the woman you've grown into, Ashie. And to see the love between you and Reece? Well, that's our greatest dream come true for you. All we've ever wanted – all any parent ever wants – is to see their child glowing with happiness as you are tonight. My wish for you is that twenty, thirty, forty, fifty years from now when you and Reece look at each other, you'll see the same love shining from each other's eyes and remember this moment with joy. Any longer than that and you'd probably need glasses to see it – but if you look for it, it will still be there.'

He paused for laughter, and looked across at me and smiled. Our eyes met and for that half a second I imagined he was reliving the same moment I was from our wedding day. For that half a second, he hadn't left me, Vanessa didn't exist, and we were still in love the way we had been back then.

Then he looked away and raised his glass. 'A toast. To Ashleigh and Reece, the bride and groom.'

'To the bride and groom!'

As I raised my glass with the rest of our guests and drank to Ash and Reece, my heart was full of the wish that they would make it through where we hadn't been able to.

Looking at them now, I thought they had a better than average chance of lasting the distance together. They certainly had a better start to married life than we'd had. When we got married, we had a four year old and Ash was on the way. There was no honeymoon, no easing into married life. It was straight into parenting, and juggling work and home. Looking back, it was probably a miracle that we'd lasted as long as we had.

Reece and Ash cut the cake, and then Neil was holding his hand out for me to join him for the waltz. He held me close as we swayed across the floor to Ed Sheeran's 'Perfect'.

'You know, this song could have been written for us,' he said into my hair. 'We were so young when we fell in love, but on nights like tonight I look at you and you're still the girl I met down at the Quay that day. You spoke to me and I couldn't believe my luck. You seemed so smart and so independent and full of dreams, and I was just this boring bank johnny. I kept waiting for you to wake up and realise, but you never did.'

I smiled into his shirt, inhaling that mix of wood, lavender and amber that was pure Neil. 'You were never a boring bank johnny to me. Well, maybe at first.'

I felt the chuckle in his chest. 'And on our wedding day, you were so perfect I thought my heart could stop right then and there. You know, you still are.'

I raised my head and looked into his eyes, feeling a jolt of desire so strong, so unexpected, that it left me shaking. 'You can't say that, Neil. Not any more.'

As I saw the same need reflected in his eyes, the goosebumps quivered across my chest.

'Katie,' he began.

'You don't mind if I cut in, do you, Kate?' Vanessa stepped in between us.

Neil released me, but his eyes were still on mine as he whirled away with her in his arms.

It must have only been seconds that I was standing there in the middle of the dance floor before Lachie stepped in to claim me. 'Smile, Kitty-cat. Whatever that was, it didn't happen.'

'I don't know what you mean,' I said.

'You know exactly what I mean. It's just the sentiment of the day; it means nothing. He's with Vanessa now, so let's not complicate things even further by getting distracted by memories.'

'You're right. I know you're right,' I said.

'Of course I'm right. And now here's your son wanting to dance with you.' Lachie dropped a kiss onto the top of my head and handed me over to Nathan.

'Anything you and Dad need to tell me?' he asked. 'You should have seen Vanessa's face when Dad was dancing with you. She's always shown us the sweet, butter-wouldn't-melt-in-her-mouth side, but the way she was looking at you just then ... it wasn't nice at all.'

'There's nothing to talk about. It's just that Ash's wedding has brought back memories of our own. It's the sentimentality of it all.'

'Are you sure? You didn't see the way he was looking at you. And on Thursday night, Dad touched your hand or your arm whenever he could. Then he turned up last night for dinner at home. If I didn't know better, I'd think there was something going on.'

'No, darling. There's nothing you need to know about. It was just nice to have the four of us together like we used to be, that's all.'

'Pity. I'd like to wipe the smile off that smug bitch's face.'

'Nathan!'

'What? You know I've never liked her – I only tolerate her for Dad's sake. But I absolutely don't trust her, and nor should you.' He paused for a few seconds, then added, 'You know, I remember your wedding. I thought you were the most beautiful creature I'd ever seen. You looked like a queen. I remember that Dad cried when he saw you, and I told him that big boys weren't meant to cry, and he told me that he felt so much love that it was overflowing through his eyes and that made it okay.'

A lump of emotion rose into my throat. That moment was so clear in my memory. Nathan and I had reached Neil, and Nathan had piped up in his high, clear four-year-old voice. 'Why are you crying, Daddy? Did you fall over?' Everyone had laughed and I'd missed Neil's answer to Nathan.

'That kind of love doesn't die, Mum. Not just because you tell it to. So if there's still a chance for you two, make sure you take it before it's too late.'

I looked up at my tall handsome son and wondered, not for the first time, why some equally amazing girl hadn't snapped him up yet.

'When did you get to be so wise?'

He shrugged. 'I don't know. I just know that kind of love hasn't happened to me yet, and when it does I won't let anything stop me.'

I patted his cheek. 'All this sentimentality is making me thirsty. How about you drop me back at the bar, and then go and talk to Reece's sister who hasn't taken her eyes off you all night?'

Outside, in the quiet of the garden, I found a bench seat, pulled my flimsy wrap more tightly around me and sat and sipped at my wine in peace. Being the mother of the bride was exhausting, but not nearly as emotionally draining as trying not to watch the father of the bride with his sparkling young partner. With Neil on her arm and the promise of a divorce just around the corner, Vanessa was back to being her most charming.

'I thought I'd find you out here,' Neil said, sliding onto the chair beside me. 'It's all a bit much, isn't it?'

'It certainly is.'

He clinked his glass to mine. 'Here's to us – the parents of the most beautiful bride in Sydney.'

'To us.'

I shivered in the night air and he took his jacket off and draped it around my shoulders. I smiled my thanks and we sat in silence for a few minutes, sipping at our drinks. Over the chatter from the function room I could hear Elton John's 'Something About The Way You Look Tonight'.

'Listen,' said Neil. 'They're playing our wedding dance.'

I punched him lightly on the arm and grinned. 'So much for your memory. We had INXS's "Never Tear Us Apart".'

'I haven't forgotten,' he said, smiling, 'but we could have had this. It would have been just as appropriate. You look so beautiful tonight that you've taken my breath away.'

'Except this song hadn't been written when we got married.' I laughed to try and lighten a mood that had suddenly become as intense as that moment on the dance floor had been.

'Come on,' he said, taking my glass from my hand and balancing it on the grass beside his. 'Dance with me.'

He held his hand out, his eyes never leaving mine, and I took it. Just one more dance, I promised myself, and then I could let him go.

He held me close, my hands in his, and we swayed together in the dark, my head burrowed into his chest. Inside the venue the song had been replaced by something more upbeat, but our pace didn't change.

'You feel so good, Katie,' he murmured into my hair. 'I told myself just one more dance and then I'd let you go. But now you're in my arms I don't want to let you go.' He stopped moving and tipped my chin up so I was looking into his eyes. 'I don't ever want to let you go again. I want to keep holding you like this for the rest of my life.'

I gazed into his gentle brown eyes, the desire that I'd felt earlier flaring through me again.

'Please, Katie, just one more kiss?'

'Just one more kiss,' I whispered into the space between his mouth and mine.

He tasted of wine and cake, and I drank from his lips thirstily. I felt the groan rumble in his throat as my tongue tentatively reached out to touch his, and my arms snaked around his neck to hold him closer, to deepen the kiss.

'Oh, Katie,' he whispered, 'I've missed you so much.'

That should have been my cue to stop this before it was too late, but I couldn't. Instead I let him walk me backwards until our progress was halted by a tree, my legs parting so he could press himself between them. And still we kissed, my hands pulling at his shirt to feel the warmth of his skin, his hands reaching under my skirt and into my pants as I moaned his name into his mouth. Oh, how his fingers still knew their way around my body.

He lifted my leg so he had better access, and kissed his way down my throat. Deep within me I felt that almost forgotten pressure building. As it burst and the stars exploded behind my eyes, he kissed me again, muffling my cries of release and his own moans as I held him firmly in my hand.

'Neil?'

Oh Christ – Vanessa.

Neil pulled my skirt back down, but stayed where he was, his body pressed into mine, his finger against my lips.

'Neil?' she said again, and I heard her soft footsteps across the grass. She paused and looked out into the darkness.

I stifled an urge to giggle and Neil shook his head slowly. We both held our breath.

After a few long seconds, she turned and walked back into the function room.

'God, I'm sorry,' Neil said, finally pulling away from me and straightening his shirt and pants. 'I didn't mean for that to happen.'

'It's fine,' I said, even though I felt anything but fine. 'You'd better go inside. I'll stay out here for a little while longer.' I took his jacket off and gave it back to him.

He nodded. 'You know that we need to talk.'

'Yes. Later.'

He kissed me again, hard, branding my lips with his. He tried to meet my eyes, but I turned away.

Once he'd left, I sat back down on the bench and ran my hand through my hair to make sure there were no leaves or bark stuck in it. Wow. That was ... unexpected. Neil had never kissed me like that before. He'd always been tender, and his kisses were always lovely, but that was something different. That was Neil kissing me in the way I'd longed to be kissed, pleasuring me in a way he hadn't done for many years during our marriage. If Vanessa hadn't come out when she did, who knows what else I would have let him do to me out here in the garden.

I closed my eyes and felt again the tree trunk behind my back, Neil's hand between my legs, and the hard throb of him beneath my fingers. We'd been like two horny teenagers. My fingers rested against my lips as if I could hold the taste of him there to savour later.

I let out one more deep breath and stood, straightening my dress, checking my hair again. Satisfied that there was nothing that could give away what I'd been doing, I walked back into the room.

Lachie spied me and, with one hand under my elbow, pulled me to the side. I could see Vanessa and Neil on the dance floor. It was a pop song so they weren't touching. I didn't think I could have borne it if they were. His eyes met mine and he smiled, taking me right back to those moments in the garden.

Lachie noticed and frowned. 'Where have you been?'

'Just out getting some air. It's hot in here.' I fanned my cheeks with my hand to lend some truth to the words.

'Really? So why do you have a leaf in your hair?' My hand involuntarily reached for the back of my head. 'Gotcha,' he said. 'There's no leaf, but you thought there could be.'

'It was just a reflex action.'

'Is that what the kids are calling it these days?'

My shoulders slumped and I gave up the act. 'Does anyone else know?'

He shook his head. 'No. I just saw you two sitting together, and then you were dancing … and then you weren't. Don't worry, once you went behind that tree I couldn't see anything, but I did put two and two together. But I don't think anyone else saw.'

I breathed a sigh of relief.

'What are you playing at, Kitty?'

'Nothing. I have no idea. It was just a kiss.' I felt warmth rush to my cheeks as I told the lie.

'From the man you've been separated from for years. The one who's dancing right now with the woman who intends to marry him once you're out of the picture and she's managed to get her hands on half of everything you own.'

'When you put it like that, it can never be just a kiss, can it?'

'No, it can't. It's also a complication you don't need.' He dragged me onto the dance floor. 'Come on, let's go join Mike. I can't let him do the "Time Warp" on his own – he's liable to do damage to innocent civilians.'

I didn't speak to Neil for the rest of the evening. Vanessa made sure of that – and, to be honest, I was glad she did. The force of what had happened between us in the garden had spun my world off its axis. Perhaps it was just that I'd been single for so long, but I'd never felt desire as uncontrollable as I had this evening – it had completely overwhelmed me. I could have convinced myself that it had been a dream if it weren't for the fact that every time my eyes met Neil's, however briefly, the need flared inside me again. Besides, I still tingled delightfully between my legs.

Ash and Reece left in a hail of rose petals and good wishes. Nathan tapped me on the shoulder almost immediately after and told me he'd see me the next morning, the tilt of his head towards one of the bridesmaids filling in the rest of that particular explanation.

Although Vanessa announced her intention to leave, Neil helped Lachie and Mike to load all of the wedding gifts into their car. I was to host the morning-after barbecue tomorrow so they'd drop the presents around then. When Neil would have hung around some more, perhaps hoping for a chance to talk to me alone, Vanessa dragged him away.

'We'll see you tomorrow,' he told me on the way out. The look on his face told me there was more he wanted to say.

As for me, I called an Uber and went home to my empty house, where I sat at my kitchen table, poured myself a whisky and decided that with everyone in my life coupled up – if only for the night in Nathan's case – I had a right to feel sorry for myself. So I did.

As I sipped at my drink, I closed my eyes and allowed myself to relive those minutes in Neil's arms – on the dance floor and in the garden. I felt again the warmth of his body and the way mine curled into his as if it remembered where it belonged. His scent filled my nose again and under the table I squeezed my thighs together.

I snapped my eyes open. I was still in love with Neil. How had I not seen that?

I let my head drop to the table. What a mess. What a fucked-up mess. And, if I wasn't mistaken, it was about to get even messier.

Nine

I dragged myself upstairs and took my dress off, leaving it on the floor, a tumble of forest-green chiffon and beads. Crawling into bed naked, I screwed my eyes shut and willed myself to sleep. But I couldn't. Not only had I realised I still loved Neil, but, more importantly, that I'd never stopped loving him. All these years that I'd convinced myself we were done came back to laugh at me, as thoughts in the middle of the night tended to do. I'd been so sure that we'd both moved on – I was single and independent with a job to match. Now I realised that although Neil had moved on, I hadn't. I'd been a fool, and it was going to take every ounce of my willpower not to be a bigger one.

Somewhere around four in the morning, I willed myself to sleep for a couple of hours. Then I got up, plastered a smile on, and prepared to face everyone again.

Libby and her husband, Russell, brought Dave and Maureen with them, and Leanne and Simon came with their eldest two children, Nicole and Amanda. Lachie and Mike arrived with the car full of wedding gifts and a couple of cases of red wine they'd syphoned away from the function room.

'Don't look at me like that, Kitty, you guys had paid for them,' Lachie said.

Nathan swaggered in just in time to help me set the table and turn the barbecue on, and Neil and Vanessa were late. When they did arrive, I tried my best to act normally, but there was nothing normal about the way my pulse raced when my eyes met Neil's. Nor was there anything normal about the way my anger flared when I watched her hold his arm and look up into his face, or when she kept her hand on his thigh even in the middle of a conversation with Mike.

It was only when Nathan asked me whether he should start cooking the sausages and I snapped at him that I realised I needed to get a grip on myself.

'Really, Mum? Is that a hangover talking?'

I rubbed briefly at my eyes. 'I'm sorry, Nath. Maybe I need another coffee. Yes, if you can get the sausages on, I'll get everything else organised.'

In the kitchen, I opened the fridge door and stared inside, already forgetting what I'd come to get. I jumped when I heard Neil's voice behind me.

'About last night,' he said.

I forced a half-laugh. 'Seriously? You're going with that as an opening line?'

He grinned. 'You're right, it's lame. But … about

last night …'

I placed my hand on his arm, felt the heat of his skin against mine. 'It's okay, I know it didn't mean anything. It was just the sentimentality of the night. We got carried away by the moment and the memories. Let's just pretend it didn't happen.'

Eggs. That's what I'd come to get. Eggs, bacon, bread and butter. Four things.

'What if it did mean something?' he said. 'What if I can't forget?'

I closed my eyes briefly as a tiny flicker of hope began to burrow its way into my heart. The beeping of the fridge door sent it scurrying back to where it belonged. I took out the food I needed, closed the fridge door and, summoning every piece of strength left inside me, looked up at him and said, 'I'd suggest you try.'

His eyes widened and something that looked as though it could be hurt flashed into them. I turned away and began loading the food onto a tray to take out to the barbecue.

'You don't mean that, Katie.'

I gripped the kitchen bench and squeezed my eyes shut. 'Neil, what we did last night was a mistake. It can't happen again.'

'Look me in the eyes and tell me that. Look me in the eyes and tell me you felt nothing.'

I swallowed hard and shook my head, unable to face him. 'You know I can't,' I said in a small voice. 'But it can't happen again.'

He was silent for a few seconds. Seconds in which I imagined I could hear my heart beating.

'We haven't finished this conversation,' he said.

I nodded once, and heard him leave the kitchen.

I didn't turn around until I heard the door shut behind him, but instead of going back outside I walked slowly into the downstairs bathroom, and looked at myself in the mirror. The face of a tired fifty-year-old woman gazed back. One who hadn't taken all her make-up off last night and now had little smudges of yesterday's liner under today's eyes.

I pinched at my cheeks to bring some colour into them, and ran my fingers through my loose curls to add some volume. 'You can do this,' I said to the woman in the mirror, and went back outside to pretend that everything was absolutely as it should be, that the sight of my husband's girlfriend touching him and smiling at him meant nothing to me.

That lasted as long as it took me to put the butter and baskets of bread on the table.

Vanessa screwed her nose up and said, 'I'm sorry, Kate, but Neil and I are off carbs at the moment.'

Any other day, in any other mood, I might have apologised and bustled around to make her a salad, but today I simply said, 'You're not the only people at this table. You don't need to eat the bread if you don't want to – there's plenty of meat and eggs.'

Nathan turned from the barbecue to look at me, his brows raised. Neil also lifted his head, and I was sure I saw a half-smile on Lachie's face.

Vanessa, though, seemed unfazed. 'I'm not really into sausages. I'm sure you wouldn't mind rustling together a salad?'

Her smile was as sweet as it always was, but I was feeling pretty sour.

'Actually, yes, I would mind. If you're after something green, you know where the veggies live.'

I resisted the opportunity to watch her reaction and instead turned to check on the progress of the sausages.

'Neil?' Vanessa almost bit the word out. 'Would you like to help me make a salad?'

'No, thanks, I'm right,' he said. 'I can resist most things, but I'm completely defenceless against a sausage or bacon and egg sandwich. Maybe I'll have one of each. Everyone knows that morning-after food doesn't count.'

'Like plane food,' offered Mike.

'And other people's chips,' said Lachie.

'Or anything off anyone else's plate,' added Nathan.

Vanessa glared. Then she noticed me smiling and glared again. I didn't care.

Nathan saw her face and decided to stir the pot some more. 'The thing is, Dad, it's about being good eighty percent of the time. Besides, you need some carbs for energy. Get into it, I say.'

Ash and Reece called in on their way to the airport – they were honeymooning in Thailand and Vietnam. Both attacked the food as if they hadn't eaten in a week.

Nathan laughed. 'I don't need the details, Ashie – that would be pretty eeeeuw – but you guys certainly look like you worked up an appetite!'

Neil cornered me again when I was in the kitchen putting together some fruit and the baked things I'd found in the freezer.

'Are you okay, Katie? You're not saying much.'

I laughed ruefully. 'It's tough getting a word in there today. I'm probably just tired.'

He shook his head. 'We're all tired. That's not an excuse.'

I shrugged one shoulder and went into the dining room to get a platter from the sideboard. He followed me, closing the door behind us.

'Last night wasn't just a sentimental trip down memory lane, Katie. We both know that.'

He moved closer, and I stepped backwards until I came up hard against the sideboard, holding the platter against my chest. That little spark of hope from earlier ducked its head up for another look. I closed my eyes briefly and pretended I couldn't feel it sitting down to make itself comfortable.

'No,' I shook my head wildly, 'you can't say that.

You want a divorce. You're going to marry Vanessa.'

'I'm not marrying Vanessa. Katie, I think I've made a huge mistake, and I'm hoping it's not too late to make it right again.'

'Please don't say that. You and I both know we're done. What you're feeling now is just a reaction to the reality of the settlement and the possibility that you'll have to commit to Vanessa.'

'You don't really believe that, do you? The part about us being done?'

'I have to. You've been gone for four years. In that time we've gotten along perfectly well, and I've even welcomed your girlfriend into the house. I have to believe that we're done.'

'But what if I no longer think we are?' he asked softly, his gaze intense. 'Last night was … oh, Katie, that kiss and everything else was out of control. I know you felt it too – you couldn't hide that.'

My hand flew to my mouth as I remembered again the insistence of his lips against mine, the heat pooling between my legs as I felt his hand there.

'You're thinking about it now, aren't you?' he whispered, taking another step towards me. The space between us now was just a breath. He lowered his head towards mine.

'Yes, no … please don't do this, Neil. Not now. Not with our kids and your girlfriend out there. Please don't.'

He must have read my face, seen the mix of desperation, frustration, lust, longing and fear there. He took a few steps back and nodded. 'Okay. You're right. This isn't the time.'

'There is no right time,' I said. 'Not for us any more.'

'I don't agree.'

'What about Vanessa?' My brain was attempting to keep this on track even as my arms were aching to reach for him.

He swallowed hard. 'No, Katie, this is about us.' My heart leaped at his answer. 'Last night proved we still have feelings for each other. I couldn't sleep for wanting you. It was playing over and over in my mind – how you taste, those moans you make that sound like they're coming from the back of your throat, the way your eyes go all dreamy and lose focus just before you come, the way you tightened around my fingers, and the cries you made into my mouth. It was gone for years, but it's back. I wasn't imagining it, I know I wasn't.'

He spoke softly, as if caressing me with his words, stroking me in the way his hands had done last night. And my body reacted in the same way it had last night. My eyes locked with his as his words made love to me.

'It wasn't just the sentiment of the night, it's something that's been growing for a while. It took facing the end for me to realise that you're the only person I can really talk to about anything that matters.

Whenever anything happens it's still you I want to tell and share it with.' He stepped closer. 'It's the way you smile, it's the way you care, it's about our history. After our talk the other week I've even been thinking about the dream we used to have of moving to the country and opening a little bookshop so I'd have access to everything I want to read, and you can run courses and author talks and get-togethers, and maybe even a little cafe. Remember that?'

I nodded, unable to speak.

He took another step towards me. 'With things as they are at work lately, I've been considering your suggestion of retiring early and doing that – before it's too late. And the only person I'd want to do it with is you, Katie. What do you say?'

I didn't know what to say. And even if I did, I couldn't have spoken. My heart had lodged in my throat and was stopping the words from getting past.

Finally he closed the gap between us and took my face in his hands. His kiss was gentle and left me wanting more.

'Promise me you'll think about what I've said,' he asked me.

I nodded.

'Say it,' he whispered.

'I promise.'

His smile was wide. 'That's all I ask. We'll talk soon, okay?'

'Okay.'

He kissed me again, then took the platter I'd forgotten I was holding and headed back out to the deck, looking back from the door.

After he left I stayed where I was for a few minutes more – just until my heart rate settled back into it's normal rhythm. I wanted to believe that he'd meant what he said, I really did, but Neil was the one who'd asked for a divorce. He was the one who'd said we needed to end whatever it was that we'd been hanging on to. I wanted to trust this feeling, but outside on the deck was the woman who intended to marry my husband as soon as he was finished with me – regardless of what he'd said his plans were.

What if Neil was running scared, afraid of the conflict and then the commitment that would inevitably come from a divorce? What if I was his safe option? And what of my life? I'd built a new life without him; I had a job where I was making a difference.

I shook my head as if it might clear the clutter of thoughts in my brain. There was no point dwelling on what-ifs now. I'd consider the options if and when Neil mentioned it again. Once the novelty of the wedding and having the kids with us was over, he'd get back into routine with Vanessa and forget all about what had happened in the garden last night and what we'd talked about today.

I only wished I could forget about it that easily.

~

Ash and Reece left on their honeymoon, Nathan flew back home to Cairns, and I attempted to settle into life in my big empty house. While this house had seen our children grow up and would always hold the memories of our family, there was no getting away from the fact that it was now too big. Ash would never again sleep in her old room; Nathan would never be home for more than a few nights at a time. Maybe it was time to sell up and buy something smaller. A house that I could manage on my own without relying on Neil to come by and mow the lawn or clean the pool. Perhaps I should get it valued and take that decision out of Neil's hands. If I was going to make a break, it made sense that it was a clean one.

When I took Nathan to the airport he refused to allow me to go into the terminal with him. 'Just drop me here, Mum,' he said. 'I don't need you to cry all over me at the gate.'

'But I'll be crying here in the car.'

'That's fine, I can't see you.'

I smiled and reached up to stroke his jaw. My tall, beautiful boy.

'Don't let her win, Mum.'

I didn't pretend to misunderstand him. 'I don't intend to.'

He nodded. 'My boss has been through this – the settlement and divorce thing – but his got pretty nasty. He said all that kept him going was remembering how much he loved his kids and how much he used to love his wife. No matter what happens, promise me you'll remember that about us and Dad – even when she's at her worst.'

'What about your dad? What if he's at his worst?'

'You and I both know that Dad doesn't do decisions well. If she pushes him too hard he'll dig his heels in – and that'll work in your favour. So stay strong.'

'I will,' I promised.

'And start dating. You need to get out there again, Mum. You deserve to be happy, and now that we've all gone, you need something – someone – that's for you.'

'Perhaps. But I've got work, and a mountain to train for – I don't really have time for a new man.'

He laughed. 'Fair enough. Perhaps you should head north and come visit me for a while.'

'Oh, Nath, that's a lovely offer, but I do need to stay here and get this sorted out once and for all.'

'Maybe I'll come and climb that mountain with you then. I've been meaning to have a look around the South Island, and at least that way I get to keep an eye on my old mum.'

I thumped his arm lightly. 'Not so much of the old, but I'd really like it if you did come.'

He smiled and swung his backpack onto his shoulders. 'It's a deal. Send me the details and I'll book it too.'

'You're serious?'

'I sure am.' He bent down to kiss my cheek. 'Love you, Mum.'

'I love you too, Nath. Take care.'

'Always.'

Ten

I was glad for the busyness of the office to distract me. After taking time off for the wedding, I had new clients to process, paperwork to catch up on, and appointments to schedule. And without anything – or anyone – to rush home for, I was happy to work late and offered to help anyone and everyone who needed it.

While I was at work, I could convince myself that those moments at the wedding and in the dining room the following day hadn't happened. That Neil hadn't touched me that way and hadn't said those words to me. None of it had happened. And while I was concentrating on someone else's problems, I didn't need to think about why I hadn't heard from him. Besides, I told myself, it had been forever since the files were properly archived.

Lying in bed each night was a different story. Then I allowed myself to indulge in the fantasies I was able to dismiss during the business of the day. In the dark I could pretend that Neil had phoned me and told me that he loved me, that he'd always loved me. If I closed my eyes I could pretend he was lying beside me, holding me the way he used to hold me.

Mari and I met on the Friday evening after the wedding at our local Italian restaurant. She and Ross were heading to Europe for an extended holiday so she was keen to catch up before they left. The first half-hour flew as we talked about the wedding and their coming trip, faltering only when Mari stopped mid-sentence to ask why I kept looking at my phone.

'Who are you expecting a call from?' she asked, never one to skirt around a subject when she could dive right in.

'No one.' I ducked my head so she wouldn't notice the heat I felt in my cheeks.

'Are you seeing someone?'

'No.' My reply sounded high-pitched.

'Bullshit.'

I shrugged.

She tilted her head to one side and examined me closely. 'A funny thing happened at Ash's wedding.'

'Oh? What was that?'

'I happened to see a look on Neil's face that I hadn't seen in years. In fact, I'd go as far as to say the last time I noticed him look like that was nearly thirty years ago when he was dancing with you at your wedding. It surprised me. What surprised me more was that he was gazing into your eyes at the time and not the eyes of his bitch of a girlfriend.'

'Maybe you were mistaken,' I said, forking through my pasta to pick out the bacon pieces. 'You know what I love about this place?' I didn't wait for her to answer. 'It's how they make the carbonara the way the Romans do, without cream. It's just the natural creaminess of the eggs mixed with a dash of the cooking water. Simple and effective.'

'Don't try and change the subject. I know what I saw. And I also know what I saw when I went to find you later to ask you about it and you'd disappeared. Then I saw Vanessa in the garden looking for Neil. It surprised me when she couldn't find him as I could have sworn I'd seen him follow you out there.' Her eyes bored into mine. 'What happened, darl?'

I moved my pasta around the plate some more, then put my fork down with a sigh. 'He came outside and we danced.'

'And?'

'And we kissed.'

'And?'

My eyes dropped to my plate.

'No way, Kate! You didn't hook up in the garden?' She half-laughed in disbelief, her hand flying to her mouth.

I failed to stop the smile spreading across my face. 'Not quite ... but it's probably fortunate that Vanessa didn't come out a few minutes earlier.'

'You didn't!'

'We did.'

She sat back in her chair, still grinning. 'Well, well, well ... I didn't know he had it in him. I didn't know you had it in you! Wow. I didn't see that one coming.'

'Me neither.'

'And he hasn't called?'

I shook my head, my smile fading. 'No. He kissed me again at my house the next day – with Vanessa sitting out on the deck having breakfast with the rest of the family. He said he wanted me to think about us starting over and buying that bookshop we always talked about. He made me promise to think about it – and not only have I not been able to stop thinking about it, I haven't heard from him all week.'

'So you think he's changed his mind again?'

'Yes. I was stupid to hope, but, Mari, it felt like he meant it.'

'I'm sure it did.'

'You sound like you don't believe me.'

'No, darl, I'm sure it did feel like that. Let's face it, it's been how long since you've had sex?'

I shrugged.

'Exactly. And this whole divorce thing – not to mention the emotional investment in the wedding – really threw you. There you are, Neil and Kate, together again watching your gorgeous offspring marry the man of her dreams. It had to bring back memories for both of you.'

'But what if it was more than that? What if he really did mean it?'

She hesitated before speaking. 'I can't tell you what to do, but just remember what you have to lose if this doesn't work. You've got a job doing something you believe in. Are you going to give that up to follow Neil and his dream?'

'It was always mine as well.'

'Yes, but now it sounds awfully like he's running away, and he wants you there to help him do it. You said it yourself – you guys were done, there was nothing left to save.'

'But what if we're not done? What if we just thought we were?'

'And what if you really are, and this little burst of passion is fear on both sides, and you end up right where you started – sitting around the kitchen table having no sex and no conversation?'

'I don't think so. Well, I didn't think so. We've been talking again over the last couple of weeks – really talking, like we used to. It's been nice.'

She scoffed. 'Nice? That's what started all this – you complained that Neil was always too nice and you wanted more than that.'

'Maybe,' I admitted. 'Or maybe I recognised his worth too late. You know what they say about not appreciating what's in front of you. Anyway, you've never liked him. Right from the start you warned me off him.'

I remembered the conversation as if it was yesterday. We were sprawled on the grass in Victoria Park behind the Law School at Sydney University. Mari had recently met Ross, an economics student, and through him was becoming more involved in the student union movement. I'd stopped going to some of the political meetings that she and I used to go to together and she blamed Neil.

'I hardly see you any more,' she complained.

'You see me all the time. You're seeing me now,' I pointed out.

'Yes, but I'm not seeing you at the events I used to see you at. I'm just going to say this once, Kate, because it pains me to say it.' She took a deep breath and raised her sunglasses so her eyes could meet mine. 'Before I know it, you'll have dropped out of uni and be languishing in domestic bliss in suburbia somewhere, saying that the issues you used to think were so important don't matter to you any more, that you're too busy making a home to think about anything else.'

'What if that stuff is important too?'

She stared at me for long seconds. 'See, it's happening already.'

'No, it's not – and you should know me better than that. All I'm saying is, what our mothers did was important too – for us. Isn't that a valid choice too? I thought that's what it was all about – having the ability to live in whatever way we choose. And before you say anything, I'll never sacrifice my career for a man. It's just that if people choose to do that, there's nothing wrong with it.'

'I suppose, when you put it like that,' Mari said. 'As long as it is a choice and not something women find themselves forced into through circumstance, or because they're opting for the easy way out. They're the ones who wake up one day, realise they're forty and they've compromised so much of who they are, and go into an almighty rebellion – and everything they've compromised for gets blown apart. Usually when the kids are off their hands and their purpose in life is gone.'

She rolled onto her back and replaced her sunglasses. A cloud moved across the sun, making it suddenly cool.

'Sounds like you're speaking from experience,' I said.

'Yeah. Mum and Dad are talking divorce.'

'Ah.'

'Yep. That word just about covers it. It turns out Dad's had something else going for a while. Mum knew about it but didn't want to rock the financial boat, so put up with it. He says it's over, but now that other people know about it I don't think Mum can ignore it any longer.' She paused. 'That's what really pisses me off. Not the affair – although there's no way that was right – but the fact that he can pick himself up and go back to work, whereas she has to start from absolute scratch because her whole life has been about him and us.'

She flipped back onto her tummy, her elbows digging into the grass, her hands cupping her face. 'At first I was so angry with her for putting up with it, and then I realised just how frightened she must have been. She must have felt trapped financially. I know she's worked a bit here and there in her friend's dress shop, but that's really only been for some play money. She certainly couldn't survive on it. If I asked her, I bet she'd say it was a choice she was happy to make to be there for us and to support Dad's career. But what he did made a mockery of those choices.'

'It wasn't really a choice though, was it?' I said. 'How could our mothers have a career? Offices didn't like to employ women who were going to leave and have babies; and there was no daycare. Our fathers always had the potential to make more money than our mothers did, so it wasn't so much a choice as practicality.'

'The thing is, it's not just our mothers though. There's still no daycare, still no pay equality, still no workplace flexibility – and until there is, women will still be the ones making that compromise and waking up one day when the kids have grown up wondering what the fuck happened to their life.' She sat up and looked straight at me. 'And that's why we can't be the ones to compromise. That's why we have to keep fighting and pushing for change. I love my parents, and will continue to do so regardless of whether or not they divorce, but I'm not my mother. There is no way I'm putting myself in a position where financial circumstances dictate whether I can leave a relationship that isn't working any more.' She began to pack the books we hadn't opened back into her bag. 'That's why I'm warning you about Neil. I don't want you to be in that situation either. He doesn't think the way you do. He's quite happy for things to unfold in the conventional order. Before you know it you'll be living our parents' life, and one day you'll wake up and be forty and not know how you got there.'

'Don't worry,' I said again. 'Neil understands what's important to me, and he knows how I feel about my career and wanting to make a difference. He'd never force me to make that choice.'

She nodded, but I didn't think she believed me. I could see her eyebrows raised under her sunglasses and her tongue pushing at the right side of her mouth.

Now, over thirty years later, Mari must have been remembering the same conversation because she said, 'I didn't want to be right, you know. And I did grow to love Neil. I still do. I just don't want to see you hurt again, and I don't want to see you give up on what you believe this time.'

'I won't,' I assured her. 'If we do end up together, and we do run away and buy our bookshop, I'll be doing what I wanted to do. And if we don't end up together, I'll be making sure that Vanessa gets nothing that belongs to my kids.'

'Just be careful, darl. And tell Neil that if he hurts you again I'll hunt him down and kill him.'

'I'll tell him. But now can we please talk about something more exciting – like Europe. You know I'll be travelling vicariously with you through your social media.'

'Let this divorce go through and you'll have the money and independence to do it yourself.'

'You really like to have the last word, don't you?'

'Absolutely.'

On Saturday afternoon, I drove to Drummoyne and parked under the Iron Cove Bridge to walk around the bay. Neil had said he'd do this walk with me. 'It's a good one to start getting your distance up,' he'd said. 'A flat seven-kilometre circuit.' But Neil was with Vanessa so I did it on my own.

It was Sunday afternoon before I saw him – at his parents' house. I'd baked some muffins and, with no one at home to eat them, packaged them up to take to Maureen and Dave. Vanessa and Neil were sitting at the kitchen table, drinking coffee, when I arrived.

Neil stood to greet me, but I waved him back to his seat. Vanessa hung onto his arm and smiled briefly.

'Kate, this is a lovely surprise,' Maureen said.

'I'm sorry I didn't call first. I had an urge to bake,

and then it was a case of what I did with the baking, so I thought of you. You can pop some in the freezer, but I know you have morning tea on Mondays so I thought you could take the rest along to that. It's a spicy ginger muffin so it doesn't need any icing – just a shake of icing sugar will do fine.' I knew I was babbling, but I hadn't expected to see Neil.

'You don't need to apologise for not calling ahead,' said Maureen, breaking the top off one of the muffins to taste it. 'We always love to see you – and especially when you bring us treats like this.'

'They look and smell pretty good,' said Dave. 'Neil, stick your nose into one of these.'

I couldn't look at Neil so I flicked the switch on the kettle and busied myself making a cup of tea.

'I'm glad you dropped around too,' Vanessa said to me. 'It saves Neil arranging a time to call over during the week.'

I raised my eyebrows at Neil. Since when did he need to arrange a time to call over?

He lowered his gaze and I understood. She was scheduling in the divorce discussion. So he'd changed his mind about not wanting to go ahead. No wonder I hadn't heard from him. Last weekend meant nothing to him – and why would it?

'Any evening suits,' I said. 'Come for dinner, I'll cook.' If I had to lose, I intended to do it with dignity.

Vanessa opened her mouth, probably to say

something about how we needed to keep this as a business discussion and dinner wasn't necessary.

'How about Wednesday?' Neil said, getting in first.

I nodded, turning away from Vanessa's triumphant smile. So that was it – the divorce was happening. We'd reached the end.

Eleven

As I contemplated the menu for Wednesday night, it felt a little as though I was preparing for the Last Supper. What to cook as a farewell meal for the man you'd spent your entire adult life in love with? Should I go with one of his favourites, or would that be too obvious? What about something that I knew would annoy Vanessa, like pasta or a pie? Maybe I should prepare a dish to remind him how we used to be. Or would it be better to cook something that had no emotional attachment at all?

Then there was the order of proceedings to consider. Would we be talking, then eating? Or eating, then talking? Or talking while eating?

As it turned out, my final meeting that Wednesday ran late so I didn't walk in my front door until almost half past six. That gave me thirty minutes to get changed, defrost a pasta sauce from the freezer and put together a green salad.

Although I tried hard not to, as I cooked this final meal for Neil I couldn't help remembering the first meal he'd cooked for me – which was also the first time we made love. We'd had spaghetti bolognaise that night too.

Neil knocked on the door right on the dot of seven.

'You could have used your key,' I said.

He kissed me on the cheek. 'It didn't seem right.'

'Yes, well, I've poured you a glass of red.' I led him into the kitchen where I had a simple cheese platter prepared.

'Oh, I need this,' he said, taking a sip of wine. 'It's been one of those days. Actually, it's been one of those weeks.' He looked at me. 'Who am I kidding? It's been one of those months.'

'Don't you mean it's been one of those years?'

He laughed ruefully. 'True. I thought things had turned around – I achieved the targets Roger needed me to.'

'So what's the problem?'

'There's now a new set of targets and I suspect the biggest of those is the one on my back.'

'They can't do that,' I said, sitting down opposite him. 'What about all those years of loyal service? What about that? They can't do this to you.'

'They can. I've told you how I've seen it happen with others of my vintage. We don't fit the demographic, and we're paid too much because we've been around for so long.'

'But they set you up to fail – surely that's not right? What about the union, can't we involve them? It's bullying and harassment at its worst. They can't get away with this. You deserve to go out with your head held high. We need to think about the best way to deal with this.'

I sipped my wine as I pondered the problem. I'd had a client not long ago who was taking action against one of the big banks for something similar. I made a mental note to dig the file out.

Neil was smiling at me. It was an indulgent smile, like he used to give me whenever I got het up about something that had happened at the kids' school, or whenever I heard about meanness or unfairness.

'Why are you smiling?' I asked. 'I can't see how you've got anything to smile about.'

'I'm smiling about you, Katie. How you automatically went to "we". It's not just my problem any more – you've made it yours as well.'

I felt the heat rise to my cheeks and downed the rest of my wine, then reached for the bottle to top up my glass. 'I'm sorry, you're right. It's not my business any more. Have you told Vanessa yet?'

'No.' He suddenly looked his age. 'You've always been the only one I can talk to about things like this. She'd want me to see an industrial lawyer and it'd all blow up in my face.'

I reached over and covered his hand with mine.

'Maybe it needs to be blown up,' I said softly. 'What they're doing isn't right. It's stripping dignity from you at a time when they should be rewarding your experience and loyalty. Stepping back and letting them get away with it might seem like the easiest option, but it's not. And just because they've done it to others doesn't make it right – in fact, it makes it even more wrong. Think about your health. I know you keep yourself fit, but this can't be doing your blood pressure any good. Then there's the precedent that's being set. If this is happening to you, you can bet your last dollar they've put someone else through this. If they push you out and you say and do nothing, you're letting them go on to do the same thing to someone else – and that someone else might not have the assets we do or be as financially secure.' I realised what I'd said and put my hand over my mouth. 'I did it again, didn't I?'

I thought for a second. 'Is that the real reason you want to get the property sorted? So you know what you have to start again with? I just assumed it was because you wanted to marry Vanessa and possibly have another family with her.'

He drained his wine and poured another. 'I told you the other day, I don't want this divorce or the settlement that goes with it. I wish I'd never asked for it – although maybe if I hadn't, I wouldn't have realised I don't want it. I wouldn't have known how much I still want you.'

I stared at him, and he stared back at me. I bit my bottom lip to stop the emotion from welling up, then stood suddenly, almost spilling my wine. I opened the drawer and got a saucepan out, filled it with hot water and threw in some salt. The whole time I was working I could feel his eyes on me. Once the saucepan was on the hob, I turned back to face him.

'You don't get to say that, Neil. You started this ball rolling – you and Vanessa. There had to be a reason for it, and that can't have changed in the last month or so. The thing is, I think I need this to happen now so I can move on. The last four years have been a weird sort of half-life for me.'

'You could have dated,' he said. 'We were separated. It wasn't as if you'd have been unfaithful by being with someone else.'

'It didn't feel right,' I said.

'What about whatever it was that went on that Christmas before I went to Everest? Did that feel right?'

My mouth dropped open. 'You knew about that?'

'Of course I did. Not what had happened or who with, but I knew you'd stepped away from me. It felt like I wasn't enough for you any more, that you wanted something different. You hadn't been interested in making love with me for ages. I still wanted you so much but I'd got to the point where I felt guilty asking you.' He paused. 'It felt like you'd given up on us.'

'I never slept with him,' I said. 'It was stupid, like a ridiculous crush.'

'Maybe, but the mere fact that you were tempted and put yourself in a position where you could have stepped in that direction was enough to tell me that there was something very wrong between us. That you were looking for something that you weren't getting from me. And then when you came back … well, that felt worse. As though you'd decided to stay with me because I was the comfortable, safe option.'

'I chose you, Neil.'

'No, Katie, you settled with me. Then you went out of your way to make sure you wouldn't be tempted again.'

I wanted to argue with him, but couldn't. What he was saying was right.

'Is that why you did Everest?' I asked.

He nodded. 'I wanted to give us both the space we needed to think.'

'But you met Vanessa.'

'Yes.'

'And then you left.'

He nodded.

'Would you have left if you hadn't met Vanessa?'

He didn't hesitate. 'Yes. I didn't want to be with someone who was settling for me out of guilt. I thought that if I left, you'd find yourself again. And then maybe you'd find us again.'

I leaned back against the counter and watched him. 'Why didn't you say anything back then?'

'What could I say? You would have denied it, and we would have fought about it. I didn't want to fight.'

'You didn't want to fight about anything – that was part of the problem. I wanted to feel like it mattered enough for us to fight about. I wanted to know that I mattered enough.'

'You mattered so much that I didn't want to make it ugly.' The sadness in his voice convinced me. 'At the end, I felt it was better for me to walk away so we had a chance of still being in each other's lives. I was hoping you'd miss me enough that you'd ask me to come back.'

'And I was hoping that you'd do the same, but then you started seeing Vanessa and I knew you were never coming back.'

I closed my eyes for a heartbeat as the possibility of what might have been ran through my head. But it was all too late.

'I need to put the pasta on,' I said, 'or we won't be eating until very late.'

'Katie –'

'No, no more … not yet. I can't … My head can't … take anything else in.'

He nodded, the movement so slight I could have imagined it. 'Okay. What's for dinner then?'

'Spaghetti bolognaise with a green salad. I've got some garlic bread to go with it, but I wasn't sure …'

'Whether I'm allowed to eat carbs, or if Vanessa would be turned off if I went home smelling of garlic?' Neil grinned and cocked one eyebrow as he correctly guessed my thoughts. 'Pop it in the oven. It sounds great. Besides, I don't see Vanessa on Wednesday nights.'

'Won't she be wanting to know how our discussion went?'

'Probably, but she can wait. I've asked her to stay out of this – to leave it to us to settle and sort. I told her I wouldn't have her upsetting you the way she did the other week. We've had a good thing these past few years where everyone's gotten on; I don't want that to change.'

'It's already changed. Once this house has sold, there'll be no need for you to come around and help me with things. She won't let you anyway.'

'I don't want you to sell the house.'

'I've been thinking that it's time,' I said. 'The kids have left, and they're never coming home. And it's quite frankly too big for me to look after and live in alone. Besides, this was our house.'

I turned to stir the sauce and check on the pasta. It wasn't quite al dente – another minute or so would do it.

'The fact of the matter is that this is partly Vanessa's business,' I went on, my tone bitter. 'You might not want to start again, but she's at the age where if she wants children she needs to have them very soon. You've proved yourself to be a good father, so why not pick you for her own kids? Plus you come with real estate, and heaven knows it's impossible to get into the Sydney housing market. You're the perfect choice. And she's going to want to make sure that, financially speaking, she and her children are covered if anything happens to you.'

His smile was wry. 'That's why I've decided that if we do go ahead with the settlement, I'll be syphoning off my share. Vanessa's been so interested in the money side of things that I'm beginning to suspect she has ulterior motives. If she wants to be with me, we can start from a level playing field – the same way you and I did. I suspect that when I tell her that, she won't be quite as keen on the idea – which would be a good thing as far as I'm concerned.'

'Don't say that. I'm sure she loves you for you.' I forced some sincerity into my voice.

'Are you? I'm not so sure. And –'

'Don't say any more.' The pasta was perfect so I poured it into the colander I had waiting in the sink. 'I can't talk about this any more.' I laughed briefly to hide the pain I felt. 'The subject's likely to give me indigestion.'

His eyes met mine and he finally nodded. 'Okay, we'll talk after dinner. But I need you to hear me out, Katie.'

'I know.'

As we ate, we talked about the kids – the photos that

Ash had posted on social media, the house she and Reece were moving into when they got home, the research project that Nathan was involved with. Anything other than what I knew we needed to talk about.

It wasn't until we'd almost finished, both of us mopping up leftover sauce with garlic bread, that Neil said, 'I don't love Vanessa, Katie. I thought I did, but I don't. I don't want to divorce you and I don't want to marry her. I haven't been able to think of anything but you since the wedding. I don't want to be with anyone else but you.'

'Then why didn't you call? I thought it meant nothing to you.'

He sighed. 'Oh, Katie, it meant everything to me. I didn't call you because I didn't think it meant anything to you. I thought I'd give you some time once things settled back down to normal to realise that it did mean something – but you didn't call, and when I saw you on Sunday you couldn't even look at me.'

'No,' I admitted. 'You were with her and I couldn't watch her touching you.'

'If you had looked at me, you would have seen me watching you.' He paused. 'You promised to think about what I'd said, so when you couldn't look at me and you seemed so anxious to proceed with this meeting, I thought you'd decided you wanted the divorce and not me.' His eyes held mine across the table. 'Do you, Katie? Do you want this divorce to go ahead?'

'It has to,' I mumbled.

His smile was gentle. 'I asked if you wanted it to.'

I dropped my eyes from his and shook my head. I thought I heard him let out a breath.

'The very first meal I cooked you was spaghetti bolognaise,' he said. 'Do you remember?'

I felt the warmth rush through my body as I remembered what happened after we'd eaten that meal.

'I do. It was the only thing you could cook,' I said.

'It was also the first time we made love.'

I looked up from my plate and met his gaze, suddenly unable to breathe normally. 'So it was. I'd forgotten that part.'

I rose and stacked the plates, then placed them in the sink, willing the memories to go back to where they belonged.

'Liar.' He'd come up behind me, and whispered the word in my ear. 'You remember that night as well as I do.'

I closed my eyes as goosebumps travelled from my ear down my neck, spread across my chest and down to my fingertips, making me lose my grip on the edge of the sink. I swayed backwards into his body, but still he didn't touch me.

'Every time we've had spag bol over the years I've remembered that night.' He breathed the words into my neck and I tilted my head to the side in an invitation for his kiss, my eyes still closed, all my other senses heightened. 'Every delicious second of it.'

His kiss when it came was feather-light, almost a whisper, and my moan almost a sigh. I moved to turn in his arms, and he stopped me, putting his hands over mine, holding me against his hardening body.

'No, Katie. Stay right there, and let's see just how good my memory is of that night.'

'I've forgotten most of it,' I said, then gasped as he nipped at my earlobe, the sensation sending more goosebumps piling on top of the ones already jostling across my skin.

'Let me refresh your memory,' he said, nuzzling his way down my neck, his hand sliding under my T-shirt to cup my breast. 'Are you remembering anything now?'

'It's beginning to come back to me.' His thumb flicked across my nipple. 'Ohhh ...'

'You were wearing these cute little shorts and I couldn't wait to get you out of them. I was so hard just looking at you that I was sure I wouldn't last until after we'd eaten.'

He deftly undid the button on my jeans. I wriggled my hips against him to help him push them down, and felt his groan through my body.

'What about if I touch you like this?' His hand slid inside my knickers, his fingers playing with me the way he had that night all those years ago, the way he had at the wedding.

I arched into him, one hand gripping the sink, the

other holding his hand in place.

'And now?' he breathed.

'Oh, Neil. Don't stop. Please don't stop.'

'Yes, that's exactly what you said that night too.'

I heard the smile in his voice as he worked me expertly to a climax that had me calling out his name in a way I hadn't done for many years.

He held me until the shudders inside me stopped. Finally, he allowed me to turn in his arms, and I reached to pull his mouth down for the kiss I'd been craving. He tasted of garlic and herbs and red wine and comfort.

'We shouldn't have done that,' I said when we paused for air.

'Probably not, but I've been desperate to touch you again since the night of Ash's wedding.'

'Me too,' I admitted, reaching between us to unzip his jeans. He closed his eyes as I held him in my hand, squeezing and releasing, loving the feel as he hardened even more in my grip.

'Oh, Katie, that feels so good.'

I released him to push his jeans and undies down. He kicked them away, and I did the same with mine.

'So what happens now?' he asked, walking me backwards until my legs hit the table.

'Oh, I remember this part very clearly,' I said. 'This is when you took me to bed.'

He shook his head, his eyes holding mine. 'Not tonight. I don't think I can wait until we reach the bedroom.' He lifted me until I was sitting on the edge of the table.

My cry of pleased surprise was silenced by his mouth. 'Shhhhh,' he said. 'Now, let me see if my memory is correct for this part.'

He stood back and looked at me, his eyes drawing a line from my breasts, only partially revealed, down my belly, and lingering between my legs. His fingers trailed the same path, slowly, lightly, leaving little spot fires in their wake. They dipped between my legs, circling through the curls there, teasing but not lingering long enough to ease the ache that was building again inside me.

I raised my hips towards him, squirming and groaning my frustration. 'Please, Neil.'

'Please what? Please do this?' He thrust two fingers inside me and I arched back in pleasure.

'Oh, yes.'

'Or please do this?' He pulled his fingers out and stroked me, back and forth.

'Mmmmm. Yes.'

'Or maybe it's please do this?'

He lowered his head and ran his tongue where his fingers had been, rolling, sucking, licking, his fingers now back inside me, pressing into that little ball of nerves until I came hard into his mouth.

'Oh god, yes. Yes!'

While I was still a mass of fabulous spasms, he

lifted my hips and slid into me, filling me, surrounding me with his heat, stroking me until I reached yet another peak, screaming out his name.

'Christ, Katie,' he groaned, 'I can't hang on any longer.'

'Then don't,' I moaned, my legs wrapping around him to pull him in tighter.

'Oh, Katie,' he cried as he released into me and collapsed on top of me.

I held him to me until it became too uncomfortable. He seemed to know the exact time and pulled away.

'Let's take this to the bedroom,' he said, pulling me to my feet and holding my hand as we walked up the stairs.

It was only when we were in the bedroom and had removed the last of our clothes that I felt shy and self-conscious under his gaze, just as I had that first time. He was used to seeing the body of a woman in her thirties who took care of herself, whereas I was fifty with a body that had given birth to two children and which I hadn't looked after nearly as well as I should have. In comparison, he was in better physical condition than he had been the whole time we were married. His stomach was flat and toned, his legs strong and muscled, his chest and arms defined. He looked fitter at nearly fifty-five than he had at twenty-three.

'Don't, Katie,' he said when I went to get a wrap to cover myself up. 'You're still beautiful.'

I shook my head. 'No, I'm not. I'm squishy and old, and I haven't waxed in forever –'

He didn't let me finish. Instead he pushed me back onto the bed and kissed me.

'Now,' he murmured, 'what do I need to do to prove to you how much I want you?'

He kissed his way down my throat to my breasts, taking one nipple in his mouth, then circling the other with his tongue.

'That will do for a start,' I moaned.

Afterwards, Neil held me close. I burrowed into his warmth, afraid to move in case it broke the connection.

'That was …' I said.

'It was, wasn't it?'

'Why didn't we …?'

'Do that when we were together?'

I nodded.

'I don't know. Maybe we got out of the habit. Maybe we took each other for granted. Maybe neither of us knew how to ask for what we wanted. Or maybe it was all those things.'

'What happens now?' It was the question I was afraid to ask, but knew it had to be asked.

'I don't know,' he said again. 'I truly don't know.'

He fell asleep soon after, his arm still around me. I lay awake for longer, enjoying his warmth, the sound of his soft snores. Soon, though, the weight of his arm around me made me feel too hot, so I eased myself out from his hold and, wrapping a dressing gown around me, went downstairs to make a cup of herbal tea.

Curling up on the lounge, I allowed myself to go back to when it all started.

Twelve

The first time I laid eyes on Neil Spence was at a Hiroshima Day rally in August 1985. Thousands of us marched up Sydney's George Street holding banners and chanting 'Hiroshima never again'. It was a big year for the nuclear disarmament cause. Not only did this year's march coincide with forty years since the bomb was dropped on Hiroshima, but it was just a month since Greenpeace's ship, the *Rainbow Warrior*, had been sunk in New Zealand.

Here in Australia, despite a member of the Nuclear Disarmament Party being elected to the Senate in the previous year's election – even if it wasn't our poster boy, Peter Garrett – there was a mass walkout of members at the NDP national conference in Melbourne in April. The party was crumbling, but it was vital that the cause remained strong. The word around Sydney University was that this year's march would be an important one – we needed as many people to join us as we could get. Besides, there were rumours that Peter Garrett and Midnight Oil might be playing down at Circular Quay after the march.

I didn't really believe that the Oils would be playing, nor did I think that marching could make much of a difference, but it was the Cold War and I did believe we needed to do try to do something about it. The actions of our parents' and grandparents' generations had put us in this predicament, and it was up to us to ensure there was still a world for our own children to inhabit and inherit.

My boyfriend at the time was a political science major I'd met during a lecture on the politics of the USSR and Eastern Europe. Miles and I were both sitting down the front – him because he was earnest, and me because I'd forgotten my glasses (again) so couldn't see the lecturer otherwise. Miles was wearing well-worn jeans that were frayed at the hems, battered tennis shoes and a brown acrylic cable-knit jumper. On the bench seat beside him was one of those canvas satchels that earnest students carried, which you could only get from army disposal stores.

The political science students had an edge that the law students didn't. Everyone in my law lectures looked fresh, clean and entitled. The majority of them hailed from the better private schools in Sydney, and the girls all looked neat and expensive and wore a lot of white. Although I was studying the same subjects as them, I had no wish to be like them. I knew that most of the girls were biding their time until they met someone suitable. I wasn't doing law for that reason, or because I wanted to make a heap of money. For me it was about making a difference. I wanted to help people who couldn't afford to help themselves; fight for causes that had been lost under the influence of the capitalist machine. Human rights and environmental issues – that's what I was in it for.

So I bought myself a canvas rucksack, tie-dyed it, and befriended arts and politics students. Sure, many of them were entitled too, but I was able to overlook that. Irene, a friend I'd met in that Russian politics class, lived in an apartment in the eastern suburbs that was filled with the latest furniture and had a sleek sound system. Her parents – both academics – were teaching in the UK, so she had the whole beautiful apartment to herself. She invited groups of us over to talk about issues. We'd smoke pot and mix tequila sunrises. It was all terribly glamorous, yet at the same time the reverse of glamour – especially the hangovers. I'd never been able to look at tequila in the same way again.

After months of me sitting next to Miles at the front of the lecture hall, it was at one of Irene's gatherings that he actually noticed me. We were standing outside on the balcony and, before I could change my mind, I launched myself at his lips. One thing led to another and I finally lost my virginity on a beanbag in Irene's spare room. The whole thing was very unremarkable.

By the time August and the march came around,

Miles's earnestness was boring me. His single-minded devotion to the nuclear disarmament cause meant that our relationship – if you could call the occasional snog and poke a relationship – came a distant second. I wanted to make a difference too, but my interests and political affiliations were wider than his. As a result, I'd already decided that Hiroshima Day would be both the first and last time I marched – at least for this particular cause – and also the last time I'd see Miles. I didn't flatter myself that he'd even notice I'd gone.

Once the march finished and the crowd dispersed, I hung around on the grass outside the Maritime Services Board. Neil was sitting just a few feet away from me reading a book – *Schindler's Ark* by Thomas Keneally. It had been on my 'to be read' list ever since. Maybe one day I'd actually read it. Dressed in a sloppy joe, jeans and sneakers, he didn't look the type to be marching.

Nevertheless, I called out to him from my spot on the grass. 'Hey, did you do the march?'

'No,' he said, looking up from his book. 'I heard rumours during the week that Midnight Oil would be playing down here. But it would seem they're not.' His voice trailed off as he looked around the Quay – all evidence of the protest already gone. 'What about you?'

'I marched.'

'So you're part of all of that?'

I shrugged. 'I guess. My boyfriend – although I think he's my ex-boyfriend now – is into it all.'

'You're not?'

I shrugged again. 'I am, but not as much as he is. Anyway, I heard that Midnight Oil were going to be here too.' Our eyes met and I grinned at him and wriggled closer on the grass. 'My name's Kate.'

'I'm Neil.' He placed a bookmark into his book, closed it, wiped his hand on his jeans and held it out to me to shake. 'It's nice to meet you, Kate.'

I leaned back on my elbows, tilted my head to the side and studied him. He looked nice. Not edgy and interesting like my uni friends, but ordinary and nice.

'You must be a fan if you're prepared to brave the crowds and the placards,' I said. 'Have you seen them play live?'

His eyes lit up. 'Yep. I was at Goat Island in January. I won the tickets on Triple J, the radio station.'

I was impressed. 'Wow. How lucky were you? I listened to the concert on the radio and watched it on TV afterwards. That moment when the fireboat sprayed water everywhere ...' I shook my head. 'That was magic.'

'You should have been there – it was amazing. And opening with "Best of Both Worlds" was an inspired choice. It's my favourite from that album.'

'Really? I'm torn between "When the Generals Talk" and "Minutes to Midnight".'

He nodded. 'Good choices. You know, *Red Sails in the Sunset* is a fabulous album, but I still prefer *10 to 1*. I think we're going to be hearing "Power and the

Passion" and "US Forces" for years to come.'

'You could be right. I even used a line from "Power and the Passion" in an economics essay. The one about the bombs never hitting when you're down so low.'

His nod was one of respect. 'Did you pass?'

'Not only did I pass, my friend, but I remembered to attribute it correctly and got a distinction. For that I can thank Peter Garrett.'

We ended up taking our discussion into one of the pubs in The Rocks.

'What I don't understand,' I slurred a couple of hours later, 'is how you can love these songs but not be moved by the message. If it wasn't for Goanna's "Let the Franklin Flow" there'd be a dam in one of the most beautiful wilderness areas in Tasmania.'

'Have you been there?'

'Well, no, but it's meant to be beautiful. Places like that should be preserved. Once it's gone it's too late. After all, we'll never ever get Lake Pedder back.'

'Let me guess – Redgum?'

'Yes!' I clinked his glass in celebration.

At around 5 pm I looked at my watch. 'Bugger, I told Mum and Dad I'd be home for dinner. I'd better call and tell them I'll be late.' I looked around the bar for a payphone.

'Do you need coins?' he asked.

'No, I have some.'

'Make your call and then I'll walk you to the

station,' he said.

After that we saw each other at least once each weekend and spent hours on the phone during the week. Neil was everything I wasn't looking for in a boyfriend. At nearly twenty-three he was almost five years older than me, but seemed much older – probably because rather than going to university, he'd got a job in a bank straight out of high school. It sounded very boring to me, but it was obvious he took pride in his work, so I resisted the urge to talk to him about capitalism and the scourges of big business and the generals of the corporate world.

He was also exactly the sort of boyfriend my parents had been hoping I'd have, from a good solid middle-class family. His mother, like mine, had stayed at home to raise her children; and Neil's own ambitions were to save for a deposit on a house, and find someone to marry, settle down and raise a family with. There was no way I was introducing him to my parents – he was too perfect for them and therefore too wrong for me. I didn't want to marry, and I didn't want to be a housewife. I had other plans for my life, and none of them involved conforming to a societal norm.

Despite that, I fell hard for Neil – right from that very first afternoon. I didn't know if it was because of the shared music, or the way he smiled slowly at me, or even the challenge he represented for me. We'd laughed that Redgum's 'It Doesn't Matter to Me' or the Oils' 'Don't Wanna Be the One' could have been written for him. Neil needed a social conscience and I was the girl to give it to him.

'You know,' I said one afternoon in the Botanical Gardens, 'that line in "Don't Wanna Be the One", about not being bothered if I don't make it to the top, was the first piece of toilet graffiti I saw in uni.'

We were under 'our tree' – the huge Moreton Bay fig that stood above the Opera House, from where you could see across the blue to Fort Denison and beyond. We spent a lot of time under the shade of that tree. I loved its tangled roots and the green canopy through which I could see the sun twinkling. It was the same tree we got married under almost five years later.

Neil was sitting with his back against the trunk, a book in his hand, my head in his lap. He idly traced a pattern on my arm with a blade of grass. 'And what did it make you think about?'

'How great it was to be somewhere the toilet conversation was more interesting than "For a good time, call …"'

He laughed and bent down to kiss me.

We did a lot of that in those days – kissing. It was as if it had been invented for us. I could have kissed Neil all day and all night. All through spring, we'd meet in the city and we'd kiss and talk and kiss some more.

Neil told me he loved me just two weeks after the Hiroshima Day march. We were lying on our backs on the grass under that same Moreton Bay fig. He reached for my hand, turned to me and said simply, 'I love you, Katie.'

I smiled. Even though I felt it too, I wasn't going to tell him so just yet. 'Oh, shut up and kiss me,' I said instead.

The closest we came to having our first proper argument was in November. It was Neil's birthday and he'd invited me home to meet his family. Although it was such a simple request, I couldn't agree.

'I don't think we're ready for that yet,' I said.

'We've been together three months, Katie. I love you and I want my family to meet you. Where's the harm in that?'

'It's not just meeting your family though, is it? Next you'll be wanting to meet mine and I'm not ready for that to happen.'

His chin firmed and he moved back into the driver's seat of his car. 'Why not? Are you embarrassed of me?'

'Of course I'm not!'

'Do you think your parents won't like me? Is it because I'm not clever like you and not studying? Is that what's wrong? Or maybe it's because I'm older?'

'Of course it isn't.'

'Well, what is it then? Because I have no idea why you're hiding me away.'

'I'm not hiding you away. It's just that ...' I let

out a breath and blurted it out. 'I think they'll like you too much, and then we won't be able to have any time together. Not on our own. It'll be all invitations to dinner and tea and everything else, and these moments – when it's just us – will be gone. It happens every time they like one of Lachie's girlfriends. They don't mean to, but I'm sure it's why the girlfriends don't last.'

I didn't tell him that I was mostly afraid of seeing approval and relief in my parents' eyes. Neil was everything I'd always said I didn't want. I was supposed to end up with someone clever and earnest and determined to save the world. Someone like Miles. We'd live together and flout the conventions of society. I didn't want my parents' life, as grateful as I was for my comfortable upbringing. I'd always announced that marriage wasn't for me, that I didn't need a piece of paper to make a commitment. I was going to live with my man, and wait until I was in my late twenties or early thirties before I had children – if I decided to have any at all. And if we did have children, they'd go to a public school and be taught about issues. I'd be an independent working woman who could have it all and do it all with a baby strapped to each hip.

None of that was Neil. He wanted marriage, a mortgage, babies, and a wife he could provide for and come home to. And he wanted it all in the proper order. I loved him, but his idea of the future and mine were very different. And meeting the parents would bring those differences out to play before I was ready to face them. But I couldn't tell him any of that.

He smiled at me. 'I love how we are too, Katie, but I think it's time we let the rest of the world in a little. If it makes you feel better, I won't push to meet your parents just yet, but I do want you to meet mine. It would be the best birthday present you could give me.'

So I met his parents and they seemed to like me, even though Neil told me that Dave was concerned I was too young, and Maureen worried that I might be too ambitious, but all in all it was a lovely evening.

That night, when Neil drove me home, we stopped the car where we always did – in the park at the end of my street. As always, we moved into the back seat so he could kiss me properly. Even though he knew I wasn't a virgin, he treated me as though I was a precious package to be opened only by him. Tonight, for the first time, we didn't stop at kisses. Neil gently moved me back in the seat until I was lying under him. I could feel his hardness pushing into me. In the past he'd apologised for it, as though it was something he should be able to control. Tonight he said nothing, and rather than cupping my breasts through the fabric of my T-shirt, he lifted it up and his hand slid under my bra to move it aside. Then his mouth was on me, licking and sucking at my nipple.

When I'd been with Miles, he hadn't really paid any attention to my pleasure. For him, sex was some perfunctory kisses, followed by a couple of fingers pushed inside me to make sure I was ready, then a bit of poking and grunting until he came. It was one of the reasons I'd been glad that Neil had always been happy with kisses. Kissing was lovely – especially the way he did it. I wanted him – I knew what that feeling of heaviness between my legs when we were kissing meant – but I was afraid that once we moved on from kissing, I'd be disappointed like I had been with Miles.

I was soon to discover that Neil was very different to Miles.

When Neil took my breast into his mouth and suckled at it, it felt as though there was a direct line of sensation that ran right through the core of me. I tried to touch him back, but he held both of my hands above my body and whispered into my neck, 'No, my darling, this is for you.'

After that? I hadn't known my body was capable of feeling so much. While his mouth was still working at my nipple, he slid his hand down my belly, across my hip, and into my pants. I gasped out loud when the pressure built inside me and I could hear myself moaning, feel myself thrusting upwards into his hand, towards something I'd had no idea existed but needed to reach.

'It's okay,' he murmured, his eyes holding mine. 'Let yourself go.'

And then he lightly bit my nipple and the world spun out of control.

He kept his hand on me until all the spasms within me settled. Then he kissed me one last time and sat back to pull my bra and my T-shirt into place. Only once I was respectable again did he lie back on the seat and hold me.

'That was ...' I started.

'It was, wasn't it?'

'But you didn't –'

'Tonight was for you.' He smiled into my eyes and kissed me again.

'I never knew it could be like that,' I said.

I was sure that if I could have seen them, my eyes would be shining with the wonder of how he'd just made me feel.

'You never got there with Miles?'

I shook my head. 'I never got there with Miles. He never made me feel like that.'

'Good,' he said, his smile almost triumphant.

We made love for the first time just a week after that wonderful moment in his car.

I knew exactly what he was asking me when he said, 'My family's away this weekend. I think it's time we had a sleepover, don't you?'

A thrill rushed through me at his words and how his voice deepened when he said them. I so badly wanted to feel the way he'd made me feel that night in his car, but was still afraid that having sex with him would be as underwhelming as it had been with Miles. Despite my fears, I told Mum and Dad that there was a uni party at Irene's house and I'd stay overnight there.

Neil picked me up from the station. He kissed me deeply, then pulled back to smile into my eyes. 'I've cooked us dinner,' he said. 'I hope you like spaghetti bolognaise – it's all I know how to make.'

I was surprised. None of the men I knew cooked. My father was like most fathers of that generation – useless in the kitchen, but okay around a naked flame as long as all the ingredients were provided to him in the order in which they needed to be cremated. It was yet another way that Neil was different to every boy I'd met before.

'I do,' I said. 'It's my favourite.'

It wasn't, but the grin that spread across his face made me glad that I'd lied.

He poured us each some wine out of a cask in the fridge, and told me to sit down at the kitchen table while he finished cooking.

It wasn't until after we'd eaten and done the washing up that he wrapped his arms around me from behind. As he pulled me closer I could feel his hardness pressing into the small of my back.

'It's been hard all evening,' he said, and the way he said it sounded like a compliment. The words sent a zing through my body that settled somewhere between my thighs.

'I love you, Katie,' he murmured into the sensitive part of the side of my throat.

Goosebumps developed on top of goosebumps and I moaned and arched my head to give him greater access to the line of my neck. One hand crept up under my T-shirt and kneaded at my breast. It felt fuller than they'd ever felt before and swelled to fit into his hand.

I tried to turn in his embrace so I could touch him too, but he stopped me.

'No, my lovely Katie, we're just getting started.' He undid the button and zip on my shorts, his hand slipping inside. He held me up when my legs would have buckled under me. 'And now,' he whispered, 'let's go to bed.'

'Okay,' I whispered back, even though there was no one around to hear me, and even though my cries just a few minutes ago had been much louder.

Once we were in his bedroom, the fears came back. Neil had told me he'd slept with other girls, so what if I was a disappointment? What if the reason I didn't enjoy sex with Miles was because I wasn't doing it properly?

He must have felt me stiffen. 'What's wrong?'

I blurted it all out. 'What if I'm crap at this? What if I don't know what to do? I don't want you to go off me. What if I don't like it?'

He put his arms around me and kissed me gently. 'It will be different this time,' he promised. 'Don't worry. I've seen the way you respond when I touch you.' I felt my cheeks warm at the reminder of how I begged and pleaded with him not to stop what he was doing to me. 'Miles didn't care about making it good for you. I do. All you need to do is exactly what you feel like doing – and trust me.'

He lifted my head and kissed me slowly, fanning the flames of the fire in my belly. He stepped back, smiling again in reassurance, and slowly undressed me, as if he wanted to make every second of our first time last.

When I finally stood naked before him, he stared and swallowed hard. 'God, you're beautiful.'

Suddenly shy, I moved over to lie on the bed. 'Your turn.'

With his eyes holding mine, he undressed as slowly as he'd removed my clothes. When he finally pushed his underwear down, curiosity won out over fear and I crawled on all fours towards him, reaching out to run a single finger down his length.

He shuddered and pushed me back on the bed. 'Oh no, you don't. I've waited too long for this to have it over and done with quickly.'

I'd got used to Neil's easy-going nature, the way he deferred to me in most things we did. I decided when we'd meet, where we'd go, what we'd do. I always knew he'd be gentle with me in the bedroom, but to have him so confident, so decisive, too? That was both surprising and a turn-on.

He sat back and ran his eyes over me, lingering on my breasts, my belly, the juncture between my thighs. Wherever his eyes touched, it felt as though he was leaving a trail of liquid heat. Finally he kneeled forward and took one breast in his mouth, his tongue circling the tip of my nipple. The breath I hadn't realised I'd been holding escaped in a sigh.

His lips left my breast and trailed down my body. When he nuzzled between my legs I pulled back in shock. He raised his head briefly. 'You'll like it, I promise,' he said. I relaxed, and immediately arched up as he sucked and licked at me. I reached down and buried my hands in his hair to hold him there as I exploded into his mouth.

He didn't wait for me to finish before sliding inside me, filling me in a way I didn't know I could be filled, setting off a whole new set of sensations.

'Okay?' he asked as he thrust slowly into me.

Unable to speak, I wound my legs tighter around his waist to force him deeper, harder, my fingers digging into his shoulders, urging him on. I called out his name when the orgasm came, sneaking up on me and taking me completely by surprise. He followed almost immediately afterwards, and slumped down on me, our bodies still joined.

'Wow,' I managed. 'Now I know what all the fuss is about.'

He laughed and pulled me closer. 'It's not always

that good.'

'Has it ever been like that for you before?'

'No,' he said. 'Just with you.'

After that night, we met as often as we could. Lachie shared a townhouse with some friends in Newtown, near the uni, so mostly we went there – or used the back seat of Neil's car. My experiences with Miles were forgotten; being with Neil was like a whole lot of new first times – and fabulous second and third and fourth times. We learned what made each other shudder and moan and gasp. If I'd thought that kissing had been invented for us, I was absolutely positive that sex had been.

I'd told Mari about Neil, and obviously Lachie knew, but I was still keeping him a secret from my parents. Although I knew they'd love him, I also knew that once they were aware of him, I wouldn't be able to get away with the lies I was telling them so I could meet him. They were too smart for that. I also knew that the time was getting closer when I needed to introduce Neil to my family.

I decided I'd talk to him about it after the Wilderness Society benefit concert. It was on just a couple of days before Christmas and I dragged Neil along to help save the Daintree, or was it Kakadu? The details didn't matter – we both were really there because Midnight Oil were playing. After the concert I'd invite him to come over to our house. Not at Christmas – that seemed way too announcey – but maybe on Boxing Day when it was more laidback.

I never got the chance. Neil beat me to it with news of his own.

When he kissed me at the station I thought he seemed different, but when I asked him he just said, 'I've got something really exciting to talk to you about.'

'What is it?'

He kissed me again and said, 'Not now, they're about to start.'

After the concert, we went back to Lachie's. His couch was smelly – as were many things about that place – and I hated to think how many people had done what we were doing on it. As he always did, Neil spread a cleanish sheet on it before we lay down.

After we'd made love, I remembered his news. 'What was it you wanted to tell me?'

'Hey, I just realised it's after midnight – it's Christmas Eve.'

'So it is. Come on … your news? What is it?'

'I've been promoted,' he said, 'to signing officer. It's a huge opportunity for me. I want to be at accountant level by twenty-five, and a couple of years in this role means I could get there.'

I had no idea what the jobs meant, but knew this was important to him.

He smiled and traced my lips with his fingers. 'You have no idea what I'm talking about, do you?' I shook my head.

'Branches have a pretty simple hierarchy,' he explained. 'The manager is responsible for everything – the lending, the results, the lot. The accountant is like an operations manager, looking after the day-to-day running of the branch – the shifts, staff issues, any performance-related stuff. The signing officer is pretty much about the tellers. I'd sign off on reports with the accountant, be the first point of escalation, and check away the cash at night with the tellers. It's the first of the leadership jobs, and I'd need to do well in it to get to the next level.'

'That's fabulous.' I reached up and kissed him. 'I'm really happy for you. Do you need to change branches?'

The look of pride fell from his face. 'Well, that's the only problem. I'm being transferred to Cooma.'

My tummy dropped and I felt the sudden heat of tears behind my eyes. 'Cooma? That's in the Snowies, isn't it? It's hours away. We'll never see each other.'

'I've been thinking about that.' I felt him draw in a deep breath. 'We don't need to be apart. We could get married and then you could come with me.'

His eyes burned into mine and I wriggled a little to get some space between us.

'I can't marry you, Neil. I'm only eighteen, I've just finished the first year of my degree, and we've only been together for four months.' My eyes pleaded with him to understand. 'I'm too young to get married. I don't even know if I want to get married. We've talked about this.'

'I didn't realise you really meant it. Every girl wants to get married.'

'Not this one. I want a career, and I want to do something that means something. I don't want to throw all that away and move to the country to be a wife.'

As I spoke, I sat up and began dressing. He watched me for a few seconds, then did the same.

'So what you're saying is, you'd be throwing your life away if you married me?'

'No, that's not what I'm saying. I love you, Neil, and if I was ever going to marry anyone it would be you. It's just that it's too soon. I'm too young. What if I regret later the chances I didn't take now?' I reached for his hand. 'Can't we just wait a few years? At least until I've finished uni?'

He pulled his hand away. 'You want me to put my career on hold until you can catch up with me? Is that what you're asking?'

'No, of course it isn't! Surely there's another branch in the city you can go to?'

'Maybe, but who knows how long I'll have to wait. Plus, when you start picking and choosing jobs, you get a name for that – and it isn't a good one.'

'So what you're saying is, you'd prefer to say no to me than to your precious bank?' I knew the tears would come later, but for now my temper had taken over.

He shook his head sadly. 'It's not about choosing between work and you.'

'It is, you know. That's exactly what it's about. If you stay, we can be together. If you go, we can't. It's that easy.'

He rested his elbows on his knees, his face in his hands. 'It's not that easy, and that isn't what this is about. I thought you'd be happy for me. I thought you'd be pleased that we could be together all the time, not just sneaking around on other people's smelly couches or in the back seat of my car.'

'What am I supposed to do in Cooma? Be happy cleaning the house and cooking you dinner and popping out a heap of your kids? You'd have your work and your ambitions, but I'd have chosen you instead of mine.'

'You're asking me to choose you over mine,' he said.

'No, I'm asking you to wait.'

'And what if I don't want to wait?'

'I don't want to go to Cooma.'

He shrugged. 'I suppose that's that then. I should have known you weren't really serious about me – you wouldn't even take me home to meet your parents. All I am to you is some fun.'

'You know that's not true.'

'Do I?' He stood up. 'I hope you find what it is you're looking for, Katie. I wish it could have been me.' He started to go and turned back. 'Merry fucking

Christmas.'

Once he'd left, the tears started. I curled up into a little ball on that dirty share-house couch and sobbed until I didn't think there were any more tears left in me. Then I climbed the stairs to my brother's room and curled up on the end of his bed.

He woke with a start. 'What? Who?'

'Shut up, Lachie. It's just me.'

'Kitty? Have you been crying?'

'Uh-huh. Neil left. We're finished and my heart is breaking.'

He sat up and rubbed at his face. 'What time is it?'

'Just after two.'

'Of course it is. Do you want to tell me about it?'

'No. Not yet. I just want to lie here.'

'Okay. You lie there, and I'll try and get a few more hours before I have to go to work. We'll talk in the morning.'

I nodded, but he was already lying down again. I stayed there, curled up on the end of his bed. When morning came, my eyes were still wet.

Thirteen

I finally returned to bed close to midnight. Neil stirred briefly when I slipped back in beside him, but didn't wake. I snuggled into him, and knew nothing more until I woke at around five to see him seated on the edge of the bed getting dressed.

I reached an arm out to stroke his. He turned and smiled at me, leaning down to kiss my lips.

'Good morning,' he said.

'Morning yourself.' I stretched, grimacing when I became aware of how certain parts of my body, not used to that sort of activity, were feeling sore.

He watched my face. 'Are you okay?'

'Mmmm. Just a little sore,' I admitted. 'I'm not used to that much ... ummm exercise.'

He grinned. 'To be honest, neither am I.' He kissed me properly. 'Not that much anyway.'

Despite my tenderness, I felt the fire stir again. 'Stay,' I urged.

'I need to get home so I can get dressed for work.'

He deepened the kiss, his hand circling the

underside of my breast. I arched into his touch.

'Call in sick,' I said, my arms going around his neck to pull his mouth back to mine. 'Just one more day.' I pulled the sheet aside. 'Come back to bed.'

He kissed me again and I began unbuttoning his shirt. He didn't argue.

We made love again, and slept some more. I woke a few hours later to the smell of coffee and Neil sitting on the bed, a tray balanced on the bedside table.

'Boiled eggs and soldiers!' I said.

'I hope they're done the way you used to like them.'

'I haven't had these for years. It looks wonderful. Thank you.'

He sipped at coffee as I ate my breakfast.

'Aren't you eating?' I asked.

'I had some toast. I've called work, and I need to go home and change my clothes, but I'll be back. I thought we might go into the city, maybe pack a picnic lunch and take a walk around the Botanical Gardens.' He smiled. 'Like we used to.'

'That sounds good.' I knew I was beaming.

I also knew this was a day away from real life, and that what he hadn't said was that he needed to call Vanessa when he got home with some excuse about why he hadn't answered her calls last night. I knew it all and none of it mattered. All that mattered now was … well, now.

I put together a picnic for the two of us that would

match the specialness of the day. A day just for us. We wandered through the gardens, and spread our picnic blanket underneath our tree – the one we were married under.

After we'd eaten, Neil lay down on the blanket and pulled me close to him. 'I meant everything I said last night. I don't want to get a divorce, and I want us to try again.'

'I want that too.'

'I'll tell Vanessa tonight.'

'No, that's not a good idea.'

I felt him stiffen. 'Why not? I love you, Katie. I want to spend the rest of my life doing that.'

'I know,' I soothed. 'And I love you too. But as soon as we tell her, or anyone else, all hell is going to break loose. I don't want those complications – not yet. I want it to be just us – at least until we know what comes next.'

'Whatever happens with us, I'm finished with Vanessa,' he said.

'I know that, but please, let's not tell her – not yet. You don't live together, so just tell her I'm being difficult about the divorce, or that you're helping me with my training or something. Neither of those are lies.' A thought occurred to me. 'Are you still sleeping with her?'

'No. I haven't since a couple of weeks before the wedding.'

'Really? Why not?'

I felt him move his shoulders. 'I'm not sure. After we told you about the divorce … well, it didn't seem right. The feelings came back, the ones I had for you – and when she began to get nasty with you, it made me look at you both in a different way. And when Ash told me how you'd stood up to her, I remembered how you'd always stood up for me, and you were still doing that. It made me realise just what I was throwing away. By then I already knew that even if we did go through with the divorce, I wasn't staying with Vanessa. I certainly didn't want to sleep with her. All I wanted was you.'

His words filled me with warmth and I moved closer to him. 'It hasn't been difficult to avoid it – we've both been working late.' He paused as if a thought had suddenly occurred to him. 'She hasn't seemed to have noticed – or if she did she hasn't said anything.'

'Every time she touched you or looked at you, it annoyed me,' I said, keen to bring his attention back to me. 'Then there were those times you looked at me and I felt funny. I didn't know what the looks meant but they confused me. I didn't realise until after the wedding it was because I still loved you.'

'I nearly told you that day we walked down at Barangaroo.'

'I'm glad you didn't. I wasn't ready to hear it.'

'But you are now?'

'I am now.' I lifted my head so he could kiss my lips.

'Do you think we might make it this time?' he asked.

'Third time lucky?'

He nodded.

'I hope so.'

So I was having an affair with my husband – while his girlfriend thought we were negotiating for a divorce. Yes, I absolutely saw that one coming. Not.

It was like when we were first together, only better. I knew my way around his body now, and he knew mine. We settled into a pattern of spending Monday and Wednesday nights together – when Vanessa had training and other activities after work and didn't normally see Neil – and a few hours over the weekend. I rushed home those weeknights, ignoring the questioning looks from my colleagues who'd become used to seeing me still in the office when they left in the evening. Neil would arrive soon after. We managed to fit an awful lot into those few stolen hours.

He'd told Vanessa we were talking our way through the settlement, but there was very little talking taking place. He'd walk into the house and I'd be ready for him. Sometimes we'd wait until after we'd eaten, and at other times we simply couldn't. In our early days together there'd been domestic duties and the pressures of work and school to contend with. Now there was freedom, laughter and the joy we found in each other.

I was still training, if you could call it that, for my hike. Neil was helping me. We did a long walk at least once on the weekend, but most of the other exercise we were doing was horizontal. We literally couldn't get enough of each other.

Lachie must have guessed what we were up to. Before Ash's wedding, he and Mike had been helping me get my financial ducks in a row as they called it. Since the wedding, I'd gone quiet on the subject of the divorce. He and Mike called around one Sunday afternoon. Neil and I had been for a long walk, then come home to make love. Neil was dozing beside me when I heard the knock on the door.

'Wake up,' I said. 'There's someone here.'

'Who is it?' He was already up and getting dressed.

'I have no idea, but I'll go down and try and get rid of them. Okay?'

He nodded and almost tripped over his jeans.

I stifled a laugh and pulled on my T-shirt and trackpants. 'Relax,' I told him.

The doorbell sounded again.

'Hold on,' I called, retying my hair into a short pigtail. 'Oh, it's you, Lachie … and Mike. It's great to see you. Unexpected, but good.'

Lachie raised his eyebrows. 'We didn't interrupt you, did we?' he asked.

'Of course not. What could you possibly be interrupting?' I laughed, and even to my ears it was forced and high-pitched.

'I don't know, Kitty-cat, how about you tell me? Why not start by telling me where Neil is?'

'Neil? Why?'

'Oh, let me see … because his car is parked outside.'

I inwardly grimaced. 'Of course it is. We've been for a walk – training for my hike. And now he's upstairs looking for something.'

'Really? And what would that be? Your lost virginity?'

I frowned and thumped his arm. 'Don't be mean.'

'Silly me. He didn't take it in the first place, did he?'

I sent him another warning look. Mike was struggling to hold his giggles in.

'Oh, look,' said Lachie, 'here's Neil now. Did you find what you were looking for?' he asked him.

'As a matter of fact, I did.'

Lachie nodded in approval. 'That's good. What was it?'

'What was what?'

'What you were looking for?'

'Oh, just something.' Neil looked wildly at me and I nodded towards the photos on the sideboard. He screwed his eyes up as he searched for an explanation that Lachie might buy. 'A photograph. One of Nathan when he was a baby.'

'Where is it then?'

'What?'

'The photograph. The one you were upstairs looking for in Kate's bedroom.'

'I didn't say he was looking for it in my bedroom,' I said.

'Didn't you? My mistake.' Lachie grinned. 'So where is it then? That photo you were looking for and said you'd found – but not in Kate's bedroom? Speaking of which, Kitty, your top's inside out.'

I automatically checked for the label – which was on the inside of my top where I would have expected it to be. I sighed loudly and gave up the pretence. 'You may as well come in and have a cuppa.'

The kitchen was a mess – something else Lachie grinned at. 'It's unlike you to leave your lunch things on the table, Kitty.'

I scurried around, collecting the bowls we'd had our soup in and packing them into the dishwasher. Neil, who still hadn't said very much, was ladling leftover soup into containers for the freezer.

'It looks almost as though you were interrupted before you could finish lunch and clean up,' Lachie said. He looked at Mike. 'What could possibly have gone on here?'

'I'm not sure, but it's a mess. Look at the way that tablecloth is bunched up in the corner,' Mike said with a huge grin.

'Okay,' I said, 'you've made your point.'

'And what point would that be?' Lachie's face was a picture of innocence.

'That Katie and I are together again,' Neil said, moving to stand next to me and putting a protective arm around my shoulders.

'I don't know, Mike, is it an affair when you're cheating on your girlfriend by sleeping with your wife?' The words sounded light, but Lachie's expression was anything but.

'Oh good, the kettle's boiled,' I said. 'Tea or coffee? I haven't done much baking over the past few weeks, but I'm sure there's something I can defrost.'

Lachie and Neil were staring at each other, the same stony expression on their faces, oblivious to my babbling.

'Just make tea, Kate,' Mike suggested. 'Somehow I don't think your baking will be appreciated this afternoon.'

No one said anything while I made tea and coffee, and placed mugs on the table.

'At the risk of sounding like a cliché,' Lachie said, when we were all sitting down, 'how long has this been going on? Since the wedding?'

I lifted one shoulder and looked at Neil. 'Sort of. It was when Neil came over to talk about the divorce and, well, one thing led to another.'

Neil smiled at me and took my hand.

'As they do when you talk divorce,' said Lachie,

a sardonic smile on his face. 'Seriously though, I'm guessing you haven't told Vanessa or you wouldn't be needing to sneak around like this? Or is it that you haven't actually decided you're back together yet and Neil still has a place in both beds?'

'It's not like that,' I said. 'It just happened, and we wanted to keep it to ourselves as long as we could.' I didn't know whether I was defending us or justifying our behaviour. For god's sake, we were adults and didn't need to do either.

'Are you still proceeding with the divorce?' Lachie looked between the two of us. 'Okay, I'll ask the question in a different way. Does Vanessa still think you're proceeding with the divorce?'

Neil nodded.

'I see. Are you sure this isn't just some way of buttering my sister up so she'll agree to a fifty percent split when we all know it should be closer to seventy percent, and sixty at the outside?'

'Of course that's not what this is about!' I looked at Neil for support. 'Is it?'

My stomach flipped when he took a half-beat too long to answer my question. And when he did, he directed his answer to Lachie.

'That's not what this is about. I don't want a divorce.' Lachie opened his mouth to speak, but Neil stopped him. 'Yes, I was the one who asked for it. It seemed the right thing to do, but that didn't mean I wanted it. I was happy with the way things were. Katie and I seemed to get on better apart than we had during those last few years together. I realised that was being selfish though. We'd been separated for four years, and I owed it to Katie to let her have a clean break. I knew she would never move on while I was still hanging around. So when Vanessa said it was time I finalised the divorce, I agreed. After all, even though she and I weren't formally living together, she spent most of every week at my place – she might as well have moved in.'

Neil placed his hand over mine before he continued. 'But then something happened. When we started talking about the divorce, I began to realise what I'd lost, and I think Katie did the same. At the same time, Vanessa started to change – maybe because she was sensing that my feelings were changing. She tried to rush the divorce through, in particular the property settlement part. The more she pushed, the more it seemed to me that she wanted the assets resolved more than the divorce itself.

'I also realised that the last thing I wanted was a divorce. But I had no choice. Katie was going along with it and said she needed the final break; and Vanessa was suddenly talking about marriage. The whole thing seemed like a train I couldn't stop. And in the middle of it all was Katie, my wife, who I realised I'd never really fallen out of love with. It wasn't until we kissed at Ash's wedding that I realised she could be feeling the same way. And it turns out she was.'

Lachie had listened to Neil's story, but his expression hadn't changed. 'When are you going to tell Vanessa?'

Neil looked at me before answering. 'Regardless of what happens with Katie and me now, I need to tell Vanessa we're over. Now that you know, it's only a matter of time before other people do too, so I'll have to do it soon. I know it sounds like a cop-out, but Vanessa's not going to be happy, and Katie and I wanted some time to enjoy each other before that happens. We've never really had that, you know – time just for us. That's what's made these last few weeks so special. If I'd told Vanessa immediately, we wouldn't have had that.'

'I see,' said Lachie, although the look on his face said that he didn't really see at all. 'And it's absolutely not because you've realised just how little you'll end up with out of the settlement? You stand to lose at least half of your superannuation, maybe more – and that's before we even get started on the assets. Maybe you've decided it's easier not to get divorced after all?'

'Lachie! That's cruel! And so far from being right – isn't it, Neil?'

Neil took a deep breath before he answered. 'I know how it looks, Lachie. I also know how it is. If we did proceed with the divorce, I wouldn't fight over the split. I'd already decided that it would be easier to start again from scratch – as long as I still had a healthy amount in my super. I couldn't risk what Kate and I have built up together for our kids.'

'I'm sure Vanessa would have loved that idea,' Lachie said. 'Do the kids know about whatever this is between you two?'

I shook my head. 'Absolutely not. And I don't want them to until we know what this is. I thought we were done – we thought we were done. The kids have gotten used to that. Above all, we have to make sure that nothing changes for them, which means our relationship as friends can't suffer.'

Lachie sighed and rolled his eyes in exasperation. 'Sometimes I think you're living in fairyland, Kitty. Let's look at the scenarios here. If you two decide to proceed with a divorce, there will be arguments over the percentage split, regardless of what your intentions are now. If you decide to make another go of it together and things go down the gurgler again, I can guarantee you that the break-up won't be as nice and clean as it was four years ago.'

'How do you know that?' I felt my chin poke out as I asked the question.

'Because sex is involved again. I'll ask you this question – were you jealous of Vanessa sleeping with Neil?'

'No.' I sent Neil a look of apology. 'I know I should have been, but I wasn't.'

'And do you know why? Because you two had allowed the intimacy and the passion to go. By the time you separated, you might as well have been flatmates. If Neil told you now that he'd slept with Vanessa, how would you feel?'

My face told the story.

'And, Neil, if Kitty went on a date with one of the many men who are probably lusting after her as we speak – lush middle-aged lady as she is – how would you feel?'

He shook his head. 'I'd probably want to kill him.'

'There you have it. Regardless of what happens now, you have a completely different scenario on your hands than the one you had a few weeks ago.'

'Oh.' I said the word, but Neil's eyes dropped to the table as well.

Mike hadn't said anything while Lachie was talking, but now he had his serious lawyer's face on. 'What I'm concerned about is something you said earlier, Neil. You mentioned that even though Vanessa never moved in formally, she might as well have done. What did you mean by that?'

Neil appeared confused by the question. 'Well, she was there most nights.'

'How many on average?'

'I don't know.' He pondered the question. 'Three or four a week, I suppose.'

'Does she have a key?'

Neil nodded.

'Does she ever buy groceries or contribute to the

utilities?'

'Yes, to the groceries. She said it made her feel less guilty for using all my power, hot water and internet. Of course I told her none of that mattered to me, but she said it suited her to make sure we were eating well and I had a habit of not really thinking about those sorts of things. Just lately she's been saying she wants to help with the utilities, but I've always declined her offer. In the last few months she's paid the electricity and the body corporate for me, when she thought I was too busy to remember – but I paid her back as soon as I realised she'd done it. I'm never that busy.'

Mike and Lachie exchanged a glance that made me feel uncomfortable, as if what Neil had said confirmed something they were hoping he wouldn't confirm.

'Did Vanessa ask you about moving in?' Mike asked.

'Of course she did. But I didn't like the idea of her moving in while Kate and I were still officially married. Maybe, if I'm being honest, it's one of the reasons I kept putting the divorce off. At the back of my mind, it always concerned me that if she moved in she could have a claim on the property, so I was careful about that. But yes, even though I never actually said the words, she probably assumed that as soon as the divorce was finalised I'd move her in properly.'

'There's a problem, isn't there?' I said when Lachie and Mike exchanged yet another meaningful glance.

'Mike?'

'There could be,' he said. 'In some cases you don't actually have to be living together to be living together. If she spent most of her time there, contributed in some way to the household – for example, if she can prove those bills were directly paid from her account – and can prove that you're an established couple, she may be able to claim it was a de facto relationship.'

'Surely not!' I looked at Neil. 'Could she? Would she?'

He shook his head. 'I don't know, Katie. I really don't know.'

I rubbed at my forehead. 'Well, aren't you two just little rays of fucking sunshine?' I said, even though I knew it was unfair to take the situation out on Lachie and Mike.

'Don't, Katie,' said Neil. 'It's not their fault. They're just trying to help you – and, I guess, us.'

Lachie nodded.

'I know it's not their fault,' I spat at Neil, but managed to stop myself before I said more.

'Katie …' His tone was a plea for me to understand, to not take it out on him, to work together to solve this … whatever it was that needed to be solved. In that one word he was asking me to not let this interfere with what we were enjoying now.

I nodded once to let him know that I understood.

'Okay,' I said, 'there's no point speculating what

she might decide to do. You can't just come straight out and finish it though, Neil. We'll need to sneak around for a little while longer until we have an idea about where she's coming from.'

'And if she asks about the divorce?'

'Tell her that Kitty's seeking legal advice regarding the split,' Lachie said. 'None of that's a lie. Mike would have acted for her in a divorce, and that's exactly what he's providing now – legal advice.'

'I can do that,' said Neil. 'Besides, there's enough shit going down at work that she needs to understand that creating more in my personal life isn't at the top of my list of priorities.' He turned to me. 'I probably should head off.'

'I'll see you out.'

In the hall, he hugged me tightly. 'I'm sorry you have to deal with all of this. I was being naive thinking I could tell her to walk away and she would.'

'Who knows, she still could.' Even as I said it, I didn't believe it. 'Are you sure this is what you want, Neil? It's not just you going for the comfortable option because everything else is so complicated, is it?'

'How can you even ask that after what we did earlier this afternoon?'

I blushed at the memory of our love-making. 'Maybe. What did you mean about the shit going down at work?'

'Nothing new – just more of the same.' As hard as

he tried, he couldn't hide the strain in his voice. 'Roger said if I considered retirement, all of this pressure could go away.' He attempted to smile, but failed.

I put my arms around his neck and pulled his mouth down to mine. 'We'll sort all of this, Neil. You and I have always been a good team. Now that we're back together, Roger Bovis won't know what hit him.'

'Katie, I'm seriously thinking about it.'

'About what?'

'Retiring. I don't want to fight with them – it doesn't mean enough to me any more.'

I pulled back and looked up into his face. 'What do you mean it doesn't mean enough?'

'I don't know what I'd be fighting for.'

'Well, your job of course. Then there's the principle of the matter. What they're doing to you – and to others your age – isn't right. If you give up, you're making it alright.'

He shook his head. 'No, I'm not. I'd be leaving with my integrity in place and my head held high. Don't get me wrong, everything they're doing is strictly legal and supposedly by the book, but I don't need that, Katie. More to the point, I don't want it. How can I continue to work for a company I no longer respect that sanctions that sort of behaviour by allowing it to continue? I missed so much of the kids' early years through work, and me working the hours I did certainly contributed to what happened to us. I'm not prepared to waste any more of my life there.'

'But what will you do?'

'It's what we do next that matters. Let's make a sea-change or a tree-change somewhere we love. Let's buy that bookshop we were always dreaming of. You can even go back and finish your degree if you want to.'

'I think after all this time I'd be starting that degree from scratch.' I laughed to disguise the little bubble of excitement that had poked its head up inside me.

He drew me back into his embrace and kissed the top of my head. 'We always used to say "one day", but what if "one day" is now? Maybe Roger's done me a huge favour by being such a prick?'

'Maybe, but I still think we can fight it if you want to.'

'Oh, Katie, I know you want me to want to take this battle on, but I really don't want to. I want to take this opportunity and do something good with it rather than try and hang on to something I should probably let go of.' He kissed me hard, with all the intensity of the pressure he was under. 'I love you, Katie, I truly do. And I want to spend the rest of my life telling you so.'

I gave myself to his embrace. 'And I love you too. I always have done.'

'None of this is going to be easy, is it? Whichever way we look.'

I held his gaze. 'No, it's not.'

There was no point in lying to him – or to myself.

Fourteen

Ash and Reece had been back from their honeymoon for just over a week, but I hadn't had the opportunity to get us all together to listen to their stories, If I was being honest with myself, it wasn't so much the opportunity that I was missing, but more that I didn't want the world – or even the family – to intrude into the bubble Neil and I had created for ourselves. Once I realised that I could delay no longer I invited them and Lachie and Mike over for a Sunday roast. Normally I would have invited Neil and Vanessa too, but this time I hesitated.

'It will be too weird,' I said to Neil. 'Don't you think?'

'Of course it will.' He threw his leg over mine in bed to pull me tighter to him. 'But it would be even weirder if you didn't. I'm not sure how long I can keep up the pretence for. She's already starting to ask questions about what I'm doing here all the time. She even suggested that she helps us with our negotiations.'

'What did you tell her?'

'That I was going slowly so that we arrived at the best and fairest outcome. I told her that I wanted us all to still be friends at the end of it all and that I wasn't losing my family over a few dollars.'

'She wouldn't have liked that.'

I felt him smile. 'You could say that. She reminded me that there was a lot more than a few dollars at stake which was when I told her that it didn't matter how long it took – that none of us were in a hurry.'

'What was her reaction to that?'

'Let's just say that she wasn't very happy, but there wasn't a lot she could say about it. She did warn me that you were trying to take advantage of my kindness.' He pulled back slightly and looked down at me. 'Are you trying to take advantage of me?'

'Absolutely.' I kissed his chest. 'Has she wondered why you haven't slept with her?'

'Yes, and I'm running out of excuses there too. We're both working late and the arguments about the divorce have helped – she's taken to flouncing out if it doesn't appear as though she's going to get her own way. I think I'm supposed to run after her and beg her to stay, but I'm not the begging type.'

'I don't know about that – I think that I could get you to beg.' I trailed my fingers idly down his arm and along the thigh he'd flung across me and felt him harden against my belly. I squirmed even closer.

'I think you could too.'

'But what if she knows just by looking at us that we've been doing this?'

He was responding so nicely to the finger-trailing thing that I kept it going, allowing them to stray down his back and across his buttock.

'Mmmm, that's nice.' He closed his eyes.

'Only nice?' I chided. 'I was aiming for something a little stronger than "nice".'

A chuckle rumbled through him. 'Seriously though, Katie, she's not going to know.'

'Are you sure?'

He rolled onto his back, taking me with him so I ended up straddling him. 'I'm very sure. Now, shut up and kiss me.'

Ash and Reece were the first to arrive. Ash burst into the house as if she'd never left. 'Oh my god, Mum, you're doing the slow-cooked lamb. We were saying on the way over that we were hoping you'd do that, weren't we, Reece?'

Reece kissed the top of her head with affection and dutifully agreed.

'We could smell it from the minute we pulled up,' she went on. 'All that garlic and rosemary.'

I smiled at her. It had always been her favourite – slow-cooked lamb with jewel-bright pomegranate seeds drifted across the top, yoghurt and a Greek salad to the side, and pita breads for wrapping it all together or for dunking into the juices. I'd gone to extra trouble today and added some crispy roast potatoes and fresh peas with mint and dots of feta.

'Well, now you're here, you can get the seeds out of those pomegranates,' I told her, 'preferably without turning the kitchen into a murder scene. And I'll take the lamb out to rest. Oh, here's Lachie and Mike.'

'Wow, Kitty, the smells coming from this kitchen are incredible,' Lachie said, kissing my cheek. 'All okay?' he whispered in my ear.

I nodded and accepted the flowers that Mike offered me. 'These are gorgeous. Thanks, guys.' I reached up to kiss Mike. 'I'd better put them into something.'

Lachie followed me into the dining room while I searched for the vase I wanted in the sideboard. 'Don't worry,' he said. 'I'm not going to say anything.'

I patted his cheek. 'I know you won't.'

'It's just that –'

I stopped him. 'I know, Lachie. None of this is ideal – far from it. And I know you're worried, but it's nice, you know?'

He nodded. 'I know.' The doorbell pealed. 'And that, my dear Kitty-cat, would mean it's showtime.'

I took a breath, squared my shoulders and went into the kitchen.

'Oh, good,' I said kissing first Vanessa and then Neil on the cheek, 'you're here. Neil, can you make yourself useful and carve the lamb for me? Lachie, you can open the wine, and everyone else can take one of these dishes out to the table.'

Ash and Reece kept us entertained over lunch with stories of their honeymoon. They described the secluded villa they'd stayed in, the romantic picnic on an otherwise deserted island, the foods they'd sampled and the sights they'd seen. Through the telling they constantly looked at each other, or touched the other's arm or leg to remind themselves they were there, sitting beside them, love shining in their eyes.

At one point it got a little too much for me and I felt my eyes welling with happiness for them. I excused myself and began clearing the table, waving to everyone else to stay put.

After a few minutes, Neil followed me with the dirty plates and stacked them in the dishwasher.

'It's beautiful to watch, isn't it?' he said.

I nodded, afraid that if I spoke the emotion would overflow. It had been hell sitting there watching Vanessa with Neil – the way she smiled at him or touched him, the hint of a shared joke. Although he didn't initiate any of the contact or touch her back, it felt as though she was putting a show on for me. I'd bitten into the side of my mouth so hard that I was sure I'd drawn blood. I wasn't brave enough to look down at my jeans to see if my fingernails had left indents in the denim. There seemed to be something very different about her today. If I didn't know better, I'd say she had almost a triumphant air.

'Seeing them together like that is everything we could have wished for,' Neil added. 'Now we just need to get Nathan settled.'

I forced a laugh. 'That could prove to be a little more difficult. He hasn't met the right person yet – and when he does, I suspect it will take us all by surprise. Him most of all.'

'I just hope he has more common sense than I do and works harder to hold on to the one he loves. Katie –'

Neil didn't get to finish because Vanessa came into the kitchen, the yoghurt bowl in her hands. 'I thought I'd bring the last of the dishes through. I'm not interrupting anything, am I?'

'Of course not,' I said. 'We were just indulging ourselves in some mutual parental congratulations about how happy Ash and Reece look.'

'Yes, she's certainly lucky.' Her tone sounded bitter, yet her expression was impassive. 'I must say, I'm surprised to see the two of you getting along as well as you are. The amount of time Neil has to spend around here in "negotiations",' she used her fingers to demonstrate the quotation marks, 'I figured you were being difficult about the divorce.'

Neil immediately looked wary.

'Did you?' I said, and smiled as sweetly at her as she was at me. 'If by making sure I'm protecting my and my children's future through a fair division, then yes, I probably am making life difficult. There have certainly been some intense moments over the past few weeks.'

Neil choked on the piece of leftover lamb he'd snuck off the plate.

Vanessa looked at him with concern. 'Are you okay, babe?'

Eyes watering, he nodded and filled a glass with water.

She turned back to me. 'The thing is, Kate, you might be thinking about your children, but what about protecting the future of any children that Neil and I might have together?'

I mimicked her tone. 'The thing is, Vanessa, any children that you and Neil might have together are none of my concern. Should that happen, I would assume you'd build a future for them from your own hard work – the same as Neil and I did for our kids. I certainly won't be agreeing to anything Neil proposes that impacts my children's future in favour of someone else's.'

I'd given up any pretence of cleaning up the kitchen, and she'd given up any pretence of helping me. We held each other's stares. Poor Neil looked as though he wanted to be anywhere but where he was.

'In fact, we've been talking about putting Neil's share of the settlement into trust for Nathan and Ash,' I added, smiling at her again. 'I'm sure you'd rather start your new life together from an even playing field?'

Her mouth fell open at that piece of news. 'No.

That's absolutely not going to happen.'

'Vanessa,' Neil said, 'I thought we'd discussed this? We agreed that the divorce and everything that goes with it is between Katie and me.'

'That was my understanding too,' I said. 'It's also my understanding that I've got a full year after we're divorced to do something about the property. Right at this minute I'm inclined to use every single second of that year – and then some. If you're hoping for a quick windfall you'll need to look elsewhere.'

I didn't think I'd ever been as angry with anyone as I was with her now. My chin stuck out even further and my shoulders squared.

'Oh shit,' Neil mumbled, recognising the look on my face. Out loud he said, 'Vanessa, leave it. It's none of your business.'

Her eyes widened at his tone. 'But –'

'No.' He didn't raise his voice, he didn't need to. 'I said to leave it.'

I hadn't seen Neil like this very often, and Vanessa probably never had. There was the time when Ash came home crying because a girl at school had thrown a Coke down the front of the new white dress she'd left the house so proudly in just a few hours before. There was also the time when she had her heart broken by some careless boy for the very first time. Then there was the time Nathan crashed the car when he was showing off in front of his friends.

Vanessa stroked her hand up Neil's arm. 'It's just that I'd like it settled to ease some of the stress you're under, babe. I hate seeing you with this hanging over your head. You haven't been yourself lately and I'm sure it's because this is worrying you. I have a vested interest in keeping you alive and healthy, you know.' She giggled and kissed him.

I turned away, unable to watch her touch him any more. Lachie was right. Now that sex was involved, this had the potential to get very messy indeed.

Neil pushed her hand away. 'No, Vanessa, I don't care what your motives are. I'm telling you to leave this one alone. If there is a settlement, it will be going into trust for my children. My existing children.'

She pouted, something I'd never seen her attempt before, but he shook his head and said, 'Don't go there. I won't say it again – this is between me and Kate. It's none of your business so leave it alone.'

Neil hadn't moved, but he seemed so distant from her in that moment there might as well have been a highway between them. I couldn't help feeling a flash of sympathy for her – although at the same time I was so turned on by this new forceful version of Neil, I was desperate to get him alone and feel his hands on my body, his mouth on mine.

'Well, now we've had that discussion, I think we'll get dessert underway,' I said. 'The others must be wondering what's going on in here. Vanessa, can you take out the spoons and the bowl of cream? Neil, can I have a quick word, please?'

Vanessa made to linger.

'Alone,' I stressed.

She looked to Neil for approval. He nodded, and finally, still looking back at us, she rejoined the laughter on the deck.

'Christ, I'm sorry, Katie,' said Neil once we were alone. 'I didn't think she'd –'

'In here, quickly,' I urged, dragging him into the bathroom and shutting the door behind us.

'What –' he began.

I grabbed hold of his jumper and pulled us both backwards until I came up against the wall. Running my hands up his chest under his clothes, I stood on tiptoes and kissed him. Hard.

He pulled back slightly, then held my head firmly between his hands and kissed me back, our tongues duelling, the desire flaming through me as his body pressed into mine.

'When you told her about the intense moments, I nearly lost it,' he muttered, taking possession of my mouth again, his hand sliding under my top to squeeze at my breast. He lifted my top and sucked at my breast through the bra, biting at one nipple and flicking his thumb back and forth over the other. I held his head in place, my hands running through his hair.

'When she touched you, I nearly threw something

at her,' I said, then gasped as he held both my hands above my head and rubbed me through my jeans, the friction of the zip catching at my clit with every movement. I arched into his hand, desperate for more.

He stopped and I groaned. 'Nooo, I'm so close.'

'Shhhh.'

He released my hands so he could undo my jeans and pushed them down around my ankles. He kissed me again, then sank to his knees and buried his face between my legs. I came fast and hard; the sort of orgasm that took the edge off, but left me wanting more.

When I had my balance back, he stood and kissed me, letting me taste myself on his lips. I reached between us, but he shook his head. 'Later,' he promised, his kiss now gentle, before reluctantly pulling away from me to straighten himself up.

I pulled my jeans back up and pulled my top back down. We'd been in the bathroom for just a few minutes, but it felt as though we'd been in another world.

'We'd better get back out there,' I said. 'They'll be starting to wonder.'

'Let them,' he said, pulling me close for yet another kiss. 'Maybe I'm being stupid, but for some reason it feels as though if we go back out there, something will shatter us.'

'It can't,' I said. 'Not now.'

He smiled slowly. 'You're right. Not now. I'll tell Vanessa tonight and deal with whatever fall-out that brings. Then we can concentrate on us. Okay?'

'Third time lucky?'

'Yep, third time lucky.'

He kissed me again before reluctantly releasing me. I felt the warmth of his smile running through every vein.

'Do I look okay?' I asked, running my hand over my hair and making sure my top was as it should be.

'You look beautiful. You always do.'

I smiled at him and patted his cheek. 'You go out first – there's a tray on the kitchen bench with the dessert on it. I won't be far behind you.'

Once he'd left, I looked at myself in the mirror. Aside from some residual brightness to my eyes and a smile that wouldn't go away, there was nothing to give away what we'd been doing in here. Yet inside me, every cell was singing.

Taking a deep breath, I followed Neil onto the deck. Other than Vanessa, Lachie seemed to be the only one who had noticed our absence. He raised his eyebrows and I shrugged a shoulder, my smile confirming what he suspected. He responded with a shake of his head and a grin.

'Wow, Mum, these look fabulous,' gushed Ash. 'What are they?'

'Chocolate mousse, but because they're made with olive oil and no cream or butter, they're dairy free.'

I'd chosen to serve the mousses in pretty espresso

cups. They looked, and I hoped would taste, decadent. I'd used extremely good dark chocolate and added salt that I'd spiced with the tiniest amount of smoked chilli to cut through any residual sweetness. I knew I'd gone to a lot more trouble than I usually would for a family Sunday roast, but I told myself it was because it was Ash's first meal here as a married woman. It had absolutely nothing to do with showing Neil what he was missing out on. I knew Vanessa wouldn't touch them. She always said no to dessert and preferred to sit there looking thirty-four, perfect and the picture of superior willpower.

Neil handed the mousses around the table. I couldn't help a little start of surprise when Vanessa took one.

'These look amazing, Kate. You've gone to an awful lot of trouble for us.' She smiled as if the scene in the kitchen hadn't taken place.

'It was no trouble at all,' I said. 'It's not every day that your only daughter comes home from her honeymoon. Besides, I've been after an excuse to try out this recipe.'

'How long did you cook them for?' Vanessa was never interested in cooking techniques. She was definitely leading into something.

'That's the thing – they don't get cooked at all. They've got raw eggs in them, so it does mean that you can't serve them to anyone immune-challenged or pregnant. But we're all okay – unless you have something to tell me about a honeymoon baby, Ash?'

'Don't worry, Mum,' she said. 'I won't be turning you into a grandmother just yet.'

But Vanessa pushed her dessert away. 'I'm so sorry, Kate,' she said, her smile telling me that she was anything but sorry. 'In that case I won't be able to eat mine.'

I stared at her for what seemed like ages, but mustn't have been more than a few seconds. I saw her placing her hand over the top of her wine glass earlier. I saw her laying her hand on Neil's arm and telling him she had a vested interest in keeping him alive. I saw the tiny smirk of triumph that had been hanging around her mouth all day, and felt some vomit rise into my mouth.

'Oh my god!' exclaimed Ash. 'She's pregnant? Dad, how could you do this!'

Vanessa smiled. 'It's not something we planned, but I'm very happy about it.'

'And Dad? Is Dad very happy about it?' Ash said. 'He didn't know, did he? You've trapped him. Oh my god, I just knew you'd do something like this. I should never have trusted you. Nathan was right about you – he had you pegged from the start.'

I could vaguely hear Ash haranguing Vanessa, but had eyes only for Neil. He was still standing, still holding the tray the dessert cups had been on. His face had turned white and the tray was shaking. I knew I should have gone to him, but I couldn't move either.

'No, Neil had no idea,' Vanessa said. 'This will be a surprise for him too, but I'm sure he'll be as happy as I am.' She was looking up at him, waiting for his reaction. 'I'm sorry you had to find out this way, babe.' She smiled and shrugged, as if completely innocent of the carnage she'd caused.

'That's bullshit,' said Ash. 'You were so obvious about not having wine – you must have mentioned it about three times. And as for the mousse, when was the last time you ever ate dessert here? You never do. You only took one today because you knew it would give you a reason to tell us all about the baby in the most destructive way possible. You wanted to upset my mother, and congratulations, you have.'

'I'm sorry you feel that way, Ash. I thought you and I were friends.' Vanessa's eyes filled and she turned again to Neil. 'Babe? Say something. Did you hear how Ash was talking to me? I don't need to stay here and be treated like this.'

But still Neil's eyes didn't leave mine.

Lachie shot a look at Mike, who jumped up from his seat, rushed over to Neil and took the tray from his shaking hand.

Neil didn't seem to notice. He was looking at me, and I was looking at him, and we were both watching all our plans for a third chance at happiness go crashing down around us.

Fifteen

Lachie and Mike managed to rouse Neil into some sort of action, and bundled him and Vanessa out of the house. I didn't recall anyone saying goodbye. I didn't recall anything very much at all. Neil might have said he'd call me, and I might have nodded, but I could have been imagining it.

As I stood watching it all unfold in front of me, the trembling started. It began in my legs, and I reached for the wall to stabilise me, but my hands were also shaking. In fact, the whole world was tipping up and down, everything swaying about in front of me.

Ash was still talking about how Vanessa had trapped her father, about how Nathan had never liked her, and how Ash would listen to him every time from now on. Reece held her as she cried.

I should have gone to her too, but just as my balance went, my lunch rose into my throat. Lachie caught me and, with his arm tightly around my waist, walked me into the bathroom, kicking the door shut behind us. I fell to my knees in front of the toilet and vomited until there was nothing left inside me. Lachie sat on the mat beside me and rubbed my back, saying nothing, just being there – as he always had been for me.

I didn't begin to come out of my daze, or whatever it was, until after I'd finished being sick. Then I collapsed back against the toilet and sobbed. I could have said I was crying for Ash and Nathan and what this new baby would mean for them. I could even have said I was crying for Neil and what this would mean for him right at the moment he'd been about to finish with Vanessa. Just as he was moving into retirement, he'd been thrown a curve ball that would force him back into the corporate trap he'd been seeking to escape. Mostly though, I was crying for myself. I'd allowed myself to hope that Neil and I could have a future; that somehow we'd work it all out and get another chance at being together. Third time lucky, we'd said. That was all gone.

Lachie reached up and flushed the toilet, then sat beside me and held me as I sobbed.

When we finally came out of the bathroom, it was to find Mike, Ash and Reece huddled over cups of tea.

Ash jumped up and hugged me, her tears streaming out again. 'I'm so sorry, Mum.'

'I know, darling,' I said. There'd be time for me to feel sorry for myself later, but for now I was Ash's mother – and even at twenty-seven and newly married, she needed me to act like it. 'But your father's been gone for four years now, and we've all known he was going to start again with Vanessa. I think it's just the way it's happened that's surprised us. That's all. When the shock of how we found out has gone, we'll be able to be happy for him and Vanessa, you'll see.'

'He's properly gone now though,' she said. 'You'll have to divorce him so he can marry her, and he won't be coming around here for family things any more. Nothing will be the same, and any hope we had of you and Dad getting back together has disappeared. Oh god, what will Granny and Pops say? And you could see from Dad's face that it's the last thing he wanted. He was horrified. I wouldn't be surprised if it's not even his.'

'Ash,' I chided gently, ignoring the lump that was in my throat and the vice that had lodged around my heart. 'Dad and I were finished. You know that.'

'I know, but I always hoped, you know? You guys got on so well – almost better than when you were together. I suppose I hoped that if something went wrong with him and Vanessa, he'd turn to you. Just lately you could tell that he'd fallen out of love with her; that whatever novelty he used to see in her had worn off.'

There was nothing I could say to that.

Reece caught my eyes and prised his wife from my arms. 'Come on, Ashie, let me take you home.'

As they were leaving, she turned and said, 'I'm never talking to him again, you know.'

I stepped forward and smoothed her hair. 'Of course you will, darling. He's still your father. And this new baby will be your half-brother or sister – whether you like it or not.'

'Well, I don't like it, and I'm never talking to her again after the way she's treated you lately – you know, pushing for the divorce and everything. And especially not after what happened today.'

I smiled weakly. 'I don't agree with the way she did it either, but it can't have been easy for her wanting to have things finalised so she can be settled. I was standing in the way of that, so when you think about it, she was fighting for her baby and her man – and I can understand that. So will you one day.'

She kissed my cheek. 'I love you, Mum. I know I don't tell you very much, but I do.'

'I know you do, darling, and I love you too.'

Once she and Reece had left, I flopped into a kitchen chair. 'Oh god. What on earth am I going to do now, Lachie?'

'Do you want me to make you some tea?' asked Mike.

'No, no tea. I need something much stronger than tea. There's a bottle of scotch in the cupboard that I'm about to demolish, but first I need to clean up out there.'

Through the window I could see my prized desserts sitting forlornly and mostly untouched in their little cups. I grabbed a garbage bag, marched out to the deck and threw everything into it, cups and all. The spoons would have gone the same way if Mike hadn't rescued them.

He held out his hand for the garbage bag. 'Sweetie, let me deal with this. I'll clean the mousse out and wash the cups.'

'No.' I didn't loosen my grip on the garbage bag. 'I never want to see them again.'

'Fine,' he said, 'give the bag to me. I'll put it in the bin right now.'

I watched as he took it around the corner of the yard to where the bin stood, only going back inside when I knew the blameless little cups would never be in my house again.

Lachie had poured whisky for us all. He offered water and ice, but Mike and I shook our heads.

'Yeah, it's not necessary, is it,' Lachie said.

I threw the spirit back, choking as it hit the back of my throat, which was still tender from my bout in the bathroom.

Lachie topped up my glass. 'I'm so sorry, Kitty.'

I made a face. 'Yeah, I know. Me too. I really thought … It doesn't matter what I thought.' I took a sip of my scotch. 'The worst of it is that Ash is right – this isn't what Neil wants. He doesn't want to start over again. He's told her that right from the start, and she always said she agreed, that she didn't want children interfering with her career. She's done this on purpose, I know she has, to push him into committing to her.

She must have felt him moving away from her, that's all I can assume.'

'It does take two to ... you know,' pointed out Lachie.

'I know.' I wondered how far along she was. Neil had told me he hadn't slept with her since before Ash's wedding, and that was a month ago.

'Don't think about it, Kitty.'

I turned on him. 'I have to! I have no choice now but to divorce him. He's going to want to stand by her – regardless of what's changed between us. Of course he'll want to.' I laughed at the irony of the situation. 'It's like history repeating itself all over again – me being pregnant before we were married.'

'Yes, but you didn't trap him – and you could have. You gave him a choice, even though I didn't agree with it at the time. Plus, he was in love with you. He's not with her any more – if he ever was.'

Lachie's tone was gentle and it brought tears to my eyes again, so I drained my glass and refilled it. I saw Mike shoot a concerned glance at Lachie.

'Don't worry,' I said. 'I'm not going to do anything stupid. I just need not to feel for a little while.'

My phone rang and I could see it was Neil. 'You get it' I said to Lachie. 'I can't talk to him just yet.'

Lachie nodded and picked up the phone, walking into the sitting room to talk. Mike and I were silent until he returned.

'He's dropped Vanessa off at her place,' he said. 'He wants to come and see you.' I shook my head. 'Kitty, he's in a bad way.'

I rubbed at my forehead, and took another mouthful of whisky. Then I nodded. 'Alright. Ring him back and tell him he can come.'

Sixteen

After Neil and I broke up the first time, it was almost exactly four years until I saw him again – December 1989. I was on a Christmas harbour cruise with the city law firm I worked for. I wasn't seeing anyone, but Shane in the finance team, with the courage that only free Christmas-party beer could bring, had decided he was the man to change that. After what could only be described as an attempted grope on the dance floor, I took myself out onto the deck for some fresh air and quiet.

The first sign I wasn't alone was when I heard someone say from the darkness, 'Katie? Is that you?'

My heart missed a beat, and then another one. 'Neil?' Although I hadn't seen him in four years, I would have recognised his voice anywhere.

He stepped out of the darkness and stood in front of me. He'd filled out a little, but his face still had the same gentleness that had attracted me all those years ago.

I stepped forward and my heel caught on one of the gaps in the deck, lurching me into his arms. He held on to me for a few seconds longer than he needed to, before setting me aside with a laugh.

'You certainly didn't have this much hair before,' he said, rubbing at his nose.

I grinned at his familiar, dear face. 'It's so good to see you, but what are you doing here?'

'I'm here with Donna Brown, but I can't tell you how uncomfortable I feel at parties like this.'

'You're seeing Donna?'

Donna Brown was the most glamorous girl in the office. Tall and blonde, she made the most of her considerable assets. Tonight she was dressed in a slip dress, with make-up and hair that looked like she'd just tumbled out of bed and was waiting to tumble back in again. She would eat the Neil I knew for breakfast.

'Not really,' he said. 'She asked me and I thought why not? I wasn't doing anything else.'

'Oh. I see. Well, when … I mean, what have you been doing? When did you get back?' There was so much I needed to ask him that I tripped over my words.

'You mean what have I been doing since you dumped me?'

Ouch. That hurt.

'I didn't exactly dump you. You'd been offered a move to the middle of nowhere and I didn't want to go with you is how I remember it.'

'I'd asked you to marry me,' he said, his eyes filling with the sadness I'd seen in them the last time we met.

'I was eighteen, Neil, and one year into my degree. I was too young to get married. You knew what I wanted from life.'

'And being married to me wasn't it.'

'No, that's not what it was about.' I almost stamped my foot as the same exasperation from four years ago threatened to take over. 'I loved you, you know I did, but I didn't want to be married just yet.'

'I'm sorry my timing didn't fit with yours,' he said, 'but I'd been offered a job that I couldn't say no to. I know we'd only been together for a few months, and marriage wasn't on my schedule for another few years either, but I knew I didn't want to lose you.'

'Or your job it would seem.'

And just like that we picked up where we'd left the argument all those years ago. By the look on Neil's face he was reliving it too.

He sighed and drained his beer. 'You know what? It was what it was. It was also four years ago. What have you been doing since then? You're at a Christmas party for a big city law firm, so I guess you're on your way to getting everything you wanted. It does surprise me that it's this law firm though. I thought you were going to stand up for the underdog, and yet here you are in a firm that works for the banks and specialises in bankruptcies and evictions.'

I shrugged. 'It's a job. And you?'

'I had two years in Cooma, and then spent a couple

of years in Canberra. Now I'm working in one of the city branches. It's a commercial credit role – that's how I met Donna. She's the account lead on a company we're taking recovery action against.'

I let out a short laugh. 'It sounds as though you're on track. I'm pleased for you.'

We stood there in the darkness for a few minutes. I had so much to tell him, so much to say, but for one of the few times in my life, I had no words to say it.

It was Neil who broke the silence. 'Are you seeing anyone?'

I shook my head.

His eyes burned into mine. 'I've missed you, Katie.'

'I missed you too. So much.' I covered the couple of steps towards him in a heartbeat and reached up to pull his face down to mine for a kiss that I'd missed for four years.

'Oh, Katie.' He wrapped his arms around me and pulled me closer, his tongue reaching out to mine. When he pulled back, we were both breathing hard. He rested his forehead on mine. 'It's still there, isn't it?'

'Yeah,' I nodded, 'it is.'

'Do you have any regrets about not marrying me?'

I stroked the side of his face. 'Yes, more than you can ever know. But it wouldn't have worked.'

His smile was gentle. 'I know you're right. What I was asking you to do was selfish – you were never suited for that life. I just didn't want to lose you.'

'And it broke my heart to lose you.'

He bent his head to kiss me again, then said, 'What happens now?'

'I have absolutely no idea, but I'd really like you to carry on kissing me,' I said.

We swapped numbers when the cruise ended and arranged to see each other the next day for lunch. Neil was to pick me up at the house I shared with Lachie in Annandale.

I spent ages deliberating over an outfit, finally deciding on jeans and a striped T-shirt. It would be fine for a pub, a picnic, or a cafe. As I did my make-up and fluffed my hair out, I tried to see myself as he would. How much had I changed over the last four years? I still weighed the same as I had back then, give or take a couple of kilos – although it had been redistributed. My breasts were definitely fuller, my tummy a little rounder. My hair was longer, and these days I coloured it – just a few streaks here and there to brighten it up.

Lachie grinned when he walked past the bathroom and saw me examining myself in the mirror. 'You're looking hot, Kitty.'

I smoothed down the striped T-shirt tucked into my best jeans, then bent to roll the hems of my jeans to my ankles. 'You don't think this T-shirt makes me look too busty?' I stood again and pushed my boobs out towards the mirror.

'Yeah, if you go around doing that. Who's this for?'

'Neil.' I didn't look at him as I said it.

'As in *Neil* Neil?'

I nodded. 'I ran into him last night.'

'Riiiiight. Did you talk?' His eyebrows were raised as he waited for my answer.

'No. Not properly.'

'Are you going to? He needs to know.'

'I know. I'll tell him this afternoon.'

'See that you do. You should have done it before now.'

I turned to him. 'You know why I couldn't. You said you understood.'

'I might have understood, but that doesn't mean I agreed.'

'I know.'

'Just don't let him hurt you again, hey? I don't want to be picking up the pieces like last time.'

'It wouldn't be like last time,' I said.

He grimaced. 'Ain't that the truth.'

I punched him lightly on the arm. 'Behave!'

'Now, where's the fun in that?'

Right on time the doorbell rang. 'It's him,' I said unnecessarily, my feet rooted to the spot.

'Go on then,' urged Lachie.

'I can't – my legs won't move.'

He shook his head at me and went to open the front door. I stood at the top of the stairs and listened to them.

'Neil, it's good to see you, mate,' said Lachie. I imagined him shaking Neil's hand, each eyeing the other warily.

'Yeah, you too. Are you and Katie sharing a house these days?'

'We are.'

Then there was silence. The reason for the silence hit me at almost the same time as Lachie's yell of, 'Kitty? Get your arse down here. Now!'

Neil was staring at the photos on the wall – a collection of memories, birthdays, picnics. My breath caught in my throat as I watched him.

'What's his name?' he asked quietly.

'Nathan.'

'How old is he?'

'Three. He'll be four in July.'

'I see.'

Lachie placed a hand of reassurance on my shoulder, picked up his keys and left quietly.

Finally, Neil turned from the wall to look at me. His complexion was pale and his eyes glistening. 'I think I know already, but I have to ask. Is he mine?'

I nodded, and let out the breath I was holding. I felt the stream of tears down my face, but let them run. There was no point attempting to stem the flow.

'Why? How?' He closed his eyes for a brief second. 'Why didn't you say?' He wiped at his eyes. 'How could you keep this from me? You had to know I'd support you?'

I nodded. 'Yes. I knew that.'

'So why?'

I put my face in my hands and rubbed at my eyes. 'You'd better come through. We can't talk here.'

'You mean here in the hallway, where I'm surrounded by photos of a son I didn't even know existed?' His voice rose as he spoke, shaking slightly at the end.

'I know, it wasn't fair, but come through and we can discuss it properly.' When he didn't move, I held out my hand. 'Please, Neil.'

He scrubbed at his eyes with the back of his hand and nodded.

As we passed the living room, he noticed the Christmas tree and the advent calendar sitting on the mantelpiece. 'Is he excited?'

I smiled. 'Yes. This is the first year he's really understood what's going on. It's all about how many sleeps until Santa comes. He stayed at my parents' last night so I could go to the Christmas party – and so they could take him to see the Christmas windows in the city today.'

I made us coffee and took it outside. He waited until we were both settled before asking, 'When did you know?'

'Not until I was about four months gone. I wasn't great after you left.' I grimaced at the understatement.

'Lachie would say that I fell apart – which probably wasn't too far from the truth. It was such an impossible choice, you see. To go with you and know that it wasn't right, or stay here and do what I needed to do but without you. I was too young, Neil.'

'I know,' he said softly. 'It wasn't fair of me to ask. But nor was it fair of you to keep this from me.'

'No. It wasn't.' I took a deep breath before continuing. 'Anyway, I wasn't eating and I was so ill – I put it down to being heartbroken. I'd never been super regular so didn't notice that I'd missed my periods until March. And even then I thought it was just because I wasn't eating properly. It was Mum who finally asked me if I could be pregnant and took me off to the doctor. By then … well, I was already into the second trimester.'

I still remembered the look in my mother's eyes. Instead of the condemnation I'd expected to see, there had been just worry and concern.

'And you weren't tempted to …'

He didn't need to spell it out. 'Oh god, no. It didn't even occur to me not to keep him. I loved him from the second I suspected he existed. He brought me back from wherever it was I'd gone when you left.' I smiled and my eyes filled with tears again. 'He's the centre of my world, and every time I look at him I see you. Oh, Neil, he's the spitting image of you.'

Neil brushed away another tear. 'I still don't understand why you didn't tell me?'

'Lachie wanted me to. Mum and Dad wanted me to. Even Mari wanted me to. I told them we were in love and we'd broken up when you had to move away for work, and I didn't want you to know because you deserved the career you'd planned. It would have been so easy to call you back, or to turn up at your parents' place all pregnant and desperate, but I didn't want us being together just because of the baby. That would have been as wrong for both of us as if I'd gone with you in the first place. I swore Lachie to secrecy, and he agreed to stay quiet as long as I promised to tell you about Nathan when the time was right.' I paused, and blew at the top of my coffee before taking a sip. 'They've been so good, all of them – Mum, Dad, Lachie. I don't know how I would have managed without them.'

'You didn't finish your degree?'

I shook my head. 'I completed the first semester of second year before I had Nathan, then took six months off with him before trying to find work.'

'But the law firm?'

I shrugged. 'Mostly admin. As I said last night, it's a job. It's amazing how much your principles change when it comes to needing to pay your bills. I figured I could go back and finish my degree when Nathan's in school. Part-time, of course. Until then I'll be doing whatever I need to.'

'How have you managed?'

'While I was living at home it was easier than it

should have been – Mum looked after Nathan every day. I was lucky – good daycare is hard to get and expensive. Since we moved in here with Lachie, it's been more of a juggle. From next year though, I want to find him a pre-school, even if it's just a couple of days a week.'

'And financially?'

'It's been tight, but, as I said, I got lucky with my family. The thing is – and you don't need to believe this – I'd decided I was going to try and find you. Not so you'd be obligated – in fact, I'd figured that by now you'd be settled down with some girl much more suited to you than I was. I just felt the time was right. Nathan understands about Christmas and Santa and family now, and I wanted him to know the rest of his family.' I shrugged. 'And this next bit isn't going to sound great, but I also figured that if you didn't want anything to do with him – or me – he's young enough to grow up knowing that as being normal. I didn't want him to deal with rejection at an age when it would really hurt him.' I reached into my pocket for a tissue and blew my nose. 'I'd decided to visit your family after Christmas and make up some story about how I wanted to catch up with you … I hadn't worked out the finer details. I just knew I needed to do it.' I attempted a lopsided smile through my tears. 'And then you were there and I didn't need to find you. I knew you'd be angry – how could you not be? I know what I did wasn't fair to you, but at the time it felt as though it was the right thing to do

– even though it was the hardest thing I've ever had to do.' I sniffed; the tears had started again. 'And that's it.'

I couldn't look at him, so I looked around our tiny garden instead. At the magpie sitting on the branch of next-door's gum tree that hung over our fence. At the noisy birds squabbling in the bush at the back fence. At the weeds I needed to pull from the pavers.

Then I felt his hand cover mine. 'Katie,' he said, 'look at me.' I turned and met his eyes.

'It wasn't fair what you did. I understand why you did it, and I'm so sorry you had to do it, but I can't pretend I don't feel as though you've cheated me of the first few years of our son's life. I can't ever get that back – and nor can I make up to you for what you had to do alone.' He gripped my hand. 'The way I figure it, I can hate you for what you've done, but that would mean I'd miss out on even more time with Nathan and that's simply not going to happen. I'm angry with you, and I'm angry with myself for not staying in touch with you – but I can't hate you, and part of me understands why you thought you had to do what you did.'

He gave me a watery smile. 'The thing is – and you don't need to believe this.' I smiled as he repeated my words. 'I've never been able to forget you, and I haven't been able to feel about anyone else the way I felt about you. I took a sideways move to come back to Sydney because I wanted to find you. I had no idea where to start – you never even let me drop you back at your door – but I was determined to find you. And then you were there.' He smiled at me again. 'Has there been anyone else for you?'

I shook my head. 'No. How could there be? And it wasn't just that I haven't had time. The thing is, I never got over you.'

He shifted his chair closer to me, and tipped my chin up so my eyes met his. 'Katie, I want to be a part of your and Nathan's life. I wish I could take the last four years back, but I can't. All I can promise is that you won't have to do it on your own any more.'

He leaned forward and touched his lips to mine. It was a gentle kiss, almost a question.

When he pulled back, he said, 'And before you bristle and get all independent, I'm not saying that because I feel I should, or out of guilt or obligation. I'm saying it because I never stopped loving you. I'm angry, and I'm hurt, but even through all that I still love you, and I'm hoping you can learn to love me again.'

'Oh, Neil …' I stroked his cheek. 'I never stopped loving you either.'

And then he kissed me properly, with all the longing that four years apart could bring.

'When will Nathan be home?' he asked when finally we drew apart.

'Not for a few hours.' I nibbled at his earlobe, thrilling at the way he drew in a quick breath. 'I don't think it's worth you going home and having to come back, do you?'

He trailed a finger from my lips down my throat and into the cleft between my breasts. 'No, that would be a waste of petrol.' He cupped my breast through my T-shirt and watched as my nipples hardened under his touch. 'Although I did promise you lunch. We can go out if you like.' His grin teased me.

'I'm not hungry,' I said, and moaned as his hand slipped under my T-shirt and into my bra. 'Are you?'

'Not for food.' He kissed me again, taking my breath away and turning my insides to liquid. 'Where's your bedroom?' he asked into my mouth.

'Upstairs.'

'I think you'd better take me up there before we give your neighbours a show.'

'I should.' I wasn't prepared to give his lips up just yet.

'Now,' he growled.

Unlike our first time together, we removed each other's clothes almost in a frenzy, pausing only when we were both naked on the bed.

'What's wrong?' he asked.

'I haven't done this for a long time. What if I've forgotten how? What if I feel different after having had a baby?'

I knew I didn't need to be embarrassed about my body. I had no scars or stretch marks, and aside from my breasts being a little fuller, and my nipples a little darker, there was no evidence that I'd given birth a few years previously. Yet lying here under his gaze, I felt shy.

'Oh, sweetheart, you look and feel pretty wonderful to me.'

He pulled me closer so we were skin to skin. His finger traced the line of my spine, back and forth, lingering to lightly feather across my buttocks, leaving little trails of sensation.

I allowed my head to fall back. 'That feels so good.' I lifted one leg to drape my knee over his to allow his fingers access to where I really needed them to be, groaning when he slid first one then another into me.

'Still think you've forgotten what to do?' he murmured into my throat.

'No … please, Neil, I need you inside me.'

'Now?'

'Yes, now. Please, now.'

Afterwards, he held me as I cried softly. 'It's going to be okay,' he soothed. 'It's all going to be okay now.'

We forced ourselves out of bed and downstairs well before my parents were due to drop Nathan off. I managed to retrieve enough ingredients from the fridge to make us some sandwiches for a late lunch. We washed them down with cordial.

Neil laughed and said it was like a pre-schooler's afternoon tea. I told him he wasn't that far off the mark.

As the time drew near I could feel him getting

tense. He laughed at things he shouldn't have laughed at; he made comments about nothing; he told me at least three times that he had no idea how to be a father.

Finally I silenced him with a kiss. 'No one expects you to know how to be a father. I didn't know how to be a mother, but Nathan knows how to be a three-year-old boy, so one of us knows what's going on.'

'Seriously though, Katie, how did you do it? Don't take this the wrong way, but you were never the most maternally focused person.'

'I know. Remember how I was going to have this brilliant career before I even thought about having a child? I was so arrogant, like I knew everything and could control the future. The one thing I couldn't control was a hole in a condom, as it turns out.' Neil laughed with me. 'I was going to show the world how a woman could have it all – be a lover, a wife, a career woman and a mother. I was going to have a kid on each hip, and smash holes in the glass ceiling with my designer handbag while my husband kicked his own goals. We'd come home each evening and compare notes about how our day was before sitting down to a home-cooked meal, our children gurgling happily before going to bed and sleeping through the night, leaving us free to sit down with a glass of red and have an intelligent conversation about what needed to be done to bring about peace in the Middle East.'

'You mean it's not like that?' He slapped both

hands to his cheeks in mock surprise.

'Actually no, it's nothing like that.'

'Tell me, what's it really like?'

I giggled. 'In one word? Chaos. I spend most of every Sunday afternoon cooking meals to stick into the freezer. Then every night when I come home from work, I argue with a toddler who's decided that even though he usually really loves cheese sticks, tonight he absolutely hates them. And that spaghetti I slaved over is so much better on the walls and on the high chair and absolutely anywhere other than in his mouth. Then when I finally get him fed, we do bath time and the bathroom's covered in water and toys. Eventually I get him into bed, we read a story and have a cuddle and he says he loves me, and I know that as exhausted as I am he's worth every single stressful second. Then, once he settles, I clean the kitchen, prepare for tomorrow, pour a wine and collapse in front of god knows what on TV. Then I fall into bed and wake up at sparrow's fart to do it all again.'

'And you don't regret it?'

I shook my head. 'No, it's the best thing I've ever done.' I corrected myself. 'He's the best thing we've ever done.' I reached across the table and took his hand. 'Don't expect to get it first go. They don't come with an instruction manual, but they are pretty good at letting you know what they need. You'll be a natural, I know you will.'

At the sound of a key in the front door, we both

fell silent.

Nathan ran into the house ahead of Mum and Dad. I bent down and he launched himself into my arms.

'Hey there, where have you been?' I said.

'We saw Santa and the elves and even the reindeers! They were busy making the presents in the shop and everything!' His brown eyes widened as he told me of the wonders he'd seen in the windows of the city's department stores.

Mum and Dad followed him into the kitchen, and Mum faltered at the sight of Neil. There was no mistaking the resemblance.

'Mum, Dad,' I said with a tremor in my voice, 'this is Neil. He's Nathan's father.'

Tears came to Mum's eyes, and Dad put his arm around her shoulders.

'What's this about, love?' he asked me, concern in his voice.

I let Nathan squirm out of my arms and run off to get a toy out of the basket I kept in the corner of the living room. 'I ran into him last night, at the Christmas party. He knows everything.'

Neil stepped forward. 'I'm sorry, Mr Howard, I had no idea that Katie was … well …' He looked across at me. 'In that predicament. I would have come back if I'd known.'

'And now?' Dad hadn't moved.

'Now, I want to make it up to her. Not that I can really do that, but I can be here. I wanted to marry her before I left – and if she'll have me, I want to marry her now. I want to be part of Nathan's life. I want to be a real father to him, and I want to be the support to Katie that I didn't … that she deserves me to be.'

I moved next to Neil and took his arm. 'Dad, it's okay. He didn't know. I was telling you the truth about that. But he's here now – and while it's too early to think about marriage,' I smiled up at Neil, 'I'm not ruling it out. The important thing is, he's here, he knows, he still loves me and he wants to be a father to Nathan.'

Nathan had come back with his favourite toy – a soft dolphin. He tugged at Neil's jeans and held it up to him. The tears that had flowed all too freely from my eyes for much of this afternoon started again.

I could see tears glistening in Neil's eyes too as he squatted down to Nathan's level. 'Who's this?' he asked.

'It's Edward,' said Nathan earnestly.

'Edward the dolphin?'

Nathan nodded and offered the toy to Neil. Neil shook one of its flippers. 'Well, I'm very pleased to meet you, Edward the dolphin.'

Lachie strolled in, throwing his keys on the hall table and stopping short when he saw the gathering. 'O-kay. This is cosy.' He looked from our parents back to me, and then across to where Neil was engrossed in conversation with Nathan and Edward the dolphin.

'Should I ask?'

Mum was the first to recover. Shrugging herself out of Dad's grasp, she walked over to Neil and laid a hand on his shoulder. 'I'm very happy to meet you, Neil, and now I think I need to put the kettle on.'

Lachie hugged me to his side. 'All okay, Kitty-cat?'

I nodded. 'Yes.' Neil looked up and beamed at me, his eyes shining. 'We have a lot of getting used to, but yes, it's absolutely okay.'

Seventeen

Lachie was right: Neil was in a bad way. Still pale-faced, his eyes red and puffy, his hand shaking as he put his keys on the table. He looked at me and shrugged one shoulder, resignation on his face.

I jumped to my feet and wrapped my arms around his waist, holding him as tightly as it was possible to hold anyone. He clung on to me and I felt his body shudder as he gave way to the emotion of the afternoon.

I heard, rather than saw, Lachie and Mike let themselves out.

'What am I going to do, Katie? I don't want this.' He almost choked the words out.

'I know you don't,' I soothed, forcing my own pain back within my body in the face of his distress. 'You'll have to marry her now. I'll make it easy for you and sign whatever you need me to sign.'

'No,' he said. 'That's the one thing I do know. I'll support this child, and be as much a part of its life as she wants me to, but I can't be with Vanessa. I didn't fight for you four years ago – I gave up on us. I'm not doing that again.'

I touched his cheek, still wet from his tears. 'I gave up on us too,' I reminded him.

'We were both wrong back then, but I'm not prepared to lose you now.'

'You mightn't have a choice.'

'I do. She might think she has me over a barrel, but I still have a choice. It's going to be tough and she's going to fight every step of the way – she told me that tonight. She probably assumes that because I'm not big on conflict I'll just roll over. But I'm not going to this time. You and I have found each other again and I'm not giving up on that.'

I smiled weakly. 'She doesn't know you very well if she thinks you'll cave in to blackmail. In my experience, any attempt to force you to do what you don't want to do just makes you dig your heels in harder.'

'It does, doesn't it. You always had a way of making me think the things you wanted were my idea.'

'You knew about that?'

'Of course I did. But not letting you know was part of the game.' He smiled and bent his head to kiss my lips. 'I do love you, my Katie.'

My smile was watery. 'And I love you too.'

'Can I stay tonight? Not to make love, but just to sleep with you?'

'Of course you can – on one condition. I don't want to talk about this any more, not tonight. I want to pretend for one night that it hasn't happened and we don't have to deal with it. Let's sleep on it, and then think about our next steps.'

'You have a deal.'

I poured us each a whisky, and we took them through to the sitting room and switched the TV on, flicking through until we landed on one of those shows where a couple escape their normal life for a new one somewhere else.

'Just like we're going to do,' Neil said. 'When I come to New Zealand and meet you there after the walk we can take some time to have a proper look around. Who knows – we might find what we're looking for there.'

'Perhaps.' I knew he was trying to make-believe that everything was as it had been earlier this afternoon.

Nathan called as I was heating up some soup. I didn't think either of us was hungry, but eating felt normal and distracted us from what was on both our minds.

Nathan didn't mess about with pleasantries. 'Ash told me. Mum, I'm so sorry. I'm not going to ask if you're okay, because Ash said you were pretty upset.'

'Yes, I was. I am.'

'How's Dad? That must have come as a surprise to him too? It's funny, because I was under the impression that he was changing his mind about her.'

It shouldn't have surprised me that Nathan had picked up on that. 'Yes, it did. He's here now if you want to talk to him.'

'He's there? Good. I hoped that would be the way he went.' He sounded relieved – and something else.

'What do you mean?'

He hesitated before saying, 'I saw you two, Mum. At the wedding, in the garden.'

'Oh.' How much had he seen? My face grew warm at the thought.

'Don't worry, I couldn't see anything once you went behind the tree. Whatever you did from there, I don't need to know – I don't want to be scarred for life.'

I could picture the mock distaste on his face. 'You didn't say anything to Ash, did you?' Through this whole thing I'd taken comfort from the fact that no matter what happened between Neil and me, our kids wouldn't be any the wiser.

'No, I figured you'd tell us if it got that far.'

'Thank you.' Having to deal with Ash was one less worry for me. 'What did you mean when you said you hoped Dad would go that way?'

'That he'd stick to his guns and choose you.'

'We don't know what we're doing yet,' I said.

'He does. He's with you now, isn't he, when he should be with her and acting like he's excited about a baby he doesn't want.'

I looked across to where Neil was pretending to be watching the TV. 'I suppose.'

'There's no suppose about it, Mum. Anyway, can I talk to him, please?'

'Sure, I'll put him on.'

'Mum, I'm really happy you guys are together, but you also have my word that I won't say anything to Ash yet.'

'Thanks, Nath.'

As I handed the phone to Neil, I wiped away a tear.

He raised a questioning brow at me as he took the phone from my hand. 'Okay?' he mouthed.

I nodded and went back into the kitchen to give them some privacy. Neil joined me soon after, leaning against the table and watching me as I gave the soup I was stirring more attention than it required.

'Well,' he said, 'I've just been asked by my son what my intentions are towards his mother. That's a first.'

'What did you tell him?'

'That my intentions are mostly honourable.'

I smiled into the soup. 'Only mostly?'

He moved behind me and wrapped his arms around my middle. 'Some of my intentions are strictly dishonourable.'

'I hope you didn't tell him about those.' I tilted my head to the side to allow him to kiss my neck.

'No, there's no need to shock the boy.'

'I don't think there's much you could say that would shock him.'

I managed to continue stirring the soup even as Neil's hand moved up and under my top to cup my breast. He nipped at my earlobe and I closed my eyes, dropping the spoon. I vaguely heard it clatter onto the stove-top.

'Except perhaps tell him what I intend to do to you right now,' Neil said.

I grinned as I imagined Nathan's reaction to that. 'Yes, that would do it.' My grin quickly turned to a soft moan when he nuzzled in behind my ear and down the line of my throat. 'I thought you just wanted to sleep tonight.'

'I've changed my mind.' He turned me in his arms and kissed me deeply, releasing me briefly to turn off the stove and move the saucepan aside. 'Are you okay with that?'

I took his hand and led him upstairs.

Later, while he held me and slept, I allowed myself to imagine a possibility where we were third time lucky.

In my dream scenario, Vanessa rang and said, 'I'm so sorry, Neil. I'm not really pregnant. It was a faulty batch of tests and I'm having that lawyer friend of mine sue the makers. I really want you and Kate to be happy.'

Yes, the likelihood of that happening was similar to the likelihood of … No, we wouldn't get into that.

In my next scenario, Vanessa said something like, 'Neil, this was my decision to get pregnant – I'm really sorry, but I flushed my pills down the toilet. The clock was ticking and it drowned out all common sense. I know you're not keen to start again, and I understand that this pregnancy is my responsibility, so I ask absolutely nothing of you. In fact, I wish you and Kate all the happiness in the world. You both deserve it.'

I smiled in the darkness, No, that wasn't going to happen either.

In the next option, Neil and Vanessa sat down to talk about the baby. 'I'd like you to be involved,' she said, 'but this was my decision, so it's my financial responsibility too. If you could help out at Christmas and birthdays, it would be appreciated. But I'd really like for you and Kate to be happy together.'

Or maybe even: 'You and Kate were meant to be together, and I don't want to intrude on that. I don't see why we can't sort something out so you're both involved in this baby's life. After all, up until the last couple of months we've all gotten on so well together.'

All my fantasies centred around Vanessa admitting defeat and wishing Neil and me well. But I knew the most likely outcome would be the one where she denied Neil access to his child, insisted on hefty maintenance payments, and cursed us both until the end of our days.

If I was being honest, I wouldn't blame her. After all, they'd been an established couple for over three years, and she probably had a reasonable expectation that she'd end up with a husband and some real estate, or at the very least a healthy house deposit. Instead, she was left with a baby. Despite the pain I suspected she was about to cause us, I couldn't help feeling sorry for her. I especially felt sympathy for her child. Every baby deserved to be born into a family where it was loved and wanted. This baby of Vanessa's was bringing with it heartache and sorrow. I knew, though, that if he got the opportunity, Neil would still want to be involved in whatever way she allowed him to be. His sense of responsibility was, after all, one of the reasons I loved him.

I reached for my phone and checked the time. How could it still only be 9 pm? So much had happened this afternoon that it felt as though it should be almost tomorrow.

Making sure the phone was on silent, I tapped out a text to Lachie. *Is it too late to call?*

His reply came through quickly. *Nope. Call away.*

I snuck out of bed, wrapped a dressing gown around me, slid my feet into ugg boots and padded quietly downstairs. Once curled up on the sofa, I called my brother.

'Hey, Kitty, all okay? How's Neil?'

'I'm fine, and Neil's upstairs asleep.'

'Of course he is. I'm sure that man could sleep through any crisis as long as he knew you were trying to fix it.'

He chuckled, but I knew there was an edge to his words. It was a criticism that Lachie had always had of Neil – how he left it to me to deal with any big decisions or potential conflicts. I used to tell Lachie that I preferred it that way, but there were times – more of them than I'd care to admit – when I'd secretly longed for Neil to take charge.

'Yes, well, he told Vanessa that he'll provide support in whichever way she needs, but that he and I are together now. I think he has this vision of supporting her from afar, and involving her and the child in our family.'

Lachie laughed then, the sound coming from deep in his belly.

'What's so funny?' I said.

'You two, my Kitty-cat. Don't you get the irony? He leaves you but stays in your life, and everything on the surface is as it always was, except that Vanessa is now on the scene – who you welcome into your home with open arms.'

'Not exactly open.'

'Not the point. Now he's decided that he wants you back and is leaving Vanessa, he's hoping to slot back in at home as though the last four years haven't happened, but this time Vanessa and her baby will be welcomed in. It's what he did with you in reverse – or not even really in reverse. It's also completely unrealistic. You know it is.'

'Yes,' I sighed. 'Which is why I'm calling you. In addition to maintenance, I'm afraid she might come after him for the property settlement she feels she was entitled to. I don't know, breach of promise or something? Is there still such a thing? Anyway, I think we need to talk to Mike to see what our options are if she decides to do that.'

He was silent for a few seconds.

'Lachie?'

'Yes, you're right. I think that's exactly what she's going to do. She wants what she thinks she's worked for the last three years.'

'That makes it sound as though she was always in it for the money and I don't think that's true – well, not at the start anyway.'

'Maybe that's a bit harsh. Let's just say that I'm sure the real estate was one of Neil's attractions.'

'That's mean! Neil's in great shape. He works out most days, he eats mostly healthy food, he still has a full head of hair. He's a hot fifty-five-year-old man. Well, I find him hot. He's definitely hotter than he was when we were together.'

'And you're hotter than you were when you were together too. But my point is, he's a healthy, good-looking fifty-five-year-old man and you're a fifty-year-old woman. Of course you can't keep your hands off him. She, however, is hot and thirty-odd. There's a difference.'

'I don't think I like the way your mind is working.'

'That's fine, Kitty, but Mike is worried she might be able to prove there was a de facto relationship –'

'Even though they didn't live together?' I cut in.

'Yes. Even though they didn't live together.'

'I see.'

'Do you?'

'What you're saying is, she might make a claim against his property on the basis that they were in a de facto relationship even though they weren't living together. And it's complicated by the fact that there's no property that's his to claim against because it's all ours.'

'Yes. You really should have gone back to finish your degree.'

'Somehow I don't think that would be helping me now.'

'True. Unless you'd studied family law, there's probably nothing that would protect you against the Vanessas of the world. If Neil had to screw around I really wish he'd chosen more wisely.'

'We don't know yet what she's going to do.'

'I think we have a fair idea, Kitty.'

I thought about something Neil had said earlier tonight. 'What would happen if Neil retired and no longer had a guaranteed income?'

'You can't be expecting that he'd try and dodge maintenance? We both know that's not his style.'

'No, it's not that, it's just that we were thinking of selling up in Sydney and buying a little bookstore somewhere. I'm wondering whether she wants Neil as a father for her child or she really just wants the settlement.'

I could hear Lachie's brain ticking over. 'I'll talk it over with Mike, but I like the way you're thinking. We'll drop over tomorrow after work and talk some options through, but that's all it can be until she decides to make a move.'

'I know that. Neil has other issues at work as well, so it's really one problem at a time.'

'And there's not much you enjoy more than having problems to get your teeth stuck into.'

'Perhaps, but I'd prefer they weren't quite this dramatic.'

Lachie laughed. 'Tell me about it. My life is a bed of rainbows and unicorns compared to yours at the moment. Now you, my sweet kitten, need to get back into bed beside your errant husband. We'll talk tomorrow. Okay?'

'Okay. Thanks, Lachie … for being there.'

'Always,' he said, and rang off.

I sat for a few moments more in the quiet dark, but there was nothing else I could do until Vanessa made her move – if indeed she intended to make one. I padded back upstairs, undressed again and slid back into bed beside Neil. He stirred slightly but didn't wake.

Eighteen

I, on the other hand, didn't drift off until the early hours of Monday morning, and was woken soon after by Neil sneaking out to head home before going to work.

'Go back to sleep,' he urged. 'I'll see you tonight.'

I yawned and struggled to sit up. 'Are you talking to her today?' We both knew who I was referring to.

'Yes.' He sat on the bed to pull his socks on. 'I have no idea what I'm going to say to her yet, but I owe it to her to at least sit down and discuss the matter.'

'It's so early in the pregnancy, there's no guarantee that she'll even –' I stopped, aware of just how cruel and heartless it sounded.

'Katie, that's not like you.' Neil spoke softly, but there was no denying that he was chiding me.

I grimaced. 'I know, I'm sorry. I wouldn't normally even think such a thing, but there's nothing about this situation that's normal, is there?'

'You're right there.' He slipped his feet into his trainers. 'I'll call her today, and maybe drop around tonight before coming back here. If it's okay, do you mind if I leave some things here? I know it's too early to talk about moving in again – we both have adjustments to make – but I'd like to have my running gear here and maybe some things for work so I'm not having to sneak out early when I'd much prefer to still be in bed with you.'

He leaned across to kiss me and the parts of me that had still been slumbering woke up.

'Of course you can – you don't need to ask. It's your home too.' I played with the buttons on his shirt. 'In fact, why don't you call in sick and stay in bed now?' My hand slipped inside the opening I'd created to slide across his chest.

He groaned and placed his hand over mine to stop it straying further. 'Don't tempt me, darling. I've got a one-on-one with Roger this morning. I suspect he's going to give me the one month's notice of intention to terminate me.'

'He can't do that!' I sat up straighter, and he put a finger to my lips.

'Legally he can. Ethically? Well, that's another matter entirely. In any case, I've decided to get in first and tell him I'd like to retire.'

'Are you sure?'

Although we'd talked about it, I needed to know that with so much other chaos going on around him, he was certain about this decision.

'Yes. I'm absolutely sure. I want us to start over again with a completely clean slate. We'll do what we always said we'd do. I don't know where, but we'll find the perfect place to settle. It'll be just us doing what we always dreamed of doing.' He kissed me again. 'What do you think?'

'I think it sounds like a plan. But what about Vanessa? I've been thinking –'

'I'm sure you have.' He smiled. 'My darling Katie, always trying to solve everyone's problems and fight their fights. Let's not try and solve everything before 6 am, hey? That will leave you with nothing to do for the rest of the day.'

I pretended to be offended but knew I wasn't fooling him. 'I love you, Neil.'

'And I love you too. I'll call you after the meeting with Bovis and let you know how it went,' he said, and he kissed me one last time and left.

Somehow I managed to get dressed and go to work. The morning was busy with administration tasks and following up on the court judgements some of our clients were waiting on.

True to his word, Neil phoned me at lunchtime after he'd met with Roger Bovis.

'I think my retirement decision came as both a surprise and a disappointment to him,' Neil said. 'I was right: he had intended on presenting me with the one month's notice, because he had someone from human resources with him – and looking mighty uncomfortable she was too.'

'As she should be. She had to know that what he was doing wasn't right.'

'Exactly. Anyway, I presented him with my intention to retire the minute I walked into his office, so after that he would have looked like a dick if he'd refused to accept it and continued with the termination.'

'You mean he would have looked like more of a dick than he really is?' I heard Neil's laugh. 'I bet he'd have pushed it if he hadn't had HR there though,' I added.

'Yes, I think he would have too. He seemed disappointed that he didn't get the chance to present me with his letter.'

'Did he want to know what you were doing?'

'He didn't ask, but the HR rep did, so I told them I was moving to New Zealand to buy a bookshop with my wife. He said he didn't know that Vanessa and I had married – he's met her a couple of times at various functions. So I told him I wasn't doing it with Vanessa, but had reconciled with my wife and this had always been our dream. I even managed to thank him for being the reason we were back together and for giving us this opportunity.'

I choked on the tea I'd been sipping. 'You what?'

'I told him that I'd confided in you about the

pressures he'd put me under, and it had made me realise how you've always been the one who's there for me. And realising that was a reminder that what I really wanted was a future with you – which didn't involve working for an organisation I no longer had any respect for and that allowed the type of bullying I'd been subjected to.'

'You said that?'

'I did. As stressful as it's all been, in a way he's done me – done us – a favour.'

'You're more generous about it than I would be, but perhaps he has. And you're okay with it all?'

Although he'd told me this morning that he was happy with his decision, the bank had been such a big part of his life for so many years that I was concerned that once the dust had settled, he'd regret not fighting for his job.

'Absolutely. I know I have the Vanessa thing to deal with, but I feel so light and free. Like there's everything to look forward to.'

'There is, Neil – we have so much to look forward.'

'Anyway, I have to go,' he said, 'there are a lot of calls I need to make. But I'll see you tonight. I'm meeting Vanessa this afternoon – she said she's too busy to see me tonight – so I should be back home by six.'

'Okay. Sounds good.'

'Katie, I'm not seeing this as an ending, you know.'

'I know.' Something that felt like joy rushed

through me. 'We're really going to do this, aren't we?'

'We really are. I'll see you tonight.'

'You will.' As he was about to hang up, something made me say, 'Neil, I love you, and I'm proud of you.'

I could hear the smile in his voice. 'I love you too, my darling Katie. I always have and I always will.'

The call came through from Vanessa late that afternoon. I'd just got home from work and was in the middle of changing into trackpants and trainers to go for a walk.

'It's Neil,' she said. 'They think it's a heart attack.'

My body went cold. There were questions I had to ask, but I couldn't get the words out.

'Kate, did you hear me? Neil collapsed. He's been rushed to hospital.'

'Who rang you?' I didn't know why it mattered, but somehow it did.

'No one rang me, I was there.' Her voice caught. 'One minute we were talking and he was telling me why he'd gone back to you, and next I knew he was on the floor and everyone was looking at me and I just froze. I had no idea what to do – someone else called the ambulance, and all I could do was wait for them to show up. The paramedics asked if I was his wife and I had to say no. I told them I'd call you.' She paused and drew in a noisy breath.

'Is he … alright?' I couldn't ask the question I wanted to ask. Is he alive?

'I don't know. He was alive when he went into the ambulance, but he's not good.'

'Where is he?'

'I should have been his wife. If you hadn't held on to him I would have been his wife.' I could hear the sob in her voice, but ignored it.

'Vanessa!' I snapped. 'Where is he? Where have they taken my husband?'

'Royal North Shore.' She almost shouted the words at me. 'But –'

I didn't wait for her to finish. I hung up the phone and grabbed my keys and bag. Once in the car, I called Ash on hands-free. I knew I should have been panicking or screaming and crying, but all I felt was a strange icy calmness.

Neil would be alright. He had to be. He was fit and healthy – he ran ten kilometres a few times a week and was careful with his diet. He even went to the gym, for god's sake. Men like Neil didn't have heart attacks. They had panic attacks that were sometimes mistakenly diagnosed as heart attacks – the symptoms were the same, weren't they? That's all this was. A scare, nothing to worry about. We were buying a bookshop in New Zealand. I was going to climb a mountain with my son, and Neil and I were buying a bookshop. Third time lucky, we'd said. He had to be alright.

Ash picked up after two rings. 'Mum, I was going to call you later to see how you are.'

'Darling, it's your dad,' I said.

'Of course it's Dad. Have you spoken to him after yesterday? I still can't believe what happened.'

'Ash,' I cut in. 'Dad's had a heart attack and they've taken him to hospital.'

The phone was silent.

'Ash?'

'Oh my god, Mum.' I could hear her crying. 'No, it can't be, he's too healthy. Maybe it's not Dad, maybe it's someone else. It can't be Dad.'

'Sweetie, Vanessa called me. He was with her when it happened. It's definitely Dad. He's at Royal North Shore – I'm heading there now.'

'I'll go too,' she said. 'Do you want me to call Nath? Oh god, what do I do?'

'Ash, calm down. Call Reece, he'll know what to do. Then go to the hospital. I'll see you there, okay?'

'Okay.'

I took another deep breath and rang Nathan, getting his voicemail. 'Nath, it's Mum. Please call me as soon as you get this.'

Who else? Lachie ... I had to let Lachie know, and Neil's parents. And his sisters. What could I tell them? I didn't know anything yet. I'd ring them when I got to the hospital and knew he was alright.

I dialled Lachie.

'Hey, Kitty, how are you feeling today?'

It was his voice that did it. The tears spilled over,

pouring out of my eyes in such a stream that I was in danger of not seeing the road in front of me. I put my blinker on and pulled over.

'It's Neil,' I managed. 'He's had a heart attack.'

'Fuck, Kitty, no!'

'I'm going to the hospital now. I don't know anything else, but I had to … Oh Christ, Lachie, I don't know what to do.'

'Where are you?'

'I've pulled over to talk to you. I have to get there.'

'I know, darling. Do the kids know?'

'I've spoken to Ash – she's on her way too. I could only get Nath's voicemail and didn't want to tell him over that.' My voice broke and I was unable to continue.

'What about Vanessa?' Lachie asked.

'She was the one who told me. He was with her – they were talking. This can't be happening, Lachie. He announced his retirement today. We were going to finally do it – run away together and buy that bookshop. This can't be happening.'

'I know, sweetie. You need to dry your eyes and get to that hospital. I'll call Nath back and also let Neil's parents know. Leave that to me, and I'll meet you there.'

'Thank you, Lachie.'

Nineteen

Neil didn't make it.

They said he never really regained consciousness, that he died soon after his arrival at the hospital.

'I'm sorry, Mrs Spence, it was a massive heart attack. There was nothing we could do.' The doctor probably said something else but I didn't hear any more.

'I want to see him.'

'Mrs Spence, I don't think –'

'I want to see him.'

He nodded once, and led me down the hall to a curtained partition. 'I'm sorry, I need to go, I have other patients. But the nurse will look after you.'

Once the curtain was closed I allowed myself to look at him. He was lying on the bed, still in the clothes he'd worn to work that morning. Someone had obviously done his shirt back up, but it had been pulled from the waistband of his pants. If he'd been wearing a tie I didn't know what had happened to it.

I approached the bed and touched his forehead, pushing his hair away like I used to when he'd fall asleep on my lap in front of the TV when we were first together. He looked as though he was asleep, but his skin was cold already.

'Oh, Neil,' I said. 'What am I going to do without you?'

A sharp pain hit my belly and I doubled over, dropping to the floor beside the bed amongst the cords and wires. The strange howling noise that filled the cubicle was coming from me.

Ash found me like that and gently pulled me to my feet, wrapping her arms around me. I don't know how long we stayed there – her holding me, me holding her – until the nurse came and ushered us from the room with kind words that neither of us remembered.

Lachie and Reece were in the waiting room, watching for us. Ash ran into her husband's arms, burrowing into his chest to sob. I sat down beside Lachie and let him put his arm around me, but I had no more tears left to cry.

It was at that moment that I saw Vanessa, standing in the entrance, all alone. I took a deep breath and stood to go to her.

Lachie squeezed my hand. 'Are you sure?'

I nodded and smiled weakly at him, before walking across to where she stood.

'Is he …?' she asked.

I nodded, and her beautiful face crumpled.

'I'm sorry,' I said, without knowing why I was

saying it to her. Aside from the fact that she must have loved him. She'd never said as much, but you wouldn't say something like that to your boyfriend's wife, would you. Of course she'd loved him – she'd wanted to marry him. With another stab of pain I remembered: she was carrying his baby.

Ash had seen us, and anger was taking over from her tears. I heard her say, 'How dare she come here!' and saw Lachie pull her back.

Vanessa looked across at Ash. 'Do you think that too?' she said to me. 'That I shouldn't be here. After all, you've got a lot of reasons to hate me.'

'No, you loved him too. I mightn't have liked that, but you made him happy for a few years when I couldn't.'

I touched her arm, intending the gesture as comfort, but she shook my hand away.

'Don't you dare patronise me. It should be me here as the grieving wife, and you standing on the outside. It would have been if you hadn't hung on to him as long as you did.'

The sharpness of her tone and the cruelty of her words startled me. I tried to tell myself it was just the grief speaking, that she didn't know what to do or how to react. I tried to remember that she'd lost someone she loved too, but the anger was welling up inside me, bubbling over the pain in my belly, entering my throat with a bitter metallic taste that made me grimace.

Swallowing it back down, I struggled for calm.

'I'm sorry you feel that way, but now isn't the time for that. You're welcome to join us – after all, you were part of this family for a few years.'

She shook her head. 'No. Just let me know when the funeral is. I still have a key to the apartment so I'll drop it back after I've collected my things from his place.'

'Vanessa, it doesn't have to be like this.'

She raised her head and looked at me, unshed tears in her eyes. 'Doesn't it?'

I watched her as she turned and left, pausing just outside the sliding glass doors to wipe her eyes, and then slowly walking down the stairs, her normally proud and upright figure slumped into itself.

I went back to join the others.

'What did she want?' Ash spat the words out.

'She cared about Neil too,' I said.

The attitude fell away from Ash's face, exposing the misery. 'I know she did.'

Yesterday afternoon, Vanessa's announcement and the events that had unfolded seemed like a lifetime ago. Since then Neil and I had cried, made up, made love, made plans, made more love, and more plans. At least I knew he'd died knowing that I loved him and we were starting over.

But where did any of that leave me? I had a whole lifetime ahead of me now – without Neil in it.

~

Lachie took charge for me, as he'd done so many times in the past. He phoned Neil's family, and stayed with me when they all came to the house, making endless cups of tea for us as we all tried in vain to come to terms with what had happened.

Although no one other than Lachie, Mike and Nathan knew that Neil and I had reconciled before he died, nobody questioned my grief or my role in it all as his wife. Nor did anyone ask where Vanessa was and why she wasn't with us. It was almost as if she didn't exist, even though she'd been in our lives for the last few years.

If this had happened even a few weeks before, things would have been very different. What would I have been if we'd actually started the divorce proceedings, if Neil was still with Vanessa? I wouldn't have been his wife or his widow – even though that's what I was legally. As for Vanessa, what was her position in this? She was neither wife nor widow, even though she'd planned a life and a family with Neil. If it wasn't all so damned sad, I could have almost giggled at the random weirdness of it all.

I said so to Lachie once the family had gone. 'Where does this leave Vanessa? It's not as though she was his wife, or even his fiancée. In the view of the world she's just somebody he used to be with, but we know she was so much more than that. I have our family and everyone's love, but what does she have?

There's no title or label for her.'

'I can think of a label for her.'

'Don't be mean, Lachie, not now. She was really upset this afternoon.'

'I'm sorry. Look, I know you feel bad for her, but if the situations were reversed she wouldn't have treated you with anywhere near the kindness you're showing to her. She'd tolerate the kids being around, have very little patience for Dave and Maureen, less for Leanne and Libby, and you'd be completely on the outer – even though you spent the majority of your adult life with him.'

'I'm sure that wouldn't –'

'It's exactly how it would have been, Kitty. And deep down you know it.'

I nodded. He was right – that was exactly how it would have been. 'That doesn't mean I need to treat her the same way. She was a big part of his life and she'll be welcome to join us.'

He shrugged one shoulder. 'It's your funeral.'

'Actually, no, it's not – it's Neil's.'

We looked at each other and laughed ruefully.

'What am I going to do without him, Lachie?'

'I don't know, but you'll find a way.'

Lachie waited with me until Nathan arrived.

'I can't believe it, Mum,' Nath said, bundling me into his arms. The tears that I'd thought had dried up at the hospital came back. 'He was so fit, so healthy.

Do they know how it happened? Was it stress or heart disease – or something else?'

'They don't know yet. I imagine they'll need to do whatever it is they do to find out.'

I couldn't say the word 'autopsy'. The idea of someone cutting into Neil was too much for me to bear.

Nathan nodded. He'd always been able to understand what I was thinking. There'd never been the need for too many words between us.

The next days passed in a blur of arrangements, tears and sympathy.

Nathan and I went to the apartment to pick up some clothes for Neil to wear to the funeral. It sounded so surreal to be saying that.

We found that Vanessa had been there before us. Neil's books, normally arranged neatly in genre and then by author, had been flung from their bookcases. It was a similar story in his bedroom, with clothes pulled from hangers and strewn across the floor. In the centre of the otherwise bare kitchen counter was a set of keys.

'That bitch!' Nathan's hands balled into fists as he looked at the mess Vanessa had left. 'Why would she do this?'

'She's hurting.' It was all I could think of to say. What I really wanted to do was march around to where she lived or worked and shake her, or slap her. This was such a needlessly cruel and petty act of vandalism.

'That's no excuse. It's not as if he died to deliberately hurt her.' Nathan's voice shook as he tried in vain to control his anger.

'Maybe not, but he'd left her for me. That had to have hurt.'

'I suppose,' he conceded. 'But even so.'

'Just leave it, Nath. Could you deal with the clothes? I don't think I can.'

I bent down to begin collecting the books into orderly stacks, straightening the dust covers on the hardbacks. Neil had always taken such good care of his books and seeing them strewn on the timber floor got to me. I kneeled there amongst them and cried, my tears forming little puddly drops on the covers.

He'd have hated that too. It was one of the things we always argued about. I liked paperbacks and was a corner-turner. On the rare occasion I read a hardback, I'd take the dust cover off to preserve it. I also liked to read in the bath, and as a result my books looked like they'd been read in the bath. Neil preferred to read on the lounge, or in bed. He used bookmarks and kept his books in an immaculate condition.

Another thing that used to annoy him was how I always had more than one book on the go at the same time. For all moods, I used to tell him.

'But how can you keep up with where you are in each of them?' he used to wonder.

'I pick the story back up within a couple of pages.'

Only last week we'd argued about how I'd changed to reading on a device rather than an actual book.

'But it doesn't even smell like a book,' he'd said.

'Perhaps not, but you can't get mad at me for turning down the corners,' I'd replied, laughing at his outrage. 'Besides, this way I can read a few books at the same time and not have them piled up on my bedside table.'

He'd looked at the pile of books on my bedside table and laughed. 'The device doesn't seem to have cured you of that habit.'

I'd giggled. 'No.'

'Well, at least on a device you can't flick to the last page to see what happens,' he'd said. 'I've never understood why you do that.'

'So I know whether I'm wasting my time. It's a huge commitment to make if the ending isn't satisfactory, or the dog dies.'

'But what about the twists you miss out on?'

I'd never told him that I also googled the endings of TV shows and movies so I didn't have to deal with the suspense. It was always easier to watch those parts when I knew what was coming.

Sitting on the floor now, amongst Neil's books, I wondered whether, if I'd been able to google the spoiler alert and seen this ending, I would still have gone down the path I had with Neil. Yes, I decided, I would have. The last few weeks of happiness, and the hope we'd had for the future – I wouldn't have missed that for anything. I wouldn't have deprived Neil of it either, even if I had already read the last page and knew what was coming.

I wiped the tears from my eyes and stacked the books.

When I looked up, Nath was standing there with a suit bag over one arm and shoes in his hands. 'Are you okay?' he asked.

I shrugged. 'She must have been so angry.'

He looked around at the mess and nodded. 'Yep. For god's sake, don't let Ash see this. She'd tear around there and confront Vanessa. No doubt about Ash: she can change her mind about a person in a split second.'

I smiled fondly. That was Ash all over – she'd always been a creature of extremes. She'd love people to pieces until they hurt her or someone she cared about, and then her enmity knew no bounds. I remembered that party all those years ago when her supposed friend had ruined her white dress. Ash had cried over it, then dried her eyes and announced that Kylie was now dead to her. 'If she can do this to me because of some boy, then she's no friend of mine,' she'd announced. I didn't think she'd ever spoken to Kylie again.

It had been the same with Vanessa. Ash had been the one to welcome her into the family, had even had a girl crush of sorts on her, but she'd turned against her the minute she'd overheard her talking to me about the divorce. Ash would have forgiven her father within a few days, but I knew she'd never speak to Vanessa again.

And no, Ash couldn't know about this. Whether we liked it or not, Vanessa was carrying a half-brother or half-sister to Ash and Nathan and so would still be part of our lives.

'Do you know what you're going to do with this place yet?' Nathan asked.

I shook my head. 'Not a clue about any of it.'

I looked around the living space. Even though Neil had been here for the past four years, there was little of his personality in the room aside from the books and a few framed photographs of the kids. The furniture, rugs and styling were simple and tastefully neutral, as if they'd come straight out of one of those reality TV shows. I remembered that when Neil moved in, he'd gone to one of the interiors stores and essentially bought the display room. He'd lived here but it didn't feel as though he'd *lived* here. And there was nothing of Vanessa here at all. Maybe she'd taken it all with her. But what did I know? I'd never set foot in here before today. This apartment with all of Neil's things in it belonged to a stranger.

'We were going to sell it,' I said, standing and dusting down my jeans. 'We were going to sell everything and move away.'

'Don't tell me you were going to finally live the dream? Buy Dad's bookshop and run your cafe and drop-in centre – or whatever it was you were going to do?'

I sighed. 'Yes. That's exactly what we were going to do.' I took a deep breath. 'Your dad announced his retirement at work that day. The last time I spoke to him he was so happy.' The lump rose to my throat as it had done so many times over the past few days, and I blinked to push the tears back. 'We were finally going to do it. We knew we'd need to make arrangements for Vanessa and the baby, but we were doing it. We didn't know where – we figured we'd know it when we saw it.' I sniffed and scrubbed at my eyes. 'Well, that's not going to happen now, is it?'

'I don't know, Mum, maybe it could still. You don't need to make any decisions just yet. You'll have Dad's superannuation and life insurance, so you'll be okay financially even if you choose to do nothing else.'

'I suppose so.'

I didn't tell him that I was still worried about Vanessa. Neil wouldn't have had an income from which he could offer maintenance, but I knew he would have wanted to support her and his child. Neil mightn't be here any more, but that didn't mean that obligation had gone away. I wondered again at the strange twist of fate that had brought Neil and me back together, and left me financially secure rather than her. Another thing there hadn't been a spoiler alert for.

'Are you done?' I asked Nathan, indicating the suit

bag.

'Yeah. I didn't know what he'd want to be, you know, wearing …' He swallowed hard, his eyes filling.

'No, me neither.'

'Dad would have hated this,' he said.

I laughed ruefully. 'I guess it's a good thing then that he isn't here to see it.'

Neither of us could say what we were really thinking: that if he had been alive, being put into a coffin would have scared him to death. Neil had always hated enclosed spaces.

Despite me calling her, and texting and emailing, Vanessa didn't come to the funeral. I would have sent her a handwritten letter if I'd known her address, but I didn't. As angry as she'd been with Neil when he died, and as angry as I was with her after what she'd done to his apartment, I couldn't help feeling that she'd wake up one morning and be filled with regret for not taking the opportunity to say goodbye to him. So I continued to text her right up until the day of the funeral.

Even though it should have passed in the same blur that the days following Neil's death had done, every single detail of the funeral was etched into my brain. Not in vivid colour, but in shades of black, white and grey, like one of those charcoal sketches where the texture is added through stippling and thousands of little dots. Somehow I managed not to cry, and sat dry-eyed and silent through the service as Nathan and Ash, Lachie, and Libby and Leanne stumbled their way painfully through their memories of Neil. Dave and Maureen seemed completely bewildered by the whole thing, still not understanding how they could possibly be in a chapel saying goodbye to their fit and healthy son.

I hadn't intended to speak. I didn't think I'd be able to, so hadn't prepared anything. Also, it didn't feel right. After all, to the rest of the world, including our family and friends, Neil and I had been separated at the time of his death. Some even knew that we'd been working towards a divorce. It felt hypocritical for me to stand up and tell everyone how much I still loved him. I certainly couldn't blurt out that we'd been planning to start again, together, somewhere new – even though I so desperately wanted to. Yet when Libby and Leanne sat down, and the celebrant made to move to the next part of the ceremony, I stood up.

'I'd like to say something too,' I said.

'You don't have to, Mum,' said Nathan.

I laid a hand on his shoulder. 'I know. But I want to.'

Once I was at the front of the chapel, the words temporarily left me. I looked around at everyone who'd come to pay their respects to Neil. All these people knew a part of him, but I was the only one who knew all of him.

'First of all I'd like to thank everyone who's come along today to say goodbye to Neil.' I took a breath and looked at the ceiling, swallowing hard. 'Neil was my best friend. Yes, he was my husband, and Nathan and Ash's father, Dave and Maureen's son, Libby and Leanne's brother, but he was also my best friend. He had been from the very first time we met on the lawn down at Circular Quay. When I looked at Neil, I still saw him how he was that day. Most of you wouldn't know this, but the reason we met was because Midnight Oil were touring America.' I smiled as my mind went back to that day. 'I was pretending to march for Hiroshima Day, but the truth was that I'd heard a rumour that Midnight Oil were going to be playing down there. Neil wasn't pretending to be there for any reason other than because he'd heard the same rumour. What neither of us knew was that they were in America.' I paused and heard a few people laugh. 'These days, with social media and everything, we would have known that and would never have met – and that would have been a great shame. We got talking and that was it. It was love at first sight for both of us. And no matter what happened over the years in between, I never stopped loving him and I don't think he ever stopped loving me.' My voice broke, and Nathan started to stand to come to me. I smiled and waved him back to his seat. 'Even though we didn't live together any more, there weren't many days when we didn't talk or text. I'll miss that. I'll miss him. To be honest, I'm not sure what I'll do without him.' I turned to face the flower-strewn coffin and this time I struggled to get the words out. 'Goodbye, my darling.'

When Nathan took my hand to lead me back to my seat, I didn't protest.

Nathan and Ash had put together a slideshow of photo memories set to a compilation of Neil's favourite music. It was the music that finally brought me undone. They'd used INXS's 'Never Tear Us Apart' – the song we used as our wedding dance – to show the story of his life, and my tears began to flow from the opening riff.

There were photos of the two of us in the Botanical Gardens, him sitting upright against the trunk of our tree, with the blue of the harbour and Fort Denison in the background. He was reading, and I was lying with my head in his lap, reading too. His free hand rested on my head. I remembered how he used to do that, play with my hair as I read. Inevitably I'd fall asleep. Then there was a photo of us under the same tree, but this time taking our wedding vows.

There we were in hospital after I'd had Ash, Neil's eyes glistening with the tears he'd shed moments before when she came screaming into the world. I could hear Ash sobbing quietly as the images flashed across the screen.

There were pictures of Neil and me, Neil and the kids, the four of us as a family. Even after we'd separated, there were photos of the four of us together – at Christmas, birthdays, and as recently as Ash's wedding.

Nathan had managed to neatly intersperse photos from the last few years as well – Neil at Everest Base Camp, Neil cycling at Lake Taupo in New Zealand, Neil crossing the finish line in one of the marathons he'd run over the last few years. Here and there were photos of him with Vanessa, but always at some family gathering, none of just the pair of them together.

The final photo was from Ash's wedding: Neil and I were dancing together as parents of the bride. He was smiling and looking into my eyes with the intensity that he'd kissed me with just a short time later. Seeing the photo, I understood why Vanessa had rushed to separate us. The longing and desire was written on both our faces.

As my tears fell silently, Nathan reached over and gripped my hand. 'Thank you,' I mouthed. Without saying anything, he'd managed to honour the love that Neil and I still had when he died.

Twenty

After the funeral, things settled back to normal – as normal as things could be when there was nothing normal about them.

Nathan and Ash helped me clean out Neil's apartment. We bagged most of his clothes for the charity bin. Nathan hesitated over a couple of Neil's jumpers and all-weather coats, but as he was taller and broader than Neil had been he reluctantly added them to the bag. I kept the jumper that was lying beside the bed, the one he'd been wearing on our last night together. If either of them noticed, they didn't say anything.

Everything else we packed into boxes and took home with us. There wasn't much – the books, and a few personal items. It was almost as though he hadn't intended staying in the apartment, as if it was an interim thing. I remembered him telling me that when he'd left he'd hoped it was temporary, that I'd ask him to come home. I wondered whether, despite being with Vanessa, he'd still been waiting for that. Of course I'd never know now.

Nathan collected Neil's ashes from the funeral home and the three of us stared at the ordinary-looking container on the kitchen table.

'What do we do with them, Mum?' Ash asked. 'Did Dad ever talk about where he'd want to be?'

I shook my head. 'As practical as he was, I think he thought that with good food and exercise he'd live forever.'

'Maybe that's why he was with Vanessa.' Ash spoke the words quietly as if she didn't need an answer to them. Then added, 'But he wasn't at the end, was he? He was with you. Why didn't you tell me?'

I didn't pretend to misunderstand her. Nor did I contemplate telling her anything other than the truth.

'Because we didn't know where it was going. We didn't want to say anything until everything had been sorted.' I smiled at both of them. 'In a way, we were being selfish too. It was the first time it had been just us since we were married and we wanted to enjoy that for a few days more.'

'Because there was always Nathan and me?' Ash said. I nodded and she half-smiled. 'I think I understand that. But then Vanessa dropped her bombshell.'

'Yes. And everything was tipped upside down again. How did you know?'

'I didn't until Reece said something the other day. There's been something playing on my mind since the funeral. Like, I knew you were upset – that's

understandable, he was your husband for so many
years and your friend for longer. Then there was
Nathan and me, and Gran and Pops, that you had to be
thinking about too – but there was something else and
I couldn't work out what it was. Then last night Reece
said something and – don't hate me, Mum, I was upset
and you know I sometimes say things I regret when
I'm upset – but I said to Reece that it was natural you
were holding it together so well for us, because you two
had been separated and were getting a divorce so Dad
could marry Vanessa.

'Reece looked at me as though I'd said something
incredibly stupid – which of course, I had – and said
that he didn't think that was entirely true. I asked him
what he meant, and he said that he couldn't believe I
hadn't noticed what he'd seen in that picture of you
two dancing at the wedding. You remember, the one
you used right at the end of the slideshow, Nath?' He
nodded but didn't interrupt her. 'Anyway, I got the
wedding photos back out and that was what had been
playing on my mind – the way you two looked at each
other. And I just knew.' Dismay clouded her eyes – eyes
that were so very like Neil's. 'I'm so sorry, Mum. It must
have been so hard for you to hold yourself together
with everyone thinking you two were separated and
that Vanessa was the one who deserved our sympathy.
I overheard a few people wondering where she was and
whether we'd excluded her.'

She turned to Nathan. 'Did you know?' Then she shook her head. 'You must have known to close the presentation with that photo. I don't know why I'm surprised – you always seem to know everything.'

He grinned. 'It's about time you admitted that. But I only knew this time because I saw them together dancing on the grass out the back of the reception. I didn't tell you because you were going away on your honeymoon, and also because I didn't know if anything else had happened.'

'I bet Uncle Lachie knew too,' Ash said.

'Yes,' I said. 'He saw us too.'

Nathan and I watched Ash closely for signs of the explosion that we figured was yet to come. Her face was expressionless – something that we'd learned over the years to be wary of. We knew what to expect when she got emotional, but Ash flat-lining could be unpredictable.

'What?' she demanded. 'Oh my god, you think I'm going to stamp my foot and throw my toys out of the cot because no one bothered to tell me that you and Dad were back together? Because I was the last to know?'

Nathan lowered his eyes to the floor, and I lifted one shoulder in response.

'Well, I'm not. Maybe I would have a few months ago, and maybe if Dad was still alive I would have. But not now. I just want to know one thing, Mum. Was he happy when he … ?'

'Yes, darling, he was. He was very happy. We both were.'

'Despite the Vanessa baby thing?'

I nodded. 'Yes. We knew there were things to work out, but we were going to do it together.'

'Is that why she didn't come to the funeral?'

'I think so.'

'Did you ask her?' Ash's tone was flat.

'I did. I phoned and texted but got no reply.'

Ash shook her head. 'And no one has heard anything from her?'

'No, not since that day in the hospital.'

'Good. As far as I'm concerned, if she can't give my father the respect of showing up to say goodbye to him when they spent the last few years together and she's supposedly carrying his baby, I don't ever want to see her or hear from her again.'

Before I could comment, Nathan reminded us why we were there.

'You said you'd never talked about it, Mum, but you must have some idea where you think Dad would want to ... you know ...'

I didn't need to think for long. 'He'd like to be under our tree. The one where we were married. We'll do it this weekend before you go home, Nath.' I thought some more. 'In fact, we'll make a thing of it – invite the family, pack a picnic, say goodbye properly.' I felt my eyes filling again as I spoke. 'I think he'd like that.'

Ash squeezed my arm. 'He would. It's the perfect way to say goodbye.'

On Saturday, almost thirty-two years since that August day when Neil and I first met, we all trooped down to the Botanical Gardens, eskies and picnic blankets in hand. Nathan carried chairs for Dave and Maureen, and Lachie and Mike had the fold-up tables.

Once everyone had arrived, we gathered around the base of the tree.

'How do we want to do this?' I asked the question of no one in particular.

Dave stepped forward and took my arm. 'How about we each do a little? You, Ash and Nath, Maureen and me, Leanne and Libby.'

I nodded wordlessly and took the top off the metal canister. I bent to tip some of the dust from it, then straightened. 'Do we need permission to do this?'

Lachie smiled. 'We're probably contravening about a million regulations, but let's go with the "apologise if we're caught" scenario.'

As I tipped the dust from the container, a slight breeze started up, sending some of it through the air across to where the harbour sparkled. I whispered, 'Goodbye, my darling,' and handed the vessel to Nathan.

Once we'd all said goodbye to Neil, we laid the food out on the tables and sat around on picnic blankets – just as we'd done that day of our surprise wedding – although Libby said that these days it was one thing getting down to ground level, but another thing entirely to get back up again. I passed around cold chicken and salads, Nathan made sure everyone had drinks, and Lachie set up the speaker and played the songs of our relationship from a playlist he'd set up on his phone. It was almost the exact soundtrack we'd played at our wedding all those years ago.

As we started eating, everyone began to talk. There were no tears today; it was as if we'd all decided to only remember happier times. I leaned back against the tree that Neil and I had sat under so many times before and looked around at our family.

Dave was chatting with Reece, Mike and Leanne's husband, Simon. Libby was bouncing her first granddaughter, Amelie, on her lap, while Simone, Libby's daughter-in-law and Amelie's mother, and Leanne's two daughters, Nicole and Amanda, were sitting on a nearby blanket with Ash. Chris, Libby's eldest son and Amelie's father, was helping Maureen pour coffees for everyone who wanted one. Nathan stood off to one side with Libby's husband, Russell, Leanne's son, Darren, and Darren's girlfriend. Adam, Libby's other son, was the only one missing – he was doing a season as a ski instructor in New Zealand. He'd come over for the funeral, but had gone back to Auckland the following day.

'You'd love this,' I whispered to the tree. 'All of us here, an eighties soundtrack, and the most beautiful day possible.' I looked at the impossible blue of the harbour, the sun glistening along the top of the water as if all the stars from the sky had been emptied into it. Below us, the Opera House forecourt and steps were full of tourists enjoying the mild winter sunshine, while out on the water the ferries chugged back and forth from the Quay.

'It's all so perfect – all it needs is for you to be here,' I said. A breeze stirred the air. 'Maybe you are.'

Lachie sat down beside me and I took the wine he offered me. 'Okay, Kitty-cat?'

I nodded. 'Do you think he can see us? Do you think he knows we're all here?'

'Fucked if I know. Do you?'

'I'd like to think so.'

He looked around at our family, and then back across the harbour towards Fort Denison. 'Yeah,' he said, 'so do I.'

Twenty-one

Nathan flew back to Cairns the following day. I drove him to the airport, and he actually allowed me to hug him tightly.

'Are you going to be okay, Mum?'

'Of course I will,' I said and smiled like I meant it.

Ash and Reece called by in the afternoon, ostensibly to return the container Ash had taken some leftovers home in yesterday, but really to check that I wasn't a blubbering mess in the corner.

'Ash,' I said, 'I appreciate your concern, but I'm okay. Truly,' I added for emphasis when I saw the look of scepticism on her face. 'It's all over now, and time we got back to normal.'

Her eyes filled with tears. 'But nothing will ever be normal again. How can it be with Dad gone?'

I held her in the same way I used to when she fell off her bike or grazed her knee or some pimply boy had let her down. These days though she had to bend down in order to burrow into me.

'I know, darling, but we need to find a new normal

now, and the sooner we get started on that the better.'

She sniffed and nodded, and moved from my arms into Reece's.

He smiled at me over the top of her head. 'Seriously, Kate, call us if you need anything.'

'I will,' I promised. 'Now, you take your wife home and hold her tightly.'

After they'd left, I spent the afternoon pottering around the kitchen making a big batch of chicken stock. While the chicken was cooking, I peeled and chopped vegetables for a vegetable soup, pouring in a packet of barley for texture. Once the chicken was done, I stripped the meat from the carcass, returned the bones to the pan to let the stock cook down some more, and packaged the meat into portion-sized bags for the freezer.

By the time I was finished, I had containers of stock for the freezer, vegetable soup for my lunches at work, and poached chicken for sandwiches or salads.

Then I went to bed and did what I'd been doing every night since Neil died. I stared at the ceiling until I finally dropped off to sleep somewhere between two and three in the morning.

August turned into September, and the new life I needed to get used to settled into a pattern of sorts. At home, I cleaned and baked and cooked, and cooked and baked and cleaned. The house gleamed, and the garden beds were all freshly weeded, trimmed and mulched. After much cursing, I finally mastered the art of starting the lawnmower and worked out how the pool vacuum and filter worked. I even gritted my teeth and dealt with the redback spiders I found in the garden shed.

One afternoon, with too many hours up my sleeve, a full freezer, a clean house and an immaculate garden, I opened the door of the linen cupboard and began pulling out towels. How did we ever accumulate so many? Sometimes I was convinced that the only reason I needed a house this big was to store all the towels and sheets and old clothes and platters and plates and books that were stored in it.

Once all the towels were on the floor in the hallway, I started on the sheets. Next was the shelf that held the tablecloths and napkins. When was the last time we'd even used cloth napkins? And those little net things that you put over salads and cheese plates or the meat from the barbecue when you were eating outside. There were even doilies, for god's sake. I hated doilies. In fact, I couldn't remember using half of this stuff. I didn't need it – any of it. Leaving the cupboard doors open and the contents on the floor, I marched back into the kitchen for garbage bags.

On the way, I passed the open door of the study. I stopped, walked inside and looked around. There was a desk and a laptop, and I kept all the household bills and paperwork in here, but I still thought of it as Neil's reading room.

This room was one of the first we'd decorated when we moved in all those years ago. We'd left the original floorboards in place, painted the walls a soft sage, and hung long curtains with a light cranberry on white floral design either side of the large window that looked across the garden. On either side of the fireplace Neil had installed floor-to-ceiling bookcases, and we'd had an old sofa re-covered in a cranberry check and filled it with mismatching cushions. Opposite the sofa sat a couple of wing-backed chairs that we'd found in a junk shop; and a round timber table – another junk shop find – stood on a rug between them and the sofa. I used to lounge on the sofa flipping through foodie magazines for inspiration, while Neil sat in one of the wing-backs and read. When the kids were smaller we used to have another rug in the corner with a beanbag where they could read, but it had been many years since either of them had ventured in here.

Even though I hadn't sat in here since Neil died, if I moved – no, when I moved – it was this room that I'd miss the most. If I closed my eyes and concentrated really hard I could almost see Neil sitting in the crimson chair, the one closest to the fireplace. He'd have a coffee on the table, probably balanced on a pile of magazines, and as the light faded he'd turn on one of the lamps so he could still read.

I shook my head to remove the image. What I

was remembering was a long time ago – before he'd decided to hike to Everest and started to spend his Sundays running or cycling to prepare for it – and way before he'd decided that we were done.

I called in on Dave and Maureen every Sunday, taking over soups and casseroles for their freezer and slices or cakes for afternoon tea. Maureen's eyes glistened whenever she talked of Neil and Dave's voice wavered. Sometimes I wondered whether I was making things worse for them by reminding them of what they'd lost, but at the same time I selfishly needed to see them to hang on to some semblance of my old life. I also needed to fill every single minute of my day. But although my body and brain were exhausted, I still lay awake every night until the early hours, staring at the ceiling.

At first Nathan rang daily, but I firmly asked him to stop.

'I'm fine,' I said. 'We all need to get on with life. I'll call you if I need you. Besides, shouldn't you be off counting whales or something?'

He laughed at that, and said the annual migration was almost over and he was going to be doing some diving with one of the organisations that monitored the health of the reefs.

'It helps to stay busy,' he said. 'I miss him.'

'I know, Nath.'

Ash was taking it all much harder. Playing on her

mind was that scene the day before Neil died – although it took her a few weeks of tearful calls to finally admit it.

She dropped over one Saturday afternoon while I was cleaning out the old sideboard that lived in the kitchen. I had all the contents on the table and was deciding what to do with them.

'Are you selling the house, Mum?' she asked.

'I don't know. I just figured I might start decluttering.' I shrugged one shoulder. 'It'll make it easier if we ever do sell. What do I need all these bowls and platters for now?'

What I didn't tell her was that I'd done this exact same exercise last Saturday, and the Saturday before that – emptying the sideboard, looking at its contents on the table, dusting them all and putting them back. It was the same with the linen cupboard – I'd emptied it and filled it twice over the last couple of weeks.

'I can help if you like,' she offered.

'No, it's okay. I might just put it all back and attack it some other time when I'm more in the mood, or at least have a plan.' I began stacking everything back into the sideboard's shelves.

'Mum, please … sit down for a minute.' It was the catch in her voice that stopped me.

'Oh, Ash, what is it?'

'You mean aside from Dad?'

I grimaced when I realised how trite my words had sounded. As if I didn't know what was wrong with her.

Ash had always been a daddy's girl, and she'd always worn her heart on her sleeve.

'I know and I'm sorry. How about I make us a coffee?'

She nodded miserably. 'Please. But no cake – or anything else,' she added as I reached for the tupperware container on top of the fridge that housed the gingersnap cookies I'd baked that morning – the same ones I'd probably throw out uneaten later in the week.

'Okay,' I said, placing two cups of coffee on the table. 'Tell me what's worrying you.'

She wrapped her hands around the cup, warming them as if we were in the depths of winter rather than a Sydney spring. 'It's what I said to you that last day ... when I said I was never going to talk to him again. I didn't mean it, you know, and I can't help thinking that's why ...' She faltered.

'Ash, sweetheart, no. Don't say that. Your words that day meant nothing. They weren't a prophecy or anything like that – just the words of someone who'd had a nasty shock, that's all. I didn't take you seriously, and your father didn't even know you'd said it.'

'But what if somehow he did?'

I shook my head and reached for her hands. 'No. Your father died knowing that you loved him. Knowing that we all loved him.'

She was briefly silent. 'You said that you and Dad had decided to be together – even though the baby was coming?'

I nodded. 'Your father knew he couldn't abandon his responsibilities, but he'd also decided he wanted to be happy. We just didn't know what that looked like yet.'

'I see. Did Vanessa know that?'

'Yes.'

She sat back in her chair, joining the dots together in her head. 'Wow. Are you sure she didn't kill him? Slip him something in his coffee? After all, she was there when it happened. And she would have felt so cheated when he told her that you weren't going to get a divorce.'

Until I saw her face, I thought she was joking. 'No! Nothing like that. Your dad had a sudden cardiac arrest – it could have happened at any time. There was no explanation, no reason, no underlying weakness. It had nothing to do with any of us.'

'But what about the stress? I saw his face when Vanessa announced she was pregnant. I saw yours too. You had to have thought he'd decide to stick by Vanessa.' She shook her head as if all her thoughts were suddenly crowding in on each other. 'But he didn't. What happened after he left that afternoon? And the next day?'

I closed my eyes briefly and went back to that terrible afternoon. 'He came back and we talked.'

'Did you forgive him?'

'There was nothing to forgive. He'd done nothing wrong, he hadn't betrayed me in any way. I thought I'd lost him, and I was angry at her – so very angry – but not with him. He said he'd been thinking that he didn't want to wait any longer – he was going to retire and we were going to start again. We were going to sell the apartment and buy a bookshop somewhere.'

'Like you always talked about when we were kids?'

I smiled and nodded. 'Yes, exactly like that. When he left me the next morning he was feeling positive. We knew we'd have some rough times with Vanessa, but he was determined that we could make it work. I last spoke to him at lunchtime. He'd told his boss that he was retiring, and had made arrangements to meet Vanessa in the afternoon. For the first time I really thought it was going to happen – and I think he did too. I told him that I loved him and he said the same to me.' I blinked and swallowed. 'And that was that.'

Ash reached for my hands across the table. Tears were streaming down her cheeks. 'Thanks for telling me that, Mum. I really think it helped me.'

'I hope so, darling.'

By the time Ash left, she was definitely more like herself – full of plans for the Christmas holidays and a story about a self-important reality TV star who'd come into the gallery she worked at.

'Oh, Mum, you should have seen her. Done up to the nines and a face full of filler. I didn't recognise her, but my boss did. She had this friend with her who seemed really lovely and pulled a face every time she said something nasty about the art – and she had something to say about every single piece. Finally she stood in front of one of the canvases, looked it up and down and said, "I could have done that." Her friend was standing next to me and had the biggest grin on his face and said, "Yeah, but you didn't." I choked on my coffee, and then realised I was drinking out of that mug we bought when we were in Melbourne. The one that says *Modern Art: I could do that … Yeah, but you didn't.*'

'That's hilarious.'

Our eyes met and the laughter stopped, as if we'd both remembered Neil at the same moment.

'It's okay to laugh, Ashie,' I said.

'I know, but I still feel guilty when I do.'

'Because you didn't think you'd ever laugh again?' I prompted softly.

She nodded.

'Your father always said how much he loved your smile and your laugh – remember?'

'Yes.'

'So if I said that he wouldn't want you to stop smiling and laughing, you'd believe me?'

'Yes.' She hesitated for a second. 'You know that he'd want you to laugh again too. He'd also want you to do more than clean and bake.'

I just smiled rather than answering her. I might be able to laugh, but I didn't think I'd ever feel anything ever again. I wanted to – mostly to release the anger that burned inside me. The anger that he'd left me forever and taken all our dreams with him. I wanted to scream and cry and rage, but although the tears still came to my eyes often, they hadn't spilled over since the funeral and part of me felt that they needed to. That unless I let them out them they'd continue to fester inside me – rather like a pond that hadn't been cleaned out in some time.

As a result of a late winter/early spring outbreak of flu, I worked more than my usual three days a week. I didn't mind – it kept me busy. Occasionally I surprised a look of pity or concern from my colleagues, but for the most part everyone left me to my own devices.

I decided that once probate came through I'd put the apartment Neil had lived in on the market – and was strangely disappointed when it didn't take as much work as I'd hoped to prepare it for sale.

I hadn't decided what to do with our family home yet. It was obviously too big for me alone, and while I was currently appreciative of the physical work and time required to keep on top of the garden, I knew it would eventually be too much for me. As it was, after a near miss involving a ladder, a chainsaw on an extension pole and the camellia hedge, I was going to need to get someone in to prune the taller hedges and trees. But it was one thing to admit the house and yard were too big for me and entirely another to decide to sell a home that held all our family memories.

Apart from that, I had no idea where I wanted to live – or what I wanted to do. I was so numb inside, and felt so little about so much, that I could have easily walked away from my life without a backward glance. The problem wasn't just that I didn't know where I wanted to walk away to, but also that I didn't know how I could abandon everyone who depended on me.

Work was usually something I could focus on, but just lately I'd even begun to feel disillusioned about that. Although the vast majority of our clients were genuinely in need and had nowhere else to turn, I'd had a few of late who seemed to want me to fix their life for them, while they sat back and did nothing but complain about the unfairness of having no man to take care of them. One woman actually told me she didn't want to learn how to budget or manage her finances. 'I'll have someone else soon,' she'd said, 'so the knowledge will be wasted on me.'

One of those decisions I couldn't make was taken out of my hands on the last Friday in September. The firm's senior partner, Barry, called me into his office after everyone else had left for the day. Never one to mince words, he kept the message simple.

'I'm sorry, Kate, the government has reduced our funding so we're having to pull back on the pro bono work we're doing. We won't be able to keep you on past the end of October.'

I should have been upset, or angry, but instead I

felt nothing. 'So this is it, after almost four years?'

'Yes, I'm sorry. You've been a part of this initiative since the beginning and we'll be sorry to see you go, but without the funding our hands are tied.'

I knew the funding had been reduced in the last budget. I also knew that because I was a casual employee he didn't have to give me any notice. I'd probably been lucky to have kept my job this long.

'What about the women who need help and rely on us to provide it?' I said. 'Who's going to look after them?'

He shrugged. 'What will you do?' He grimaced as he finished asking the question, probably conscious of the fact that I hadn't had a chance to think about that yet – and not knowing that I'd done little but think about it for weeks.

'I'm not sure, Barry, but I'll be fine.'

As I lay awake again that night, I realised that every tie I'd had to my previous life had been loosened or removed. Other than my responsibilities to Dave and Maureen, and Ash and Reece, there was nothing keeping me in Sydney now. Yet rather than feeling free, I felt trapped.

Mari and Ross arrived home on a Thursday morning at the beginning of October. Lachie had posted the news about Neil and the funeral arrangements on Facebook and Mari had immediately offered to cut their holiday short, an option I'd firmly refused.

'You can't do anything,' I'd told her.

'I can be there for you,' she'd replied.

'I appreciate that, but I'm fine. Really.'

I was getting ready to go to work when she phoned on their way home from the airport.

'I just wanted to give you a call before you go to work and I collapse into bed for the next thousand years,' she said. 'God, why does Australia have to be so far away from everywhere? Those overnight flights just get worse.'

I grinned. It was good to hear her voice. 'I thought you were sitting further up front this time. Didn't Ross say his knees were too sore to fly cattle class any more?'

'Only premium economy, you know what I think about anything posher than that – we all get there at the same time. And whichever way you look at it, I don't think it's possible to sleep well at that altitude. Anyway, enough about me – how are you going? Has everything settled down? I haven't heard from you since the funeral.'

She'd sent me a few 'thinking of you' texts leading up to the funeral, which I hadn't responded to. I'd appreciated the gesture but hadn't wanted to talk to anyone at the time. I still didn't, but knowing Mari as well and as dearly as I did, I suspected that she wouldn't be put off.

'Everything is as fine as it can be in the circumstances,' I said. 'I lost my job last week – funding cuts. I finish up at the end of the month.'

'Oh no, Kate! That's just what you don't need –
not on top of everything else. Just bloody typical to cut
funding for a service primarily used by women.'

I shrugged. 'I know. But it is what it is, I suppose.'

'I bet they would have upped the funding if it was
for men – or thrown in free Viagra for every client.'

I giggled and changed the subject. Once Mari got
started on that particular soapbox there was usually no
stopping her – not even after an all-nighter in a plane.
'I'm looking forward to hearing about your trip, and
I've got the professional photos from the wedding to
show you.'

She hesitated, and I knew she was deciding
whether to call me on my obvious diversion or to let it
rest until she saw me. She chose the latter.

'Okay, I'll see you tomorrow afternoon. Just so
you know, I'm starting back on my diet tomorrow so
under no circumstances are you to bake.'

Of course I ignored the message about not baking
– as I was intended to. Mari was always absolutely
positively giving up sugar, starchy carbohydrates and
alcohol ('I really mean it this time') the following day,
the following Monday, the first of the month.

Although my freezer was full with all the baking
I'd been doing in my evenings and on weekends, I
got up early on Friday morning and prepared a batter
for honey and lemon madeleines. I sat it in the fridge

to rest for a few hours – I'd pop the madeleines in the oven as soon as Mari arrived – and busied myself putting together a honey and lemon syrup to drizzle over the top of them.

Once that was done, I decided that Mari needed more than some little bites of honey cake to welcome her home after three months away, even if the madeleines were intended to remind her of Paris. What Mari needed were pastries that flaked and stuck to the top of your lip, and drifted down to cling to whatever you were wearing. Pastries rich in butter and nuts and scented with cinnamon.

For half a second I debated making my own puff pastry. I'd never attempted it before, but they did it all the time on those cooking shows. Rough puff they called it, and it was made in minutes – or so it seemed. I checked my watch – no, I didn't have time for that.

Instead, I took a few sheets of frozen puff pastry out of the freezer, set about melting some butter, and peeled and cubed a couple of apples. I brushed the first sheet of pastry with melted butter, sprinkled a mix of brown sugar and cinnamon over the top of it, then placed another sheet of pastry on top and repeated the process until I'd used up all the pastry. Finally, I scattered the chopped apple and a good handful of flaked almonds across the top and rolled it tightly like a swiss roll. I brushed the top with an eggy-milky wash, then cut the roll into slices that I laid flat on the baking tray. I brushed some more eggy wash across the top, sprinkled over the last of the cinnamon sugar and almonds for good measure, and popped the tray in the oven.

Once the pastries were golden and flaky and smelling fabulous, I brushed them with a honey and vanilla glaze and sprinkled over a little more caster sugar, before putting them back in for another few minutes. Finally, I piled the cooked pastries and madeleines onto pretty china plates to serve, and set the table ready for Mari.

The doorbell rang. I checked my watch – it was unusual for Mari to be early.

It wasn't Mari; it was a man in a courier uniform holding an envelope.

'Mrs Kate Spence?' he said.

'Yes, that's me.'

'I have a delivery for you. Can you sign here, please?'

I signed the device he handed me and accepted the envelope, taking it back into the kitchen. I opened it and read the contents – and the bottom dropped out of my world again.

Twenty-Two

I was still sitting at the kitchen table, holding the letter, when Mari opened the back door fifteen minutes later.

'Oh, you are here,' she said. 'I rang the doorbell and knocked. Your car's in the driveway and there's an amazing smell coming from the house so I knew you had to be in here somewhere. I thought I told you not to bake – but this all looks amazing. How many of us did you say were coming for afternoon tea?'

When I didn't stand to greet her, her voice became concerned. 'Kate, are you okay?'

I looked up then. 'I have no idea.' My hand shook as I held the letter out to her.

'What's this?'

'Read it.'

She took the document and started to read, sitting down when she got part way through the first page. 'What the fuck?' She looked at me, her nose screwed in confusion.

'Just keep reading.' I roused myself sufficiently to stand and put the kettle on.

'Is this what I think it is?' Mari asked, folding the letter and placing it back in its envelope.

'Vanessa's suing me for Neil's estate? Yes, I think so.'

'But why? Didn't the settlement go through before he died? I thought she would have got that anyway?'

I poured water into the teapot. 'A lot has happened while you've been gallivanting around Europe.'

'You mean apart from your ex-husband dying?'

I nodded. 'Yes, apart from that.' I set the teapot down on the table and, without meeting her eyes, said, 'Have a pastry.'

She took one of the scrolls and bit into it, the flaky crumbs sticking to the front of her shirt. 'These are good. Are you having one?'

I shook my head. 'I'm not hungry.'

'But you've made all this food.'

'I know, but what you don't eat I can take to Dave and Maureen. Or Ash or Lachie might call in tomorrow. Someone will eat it.'

She looked at me keenly. 'You've lost weight, Kate.'

'Thanks.'

'It wasn't meant to be a compliment.'

'I haven't been trying to – there's just been a lot to do around the house, and I don't really feel like eating. Anyway, we're not here to talk about my weight.' I forced a smile. 'I want to know all about your holiday. The photos you shared on Facebook were fabulous – it looked like you were having an amazing time. But the time has all gone so quickly.' I knew I was babbling.

'We need to talk about this,' she said. 'Why is Vanessa disputing probate? Surely Neil made mention of her in his will?'

'No, he didn't. He hadn't updated it.'

'What about his superannuation or life insurance?'

'No. None of it.'

'I see.' But she said the words slowly, as if she didn't understand at all. 'Weren't they going to get married? I thought that's why Neil wanted to get the divorce finalised.'

'I thought so too – at least, when he first told me he wanted to formalise our separation. She was pushing him to do it – I think she thought it meant he'd commit to her. But he'd never asked her to move in and said he'd never spoken to her about marriage either. He told me he was going to put his share of the assets into a family trust so the kids would be okay if anything happened to him. That way he'd be going into any new relationship starting from scratch, except for what was left of his superannuation.'

'She wouldn't have liked that.' Mari pondered for a few seconds. 'Did Neil think she was after him for his money? Not that it hadn't occurred to me as well, of course. I loved Neil to bits but, well, you know what I mean.'

I nodded. I knew exactly what she meant.

Mari reached for a madeleine. 'So if they weren't engaged and she'd never moved in, what gives her the right to think she's entitled to anything?'

'She's having his baby.'

Mari choked on the cake, and gulped down a mouthful of tea before saying, 'Since when?'

'She announced it the day before he died. Neil didn't know – it was a shock to him too. He'd planned to tell her that evening that they were finished. I think somehow she knew that and got in first.'

'Christ, that's messy.'

'Yeah, you could say that. That's where he was when he died – they'd met up to talk through what was going to happen. She was the one who called and told me.'

'Oh, Kate.'

'Yep. There was a bit of a scene at the hospital and I haven't heard from her since. I told her about the funeral, but she didn't come. When Nath and I went over to get some clothes for Neil to … ummm … wear, she'd been there already and trashed the place. She must have been so angry.'

'Sweetie, you need to get some legal advice and quickly.'

'I know.'

Without warning, bile rose in my throat. I tried to swallow down its bitterness, but following too closely behind it was a wave of pure anger. After spending the last couple of months feeling nothing, I was surprised by both its appearance and its intensity. I wanted to pick my teacup up and slam it against the wall. I wanted to sweep the pastries and the cakes from the table. I wanted to cry and scream and throw things.

Instead I pushed my chair back from the table and walked into the hallway where I opened the doors to the linen cupboard and began pulling things out. Once the contents of the cupboard were on the floor I began rolling towels and placing them back on the shelves. At some point I became aware that Mari had followed me. I ignored her and picked up the next towel.

'What's going on, Kate? There's obviously more to this than Neil dying and Vanessa wanting in on the estate.'

I rolled the towel and shoved it into the cupboard.

'Kate?'

'I don't know any more,' I muttered, grabbing another towel and pushing it into the available space.

'What? I didn't hear you.'

'I don't know any more.' I must have shouted because Mari took a half-step backwards.

I shook my head in apology, took a deep breath and exhaled loudly. 'We were in love. We were back together, and ready to sell up and move away and start again. Just us. Then he died.' I felt the tears rush towards the anger in my throat and mingle with it. 'It was to be third time lucky for us. A happy ever after. And he died. He fucking died, Mari. And now …'

I paused and shook my head again as I tried to stop the tears and the emotion from spewing out. 'Now I don't know any more. And I'm sick of everything. I was sick of my job, so thank god that's gone now. I'm sick of mowing the lawn and weeding the garden. I'm sick of pretending that I feel nothing because as far as the world knows it was my ex-husband who died – not the man I still loved. According to everyone else, we were separated and he was loved up with his pregnant fucking girlfriend.'

By now I'd given up the fight and the tears were rolling freely down my face. 'There's so much stuff in this house and I'm sick of it all. I'm drinking way too much and not eating enough. I watch the clock until it gets to five and then I open a bottle. I have one glass and then another and I still can't fill the great fucking hole that's inside of me. When I'm on my own, I want to be with other people – and when I'm with other people, I want to be on my own. I spend every weekend emptying out this cupboard and filling up the fucking freezer with meals for one that I never bother defrosting, and every night I clean until there's nothing left to clean, or watch TV even though there's nothing on that I want to watch, and then I go and lie in bed and stare at the fucking ceiling for hours until I finally go to sleep. Then when the alarm goes off, I want to pull the covers over my head and lie there and never come out.

'I know that I have to sell this house, but I don't know what else I can do or where I want to go. I don't know anything any more except that I don't know anything and I can't feel anything and I'm tired of holding it together for everyone.' I was sobbing so hard that I would be surprised if she'd made any sense out of what I was saying. 'I was in love again, Mars. And now he's gone and I don't know what the point of any of it is any more. I feel like I could disappear and no one would notice.' I punched at my chest as I struggled to breathe and sob simultaneously. 'I hurt so badly that I can't even feel the hurt any more. I just want it to be over. But it's never going to be over because Vanessa will never let it be over, and now she's having his baby.'

'Oh, sweetie.' Mari pulled me to her and held me tightly and rubbed my back as I cried the tears that had been building up inside me for months. 'Ash might be married now, but she still needs you. As for Nath, he's always going to need you – and you hardly feed him at all any more.' I managed a laugh through my sobs. 'Lachie and Mike need you, and Dave and Maureen need you. I need you – although if you weren't constantly baking for me I might finally lose some weight.' My half-laugh turned into a sniff and I wiped aimlessly at my nose. 'We all need you – and we're all going to help you fight this thing with Vanessa. You don't have to do it alone.'

She pulled back and I could see that she'd been crying too. 'Now how about we use some of these useless-as-all-crap napkins to blow our noses and wipe our faces and then you can tell me all about you and Neil getting back together.'

I smiled through my tears and passed her a napkin. 'You're right, these napkins are useless. As are these net things for keeping the flies off.'

'And this round tablecloth – what's that about? When did you last have a round table?'

'In 1992, I think.'

We looked at each other and burst out laughing.

'What am I going to do with all this crap, Mars?'

'Put most of it in a bag for the charity shop, I suspect – except for these snotty napkins. We'll wash these first, hey?' She looked at the piles on the floor. 'How about we shove all this back in the cupboard for now, and I'll come by on the weekend and help you sort it?'

I nodded, and we both picked up armfuls of fabric and forced it all back into the cupboard, firmly closing the door on it all.

By unspoken agreement we both resumed our places at the table. I took a sip of my tea and grimaced when I found it had gone cold.

'How about I reboil the kettle and you have one of these delectable pastries,' suggested Mari. 'Then you can start talking.'

'But –'

'No, sweetie, you need to eat.'

I selected the smallest scroll and took a nibble out of the corner. Flakes of pastry dropped over the table and clung to my bottom lip. I used my tongue to lick one off, and smiled as I tasted the sweetness of the vanilla honey glaze. I took a bigger bite, and then another.

Mari watched me eat. 'They're good, aren't they?'

'They are,' I agreed, and reached for another. 'I don't know why I'm so surprised.'

'So, you and Neil,' she prompted. 'Last I heard was you'd had those couple of moments, but he hadn't rung so you'd decided the divorce was back on.'

I nodded. 'Okay, well, I saw him and Vanessa that Sunday – at Dave and Maureen's. We agreed he'd come over on the Wednesday night to talk about the divorce, and one thing led to another and we ended up in bed. It was lovely, Mars. Just like when we were young. He gave me goosebumps and heart flutters, and the sex – oh my god, the sex. I was feeling everything that I'd thought was long gone.'

'Maybe you'd wanted it to be gone,' she suggested softly.

'Maybe. We didn't tell anyone for a few weeks, we just kept it to ourselves. Lachie was the first to put two and two together, and it turned out that Nath had seen us at the wedding, but it was lovely having it as a secret. Neil had decided to retire early and we were going to sell up and start again somewhere – buy that bookshop we'd always talked about and be together. It's not as if the kids needed us any more – it was time for us, you know? That's why we didn't tell anyone when we first got back together. Aside from us not knowing where it was all going, we were enjoying being together without any other responsibilities for the first time ever. And, oh, Mars, it felt like it did when we were first together all those years ago. It wasn't just the sex – even though that was the sex I never thought we could have – it was more than that. It was us being us, not parents, but lovers.'

'Did Vanessa know?'

'No, but I think she guessed. Right from the day they talked to me about the divorce, she stopped all pretence of being nice and let the inner bitch shine through. So yes, I think she knew. But you know what Neil's like with conflict.'

'I do. He avoids it as much as possible.'

'Exactly. But once Lachie knew about us, we admitted we'd have to go public. Neil was going to tell her the day before he died – but she got in with the baby news first.'

'I would have thought that would put an end to your plans, but you said he'd met her to talk through what he wanted to happen?'

'Knowing Neil as I did, I thought he'd do the noble thing too – but he told her that we were going to be together. That he'd still support the baby but his life was with me.'

'And the baby? How was he going to support it with no income?'

'We hadn't got that far, but I'd suggested we put money aside for her as a one-off settlement.'

'To make her go away?'

I shrugged. 'Maybe. I don't know.'

'And now?'

'Now I need a lawyer.'

Twenty-three

I waited while Mike read the letter I'd received from the probate solicitor, then said, 'Well, what does it mean?'

'She wants a share – quite a large share – of Neil's estate.' His brow was furrowed as he re-read a couple of paragraphs. 'Actually, she's asking for whatever she thinks Neil should have got from the divorce settlement.'

'On what grounds?' I paced the kitchen as I spoke.

'On the grounds that she was his common law wife for the past three years and now requires maintenance for his child.'

'But they didn't live together. They never lived together.' The anger I'd felt earlier that afternoon still bubbled away inside me.

'According to this, that's what you'll need to prove in court.'

'But I bought that unit with my inheritance just before he moved out. And he had no right at all to the holiday house because that's ours, Lachie. All he was asking for in the divorce was half his super and a lot less than half of this house.'

Out the side of my eye, I saw Lachie's eyebrows rise. 'What?' I demanded.

'Nothing, Kitty.' When I stopped pacing to stare at him, he relented. 'I was just thinking that –'

'I'll say it,' broke in Mike. 'We were thinking that it's no wonder he changed his mind about the divorce.'

What. The. Absolute. Fuck?

'Seriously? You think we only got back together again because it was financially more lucrative? Do you really think that?'

'Hasn't the thought ever crossed your mind?' Mike asked.

'No! Of course it hasn't. Not before you mentioned it anyway.' I snatched the letter from Mike's hands and glared at both of them. 'I can't believe that it's crossed yours.'

I turned the glare up a notch as I focused it on Lachie. 'I especially can't believe you thought that. It was just the finality of the divorce that made us both realise we still loved each other. We told you that – the day you found us out. Besides, Neil had already decided that his portion of the assets were going into some sort of trust for our kids so that if he died,' my voice broke on the word, 'before Vanessa, Nath and Ash would still get what they're entitled to. If he married again, he would be starting with someone else from scratch.'

'And what about you? Was he expecting you to do the same thing if you started a new relationship?' Mike asked.

I frowned and took a step backwards. 'I don't know. We'd never talked about that. I'd never thought about the possibility of even being with anyone else.'

Lachie shrugged one shoulder. 'We're sorry, Kitty, but this is the sort of stuff that's going to come up in court. Had you and Neil talked about what would happen regarding maintenance of the baby? Neil wasn't the type of man to walk away from his responsibilities.'

'He did once. He left me with a mess to deal with back then too.' I regretted the words as soon as I'd said them.

Lachie shook his head slowly. 'That's unfair. You didn't give him the chance to make that decision when you were pregnant with Nathan. Don't go there.'

I turned away and sighed. 'No. You're right, of course. He didn't choose to leave this time, but he's still left me to pick up the pieces.'

Lachie gave me the sort of look he used to give me when we were growing up and I was taking an argument too far.

'We'd sort of talked about it,' I said. 'He was retiring from work so I thought we should offer her some sort of financial settlement. He thought that was a good option. If she still wanted him to be involved with the baby we figured we'd deal with that when it happened.

But when she just walked away after he … died, I guess I thought she'd lost the baby, or something.'

I wondered if I'd ever be able to say that Neil had died without my voice breaking.

Mike nodded. 'A settlement is what I would have suggested too. Are you still interested in doing that?'

'I would have said yes, but after seeing this letter I'm not sure any more.'

Lachie's look was one of concern now. 'I know you're angry, Kitty, but the baby is innocent in all this. Think carefully about that before you decide to fight.'

'It's not just that either,' said Mike. 'This will be drawn out for some time, and while it is, you can't make any financial decisions about your future. Even if you sell this house, you won't be able to do anything with the proceeds until the legals are concluded. Don't ignore the legal costs either. I'll do this affidavit work for you now, but if you go to court to fight it, we'll need to brief a barrister and pay for their time – and that's expensive.'

'When you say "some time" what do you mean?' I asked.

Mike held his hands out, palms up. 'Who knows? It could be years.'

'And I'm stuck in a holding pattern for as long as it takes?'

'Yes.'

'I see.' How dared he leave me with this? 'It would

have been cheaper and easier if we'd divorced, wouldn't it?' I said bitterly.

Mike lifted a shoulder in response.

'So what do I do?'

'We'll prepare a response to this now,' he said. 'That'll give you time to think about what you want to do.'

'Right now I want to run away and pretend none of this is happening. Somewhere a long way away.'

'I don't blame you, Kitty.' Lachie put his arm around me.

I rested my head against his chest. 'I just want it all to be over.'

'I know you do,' he said.

That night as I lay in bed and stared at the ceiling, different thoughts found their way into my brain. Thoughts that had no right to be there, but had been let in when Mike and Lachie questioned me about Neil's motivations for us to be together. Now they'd made themselves comfortable, I couldn't think of anything else.

What if Neil had done the calculations and decided he wouldn't have enough to start over? He knew he couldn't touch the holiday house, and would have received the same advice I had regarding my inheritance – although even that was unclear. Mike had said that if we'd completed the financial settlement at the time we'd separated it was likely that the apartment would have been excluded from consideration. Given that Neil had lived there for the past few years and maintained it, the waters had been muddied. They'd been further stirred up by the fact that instead of paying rent, Neil was paying the mortgage on the unit and also taking care of the utilities. Through being civilised about the whole thing we'd put ourselves at a disadvantage when it came to formalising the finances. What if Neil had worked that out and decided the practical solution was to stay together?

I knew he would have hated the conflict of a drawn-out settlement negotiation. When we were together, I was always the one who had to play 'bad cop' if there was a tradesman or one of the kids' teachers to be dealt with. I was the one who'd told the telemarketers where they could go, and the one who did the haggling over ten-dollar sunglasses on our Asian holidays. What if getting back together was Neil's idea of the easier solution?

In the way that such thoughts normally went about their business, by the early hours of the morning I'd gone from wondering whether Neil was avoiding conflict and financial ruin by getting back together to wondering whether the whole thing was some elaborate plan to leave me again and this time get his hands on the apartment as well. Maybe he and Vanessa were going to stay together, and once he'd conclusively proved financial contribution, or whatever it was he had to prove to bring my inheritance back into consideration, he'd file for divorce again.

Even though my logical mind knew that these squatter thoughts were rubbish, I couldn't get images of Neil and Vanessa plotting together out of my head. Think about how she announced her pregnancy, urged Reason. She wouldn't have done it that way if she wasn't frightened of losing him. Then there was the way she'd trashed the apartment, whispered Rationality. That was the act of someone who was seriously pissed off that things hadn't gone her way.

I tried to listen to Reason and Rationality, I really did, but the squatters were so loud and so insistent that even putting earplugs in didn't drown them out. I tried to think about what Neil would do, to conjure up a picture of him in my head – the way I did every night – but tonight I couldn't find him. I couldn't see him behind Vanessa.

When I finally did sleep, it was to dream of a hugely pregnant Vanessa smiling as she moved into my house, and me standing on the side of the road with a backpack full of vintage china and a few family photos.

Nathan phoned on Saturday morning for his weekly check-in. I hadn't yet worked out how to tell the kids about this latest drama so said nothing about the letter I'd received. Instead I told him that Mari was back from holidays and how she was going to help me begin to clean out some of the clutter.

'Have you thought any more about what you're going to do with the house, Mum?'

'No, not yet. I've got plenty of time.' Potentially years if this court case dragged out.

'Hey, I almost forgot,' he said, 'I received an email the other day from the hiking company letting me know that we're just six weeks out and giving tips on training.'

'Six weeks out from what?'

'Our trek, Mum. Milford Sound. Remember, the mountain you decided you were going to climb to prove to Dad that he wasn't the only one in the family who could climb a mountain?'

I let out a breath. I'd completely forgotten.

'You've forgotten, haven't you?' His tone had an edge that immediately made me feel ashamed.

'It's not that. It's just that it –'

'Slipped your mind?' he finished for me.

My silence said it all.

'Mum … is it just house stuff that's worrying you?'

I nearly told him then about Vanessa suing me, but how could I? I knew that Nathan and Ash deserved to know what was going on – it was their inheritance that was at stake – but the baby was also their half-brother or sister. I'd tell them once Mike had looked into it and once I'd decided what I was going to do. There was no point worrying them before that – they were still coming to terms with having lost their father.

'I'm fine, Nath,' I said. 'I'm just not sure I'm up to

walking up a mountain.'

I had too much to think about as it was, and felt angry about throwing climbing a mountain into the mix.

'You're not getting out of this, Mum. I think it'll do you good to get out and start walking again. And it'll do you good to get away – you might be able to think more clearly about the house and what you want to do while you're away from it. Besides, you'll be between jobs, and you haven't taken a holiday since well before Dad left.'

'I know, but –'

'No buts – we're doing this.'

I couldn't remember any more why I'd booked the hike in the first place. I'd never really had any burning desire to walk for miles and miles through a rainforest and up and down a mountain, had never felt the need to push myself to that level. It had been a reaction to Neil's news that he wanted a divorce, I supposed. A way to show that I didn't care, that I had my own life goals to pursue while he got on with his life with Vanessa. But then Nathan had jumped on board, and Neil had been so encouraging.

I'd even asked if he wanted to come too, with Nath and me. He'd thought for a few seconds and then shaken his head. 'No, love, this is something for you and Nath to do together, and for you to prove to yourself. I'll meet you in Queenstown afterwards and we'll have a look around together. It'll be like the honeymoon we never had.' I'd laughed and agreed and continued to huff and puff up the hill a few blocks from our house.

But now? I hadn't walked since Neil died. I knew that Nathan was looking forward to the hike, but I could no longer see the point. I had nothing to prove to anyone. Besides, Nathan had said from the start that he was only doing it this way – the guided walk – because of me. If it had been up to him, he'd do it with a couple of mates and they'd carry their own backpacks from hut to hut.

I reminded him of that now. 'I know you're only doing the guided walk to keep me happy, but if you want to do it your way, as a freedom walker, with people your own age, I'm absolutely okay with that.'

He laughed. 'I'm sure you are, and nice try – but you're not getting out of this, Mum. We might be doing it for different reasons than when we first booked, but we're still doing it.'

'Why are you doing it?'

'I was originally going to make sure you had company,' he said.

'To look after me, you mean?'

'That too. But now? I'm still going because of you, but I'm also doing it because of Dad. He came back from Everest Base Camp a different man and –'

'That's because he met Vanessa there,' I interrupted.

'Perhaps. But I'm wondering if maybe I'll feel

closer to him up there. I know it sounds stupid, but now it feels as though it's something I need to do for him and not just for you.'

'Oh.' My voice was small. I'd been so tied up in the anger that continued to simmer inside me that I hadn't given a minute's thought to how Nathan had been feeling.

Ash was easy – she wore her heart on her sleeve. You always knew what was going on with Ash because she'd tell you in no uncertain terms. But Nath was different. I didn't know whether it was because he always seemed strong and confident, or whether it was because he was independent and lived away, or something else entirely, but I often forgot just how much he felt things – and how much he hid that sensitivity. He'd always been the same: he'd present a happy smiling face to the world and rarely showed what he was really feeling. It was easy to assume that because he acted as though he was okay, he was okay. He'd been my rock since the day he was born, but I wondered now who was there for him.

'I think it would help you too, Mum,' he said quietly. 'The walking, the quiet. I think it would help.'

I didn't know how it could. Going for a walk in New Zealand wasn't going to bring Neil back or make Vanessa go away.

'It might help put things in perspective,' he said, almost as if he'd read my mind.

'Yes, it might.'

I could only hope that would be the case.

Mike responded on my behalf to the letter from Vanessa's solicitor. I was so angry with the entire world that I'd decided to take the fight right back to her, even though Mike reminded me that it could result in me being unable to do anything in regards to the house for a very long time, maybe years.

I shrugged. 'So what?' If all she wanted was money, I was going to make her work for it. I could last longer than she could.

Lachie had frowned. 'That's not like you, Kitty. Think about what Neil would do if he was here.'

'If Neil was here, we wouldn't be having this conversation!' I yelled, before sitting down with a thump.

I didn't blame Lachie and Mike for the step back they'd taken. I wasn't the yelling kind, but nor was I about to apologise.

'If Neil was here,' I said, my tone now completely flat, 'he'd give her what she wanted so she'd go away and he wouldn't have to deal with the conflict.'

'That's not fair,' Lachie said.

'Perhaps. But it's true.' I let out a breath on a long sigh. 'Who am I kidding? Even if Neil was here, she'd still be suing for maintenance or something. Wouldn't she?'

'Probably,' Lachie agreed. 'Maybe you need to think about the baby. It hasn't asked to be brought into this situation, and you know that Neil would have accepted his responsibilities.'

'I am thinking about the baby. But my babies, not hers.' I felt my chin jut out. 'Why should my children suffer because their father –'

Lachie held up his hand. 'Don't say it, Kitty. I know you're angry, but that's beneath you.'

I turned to Mike. 'Just do it. Send the letter. Let's see what her next play is.'

Mari's reaction was similar. 'This isn't like you,' she said.

We were finally cleaning out the linen closet. I'd taken to sorting and discarding with a manic energy that I should have been applying to my hiking training.

'Throwing stuff out? Decluttering? Vanessa has no claim over anything in my house – well, not as far as I know anyway.'

'No, darl, not that; this decision to fight Vanessa. We both know that Neil would want to provide for his child, regardless of what his ex has done.'

'Yeah, well, Neil isn't here. And if I know the way Vanessa's mind works, she'll want more regardless of what I offer, so I might as well take the option that's going to cost her money and keep her tied up for as long as she's got me tied up.'

'That's what I mean – it's not like you to be so

bitter and full of revenge. You can't move forward either while this is going on, and you'll probably still have to give her something at the end of it all. In the meantime, you're in a holding pattern too.'

'Perhaps, but I'm not the pregnant one who needs the money.'

When I glanced up from the garbage bag I was shoving towels into, Mari was looking at me as if I was a stranger. I didn't blame her – I didn't know me either. I didn't know the person I'd become. The anger was bone-deep, and had consumed me. Its bitterness scalded the back of my throat and made me feel ill every time I attempted to eat.

'If your mother was here, she'd tell you not to bite your nose off to spite your face,' she said quietly.

'You know what? I'm sick of people telling me what Neil would do if he were here, and now you're bringing Mum into it too. Neither of them is here and never will be again. So what they would think, say or do means nothing. There's just me.' I tapped at my chest for emphasis. 'Vanessa wants to take her revenge on me and my family, and I'm not going to let her. That's what this is about. And I don't care that I sound like a bitch in the process.'

Mari silently folded a pile of pillowcases and put them back into the cupboard. 'Have you told the kids yet?' she asked.

I shook my head.

'Are you going to?'

'When the time is right.'

'You don't think they have a right to know? This is their future you're playing with – and it's their half-brother or sister too.'

I wasn't looking at her, but I heard the disapproval in her voice.

'I'll tell them when I'm ready,' I said firmly.

As well as decluttering like a woman possessed, I was trying to lose myself in the walking I was doing. Regardless of the weather, every evening after work and each day on the weekend I'd throw on a pair of black tracksuit pants, an old shapeless grey T-shirt and trainers, and shuffle with my head down – at first to the end of the street and back, but further as my physical strength grew. But still I spent my nights lying in bed staring at the ceiling.

Vanessa responded via her solicitor to say she'd see me in court. I stuck my nose in the air and refused to budge.

My resolve wavered a little when Mike told me that because Vanessa was claiming financial hardship because of the baby, we'd be able to get a court date sooner rather than later. It was one thing to talk about standing firm, and another to know that I could be standing in court having the laundry of my relationship aired in public before I'd even finished grieving for the end of that relationship. Nevertheless, I pushed my chin out and told Mike to brief a barrister.

The day before I left for Queenstown, Lachie and Mike turned up with containers of takeaway and huge grins.

'You'll never guess the news we've got for you,' Lachie announced as he kissed my cheek and set the food on the table.

'Probably not,' I said, returning his smile and laying the table.

'It's about Vanessa,' he teased.

I stopped what I was doing immediately. 'What about Vanessa?' I turned to Mike. 'Have we got a court date?'

'We do – a mediation session has been set for the beginning of December. But that's not what our news is.'

'You're as bad as he is.' I pulled a bottle of wine from the fridge and held it up in silent question. They both nodded. 'One of you needs to tell me what's going on,' I said as I poured the wine.

'Well, Mike was talking to one of the associates in his office – Aaron, I think his name is … is that right?' Lachie looked to Mike for affirmation. 'Anyway, Aaron was saying how a mate of his in another firm has been seeing this girl for a while … how long did he say?'

'Why doesn't Mike just tell me himself?' I struggled to keep the impatience from my voice.

Lachie looked across to Mike, who shrugged. 'Okay. Well, Aaron was telling me about this friend of his who's been seeing this girl for about a year on and off – you know how it is.'

I shook my head. I had no idea how it was in this swipe-right – or was it left? – generation.

'Anyway, she's pregnant and this guy doesn't know if it's his or the dude's that she used to be with. His words, not mine,' he added when I raised my eyebrows at the use of the word 'dude'. 'What got me interested was when Aaron said that she's a physiotherapist who does some work at the gym he goes to, and the old dude she used to be with – again, his words – had died.'

My eyes widened.

'I thought that would get your interest,' said Lachie.

'Aaron's mate said she's suing the old guy's wife for maintenance. She reckons he cheated on her with his wife, so she's owed it – regardless of whether or not the baby's his. Aaron's mate reckons it will be a guaranteed house deposit at the very least.'

The prawn I was holding to my mouth dropped from my chopsticks back into the bowl. 'Do you think it's Vanessa?'

'I know it is,' Mike said. 'I asked Aaron for his mate's name – it's Brandon someone or other – and then Lachie and I did some social-media stalking. While we found nothing on her feed, we found these pics on his.'

He handed his phone across and I scrolled through the pictures of Vanessa with a very good-looking guy – of around her own age. In one photo they were kissing; in another they were looking loved up. The most recent was last week and the earliest dated back to January this year – eight months before Neil died. Vanessa had been cheating on Neil. Although he was gone, my heart went out to him.

'The baby mightn't be Neil's?' I asked, faint hope mingling with my words.

'There's absolutely enough doubt here to muddy her case – and to insist on a DNA test to confirm parentage.'

'Wow,' I said softly. What else could I say?

For the first time I wondered whether the baby mightn't be Neil's. Although I'd fallen pregnant twice by accident, we'd tried for a third baby and nothing had happened. We already had two healthy children so hadn't worried about taking it any further. What if this baby wasn't his?

Mike and Lachie looked at each other.

'Is that all you have to say?' Lachie sounded disappointed.

'At the moment, yes.' I reached across to touch the back of first Mike's and then Lachie's hand. 'This is huge, and thanks for telling me, but I just don't know what to do with it yet.' I smiled as the weight that had been on my chest lifted just a little. 'I'll think about it on the walk and we can talk when I get home. Until then, keep those screenshots safe. I bet if Vanessa knew that we knew about this guy she'd make sure any evidence was deleted.'

Twenty-four

Nathan and I flew into Queenstown on Saturday afternoon, the clear skies allowing magnificent views of the mountains below.

'Look down there, Mum,' he said, pointing. 'I think that's where we'll be walking.'

His voice was excited, so I looked at where he was indicating and smiled. Something stirred within me at the view – fear perhaps – but otherwise I felt nothing.

On the way to our hotel by the lake, the cab driver asked if it was our first trip to Queenstown.

Nathan was in the front seat, so answered for us. 'Yes. My mother and I are here to do the Milford Track.'

The driver nodded. 'Will you have a chance to look around before or after?'

'We head out on the hike on Monday, but we'll have a few extra days here when we get back.'

'Be sure you get out to Glenorchy and Paradise then – and the wineries. We have some great wineries.'

'We'll bear that in mind, won't we, Mum?'

I half-smiled and continued to look out the

window as Nathan and the driver chatted lightly for the rest of the short drive.

'I'm going to pop my bag in my room and go look at the lake,' I said once we'd checked in.

'Do you want me to come with you?' There was no mistaking the concern in Nathan's voice.

I patted his arm. 'It's okay, Nath. Get settled, and come and find me.'

As I walked down the lawn and through the rose gardens in front of the hotel to the edge of the lake, the clouds moved to display the mountains to the left, instantly changing the colour of the water from a nondescript grey to a deep blue. The willows beside the Bathhouse Cafe rustled in the breeze, and a few seagulls glided past. In the middle of the lake, a steamboat was puffing black smoke into the air; and to my right along the lakefront, a small cruise boat was getting ready to head out.

Blocking all other noise out, I focused my attention on the lake – and that sensation I'd felt deep in my belly at the first sight of the view from the plane shifted again.

'Mum.' Nathan's voice brought me back to the present. His face had that look again – the one that said he was worried but didn't want to say it out loud.

'Isn't it meant to be summer?' I said as I wrapped my scarf around my neck.

'Are you glad I talked you into buying the thermals

now?' He grinned. 'I reckon you'll be needing them – and the pack cover. Rain is forecast on and off for the next few days. How great would it be if we got some late season snow too?'

'You think?' I allowed my mouth to curl into a smile.

For much of the time since receiving the letter from Vanessa's solicitor I'd been numb, aware only of the dull thrum of anger in the pit of my stomach and the occasional rise of bitterness to the back of my throat. While I didn't relish walking in the cold and the rain, being here in Queenstown and experiencing both the wonder of the lake and its four-seasons-in-one-day weather had already begun to weave a spell on me.

On Monday, we met up with the other walkers. There were a couple of groups of two or three; one largish bundle of five women, all of whom appeared to be in their sixties; another six people who seemed to be travelling as a family; a couple in designer hiking gear who looked super fit – the wife reminded me of a gazelle; and a single man standing off to the side. My gaze flickered over him – as it flickered over most people these days – then something made me turn back and I saw him smiling at me. About my age, I'd guess, maybe a little older, closer to Neil's, his hair peppered that steel grey that only the blackest of hair goes. I smiled back and shifted my focus to Nathan, who was suggesting we load our walking poles and bags onto the bus.

Once everyone was on board, the guides introduced themselves. Kelsey, a bubbly blonde, and Cody, tall and thin with a blond ponytail that made him look as though he'd be more at home in the surf than the mountains, looked to be in their early twenties. Jess seemed older – mid to late twenties perhaps? All three appeared strong and fit, but Jess had a vitality that went beyond fitness – as if even sitting on a coach for two hours was to unfairly restrain her. I noticed Nathan glancing at her every so often and smiled to myself.

I spent the drive to Te Anau gazing out the window at the landscape. I could hear Nathan chatting to the older couple sitting across the aisle from us and the daughters from the family group who were diagonally across. And from time to time one of the guides – usually Jess – would interrupt my thoughts with information about The Remarkables, the mountain range we were driving beside, or Lake Wakatipu, which was on our right for the first forty-five minutes or so of the journey. But as magnificent as the views were, my thoughts were back in Sydney.

I still had no idea how I was going to use the information Lachie and Mike had given me. On one hand, it was enough to bring Vanessa's alleged position as Neil's common-law wife into question, as well as the parentage of the baby; on the other hand, I couldn't help wondering whether I could stoop so low as to use it. Sure, I'd do anything to preserve my children's inheritance, but would they – and would Neil – approve of the actions I needed to take to do so?

As the scenery flew by, I again – for the umpteenth time – went through every potential scenario in my head, arriving, as I always did, at the conclusion that there was no right answer.

We stopped for lunch in the lakeside town of Te Anau at a cafe inside a large store selling souvenirs and snow clothes. Tables had been laid with salads, cold meats and bread rolls, fruit, jugs of juice and some tray-baked slices.

Nathan and I loaded our plates and found a table to sit at. The family of six joined us. They introduced themselves as Janelle and Dale from Arizona in the US, their three daughters, Georgia, Skye and Elise, and Skye's husband, Rick. During the bus trip, Georgia and Elise hadn't been able to take their eyes off Nathan.

'My girls certainly seem taken with your boy,' Janelle said to me, her eyes dancing. 'Oh, to be young again.'

'To me, you're the same age as when we met,' said Dale.

Janelle smiled fondly at him. 'I hardly think so, but it's a lovely sentiment. We've been together since we weren't much more than kids,' she told me. 'It's why when Skye told us she was in love with Rick, even though all our friends and family said that at twenty and twenty-two they didn't know what love was yet, we knew better. When we were that age we thought we'd invented love'

'I know,' I said. 'At that age, it was as if no one older could possibly understand love; and now we're our parents' age, we have to stop ourselves from believing that at their age they don't get it. My daughter recently married her childhood sweetheart and I have to believe that they'll make it.'

'What about you?' Janelle asked. 'Is there a Mister Kate?'

'There was, but he died a few months ago.' I didn't even trip over the words. One thing the anger had done for me was harden my tone – and my heart.

'I'm sorry to hear that. Was it sudden?'

'Yes. A heart attack. One minute he was there and the next he wasn't.' I looked across at Skye and Rick. 'I was eighteen when we met, and he was twenty-three. It's funny how a five-year age gap seems so much at eighteen, and nothing at fifty.'

'That's why we're here now,' said Dale. 'Janelle had a cancer scare a few months back.'

'It was a timely reminder that we need to do more things as a family before it's too late. It's an expensive trip, but you can't take it with you, can you, honey?' She linked arms with Dale as she spoke.

'You certainly can't,' he replied. 'Anything's worth it to see the smile on Janelle's face. I thought I'd lost her there for a little while.' His smile was gentle. 'I used to work too many hours; now I don't want to miss a single minute of the extra time we've been granted. I've retired, and we're finally doing all those things we promised ourselves we'd do when we had the time and money to do them.'

I nodded, but didn't say what I was thinking. Neil and I didn't get that chance.

After lunch, we all piled back onto the bus for the drive to Te Anau Downs harbour.

'Okay, guys, this is where the adventure starts,' announced Jess. 'The boat will take us up to the head of Lake Te Anau – and the official start of the track. From there we have just a short walk – around a mile – to get to the lodge. For those of you who are wondering, all the distance markers on track are in miles. You can forget about kilometres until we are back in Queenstown. You'll have time to leave your backpacks in your rooms and then we'll gather at the front of the lodge for a group photo – in the rain, by the look of those skies – and then for those who are interested, we'll take you on a short walk through the forest and point out some of the plant life and birds that we might see on track. Kelsey has just graduated from university where she learned about all of this stuff, so who are we to deny her telling us about it? Any questions? No? Let's go then.'

It drizzled the whole time we were on the lake. I stood outside in the cold – under the canopy to protect me from the rain – and watched the palette of grey blue go past, the mountains in the distance almost navy in the rain.

'I can see why you're braving the cold. There's a wildness about the country beyond those shores.' It was the man with the steel-grey hair. He was indicating the shoreline we'd just passed – a tumble of rocks below a heavily tree-lined steep slope. 'I'm glad we're not walking up that.'

'Me too.'

I looked closer at him. The planes of his face were angular, as if he'd been chiselled from a piece of granite. Yet his eyes crinkled at the edges, the deep lines around them and his mouth showing a good fifty years, maybe more, of experience and laughter.

He smiled and held out his hand. 'I'm Tom,' he said.

My hand was cold and wet from holding on to the railing of the boat, so I wiped it on my leggings before taking his. 'Kate.'

'Nice to meet you, Kate. Is that your son you're walking with?'

'It is.' My eyes went to the cabin, where I could see Nathan inside chatting to Georgia and Elise. 'Although something tells me I won't be seeing too much of him over the next few days.'

Tom grinned, his eyes alight.

I shivered and dropped my gaze. 'I think I might

go in and warm up.' As I walked into the cabin, I could feel his eyes on my back.

Soft drizzle accompanied us on the short walk to the lodge, and held off while we were having the obligatory group photo. It didn't set in with any seriousness until everyone left on the group walk.

I elected to stay back and settle into my room. Nathan had said it would do me good to meet other people again – and I knew he was right. I needed to be dragged out of my self-imposed isolation, but managing the tumble of names and personalities all at once was producing too much noise in my head for now.

When I joined the others for a drink before dinner, Nathan was talking with Tom and the girls from Arizona. As I approached the group Tom headed off to the bar, returning a few minutes later with a glass of red wine, which he offered to me.

'Nathan mentioned that you're a red drinker, but if you'd like something else I'd be happy to get it for you.'

'Thank you,' I said. 'That's lovely.'

I sipped at the wine and listened to the two American girls vying for Nathan's attention.

'He's not really as oblivious to their attention as he's making out, is he?' Tom asked in a low voice.

I shook my head. 'No, but I don't think either of them is his type.'

'I see. Well, they'll both be disappointed then.'

I saw from his face the direction that his mind was heading. 'I don't mean that he's gay, just that he's never been the sort that flirts if he thinks someone might be hurt in the process.' I looked around the room. 'If I was to match him up with anyone it would probably be Jess.'

As I spoke, I saw Nathan's eyes wander across to where Jess was helping prepare the tables for dinner.

Tom noticed as well. 'It would seem that your instincts are spot on.'

'Not always, sadly, but where my children are concerned, yes, they usually are.'

'Do you have other children?'

'Yes. A daughter, Ashleigh – Ash, we call her. She was married a few months ago to her childhood sweetheart.'

I waited for the inevitable follow-up question.

'And Ash and Nathan's father?'

There it was.

'He died. Not long after the wedding.'

He was silent for a few seconds as he absorbed the information. 'I'm sorry. It's so recent – you must miss him.'

'I do. We all do.' I squeezed the words past the lump that had suddenly formed in my throat. I hadn't felt this close to tears since I'd found out about Vanessa contesting the will. Maybe it was the change in environment, or the sympathy I saw in his brown eyes.

I forced a smile to my face. 'What about you? Do you have a wife and children somewhere?'

'Yes. I have three children – all in their twenties. Chelsea and Brodie are in Auckland, and our youngest, Brooke, is at university in Wellington. She lives with her mother – I see her as often as we can manage it.'

'And you? Where do you live?'

'Here.' At my raised eyebrows, he corrected himself. 'Sorry, Queenstown … well, just out of Queenstown. When Shellie – my ex-wife – and I finally decided to call it quits, I took it as a sign to make a change. So I traded my partnership in a law firm for a winery.'

'That's quite a change.'

'It certainly has been.'

I would have asked more questions but Kelsey called us in to dinner. Somehow, during the course of our conversation, we'd become separated from the rest of the group. As if by unspoken agreement, we moved towards a table where Nathan and the Arizonas – as I'd christened the family from America – were already sitting.

'I'll go get us another drink,' Tom said once I was sitting down.

'No,' I made to stand back up, 'it's my turn.'

He motioned for me to stay where I was. 'You can get the next one.'

I felt my cheeks grow warm as I saw Nathan watching the exchange. Once Tom had gone to the bar he leaned in and whispered, 'It's okay, Mum. Just relax.'

Over a surprisingly good dinner the Arizonas filled us in on their lives in the US and the girls continued their flirtation with Nathan. Following dinner, we all assembled in the lounge area.

'Grab a drink if you want – we've got a bit to get through this evening,' said Cody.

Once we were all settled again, Jess called us to attention. 'Okay, guys, we'll be spending a lot of time together over the next few days, so I think we all need to get acquainted a little better. If we could maybe start with your name, where you're from, something about yourself and why you're doing the walk.'

As we all shuffled in our seats, she grinned. 'I'll go first. My name is Jess – I guess you all know that by now. I used to do a lot more guiding than I do now, but I also run a cafe in town – down on Beach Road. I hope to see some of you in there when we get back. I reckon we do the best breakfasts in town, but I could be biased. Why do I still guide? Because I love these tracks – and I love seeing people accomplish things they didn't believe were possible. Cody, over to you.'

As Cody and then Kelsey told their stories, I watched Nathan watching Jess. Yes, she was very much his type.

We did the rest of the introductions in order of country. Aside from the Arizonas, there were another two couples from the US; and three brothers in their late thirties or early forties from London who had done the Queenstown marathon and stayed on to walk the track. From New Zealand there was an accountant and his wife from Auckland, and Tom.

He introduced himself by saying he was an ex-lawyer from Wellington who was now a winemaker in Queenstown. 'As part of my tree change I figured I'd better have a look at the country down here too. Then I met Jess at a rugby club function and she convinced me I hadn't seen anything until I'd been out here. So here I am.'

Finally it was Australia's turn. First up was a mixed group of nine hikers from the same walking club in Melbourne. The youngest of the group would have been in her mid-sixties. Some were partnered up, others were single, but all were seasoned hikers – or trampers, as Jess said it was called here. They'd set themselves the challenge of completing the Milford Track plus the Greenstone and Routeburn Tracks. I was in awe of their energy and optimism. Other than them, there were two best friends from Sydney – Marg and Deb – and a married couple from Brisbane, Bob and Penny, who I'd noticed keeping to themselves earlier. A similar age to me, Penny didn't appear to have the enthusiasm for the venture that her husband did.

As the others introduced themselves one by one, I wondered what there was for me to say. 'I booked this walk to show my husband that I didn't need him in my life, that I didn't care that he was divorcing me for a younger model, that if he could climb a mountain and walk away from our life, then so could I.' Those were my original reasons, but now? Now I was here because Nathan had told me I needed to be here, and because he felt that doing this would make him feel closer to his father.

When it was my turn I fumbled for the words. 'Hi, I'm Kate and I'm from Sydney. I'm walking with my son, Nathan.' I smiled at him. 'This started because I decided I needed a challenge and Nathan said he'd come with me to make sure that I didn't slip off the edge of the mountain. Since then I … I've lost my husband, so I'm not really sure any more why I'm doing this. Maybe to walk through the sadness.' I attempted a half-smile and Nathan gripped my arm in reassurance.

'I'm Nathan and I'm a marine biologist from North Queensland. I was originally coming along with Mum partly to make sure that she didn't slide off the mountain, but also because I've wanted to do one of these great walks and Mum gave me an excuse. Since we lost Dad though, I think these few days will help both of us process that.'

His eyes were shining and I was suddenly proud of the strong, yet sensitive man that Neil and I had raised together.

Looking at him, I knew I'd been wrong to try and protect him from what had been going on with

Vanessa. He and Ash were both adults and deserved to know. It was as much their business as it was mine.

I'd tell Nathan before we went home, and I'd tell Ash as soon as we got back. We'd decide what to do about it together.

Twenty-five

It rained steadily all night. As always, I'd lain awake until the early hours, staring at where I knew the ceiling to be. The generators had all switched off at 10 pm so it was completely dark, and, other than the sound of the rain hitting the roof, completely quiet.

The pitch black and perfect quiet were ideal conditions for my doubts and fears to emerge and cluster together. I hadn't prepared well enough for this walk. What was I thinking of? Not only was I likely to fall off the edge of the mountain, but I was likely to take Nathan with me. The whole project was irresponsible, a reaction to Neil's intention to divorce me. It wasn't something I really wanted to do.

And if anything happened at home, how was anyone to contact me? I was in the middle of a court case. I should be at home in Sydney, sorting out the will and dealing with Vanessa, not in a lodge in the rain in a New Zealand forest.

If I hadn't over-reacted when someone other than Neil paid me a little bit of attention all those years ago, none of this would be happening. That's why Neil had gone off and walked up his mountain, met Vanessa, left me, and decided to divorce me. If he hadn't wanted to get divorced, we would never have got back together, Vanessa wouldn't be pregnant, Neil wouldn't be dead, and I wouldn't be somewhere I absolutely shouldn't be.

Everything that had happened was my fault and instead of fixing it, I was stuck here without phone reception or power in the dark with the rain pouring down outside. Tomorrow I had to walk sixteen kilometres, sorry ten miles – probably through more rain. I hoped it hurt. I needed it to hurt. It would be no less than I deserved.

I must have dropped off to sleep sometime around two, so when the power came on with a rush four hours later, I felt as though I hadn't slept at all. I showered, dressed and packed, and made my way down to breakfast.

Everyone else appeared to have spent a much better night than I had. They were full of the excitement of getting started on the track. It was still raining. I sighed and went over to where the makings for breakfast had been set out.

Nathan came and kissed me on the cheek. 'Okay, Mum?'

I managed a smile. 'Absolutely.'

His eyes narrowed with concern as he saw the shadows under mine. 'Are you sure?'

'Of course.'

Tom was over at the urn pouring himself a cup of coffee. He smiled and I acknowledged him, but took my cup of tea and toast to a table away from him.

Nathan and I set off soon after breakfast. We walked together in silence for the first twenty minutes or so, greeting other walkers from time to time.

'You know you don't need to walk with me,' I said. 'If you want to go on ahead that's okay.'

He turned to look at me, drops from the top of his hood landing on his jacket. 'We're doing this together, Mum.'

'I'll be glad of your presence tomorrow when we walk up that mountain, but today I think I need some time alone. Is that okay?'

His eyes sought mine and finally he nodded. 'If you're sure.'

'I am. Now why don't you catch up with those two American girls? I don't think they're too far ahead – they seemed reluctant to pass us, and I don't think my company was the reason why.' When he still hesitated I said, 'Go on. I'm fine. If I don't see you on the track, I'll see you at the lodge.'

'Okay. See you there.'

He picked up his pace and I watched him until he was out of sight. Then I walked. Step after step. In the rain. All around was water. Below, to my right, was the river. I could hear it constantly, and every so often when the path ran close enough I'd see it too, rushing past, carrying branches in its torrents. Springing from the mountains were thin streams of silver waterfalls, almost as if they were crying lightning bolts of water.

The rain got heavier and still I walked. Through a beech forest dripping with moss and lichen, through puddles that filled my boots and mud that was always deeper than it looked. As I walked, the thoughts from last night returned and brought with them regret and guilt. Regret for what had happened between Neil and me, for how we'd lost our way at some point over the years; and guilt for my part in that. He might have been the one who'd left, but knowing what he did about my almost-affair, he might have thought it was the only action he could take. That leaving was the only way to salvage at least a friendship out of the desert our marriage had become.

I didn't know if things would have been different if I'd gone back to university and finished my degree; if I'd had a purpose in life so I didn't resent his. If I'd had something more to do when the kids no longer needed me and Neil was spending so many hours at work. If I hadn't sought to fill the gaps within me with someone else rather than *something* else. If I'd worked harder to keep us on track. If I hadn't forgotten that we'd already been given one second chance at getting it right. If I hadn't forgotten how much we'd loved each other, how it was when we first met and the way we were convinced that no one else could possibly love each other as much and as hard as we did. All the if-onlys.

As I walked, I saw myself for what I was – someone who had hurt the man she loved, who had ruined a perfectly good marriage, and then, for good measure, allowed the world to blame him. He was the one who left and I was the one left behind – therefore the breakdown of our marriage had to have been his fault. He was the one who had a midlife crisis and climbed a mountain. All I did was kiss someone I shouldn't have – but no one else knew about that, so in their eyes I was the one to be pitied.

Then there was the mess with Vanessa and the fear that I could lose up to half of what Neil and I had worked to build all those years, that after all the sacrifices we'd made, the hours at work, time together that we'd never get back, our children's inheritance could go to her child rather than Nathan and Ash. How was it fair that just as we were on the brink of enjoying our regained time together, Neil had died and Vanessa got to waltz in and claim half of everything? She'd only had a couple of years with him? How was that fair?

Could I have dealt with it all differently? Should I have dealt with it differently? Because of my actions, my kids were going to lose out. Everything was my fault.

At some point, my guilt and regret became one with the rain. I climbed over a fallen tree, slipped on the mossy top and slid down the other side to land heavily on my bum, twisting my knee slightly. And then I was sobbing. I brushed at my eyes but didn't know what was rain and what were tears. Blood smeared on the back of my hand and I felt a smarting at the top of my mouth. A branch must have scratched my face on my way down.

My chest heaved with the effort of my sobs and I used my poles to struggle to my feet. My pack weighed heavily on my back and I struggled out of it, remembering from somewhere what Jess had said about leaving it on the path to let anyone passing know that I'd left the main track.

I stumbled down a narrow path that led to the river. Once I was out of sight, I sank to my knees in the mud and gave way to the grief that erupted from the very core of me. I cried for what I'd lost, for what we'd lost – Neil and me – and I cried for the parts we'd both played in that. I wished that we'd talked about it, that I'd been able to tell him of my discontent, that he'd listened to me rather than pretending that everything was okay. I wished he'd asked me about the kiss so we could have acknowledged it rather than leaving it undealt with all of those years. I cried for everything we could have said but didn't.

I had no idea how long I cried for – I simply let it have its way, until all the regret and guilt had left my body. Then the vomiting started. It was as though my body needed to be rid of everything that was poisoning me from the inside. The rain mixed with my tears and my blood and my vomit and washed it all away. And still I sobbed and heaved.

Finally I was done. I reached for the poles I'd dropped and levered myself out of the mud and back into a standing position. After the onslaught I felt empty. I knew the anger would find its way back in, but for now I had nothing left.

I made my way back to the main track and manoeuvred my pack onto my back, leaning forward to get it to sit right and fastening the strap around my waist. Straightening, I saw Tom sitting on the log I'd fallen from, the hard edges of his face softened by the rain streaming over them.

'How long have you been here for?' I asked.

'Long enough,' he replied, his eyes full of concern.

'Did you see?'

He nodded. 'Yes, but I thought you needed to let it go, so I waited here until you were ready to come out.'

'Thank you.'

'Are you right to start walking again?'

'Yes.'

So we did.

After we'd been walking in silence for a while I said, 'I suppose you think I'm some sort of mad woman.'

'I don't think that.'

'You probably want to know why I was crying?'

'Only if you want to tell me.' He turned his head to look at me through the rain. 'If you don't want to tell me, I'll wait until you do.'

'I don't want to talk about it.'

'That's fine then.'

We covered the next mile without speaking. The rain continued to come down.

'You don't need to walk with me, you know,' I said.

'I know I don't, but I'm in no hurry and I want to walk with you.'

'Okay then.'

After another long silence, I struggled for something to talk about. 'You said last night, in the introductions, that you're here because Jess convinced you to do the walk. Do you know her well?'

I could hear the smile in his voice as he acknowledged my effort. 'No, not really. We got talking at a rugby club event and she mentioned that she's a keen tramper. Her brother recently came back from England and apparently his partner now helps out in the cafe, so Jess can do a few more tours in the summer. She said that if I was going to settle in the area I really should do at least one of the great walks. She can be very persuasive, so here I am.'

'How long have you been in Queenstown?'

'Just over a year. Shellie and I split soon after Brooke finished school. We'd hung on until the last school fees were paid, but we both knew it was over. When it's done, it's done. She's married again and is happier than when we were together.'

'Do you two still get on?'

He hesitated for a second before answering. 'We're fine now, but at first, no. I was pretty angry and so was she. We both blamed each other, but really it was both our faults. It always is, you know?'

I nodded, but I didn't agree with him. Our split was all my fault.

'She fell in love with someone else.' He said it so softly that I turned to look hard at the set planes of his face, the rain streaming over his cheeks.

'How can you take any of the blame then?'

'I didn't at first. It was only much later that I realised she'd given me so many opportunities to talk about what was wrong between us, but I was always too busy or didn't want to stop and listen. If I had listened, it would have meant that I needed to do something about it and I told myself I didn't have time for that. She'd get over whatever midlife crisis she was having. She gave me so many chances to make it right and I didn't take any of them. So yes, the failure of our marriage was as much my fault as hers.' He shrugged one shoulder and smiled at me briefly. 'As I said, it's a rare divorce that can lay the blame wholly and squarely at one person's door. In any case, she's happier than she's ever been and I'm enjoying life too. I never would have followed my dream if we hadn't separated. It was painful, but we're both better for it now.'

'Neil's dream was to buy a bookshop in a country

town somewhere.'

'Was it yours too?'

I nodded and the rain on my hood flew off in big fat drops. 'He loved books, but I wanted to offer a service in the shop too – make it somewhere for people to research and learn and write and meet up. Like a library, bookshop and evening college all in one.'

'If he hadn't died do you think you'd have done it?'

'Yes. He'd announced his retirement the day he died. We had plans of selling up and moving away. We didn't know where, but it was to be the start of a new life for us. Another chance.'

'You can still do it,' he said.

'Perhaps. I don't know. There's still a lot to sort out. Things are complicated.' I looked away, and saw that we were just past the seven-mile marker. 'Look, here's the hut and there's Nathan.'

I felt Tom's eyes on me, as if he saw my relief at ending a conversation that had become more personal than I was comfortable with.

Nathan had obviously been waiting for me. 'I was beginning to wonder where you were.' He looked me up and down, taking in the scrape on my mouth and the mud on my clothes. 'What's happened to you?'

'I had a bit of a fall off the top of a log. I'm dirty, but no harm done.' I couldn't help sending a look to Tom.

'I came across her soon after,' he added. 'She's

walking fine, there doesn't appear to be any problem.'

Nathan searched his face and, seemingly satisfied, nodded. 'Okay. Now I know you're fine, Mum, I'll keep going. See you at the lodge. And watch where you're putting your feet, hey?'

'I will,' I promised.

Inside the hut, Jess offered us a hot drink. 'Sorry, I can't stop the rain, but I can give you something to warm you from the inside.'

I smiled gratefully, took my pack off, accepted the mug of hot chocolate and sat down on a bench to eat my sandwich.

Tom did the same, but took a seat on the other side of the hut. I didn't blame him for wanting to get as far away as he could from the mad woman. My cheeks burned at the thought of the breakdown he'd witnessed.

Twenty-six

Dale and Janelle arrived soon after, followed by Marg and Deb, and the accountant from Auckland and his wife. As we were finishing our sandwiches, Cody arrived with Bob and Penny from Brisbane. Penny complained loudly about the rain and how cold she was while Bob scurried around to get a hot drink for her.

Tom and I exchanged glances and I found myself holding back a complicit smile.

While Penny used the facilities, Jess asked Cody if he was right to finish up.

'Sure,' he said. 'You go on ahead. I don't suppose you've heard if the leaders have made it to the river yet?'

'No, but they can't be too far from it. I don't think we've had enough rain to flood the crossing, but we'll definitely need to help people across. I'll head out with Tom and Kate, and then push on to take over from Kelsey with the first group. You'll be right with these guys?'

'I sure will. See you back there.'

As Tom and I stood to zip our rain jackets back on and replace the packs on our backs, Jess did the same.

Back on track, Tom and Jess chatted lightly – about people they both knew, and Jess's cafe and the function she'd agreed to cater for at Tom's winery just before Christmas.

'Between Dan – he's my chef,' she explained to me, 'and Max – she's my brother Richie's partner – we'll be fine. I haven't done many functions up until now because my previous baker was quite unreliable. When Richie came home after spending way too many years in England and brought Max with him, I couldn't believe my luck. Not only because Richie's happy and might actually stay put – especially now that Max is pregnant – but because Max is brilliant in the kitchen. It frees me up to spend some time on track, but also to take the business in a slightly different direction. Max is right into the seasonality of the produce, so we're moving more down that line.

'Nathan was saying that you're quite the baker too,' she added. 'He was telling me about your soups and stews as well, and the platters you used to put on for family gatherings.' Was I imagining it or did I see some pink in her cheeks at the mention of my son's name? 'He said you did a whole Victorian high tea theme for his sister's kitchen tea. Maybe I can convince you to stay around in Queenstown too.'

I smiled but didn't reply.

We came out of the forest into a clearing. The rain had lightened to misty instead of torrential. I raised my face to the sky and felt raindrops slip under my hood and drip down below my jacket.

Jess pointed ahead. 'Through there, that's Mackinnon Pass. We'll be going up and over that tomorrow.'

I pushed my hood back and the three of us gazed at the mountain in the distance and the low clouds and mist swirling around it. Both Tom and Jess had looks of excitement on their faces. I felt the acid taste of panic rising within me.

'Don't worry,' Jess said to me. She must have seen the same look of trepidation on hundreds of faces. 'You take it at your own pace and there'll always be someone with you.'

'Why doesn't that make me feel better?'

She laughed. 'Okay, guys, if you two are fine, I'm going to shoot on ahead and help Kelsey out at the crossing.' With a wave she was off.

'You can go on ahead too if you want,' I told Tom.

'Haven't we already had this conversation?' He grinned at me, the hood no longer obscuring his eyes.

Suddenly I wished it would rain again. I felt much more comfortable when I couldn't see his face properly. 'I guess so.'

'Unless you don't want my company,' he added. 'And it's absolutely fine if you don't. I won't be insulted, but I will be disappointed.'

'In that case you'd better hang around then.'

I ducked my head, but not before I'd noticed how his smile reached his eyes.

'I don't suppose you know whether Jess is single?' I asked, a half-mile or so later.

'I thought I saw her cheeks looking a little brighter than normal when she mentioned Nathan,' he replied. 'She is. From what I can understand, she tends to fall for short-term men. I think Dan, her chef, is keen on her, but they've been friends since school so I don't think she'll ever notice him in the way he wants her to.'

'Nathan is only passing through too,' I pointed out.

'True. I have the feeling that could be a very great pity.'

'Perhaps.' There was definitely chemistry between them – even as soaked to the skin as we all were.

The track had brought us out into open prairie country. I imagined that on a good day we'd be able to see for miles, but today there were more waterfalls streaming from the mountains than I could count. Despite the way I felt, I couldn't fault the beauty around us.

'It's pretty spectacular, isn't it?' Tom said softly.

'It certainly is.'

'Kate, why did you really decide to come on this walk? I couldn't help seeing your face when Jess pointed out the pass – you looked terrified.'

Even to me, my giggle sounded uncomfortable. 'Like I said last night, I needed a challenge.'

'Come on, there's more to it than that, isn't there? You've obviously never done anything like this before – and I don't mean that nastily. It's just that you're not comfortable with packs and rough paths.'

'No, I'm definitely a city girl.' I paused. This man had seen me vomiting and sobbing; I couldn't possibly appear any worse in his eyes. 'I'm here because I wanted to prove a point to Neil. I wanted to show him that I didn't care that he wanted a divorce, and there were things I wanted to do with my life that didn't involve him. If he could climb a mountain and come back a changed person, so could I.'

'Hang on, you guys were divorcing when he died?'

'Yes and no. We were – then we weren't. It was a bit complicated.'

His raised eyebrows told me he considered that an understatement. 'Why don't you tell me about Neil?' he said.

'Do you really want to hear it?'

'Yes, I do. But only if you want to tell it.'

After a heavy sigh, I said, 'I met Neil when I was in my first year of university. I was going to be a lawyer and stand up for the poor and downtrodden, take a stand against the capitalist oppressors – that sort of thing. And then Neil came along. He was older than me – twenty-three to my eighteen – conservative, a banker, and he didn't care about politics. He was everything I was determined not to end up with so of course I fell for him hard. Then he was promoted and transferred to a small town in the country. He asked me to go with him – he wanted us to get married. I said no – I had a degree to finish and a brilliant career to contemplate and neither of those were going to happen as the wife of a banker in a small country town. So we broke up.'

The rain had started to come down again so I pulled my hood back over my head. It made it easier to go on talking.

'He hadn't been gone long when I realised I was pregnant with Nathan. I could have told him and he would have come back, but that would have meant losing his job and his job meant so much to him. So I didn't tell him. I made a deal with myself that I'd find him when Nathan was two; and then when Nathan was three; and then before Nath started school. I knew Neil would be angry and would want to know, but ...' I shook my head and raindrops flew everywhere. 'I had no real excuse. As it turned out, I didn't need to find him – I ran into him at a Christmas party when Nath was three, and the feelings between us were still there.'

'How did he take the news?'

I shrugged. 'Pretty much as you'd expect any decent man would take it – he was furious with me. But he also still loved me. We never spoke of it again. There was a lot over the years that we didn't talk about, but that was the first time I understood that Neil's way of moving forward was to bury things in the past.'

'And you never finished your degree?'

'No. That joke was well and truly on me. The law degree and brilliant career that we'd broken up over never materialised. I don't know, maybe I resented him for that – subconsciously, of course.'

'Were you happy?'

'Yes. Not deliriously so – I don't think that's possible. But we were content, and he was my best friend. It was my fault what happened next.'

'I'm sure it wasn't all your fault,' Tom said. 'As I said earlier, no one party is usually to blame in these situations.'

'In this instance, it was all on me. The kids were pretty much grown, and I had time on my hands and started to wonder if what we had was all there was. Neil and I had settled into ... well, I'd been tired a lot and he didn't seem interested any more.' My cheeks grew warm as I hesitated over how to explain my sex life with my husband to this man I'd never met before yesterday. 'We were never just us. We were parents right from the start, and we'd both had to work long hours to pay for the kids' schools, and ... well, you know how it is.'

'I certainly do.'

I hesitated before speaking again. Too much of what I was about to say might remind him of his and Shellie's story. 'Anyway, I decided that I wanted more.

I probably should have gone back to university, but instead I began a flirtation with a man at work. It didn't go anywhere past a kiss, but for a time I wanted it to. I wanted to feel as though I was something other than a wife and a mother, that I was still a woman worth noticing – in that way. Afterwards, I threw myself into trying to be the best wife possible. Neil told me before he died that he knew there was someone else, but we'd never talked about it. If he'd asked, I would have confessed; but he never asked. It wasn't long after that when he announced that he wanted to hike to Everest Base Camp. I'd been so tied up in my own boredom and then in trying to be Super Wife that I hadn't noticed he wasn't happy either. I thought it was just me who was trying to fill the gaps and … Well, you don't need to know all that. Actually, you don't need to know any of this. I have no idea why I'm telling you.' I stopped walking and looked at him. 'Why am I telling you?'

'Because you need to talk, because I'm here, and because I don't know you,' he said. 'Also because I'm interested,' he added softly.

'Even though I kissed someone who wasn't my husband?'

'And, by the sounds of it, have beaten yourself up about it ever since.'

'Maybe. Anyway, when Neil came home from Base Camp he was different. He said he'd spent the time up there thinking about us and had decided we'd be better apart.'

'Were you angry about that?'

'I don't know. No … maybe … yes … I thought we'd continue as we had done forever. That what we had was preferable to being alone. He didn't agree. He thought that separating was the best way for us to stay friends, and although I was upset, I agreed with him. We were done. We loved each other, but we weren't in love. Anyway, he began seeing this girl – and she was a girl, not much older than Nathan – who he'd met on the trek. Vanessa. I pretended that I didn't care and welcomed her into the family, because that's what civilised people do if they don't want to split up their family.' I looked sideways at him and saw his raised eyebrows. 'I know, it's totally dysfunctional, but it sort of worked. Neil was with Vanessa, but he'd still come by most weekends to mow the lawns and look after the house, and both of them would come for family dinners.'

'Seriously? I don't know that I could have been that generous. When Shellie and I split there was a lot of very healthy anger that eventually settled back into friendship, but there's no way I'd be inviting her new husband around for a meal.'

'Yeah, our friends couldn't understand it either. Although once Neil started seeing Vanessa, I lost most of them anyway. Apparently it's far easier to socialise with couples than with singles. Earlier this year, not long before Ash's wedding, he asked me for a divorce.

It hit me like nothing had ever hit me before – although I pretended it made sense. That's why I decided to do this walk – to prove to Neil that I could do something challenging with my life too. Not that it mattered. Talking about divorce made us both realise that we still had feelings for each other – and it was just like it had been when we first fell in love, before the kids came along. We had all these plans. Neil was going to retire, and we were going to sell up in Sydney and buy that little bookshop I was telling you about. One minute we were planning our glorious future together, and the next he was dead.'

As we'd been talking the track had begun to climb. The rain continued and I struggled to breathe and talk at the same time. If I was like this on this slope, what was I going to be like with two uphill miles of zig-zagging paths tomorrow?

'It wasn't all your fault, you know,' Tom said softly.

'How do you figure that? I kissed someone who wasn't my husband.'

'Yes, but you did that because you felt you weren't satisfied in the marriage. You say that maybe you should have talked about that with Neil, but you've also said that you didn't think he'd listen. Do you believe that?'

I nodded slowly. 'I do. Neil didn't like to argue or confront anything. He usually hoped it would all go away or get fixed on its own – usually by me.'

'But this time it was you who needed to be fixed.'

I paused on the track and turned to face him, forcing the breath into my lungs. 'I thought you were a lawyer not a counsellor.'

He laughed ruefully. 'I only see it because I did the same. Shellie needed me to step up and I stepped away instead; so she found someone who could give her what she needed. It wasn't her fault, it wasn't mine; we both had a part to play.'

I searched his face, but the hood of his jacket was partially obscuring his eyes. I turned away and continued trudging up the hill.

He caught up to me within a couple of strides. 'Do you think you would have made it work this time? If he hadn't died?'

I hesitated over my answer.

'Kate?' he prompted.

I swallowed hard. 'See, that's the problem. I honestly don't know whether we would have. I lie awake at night wondering whether we took the easy option by falling back into bed rather than getting divorced. Would we have bought the bookshop, or would we have been unable to decide where we wanted to be? I loved Neil, and he loved me, but I honestly don't know if we would have made it work. I can't help thinking that we might have ended up exactly where we were before, just in a different place. Maybe we were kidding ourselves that it was going to work this time.'

We stopped at a small shelter, somewhere people

could wait if the river was too high to cross. Ahead was a wide bank where a tumble of grey rocks sat above the water that was pouring over them and down towards the raging river. Jess was there to help us across if we needed it. I could see Nathan as well. He would know how scared I was at the idea of balancing my way across on rocks.

'There's something else keeping me awake night after night too,' I confessed. 'The idea that I took Neil away from Vanessa just because I didn't want her to have him, because I didn't want to lose what we'd built for our kids. Guilt about the child she's carrying is eating me up inside.'

'She's pregnant?'

I nodded. 'We found out the day before Neil died. And now she's suing me for the portion of his estate that she says she would have got if we'd divorced.'

'What did you say? Your husband's ex-girlfriend is suing his estate?'

'Yes.'

He rubbed at his forehead, his hand coming down to cup his chin. 'Fuck. No wonder you're so upset. But –'

'Don't say any more,' I said. 'Nathan doesn't know the part about Vanessa disputing probate.'

'That's not the kind of thing you should be keeping from your children,' Tom said. 'I can imagine what mine would have to say.'

'I know it's wrong, but I haven't been thinking

straight and the whole thing is now out of control, so please, don't say a word.'

He watched my face as my eyes left his and focused on where we needed to walk. I didn't know how I was going to get to the other side of the river without falling, without twisting an ankle or a knee, and without embarrassing myself more than I had already today.

'Okay, but the subject isn't closed,' he warned.

I nodded, and then Nathan was beside me to help me across the rocks and for the short walk to the lodge.

In my room, I took the cover off my pack to see what damage the rain had caused to the contents. I'd taken the precaution of packing everything into a separate liner bag, and as a result it was all thankfully still dry. I took my time in the shower, then spent longer than I needed to washing my clothes and hanging them in the drying room. My boots were soaked, but we'd been warned that the heat in the drying room could damage boots and packs; and not to leave them outside our rooms either, as the cheeky keas – a large, noisy and very naughty alpine parrot – would ruin them. I brushed the mud off my boots as best I could and left them inside my room.

Unable to avoid it any longer, I wandered down to the common area. Nathan saw me and waved me over. He was engaged in a game of Scrabble with the Arizonas, so I poured myself a cup of tea and went to join them.

Tom, I noticed, was sitting at the opposite end of the room talking to the couple from Auckland. His eyes caught mine and he smiled. I forced a smile in return and sat down in the space Nathan had left for me. Now that I was clean and dry I felt mortified that Tom had seen and heard me at my absolute worst. Not that I knew why it mattered, but somehow it did.

'Tom seems nice,' Nathan commented.

'Yes, he is.' I looked at Nathan, but his eyes hadn't strayed from the Scrabble board. 'Don't go thinking that,' I warned.

'I wasn't thinking anything.'

'Yes, you were, so don't. I like his company but that's all.'

'If you say so.' He didn't sound convinced.

'I do say so.' I leaned forward to move his letters around. 'There you go – you can put "chided" on that triple word score.'

He grinned at me. 'And I'll consider myself chided too.'

The back wall of the lounge area was made up of floor-to-ceiling windows that looked out across the forest and to the mountains that surrounded us, all of which were streaked with silvery streams of water. It felt as though the lodge had been airlifted in and dropped in the clearing. It had stopped raining – for now – and a huge olive-green bird flew past the window, flashes of bright orange visible under its wings. A kea.

It settled on the deck outside the common room and began attacking an old boot that was attached to a pole much like one a cat would scratch on.

Another bird flew past and settled in the same spot. I wandered out to the deck to watch them wrestle with what was left of the boots, their sharp curved beaks ripping into the leather uppers. A third bird arrived and proceeded to tear into the already damaged rubber soles of another boot.

'And that's why we don't leave our boots or our packs outside,' Tom said. He'd come out to watch the birds too. 'These guys are clowns, but destructive ones. Everyone has a story about tourists coming back to their car to find the windscreen wipers have been stripped, or trampers whose boots have been ruined overnight.'

'They're hilarious. Do they only live down here?'

'Only in the alpine areas on the South Island. There's a spot near the tunnel on the road into Milford Sound where you always see some. Tourists stop there a lot because the views are great, and these guys,' he indicated the parrots, 'are smart. They've learned that where there are tourists, there's fun to be had.'

We watched the birds' antics a few minutes longer. Over on the railing, two birds were hanging off the same boot.

'I got the impression that you were avoiding me before,' Tom said.

I attempted to look perplexed. 'Really? When?'

He raised his eyebrows slightly. 'You know perfectly well when.'

I lowered my gaze. 'Maybe. Yes, I suppose I was.' I raised my eyes and met his. 'I owe you an apology. I have no idea what got into me today, with the crying and the vomiting and then the offloading. I must have seemed like a mad woman and I'm not – not really.'

His smile was gentle. 'You didn't seem mad – just very sad. There's obviously a lot on your mind. If I was in the same position, I don't think I'd be dealing with it as well as you are.'

'Thank you for that,' I said, 'but I don't think I'm dealing with it at all well. I'm tired and I'm angry and I can't seem to pinpoint exactly who or what I'm angry at – it comes in waves.'

'Are you sleeping okay?' He shook his head. 'Ignore that, it's a stupid question. Of course you're not sleeping properly.' He paused. 'I know it's not why you booked this trip, but is that one of the reasons you're here now? To punish yourself?'

I drew in a deep breath and let the possibility of what he'd said wander around in my head. Finally I nodded. 'Perhaps.'

At that moment Jess came out onto the deck. 'Just how funny are the keas? Now you know why we tell you not to leave your gear outside!'

'We sure do,' I said.

'Just letting you know that the bar is open. Dinner will be at six, and we'll do the briefing for tomorrow after that.' She looked out into the mist where the rain was starting again. 'Unfortunately I think we'll have more of the same tomorrow. Heavy falls are forecast overnight and it's going to make the climb and the descent difficult. Part of the main track down was taken out by an avalanche during the winter so we have to use the emergency track, which is much steeper and tougher going, especially in the wet.'

'How to sell it to us, Jess,' Tom said.

'I know.' She looked at me and must have seen the concern on my face. 'Don't worry, Kate. We'll get you up and back okay. Anyway, you guys are into drinking time and I have some tables to set.'

As if on cue, the rain came towards us in a sheet. The birds took off loudly, and Tom inclined his head towards the door. 'Perfect timing. After the day you've had, it's my shout – no arguments.'

'I wouldn't dream of it.' Besides, I was hoping that the wine would take my mind off the climb we had to do tomorrow.

Twenty-seven

It rained again all night, beating against the roof of the lodge incessantly. As it rained, the squatters inside my head took up their usual positions.

'This whole thing was a ridiculous idea,' one said.

'What made you think you could do this?' asked another. 'What if you slip off the mountain or down a waterfall?'

'You know you could die up there and what would happen to the court case then?'

'How could you keep something like this from your kids? They're not children any more, they're grown adults. Tom was right – they have a right to know what's going on.'

I popped in some earplugs and lay on my side with my hand clapped over the other ear. It muffled the rain but not the voices.

Over a breakfast that I was unable to stomach, Nathan announced his intention to walk with me all day. 'I want to hit the top of that mountain with you, Mum.'

I smiled weakly and didn't argue. I suspected I was

going to need all the support I could get today.

Tom brought his coffee over and sat beside me, setting the brown paper bag containing his lunch on the table. 'Ready for today?'

I shook my head. My empty stomach was churning so badly that I wasn't sure I'd even keep my tea down.

He took a look at the breakfast I'd barely touched. 'Nervous tummy?' he guessed.

'Yes, ridiculous, isn't it?' I attempted a laugh but it came out strained.

He shook his head. 'No, not at all. I'm guessing that after yesterday you probably didn't sleep well either?'

'Do I look that bad?'

The face I'd seen in the bathroom mirror this morning certainly wasn't pretty. My eyes looked as weary as I felt, and the shadows below them were heavy and dark. My face had no colour and my hair no life. I'd run my fingers through my short curls in an attempt to give them some spring, but figured they'd soon be flattened by my beanie and the hood of my jacket anyway.

'You look tired,' he said, 'and like a woman who is about to climb a mountain with the weight of the world already on her back.'

'Something like that.'

He sipped at his coffee. 'Are you going to eat any more of that?'

'No.' I pushed my plate away.

'Okay, then I want you to fill your pockets with barley sugars and chocolate. You're going to need something in your tank, and I remember Shellie always used to make the kids suck on barley sugars for motion sickness so it will help with that too.'

'Thanks, I'll do that,' I said.

Nathan joined us, two bulging brown paper bags in his hand. 'I'm a growing boy,' he said when I raised my eyebrows at the amount of food he had. 'I'm sticking with Mum today,' he said to Tom. 'Are you walking with us too?'

'If that's alright with you two?' Tom directed his question to me, but Nathan answered.

'Absolutely.' His face was pure innocence, but there was something dancing in his eyes. If I didn't know better I might have thought he was trying his hand at a spot of matchmaking.

I shrugged in resignation. 'Okay. Well, the sooner we get out there, the sooner we can get this thing over and done with.'

'Come on, Mum, where's your sense of adventure. It's not just about getting to the top and back down again – it's about the journey.' Nathan grinned. 'Besides, this was all your idea in the first place, remember?'

Four hours later, I was wishing I could blame someone else for the idea.

We'd been climbing steadily – or, in my case,

unsteadily – for hours. It was still raining and the rocks underfoot were slippery. Waterfalls ran down the mountain and over the path we were walking on. Every so often I'd look up and see nothing ahead but endless switchbacks.

Nathan and Tom kept up a constant stream of conversation, talking about everything from wines to rugby to the conservation work Nathan had been doing. I listened but didn't contribute. I could think, breathe and walk at the same time, but talking as well was one task too many. My thighs burned and as comfortable as my pack was, it was weighing heavily on my hips as we continued to tramp uphill. Every so often I unwrapped a barley sugar and sucked on it, the sugar giving me a quick surge of energy. At first I stopped at the end of each switchback, but as the time wore on and the rain came down, I was stopping every couple of hundred metres. Neither Tom nor Nathan commented, just paused their conversation until I was ready to walk again.

We'd started climbing under the cover of the beech forest, but now emerged into alpine country. On the one hand we could see more clearly where we were going, but on the other we were so much more exposed to the elements. Luckily, the rain had changed from a steady downpour to a soft barely-there drizzle.

'How many of these things are there?' I asked at one point.

'Zig-zags? I don't know,' said Nathan, sounding way too cheery for someone who'd walked miles uphill on a rocky path in the rain. 'Eleven? Maybe fourteen?'

'There's a big difference between eleven and fourteen,' I grumbled.

'Didn't they say last night that a couple of them have an A, B and C?' Tom offered. 'I think that's where the fourteen might come from.'

'I wasn't listening last night,' I admitted, my hands on my knees and my back hunched as I fought to get air into my lungs.

After dinner, Tom and I had taken our wines to a lounge at the edge of the room. Although I'd kept one ear on what Cody was telling us we could expect today, in truth I hadn't wanted to know. I'd listened up to the part about walking uphill for two miles over a series of switchbacks, or zig-zagging paths; and after that I'd concentrated on my wine and what Tom was telling me about the challenges of winemaking in a cold climate.

'Well, there you go,' said Nathan. 'That'll teach you to drink wine during an important briefing.'

'How many do you think we've done?' I asked, placing a hand on my lower back to support myself as I straightened.

'I don't know,' said Tom. 'Maybe nine. We should be able to see the top soon. But check out how far we've come.'

The three of us looked back down the pass into

the valleys. Waterfalls sprang from the sides of the mountains around us, and as if on cue the clouds parted to show a glimpse of bright green way below. Some white flowers clung to a crevice in the side of the rock, raindrops hanging from their delicate petals. The sun broke through briefly, lighting the lichen on the trees and turning the waterfalls to silver.

'It's beautiful,' I managed.

Although there were people on track in front of and behind us, it felt for those few minutes as though we were the only people on earth. Other than the rustling of the trees and the constant drip of water falling from the leaves, or trickling through the rocks and down the side of the mountain, there was nothing. Just two men and a heavy-breathing middle-aged woman.

Jess found us like that. She bounded around the corner and grinned when she saw us. 'I wondered where you guys were.' She turned to me. 'How are you going?'

'Next question?' I attempted a smile but didn't have the energy for it.

'The good news is you've not far to go – in fact, around the next switchback you'll see the memorial. But we won't get there hanging around here.'

She led off, Nathan with her, while Tom and I fell a little behind.

'How are you doing?' he asked.

'It hurts,' I admitted. 'A lot.'

'You've hardly said a word this morning.'

'You two were chattering away so I couldn't get a word in.'

'I'd hardly call it chattering.'

'Well, that's how it seemed to me.' I knew I sounded churlish but couldn't seem to help myself.

He was silent for a few seconds, then said, 'What's wrong, Kate?'

'What could be wrong? I'm under-prepared for a hike that everyone says is perfectly doable for anyone with average fitness, and I'm hurting like I've never hurt before. I'm wet through for the second day in a row. I shouldn't be out here doing this – I've nothing to prove to anyone any more. I should be at home preparing for a court case, not playing at being an adventurer out here in the middle of nowhere.'

'And that's what's been going through your head all morning? You want it to hurt so you can add that to your list and beat yourself up a bit more. It's not your fault Neil died, Kate.'

'Do you think I don't know that? But I *want* to blame myself – or Vanessa. I want someone to blame so I don't have to feel angry with Neil because he's not here any more for me to feel angry at. And I'm so very angry with him, Tom. Not just for leaving me, but for leaving me with this mess.'

Hot tears had come to my eyes and I let them run. A lump rose to my throat and made breathing hard. I pounded at my chest through the layers of rain jacket and merino to try and shift it. Crying was the last thing I should be doing. Not only did it make it harder to breathe, it made it impossible to see where I was placing my feet.

'I know I shouldn't be angry with him,' I went on. 'But, for Christ's sake, how unlucky can one man be? Nathan was an accident – the most delightful accident in the world, but an accident. I didn't know I was pregnant with him until after we'd broken up and Neil had left town. Then Ash was an accident – a reunion baby. I was four months pregnant when we got married. Now, just when things were falling into place for us, he had another accidental pregnancy – and left me with the mess to clean up. One I understand, but three times? And the biggest joke is, now we don't even know if the baby's his or not, but I still have to go to court and argue about it.' I stopped and took some deep breaths. 'I'm sorry. I'm tired and I'm hurting and I just want everything to be over – especially this fucking climb.'

My voice rose on the last sentence, and as we rounded the bend towards the memorial stone I walked straight into Nathan. His face was pure stone.

'Mum – what do you have to go to court to argue about?'

Tom stepped back, and joined Jess who was standing to one side. I kept walking towards the memorial, Nathan beside me.

'Mum?' he prompted.

'I should have told you and Ash, but I didn't know how.'

'Told us what?' His voice was as expressionless as his face.

'Vanessa is suing your father's estate for what she thinks he would have got if he and I had divorced. She's saying it's in lieu of the maintenance your father isn't around to pay.'

'What the absolute fuck? That fucking money-grabbing bitch! I fucking knew it would come to something like this. I thought we'd gotten off lightly. How long have you known?'

'About six weeks, I suppose.' My voice was small. Nathan's anger was currently directed towards Vanessa, but I knew that it would be directed to me at some point – and deservedly so.

'Who else aside from him,' he nodded towards Tom, 'knows? And why does he know?'

'It all got too much for me at one point yesterday on track. It's helped to talk about it with someone who knows nothing about us. As for who else knows? Mari was there when I got the letter, and Lachie and Mike have been helping me with the legal stuff.'

'And at no point did it occur to you that you should tell Ash or me? After all, it's not like it's any of our business. It's not as if we're two grown adults. It's not as if we care about you and would want to help you.'

We'd reached the memorial. Nathan took his backpack off, almost throwing it to one side, and stalked across to the edge to look out into nothing. The clouds were swirling around our heads and the mountains around us came in and out of visibility. I took my pack off and walked over to join him.

'I'm sorry, Nath, I really am. I just didn't know how to tell you. I didn't know where to start.'

He looked at me blindly, tears in his eyes. He used the back of his hand to scrub them away. 'Why do you think you've got to take care of everything all the time, Mum? Ash and I want to help you, we really do, but you don't let anyone in. I don't know whether it goes back to when Dad was gone that first time and you had to look after me on your own, or whether it's just that you feel you need to control everything. But sometimes, Mum, there are things you can't control, and that's when we want to be there for you. The way you always were for us.' He shook his head, more tears in his eyes. 'Over the years there were so many things neither of us told you about because we just knew you'd march in and want to fix them for us, and we knew we had to learn how to do that for ourselves.'

He paused. 'I've seen how hard it's been for you over the last few years since Dad left, pretending that everything was all happy families when I knew how upset you must have been. I've seen you try and hold it together since he's been gone, but you don't have to do that, Mum. You really don't. You've been looking after someone since you were nineteen years old, and while I appreciate it and Ash appreciates it and everyone you feed and care for appreciates it, it's time to let someone care about you and look after you now – and that's never going to happen as long as you push us all out of the way.' He brushed at his eyes again. 'You know, I'm so fucking angry that Dad went and died. And if she's suing us, it could be years before you can move on. How dare he leave you with that? How can you not be angry with him?'

'Oh, Nath, I'm furious with him, but I'm trying so hard not to be – partly because I loved him, partly because he's not here to be angry with, and –'

'And if he was here, he'd be expecting you to clean up the mess anyway – the way he always expected you to. Face it, Mum, even if he hadn't died, you'd be dealing with a court case. Dad would let you make the decisions and call the shots and he'd carry on as if everything was fine. I loved him too, but I also know what he was like.'

I sank down on a rock away from the memorial stones, absently noticing the tiny white lilies growing out from a crack. It felt like we were on the top of the world, up in the clouds; how could something so beautiful and as delicate as these flowers possibly survive up here?

I looked up at Nathan; the tears were flowing freely down his cheeks now. I could see out the corner of my eye that Jess and Tom were sipping something out of cups. They were far enough away to give us space and also as warning for anyone else coming up the track.

'I miss him, Mum,' Nath said.

'I know. I do too.'

I got to my feet and wrapped my arms around him, feeling his sobs echo through my body. When I felt him take a deep breath, I stepped out of his arms and turned to look over the valley, giving him the opportunity to recover himself. The clouds had cleared, almost miraculously, and displayed a view down the valley that we'd walked through in the rain yesterday.

'I wish Dad was here to see this,' Nathan said.

'Me too. He'd love it here.'

I knew it made no sense at all, but as I looked out over the precipice it felt as though Neil was standing beside me. I turned to where I imagined him to be and saw him smiling at me in that slow, gentle way.

'I love you, Katie, but it's time to let me go,' he said.

The tears ran silently down my face and I nodded once. 'I know,' I whispered. 'I love you.'

As the wind blew the clouds around I could have sworn I heard him say, 'Goodbye, my darling Katie.' And then he was gone.

'Goodbye,' I said to the empty space.

'It feels like he was here, Mum,' Nathan said. 'With us. Saying goodbye. I know he can't be, but it felt like it.'

'Yes, I felt it too,' I said. 'But now he's gone.'

We stood in silence for a little while longer, then Nathan looked to where Tom was standing with Jess and said, 'Don't close yourself off, Mum. Dad would hate that.'

I didn't reply, but he was right. Neil would hate it if he thought I was closing myself off to the possibility of living my life. As I looked at the vista spread out before us, I finally understood what it was that he'd learned on his mountain. He always used to say that all he ever wanted was for me to be happy. He'd said it when he left too, and I'd wailed that I couldn't be happy without him. He'd smiled sadly and said that we weren't happy together any more and that was why he was leaving – to give me a chance to live my life before it was too late. If I didn't take that opportunity now, what would it all have been for? When Neil climbed his mountain, he'd found the courage to let go of me. Now, on my mountain, I had to do the same for him.

Jess signalled to us, and I looked down the track and saw that the couple from Auckland were approaching. I rubbed at my eyes until all signs of moisture had gone, picked up my pack and went to join Jess and Tom. Each held a steaming mug of hot chocolate. I took mine from Tom and smiled gratefully at him.

'Okay?' he asked.

The smile I gave him was genuine. 'Yes. It is. Well, I think it will be.'

He nodded and smiled back, the warmth reaching his eyes. 'I'm glad. You've done a good job there. With Nathan.' He inclined his head towards where Nathan and Jess were standing.

'I know. Some of my best work.'

Twenty-eight

The emotion at the Mackinnon Memorial seemed to have left Nathan and me drained. During our lunch stop at the hut, we sat mostly in silence while we ate our sandwiches. I took advantage of the relative privacy to duck into a side room and strip off my wet merino and equally wet base layer, swapping both for a dry version. There was nothing I could do about my bra, which was soaked through, but for now I was as warm and dry as I could be in the circumstances.

We all took turns using the toilet with the best view in the world, leaving the door open so we could see all the way down the valley. When we left the hut, Jess stayed behind to wait for Kelsey, who was with Bob and Penny and Dale and Janelle. She said she'd catch up once she'd done the handover.

If I'd thought the way up was physically tough, going down was mentally exhausting. The emergency track was steeper than the ascent and seemed to be mostly rubble. Every rock was slick with water, and a false step promised at best a turned ankle and at worst a slide off the edge. It took most of our concentration to pick our way gradually down and we took it slowly, Nathan going first, and helping me where necessary, and Tom bringing up the rear.

On the way up I'd hurt from the physical effort of the climb; going down, my knees burned and my toes pushed painfully against the ends of my boots. The rain had started again and at times it seemed as though we were literally walking down a waterfall. A constant fear of falling made me overly careful and I deliberated over every foot placement, continually apologising to Nathan and Tom for slowing them down.

'Mum, enough!' Nath said. 'We get it – you're sorry for slowing us down.'

'It's fine, Kate,' said Tom. 'We have plenty of time.'

After we'd been walking for around ninety minutes, Jess caught up with us not far from the shelter spot. We took our packs off and dug out our chocolate bars. Despite having changed up at the pass hut, I was again soaked through. My knees felt like knives were being driven into them and I hated to think about the condition of my feet.

Tom looked as though he felt the same. He glanced at me and grimaced. 'Knees?'

'Yep. You?'

'Uh-huh. Jess was just telling me that she's had word the older group are already back at the lodge. All I can say is they must have joints the age of Jess and Nathan.'

'Or have a lot of hiking practice.'

His chuckle was rueful. 'Are you feeling better for having talked to Nathan?'

'Yes, much better.'

It was true. Despite the weight of my pack, I felt as though my load had lightened substantially. The emotional flare-up between Nathan and me was overdue, as were, I suspected, his tears. Ash had let her feelings out months ago – plus she had Reece. Nathan had no one he could share his with.

'At the risk of apologising again, you must be wondering just how much more drama there is to come,' I said.

Tom smiled at me. It was a gentle smile and warmed my freezing core. 'Not at all. I am, however, interested in your comment before about how you're no longer certain that Vanessa's baby is Neil's.'

Nathan turned from his conversation with Jess. 'Yes, I'd forgotten about that. What's the story there?'

'How about we walk and talk?' suggested Jess. 'I'd like us to get to Quinton Lodge at some point this afternoon. We still have about another two hours to go, and for much of that we'll be tracking beside the river.'

So we put our packs on and started walking again. We were back in the beech forest and the moss and ferns made it feel as though we were walking through a fairyland dripping with green. I put my rain hood back on over my beanie and told them how Lachie and Mike had found out about Vanessa seeing someone else and had obtained the proof via social media.

'I just don't know how to use the information,' I said once I'd finished the story.

'I know how I'd like to use it,' muttered Jess. 'Not that it's any of my business of course.'

'I'm with Jess,' said Nathan.

I wondered if he realised what he'd said, but Jess ducked her suspiciously pink face.

'You've definitely got enough information to cast some doubt on both the common-law wife argument and the parentage,' Tom said. 'At least enough to insist on a DNA sample – if you wanted that. It would delay proceedings, which might also be a tactic that would work in your favour, especially if she is desperate for the money.' He paused and studied my face. 'But I'm guessing that you're not sure about using the information because you don't think it's what your husband would have wanted.'

I nodded at his astuteness. 'Exactly. I'm angry enough with her that I don't care how long it takes or how much it costs. But my mother, if she was here, would tell me that's biting my nose off to spite my face. I can't move forward as long as the proceedings are still happening.'

'What do you think Neil would do?'

Nathan laughed at that. 'I tell you what Dad would do. He'd eventually tell Mum what was going on –

usually once it was far enough down the track to be a real problem – then he'd wait for her to fix it. I loved him to pieces, but Dad did like to bury his head in the sand – or in his case, a book – and pretend the real world wasn't going on. Having said that, he had more integrity than anyone else I know. He would never have walked away from his responsibilities. Even if he was here, I suspect we'd still be dealing with this. What do *you* want to do, Mum?'

I sighed heavily before replying. 'I thought I wanted to fight, but I actually just want it all to be over.'

'But what if you could win?' Nathan asked.

'At what cost? I don't like her any more than you do, but when all is said and done, your father loved her for a time, and she must have loved him too. If he was still alive, we would have offered her a capital settlement in lieu of maintenance – just so we could get on with our lives.'

'Then that's what we'll do now,' decided Nathan.

'Just like that?'

'Yep. We'll need to talk to Ash first, of course – and you know she's going to fly off the handle – but it's what Dad would have done. And not just because it's the easiest way out, but because he would have thought it was the right thing to do.'

'From what you've told us,' offered Tom, 'there are plenty of reasons for her to take a settlement that's substantially less than the amount she's asking for.'

'That's decided then,' said Nathan. 'We wave Vanessa goodbye, and then we find you a bookshop to buy.'

The track had narrowed again and Nathan and Jess walked ahead. By unspoken agreement Tom and I held back.

'Tell me about the bookshop,' he said. 'You mentioned yesterday that you wanted it also to be an evening college. What's that about?'

'I've often wondered whether I would have been as restless as I was if I'd had something to occupy my mind – something to bring me some sort of creative fulfilment. Instead of looking outside my marriage, or blaming it for how I was feeling, it would have been great if I could have found what was missing inside me within the structure of what we had. I'm certain there are other women out there – not just at my age, but older and younger – who want to learn but have neither the money nor the ability to study formally. Perhaps they're in a town without those facilities, or perhaps they're home with children, or perhaps they just want to gather information or meet up with other people who share their interests. So while Neil wanted to sell books and have a couple of chairs around for browsing and reading, I wanted a space that we could use for writers' groups, or offer at a low cost to people who wanted to run creative workshops, or meet-ups for people new to the area, or people into family history or photography or whatever. I wanted it to be a true community space at an affordable price. Maybe have a cafe attached selling coffee and tea and a simple range of scones or soups. Possibly even a secondhand or swap type of shop – almost like a community library. You know, bring a book, take a book. That sort of thing.'

'That's a great idea,' Tom said, 'but not one for the city. It would work brilliantly in a place like Queenstown, where the population can be quite seasonal and transient. It's actually difficult to meet people and make friends because of that. Maybe you should explore the area while you're here.'

'That's what Neil had suggested. It's why I added a couple of days to the end of the walk – so we could have a look around.'

'Well, there's no reason you can't still do that. Let me show you around.'

The warmth that filled my face confused me and I tripped on a tree root. He grabbed my arm to steady me and didn't let go straight away.

'Don't feel uncomfortable, Kate,' he said. 'I know it's early days, but I like you and I want to get to know you better. There's no pressure and no expectations. Okay?'

I nodded slowly. 'Okay. That sounds nice then.'

In the lodge that evening I spent a long time under the shower, trying to warm all the parts of me that had been so cold and so wet for so long. When I took my boots off, my feet were swollen and crinkled from water, the toes throbbing from banging against the ends of my boots during the long, slow descent. I suspected I'd be losing at least a few of those toenails.

I rinsed my clothes out and hung them in the drying room, sparing a moment to think about the freedom walkers who would tomorrow be climbing back into today's wet clothes.

As cold and as sore as I was, there was the spark of something deep inside me that could have been hope – although it had been so long since I'd felt anything other than numb or angry, I didn't know whether to trust the feeling. I'd felt broken after Neil left and so hurt after he died that I'd feared I'd never be able to feel anything good again. Tom had been spot on – I'd wanted the walking to hurt. Not only did I want to punish myself, but I wanted to feel *something* other than numb and broken. It wasn't so much that I wanted to lose myself in the pain of the walk, but that I wanted it to completely break me open so I could see inside and find myself again.

For those few minutes when the clouds had cleared at the top of Mackinnon Pass, I'd seen it all clearly. I'd felt Neil's presence so strongly – as if he was standing beside me at the edge of that precipice, close enough for me to say goodbye and mean it. I'd even convinced myself that I'd heard the same loving farewell from him. Everything Neil had ever done was to make me happy. I owed it to him to do my best to *be* happy. Maybe not now, maybe not next week, but sometime soon.

That night, for the first time since Neil died, I had an appetite. I managed to eat all of my dinner, including dessert.

And when the lights went out, despite the throbbing in my toes and knowing that I had the equivalent of a half-marathon still to walk tomorrow, I went straight to sleep, waking only when the generator and lights came back on the next morning.

Twenty-nine

Tom commented at breakfast that I looked as though I'd slept better. I was able to honestly tell him that I felt great. Then I tucked into a cooked breakfast, and set off with a spring in my step. Despite the pain in my body, and the pack on my back, I felt lighter than I had done in I couldn't remember how long.

The Arizonas had seemingly admitted defeat in their quest to win over Nathan, and set off with him this morning chattering and giggling to each other. It made a change from all the hair flicking, big eyes and meaningful silences he'd been getting over the last few days from them. Jess was waiting behind to walk with the slower walkers, so Tom and I set out somewhere in the middle.

Although the distance today was the longest, there was no climbing, no nasty descents, and nothing terribly challenging – just a muddy track and plenty of sandflies. We left the lodge in drizzle, but by the time we arrived at our morning-tea stop the sun had come out and it was warmer than it had been all week.

We shed beanies, gloves, rain jackets and top layers, pushing them into our packs and spraying every inch of exposed skin with insect repellent before hitting the track again.

Although I'd seen Tom without his many layers in the lodge each night, he'd been wearing long-sleeved T-shirts. Perhaps I'd been too preoccupied to notice him before, but I was certainly noticing him now – and very much liking what I saw. Well-toned biceps peeked out from the short sleeves of his tee, and his stomach appeared to be completely flat. Neil had the physique of a man who worked out and ran regularly; Tom's body was that of a man who did physical labour.

I tried not to think of the picture I presented to him: a middle-aged woman with shortish curly hair that had been flattened under a beanie all week, eyes that were still shadowed, and a body that was decidedly squidgy. Not that it mattered how I appeared to him. Still, I was looking forward to getting back to Queenstown and washing my hair and putting on some make-up and decent clothes that hid the lumps and bumps rather than highlighting them.

Aside from breaks and when we stopped by the falls for lunch, Tom and I walked most of the way without company. The scenery was fabulous and with the sun shining the miles flew by. We chatted lightly and easily, segueing from subject to subject. I told him how I couldn't hold a note to save myself, but still sang loudly when I was cooking or cleaning; and he told me how he could never remember the punchline to a joke. We talked about our parents, our siblings, our childhood dreams, our marriages. We talked about books (he was a corner-turner like me), movies (I liked romcoms, he preferred more action) and TV (we both liked *MasterChef* and British police dramas). We talked about where we were when we heard about John Lennon dying, Princess Diana, 9/11, the sinking of the *Rainbow Warrior*, Tiananmen Square. We talked about the issues of the day and found that politically we were aligned. When we thought that we'd exhausted every possible topic, we found even more to talk about.

By mid-afternoon we arrived at Sandfly Point, the official end of the track. Kelsey was there, with a swarm of sandflies, to greet us and congratulate us for finishing.

Nathan and the Arizonas had also waited until we arrived so we could all board the boat for the short trip across to Mitre Peak Lodge together. Nathan hugged me and shook Tom's hand. In the jubilation of the moment, the pain of yesterday's climb and descent felt like it had been experienced by someone else.

My room overlooked Milford Sound and the view of the remarkable Mitre Peak rising above it. Even more wondrous than the view was the bath.

I said to Tom, who had been allocated a room just down the hall, 'I'll see you sometime next year. I don't intend to come out of that bath for some time.'

He laughed and replied, 'But then you'll miss out on the red wine downstairs.'

Although we'd had the option to send a bag containing clean clothes and make-up along with the bus that had arrived today to drive us back to Queenstown tomorrow, at the time I hadn't seen the point. I regretted it now. I languished in the bath for ages and was at least able to rinse out my hair, but other than that there was little I could do to make myself look more presentable.

Some of the others had made much more of an effort – the guides especially. Nathan stopped still when his eyes hit Jess. Her light-brown hair was out of its usual ponytail and had been straightened. She'd applied some make-up – not too much, just some mascara and lip gloss – and was wearing a short strappy dress that showed her toned legs and arms to their best advantage.

'Wow, Jess, you look … just wow,' he said.

She lowered her eyes and pushed a strand of hair behind her ears. 'I was thinking, when we get back to Queenstown – if you're not busy tomorrow night – you might like to come down to the rugby club with me?' She lifted her head and met his gaze.

'I'd like that,' he said softly.

They both grinned at each other and then Jess said quickly, 'Good. That's sorted then. I'll talk to you later.'

I watched her whirl away. 'That girl has way too much energy.'

Nathan was watching her too, still smiling. 'She does, doesn't she?'

The rest of the evening had a convivial party atmosphere. We'd all walked the equivalent of a half-marathon today on legs that were sore from the previous day in boots that hadn't been dry since Monday. It was an experience that we all had in common.

For me, and I thought for Nathan, it had been more intense than that. We'd each confronted our grief and left what needed to be left behind up on the mountain. Now the healing could begin.

Before we boarded the bus back to Queenstown, a cruise of Milford Sound had been scheduled. The blue sky from the previous day had held and the scenery was picture-perfect magnificent.

Jess joined Tom and me on the deck. 'You know, we're lucky – they have so much rainfall down here that days like this are remarkable. Although it's just as amazing seeing it in the rain with the waterfalls from every mountain.'

'You must get sick of seeing it all the time,' I said.

'Absolutely not. I love the tramping and the scenery. I used to guide all season, but since I bought Beach Road I manage only a couple of tours a year. Now that Richie's back, I can leave the cafe more often in Max's capable hands and get on track again.'

'Do you just do the Milford?' asked Tom.

She shook her head. 'No, I do Routeburn Track as well – and the occasional Greenstone Valley–Routeburn double. Richie's keen to do more tramping so he and I do the occasional run up Queenstown Hill. We did Ben Lomond the Sunday before last – it's a steep climb and took us most of the day. He's not into the multi-day tramps at the moment – he doesn't like to be away from Max for too long.'

'You mentioned the other day that she's pregnant,' I said.

'Yes. Deliriously so. They're so wrapped up in each other it would be disgusting to watch if I didn't love them both so much.' She laughed but there was a wistful expression on her face for the briefest of moments. Then it was gone and the smile was back. 'You'll have to drop into Beach Road over the weekend and try some of her baking. She's started doing this lemon cheesecake that sells out almost as soon as I put it out!'

'I'll make sure we do.'

'Okay then, I'd better go make sure that everyone else is under control. We're coming up to the Falls, so if you don't want to get soaked I'd advise putting on a jacket or going inside.'

On the bus back to Queenstown, Nathan moved up the front to sit beside Jess, and Tom took his place beside me. We ate our lunch and chatted for most of the way to Te Anau, where we stopped for toilets and coffee. Once back on the road I lay my head on Tom's shoulder and slept, waking with a jolt when the bus came to a stop. I blinked a few times as I tried to work out where I was, and felt my face grow warm when I realised that my pillow was a beautifully muscled male arm.

'Oh god, I'm so sorry,' I said.

He laughed at the horror on my face. 'It's okay. I dozed for a bit as well, and it's been a while since I slept with a woman too.' As my face grew hotter at both his comment and the picture we must have presented with our heads so close together as we both slept, he said, 'That didn't come out quite the way I intended it to.' We met each other's eyes and giggled.

He took a deep breath. 'You're probably too tired, but I thought that if Nathan was out with Jess tonight, you might like to have dinner with me. It wouldn't be anything fancy – but what do you think?'

'Are you sure you haven't had enough of me over the last couple of days?'

'This is going to sound weird, but I'm too old to be playing games. The thing is, I can't imagine having enough of you and I'm conscious of the fact that you're going home again in a few days, so I want to make the most of that time.'

I opened my mouth to say that it was all too soon, that I liked him too, but … But I couldn't think of the excuses I should have used.

'I know that it's probably too soon for you,' he went on, 'and I'm fine with that. If it makes you feel better, let's just be friends until you're ready. There's absolutely no pressure and no obligation.' He smiled at me, and his offer felt as comfortable as his arm had been a few moments ago.

'Dinner sounds lovely,' I said.

Dinner was lovely. He picked me up from my hotel near the lake and we walked around the foreshore to a casual restaurant specialising in Asian-style street food. We ate and talked until I couldn't hide my yawns.

'I hate to admit it,' Tom said, 'but I'm feeling it too. And it's not even nine!'

'We must be getting old,' I said.

'Either that or we've just walked nearly thirty-five miles over the last few days.'

'No, that would have absolutely nothing to do with it.'

He walked me back to my hotel and left me at the front entrance. 'I'll pick you up at nine tomorrow,' he said. 'We'll go have breakfast at Jess's cafe and then I'm taking you for a drive.'

'That sounds good,' I said, and went inside and straight to bed – where I fell asleep immediately.

Beach Road was busy when we arrived the following morning, but Tom managed to find us a seat at the counter. He placed our order with a blonde woman who greeted him warmly in a soft English accent.

'Tom! You're back! How was it?'

'It was great. Fabulous scenery – just as Jess described. The weather for the first few days was dire though.'

'Yes, it wasn't nice here either – I wouldn't have liked to be walking in it.'

'No Jess this morning?'

'No. She called me early and asked if I could help out until she made it in. Richie and I met up with her last night – she was at the rugby club with a very cute Aussie, but don't tell Richie I said that. Anyway, between you and me I wouldn't be surprised if … well, you know.'

Tom laughed and turned to me. 'Did Nathan come back to the hotel last night?'

'I don't think so. He texted me very early this morning telling me he'd see me later this afternoon.' So, Jess and Nathan had spent the night together.

'Max, this is my friend Kate,' Tom said. 'She's over from Sydney – we met on track. Her son Nathan is who Jess was out with last night.'

'I'm pleased to meet you,' I told Max. 'I've heard amazing things about your baking. Apparently there's a lemon cheesecake I have to try.'

Her pale skin tinged pink and she lowered her eyes briefly. 'Oh, that's nice of you to say. I'll set some aside for you. And I'm sorry about what I said about your son.'

I smiled to ease her obvious embarrassment. 'Don't be sorry. I've been told the same by plenty of people. I can't see it myself ...'

The colour in her cheeks faded. 'I'd better take some orders and work through this queue. What can I get you guys?'

'A couple of trim flat whites please and,' Tom turned to me, 'you have to try Dan's eggs benedict.'

I nodded. 'Sounds good to me.'

'Two egg bennies and a serve of cheesecake afterwards – with two spoons, please.'

'Done,' Max said.

The food was fabulous and I immediately asked Max for the cheesecake recipe. She blushed again and asked for my email address so she could send it through to me.

As Tom and I were leaving, Nathan and Jess arrived.

'Mum! I wasn't expecting to see you here,' Nathan said.

'I'm sure you weren't.' I turned to Jess and smiled. 'You have a wonderful place here. I don't think I've ever had a better hollandaise – and I love how the eggs are served on a potato rosti rather than muffins. It makes for a lovely change.'

Jess looked pleased. 'What did I tell you? And did

you try the cheesecake?' She looked across to the cake counter where there was just one piece of cheesecake left and nodded to Max, who immediately placed it to one side – presumably for Nathan and Jess.

'I did. Max is going to send me the recipe.'

'I've got a better idea. Move over here and Max can make it for you.' She turned to Tom. 'There's your challenge – find the perfect place for Kate to have her bookshop and convince her to stay.'

I felt my cheeks go as pink as Max's had earlier and couldn't look at Tom.

At that moment, a tall, dark and very handsome man approached us. 'Don't listen to my sister,' he said. 'She always rattles off without thinking. How's it going, Tom? You made it safely across the pass obviously.'

Tom shook his hand. 'Good to see you, Richie. Max is looking well.'

Richie's eyes softened as they settled on Max. She looked up from her customer and smiled at him. 'She is, isn't she? Even though my sister does take advantage of her. What's this about ringing us in the middle of the night so Max can work and let you have a sleep-in, you lazy bugger? Or was that more to do with you?' He turned to Nathan and shook his hand in greeting. 'I might have been looking forward to a lie-in myself,' his eyes went again to Max, 'but it's good to see that Jess is in a better mood this morning than she has been in ages.'

Jess reached across and punched his arm. Rubbing where the punch had landed, Richie turned his attention to me.

'You must be Kate,' he said, holding out his hand for me to shake.

'And you must be Jess's brother, Richie.'

'I am. Jess was saying that you only have a few days here before you fly home.'

'I do. Nathan needs to be back at work on Tuesday.'

'And you?'

'No, I don't.'

'There you go then. Stay longer. Let Tom show you around. Where are you off to today?'

Jess and Richie were as bad as each other. I wondered how Max kept up with them.

'I'm taking Kate out to Glenorchy for a look,' said Tom. 'I thought we might have lunch at the pub out there. Tomorrow I was going to show her the winery and maybe do some tasting. If we have a chance, we can go to Arrowtown or across the hill to Cardrona.'

Richie nodded. 'Good choices. Anyways, I'm going to rescue Max from behind that counter so I'll see you later, Tom. Hopefully I'll see you again too, Kate.'

I said goodbye to Nathan and Jess, waved to Max, and let out a breath when we made it outside.

Tom noticed and laughed. 'Richie and Jess can be a bit like that. When they're together it's tough to get a word in, but they mean well.'

~

Neither of us mentioned what Richie had said about me staying longer, but as the day progressed I realised that I didn't want to go home. Home meant decisions and Vanessa and settlements and possibly court. Here was scenery like nothing I'd seen before and the company of a man who I was not only beginning to care about, but whose touch was making my heart race in a way I'd thought it never would again. He was treating me carefully, as if I was a flighty young horse that could be frightened off at any moment, but that didn't stop the butterflies that were set free in my belly every time our eyes met or he placed his hand in the small of my back to guide me or support me.

The road into Glenorchy was one of the most picturesque I'd seen, the scenery breathtaking in its beauty. Tom stopped the car at a lookout point so I could get out and take some photos.

'It gets most people like that,' he said when I found myself lost for words.

As Tom had told Richie, we had lunch at the pub in Glenorchy. When we were leaving the bar afterwards, the backs of our hands brushed together. Neither of us looked at the other, and neither of us moved our hands away or made to hold hands.

When Nathan's text came through, we were

heading back to Queenstown and then out to historic Arrowtown, about twenty kilometres away.

Hey there, hope you're having a great day. I was going to have dinner with Jess tonight if that's okay and will probably have another sleepover – she doesn't need to work tomorrow. If you need me though, it's no biggie to change our plans.

I smiled as I read the text, but I was also concerned that one or both of them were headed for heartbreak when Nathan went home on Monday morning.

'Is everything okay?' Tom asked.

'Yes, it's fine. Nathan was just telling me that he'll be out again with Jess tonight.'

The concern I felt must have come through in my voice, because Tom said, 'You don't sound too happy about it.'

'Oh no, I'm pleased for them. It just worries me that they're going to get hurt when we go home on Monday.'

'They're young,' he said. 'It's different. And they have other ways to stay in touch these days. Besides, it's a short flight.' Something in his tone told me that he wasn't just talking about Nathan and Jess. His next words confirmed it. 'I'll miss you when you go too. But I'm hoping that it won't be goodbye for long.'

I turned to look at him. He was focused on the road, but a little pulse beat in his jaw. There were so many things I should have said. I should have reminded him that my husband had died only a few months ago, that I had a court case that needed to be settled, a house that I needed to sell, and decisions to make about my future. Instead I said, 'Me too.'

He didn't take his eyes from the road but his smile was wide, his eyes crinkling at the edges in a way I'd begun to look for.

'If Nathan is out, why don't I cook us some steaks at home?' he said. 'I can drive you back afterwards.'

His home. That meant seeing where he lived, and where he slept. As much as parts of my body might have disagreed, I wasn't ready to sleep with another man. Not yet, anyway. I hadn't slept with anyone other than Neil since I was eighteen. What if I couldn't respond with anyone else? What if my body only worked in that way for Neil?

'Has anyone ever told you that you have a very expressive face?'

I groaned and placed my face in my hands.

'It's just dinner, Kate. A steak and a couple of glasses of wine. Maybe a salad. Nothing else, and absolutely no sex. I promise that I won't even kiss you – not until you ask me to.'

I knew that I shouldn't have been, but part of me was disappointed.

Thirty

Arrowtown was delightful, and we spent a couple of hours wandering around the shops and some of the streets in the blocks behind. Many of the miner's cottages had been preserved and I could imagine what a picture the town must be in autumn when the leaves turned. I said as much to Tom.

'It's beautiful,' he agreed. 'And yet another reason for you to come back to see it.'

We turned into a street where flags and signs advertised a cottage that was open for inspection. Sitting in an English-style garden behind a low drystone wall, the single-storey stone cottage could have come straight from the pages of a magazine. Behind it rose a hill covered in deciduous trees that would be a blaze of colour come April.

'Oh, how beautiful!' I said. 'Let's go and take a look.'

Inside, the cottage was small but immaculately restored. It consisted of two bedrooms, a bathroom, a large combined lounge and dining room, and a well-proportioned kitchen. Each of the rooms had fireplaces. Beside the main cottage was a wooden cottage with another two bedrooms, a sitting area, a modern bathroom, and a kitchen that opened onto a wide verandah and outdoor area. In the garden was yet more accommodation – a self-contained studio with attic.

Even though I knew I was in no position to make plans, my mind was whirling. I could see the stone cottage turned into a small bookshop – new books in one room and secondhand or swaps in the other. The lounge and dining space would make a fabulous tearoom and sitting or reading area. I could live in the wooden cottage next-door, and the studio would be ideal for workshops.

I said nothing to Tom, but walked through each of the rooms again. The garden would be perfect for a kitchen garden, and if I closed my eyes I could see it lit with lanterns or fairy lights on a warm summer night, a single long wooden table down the centre and people gathered around the table eating and drinking. Pop-up dinners centred around a single seasonal ingredient. I could even …

I shook my head to clear it of the images. I had no right to even think of the possibilities – not until I was free of the court case.

'Are you ready to go?' I asked Tom.

'Sure.' If he was confused by my rapid change

from interest to departure he didn't show it.

I was quiet for the short drive to Tom's house in the Gibbston Valley. The property in Arrowtown was perfect – for both a business and for me. There was enough room in the second cottage for me, and I could convert the attic to additional rooms for when Nathan, Ash and Reece or Lachie and Mike came to stay. It was currently being used as holiday accommodation, so I'd need to make sure I had the appropriate permissions to run it as a commercial enterprise, but ... Enough, Kate!

Despite ordering my brain to stop, I was still picturing the cottage and how I'd make it mine when we turned up the long drive that led to Tom's house. It was set high with views over the valley, its exterior a mix of timber and stone with plenty of windows to grab both the light and the view.

He led me through a wide timber door into a sitting room with a massive fireplace made from the same stone that was on the outside of the house. The furnishing was simple and functional yet luxurious at the same time, with plush rugs on the timber floors.

'This is gorgeous,' I said.

'Thanks. I didn't have to do too much to it, and everything in here has a purpose.'

'Or is beautiful,' I said, pointing to the painting of a highland cow hanging on one wall. 'You have some great art.'

He smiled as I wandered around drinking it all

in. In one corner of the room was a wingback chair covered in a storm-blue tweed. The wall beside it was lined with bookcases. Neil would have loved it. I quickly moved away before I could dwell too long on that idea.

'Let's go into the kitchen,' Tom said, 'and I'll get you a glass of wine.'

His kitchen was functional and stylish. Although the cabinetry was mostly cream, it was accented with timber and stone to blend in with the rest of the house. An island bench ran along the centre of the room, and glass doors opened up to a pergola, a barbecue and outdoor table and chairs, and more views down to the vines.

Tom indicated the stools under the bench, and poured red wine into an oversized glass for me.

'One of yours?' I asked before putting my nose into the glass to savour the aroma.

'Yes. One of our pinots.'

I took a sip. 'I know very little about wine, but I do like this.'

'Hopefully I'll get the opportunity to teach you some more,' he said.

I was grateful that when he spoke he was turned away from me and fossicking through the fridge. He emerged with a couple of steaks and the ingredients for a salad.

'Can I at least take care of the salad?' I asked.

'Sure.' He pushed a board, a knife and a bowl

across to me. 'Help yourself to whatever you can find in the pantry by way of dressing ingredients. And while you're chopping, you can tell me all the reasons why you walked away from that cottage when it so obviously excited you.'

I paused mid-chop. 'I don't know what you're talking about.'

'Come on, Kate. We mightn't know each other very well yet, but as I said earlier, there are times when you forget to hide what you're thinking or feeling.'

'Have you got any garlic?' I asked.

'Sure.' He tossed me a bulb. I broke off a clove and set about chopping it finely. 'I can't think about it, Tom. It's more than I could ever have hoped for. I even have these visions of a kitchen garden and running a little cafe out the back. And midsummer pop-up dinners along a long table lit with lanterns or fairy lights. And that's the problem – it's perfect and I can't do a thing about it until I take care of Vanessa. If she accepts the offer I'm going to make her, I'll have enough to buy it and set it up as I'd like, with plenty to live on if things don't work out. If she doesn't accept the settlement, we could be tied up for years.'

He was grinning.

'What's so funny?'

'You. You hadn't even been here before last weekend and now you're talking about settling. What would your family say?'

'That's the other problem. I have responsibilities to Neil's parents – although they also have their daughters, Libby and Leanne. I know Nathan isn't in Sydney any more, but Ash and Reece are, and I don't know how Ash would take the idea of me moving away and not being there if she needs me. Then there's my brother, Lachie, and his husband.'

'What about you? What do you want?'

I swallowed hard. 'I want that cottage. It's everything I always dreamed of and more.' I blinked as tears rose to my eyes. 'Neil's death has shown me that you can't wait around for things to happen – tomorrow might never come. I know it's quick, but as you said, we're too old to play games, and I want to be here – not here exactly, but in that cottage. And I want to learn more about wine.'

I didn't say the rest of what I was thinking: *I also want to know more about you.*

He looked up from seasoning the steaks and washed his hands under the tap, then wiped them dry on a towel. 'Anything else?'

'Yes. It's way too early for anything else, and I'm way too scared for that anyway, but if it's okay with you, I'd really like for you to kiss me.'

Thirty-one

On Sunday night, Tom, Nathan and I went to Richie and Jess's parents' home for dinner. The invitation had apparently come when Jess's mother had walked in on Nathan and Jess kissing on Sunday morning. Nathan said she'd simply turned her back while they made themselves presentable and said, 'I'm Milly and you must be Nathan. I've heard a lot about you – and your mother. All good, of course. Come for dinner tonight.'

After roast lamb served with a potato bake that Nathan announced was better than mine, and a fragrant lemon and thyme drizzle cake, I found myself talking about the property in Arrowtown. Despite the hurdles I knew I still needed to get over, I was even more convinced than yesterday that the place would be perfect for me.

Milly and Fletch – Jess's father – listened as I talked about my ideas for the shop. The two younger couples were at the other end of the table, discussing day walks around Queenstown.

'I think the learning centre would be a great idea

for this town,' said Milly. 'I could really see it working and I'd love to be involved. What do you think, Fletch?'

He rubbed at his chin and nodded slowly. 'Yes, I agree. One of the problems with this town is that the population is constantly changing with the seasons. It can be a lonely place to come into, especially if you're past the age when you're into clubs and seasonal relationships.' He turned to Tom. 'I know you haven't been here for long either, so let me know if you need help with any of the planning and permissions, Kate.'

'I haven't bought it yet,' I protested.

'You will,' said Milly.

Nathan went back to Australia as planned on Monday. I'd ended up organising to stay an extra week. Before he left the hotel for the airport, I asked him about Jess.

'I think this could be it,' he confided. 'I think she's the one – which is typical given she lives in a different country to me.'

'How does she feel about you?'

He lowered his glance briefly in a vain attempt to hide his grin. 'She said she feels the same. We both know it's early days though, so we'll wait and see what happens. I might be able to get some work at one of the research projects over here, so who knows?'

I patted his cheek. 'For what it's worth, I like her for you.'

'So do I.' He tilted his head slightly. 'And you?

What's going on there.'

'Nothing. It's still too soon for me, but Tom seems happy to wait for me to catch up. He's a nice man, I really enjoy being with him.'

I smiled as I recalled his kiss the other night. He'd held my face in his hands and tasted my lips gently at first, pulling back to check that it wasn't too much for me. It was me who'd pulled his head back down so we could kiss properly. He had gently turned the kiss into a hug just as the desire was flickering between us, and held me close for another few heartbeats before releasing me.

'This isn't getting the steaks cooked,' he'd said, his eyes crinkling as they looked down at me.

'Or the salad chopped.'

'True. And the salad is very important.'

We'd looked at each other and giggled as we realised how inane the conversation was.

'That was nice, Kate, but I'm not going to rush you.'

I'd nodded. 'Thank you.'

After Nathan had left, I accepted Jess's offer of the spare bed in her house and moved out of the hotel. Tom had also offered me a room, adding that I'd be perfectly safe there with him. When I refused his offer I didn't tell him that it was myself I didn't trust. Each time he kissed me it was becoming harder not to give in to the desire I knew we were both feeling. My body might be ready, but my head and my heart absolutely weren't.

Although he had to work, I saw him each day. He showed me the winery and talked me through the winemaking process. We explored Arrowtown some more, the Gibbston Valley, and took a drive out to Cromwell, where we walked through hills covered in wild thyme, the fragrance rising around us with every step.

When it was time for me to go home, Tom took me to the airport and kissed me gently. 'Thank you,' he said.

'What for?' I was genuinely confused.

'For this last week. For trusting me.'

I reached up and kissed his lips, suddenly unable to say anything back.

'See you soon?' he asked.

I nodded. 'Yes, I'll see you soon. And I'll let you know how we go with Vanessa.'

I'd been dreading the conversation I needed to have with Ash about Vanessa – and rightly so. To say that she was furious was an understatement.

Nathan had dialled in for the discussion, and Lachie and Mike were there too, to help us talk through our options. I didn't know who Ash was angrier with: Vanessa, for what she was doing to us; her father, for leaving me to clean up the mess; me, for not telling her; Nathan, for not ringing her the second he found out; or Lachie and Mike, just for being there. The only person she didn't take her anger out on was Reece.

Nathan joked that was only because she couldn't come up with a legitimate reason to yell at Reece. That comment didn't go down well.

When Ash had finally finished stalking around the kitchen, she sat down at the table, looked at me and burst into tears. 'I'm so sorry, Mum. It's so unfair that she's done this, and you shouldn't have had to deal with it on your own.'

I reached out and covered her hand with mine. 'I know, darling, none of it seems right. But not telling you and Nathan was my decision – and that wasn't fair to either of you.'

'We're all grown up now, you know,' she said with a watery smile. 'You don't have to protect us from everything any more.'

'I know that – but it doesn't stop me from wanting to.'

Ash turned to Lachie and Mike. 'Okay, now that's over with, what are we doing about stopping the bitch? I don't personally know anyone who could take her out, but I could ask around.'

It took a second or two for us all to realise she was joking, but the laughter took us back to where we needed to be.

'That's perhaps a little extreme,' I said. 'I'll let Lachie and Mike tell you what they've found out about her, and then we can talk about what I think we should offer.'

'What do you think you have on me?' Vanessa said, sitting down opposite me without bothering with a greeting.

I'd sent her a text yesterday afternoon suggesting that we meet today. The coffee shop near her practice was her choice.

'Hi, Vanessa, you're looking lovely as always. Pregnancy suits you.'

She was blooming, her tummy a perfect beach ball. From the back she probably looked as slim as she always did.

'Thank you,' she said. 'I don't know what you have to say to me that you can't say to my solicitors. We have mediation next week. Whatever ridiculous offer you have for me, you could have saved it until then.'

'Do you want something to drink?' I indicated the tea in front of me. 'Or a coffee maybe? Although I remember not being able to bear the smell of coffee when I was pregnant.'

'What is it with you and this need to feed people? I don't want anything to drink or to eat. I just want to know what you think you have.'

I sighed. 'I don't understand why you're like this.

What did I do to you? I welcomed you into my house, accepted you as part of Neil's family.' I shook my head. 'I know things between you and Neil didn't work out the way that you wanted, but we've both lost him. To do what you did to his apartment and then not even come to the funeral, that was just cruel.'

Her pretty face was screwed up, her nose wrinkled as if she was struggling to keep control of herself. 'You really don't know what you did? You didn't let him go. That's what you did. I knew I was always second choice. Sure, I was young and beautiful and he liked having me on his arm and in his bed – why wouldn't he? But he never really talked to me or shared anything with me – that was always for you. Every weekend he'd find an excuse to be at your house – mowing the lawns or fixing something up. There was always something happening with his parents or something going on with the family – which you'd ride in and fix. "It's okay," he'd say to me, "Katie's on it." Then there was Ash's wedding and you two were brought together even more. It should have been my wedding. Everywhere I turned, you were there. Saint Kate, the perfect wife who could prepare a perfect meal and set a perfect table, and was never fazed or stressed. Always in control, always there for everyone. I could never compete with you. The only thing I could do that you couldn't was fall pregnant – and you even took that glory from me.'

She glared at me. 'I knew exactly when he pulled

back from me. I'd convinced him that it was a good idea to divorce you – not because he was going to finally marry me, but because I told him you wanted to be free. I told him that it was unfair to you and you deserved a chance at happiness. He was doing it for you, not for me. Everything was always for you. It was always about making you happy.' She flicked her hair back from her face. 'I had no doubt that I'd be able to talk him into moving me in once you were off the scene. But then you had to go and fall for him again. You think I couldn't see it happening? The whole family was cheering for you from the wings. "Oh, poor Vanessa," they must have been saying. "He's only gone and fallen for his wife again." Do you know how humiliating that was? Look at me and then take a look at you.' Her glare became a sneer. 'It would be one thing if he'd traded me in for a younger model, but to go back to the old family station wagon? That's just embarrassing. He deserved to have all of that destroyed. No one rejects someone like me for someone like you. I couldn't have choreographed that pregnancy announcement better if I'd tried. I only wish I'd captured the look on your face. I made sure that if he chose you, the cosy little life the two of you were planning would never happen. He was going to pay – and now that he's not here, you can.'

As she spoke, my anger was building. It started as an irritation, like a spark, then began to smoulder. Each of her words added fuel until it was a fire raging within me. This woman had actively plotted to destroy my family. She deserved none of my sympathy.

'You want me to believe that's why you cheated on Neil with Brandon?' I said. 'Because he chose me? Maybe I could understand that – if I didn't know you'd been seeing Brandon for months before you convinced Neil that divorcing me was a good idea. Or was Brandon your Plan B?'

She couldn't hide her surprise at the mention of Brandon's name, but quickly recovered. 'I don't know what you're talking about.'

'Your solicitor friend, Brandon. The one who's helping you "sue the old dude's wife for what you're due".' I used my fingers to make quotation marks. 'Apologies if I didn't get the wording right. What I heard was that Brandon doesn't know whether the baby's his or Neil's, but it doesn't matter, because you're owed and you're going to make "the wife" pay. He doesn't care whose baby it is as long as there's a house deposit in it. I'm guessing all that must have been his idea? I know you truly loved Neil for more than his money.'

She shrugged. 'I don't know what you think you heard, but you have nothing.'

'Except photos of you and Brandon looking very loved up. The earliest I have is date-stamped in January and there are regular additions to his Instagram account all the way through to now.' I settled back in my chair. 'What happened? Did you stop your pill hoping to trap

Neil, and forgot the condom with your boyfriend? Or did you fall pregnant with your boyfriend and decided it would be more fun to try and pass it off as Neil's and in the process totally destroy his life?'

I paused briefly; did I dare go there? I did.

'What would you say if I told you that Neil had a vasectomy years ago because contraception didn't suit me?'

Her mask slipped, but was again recovered quickly. 'I'd call bullshit. There's no way you'd be taking this to court if you could produce a certificate.'

'I don't know,' I mused. 'You've just told me how you wanted to ruin our lives. Maybe that's what I want to do to you? This hasn't cost me a cent so far, but I know exactly how much that expensive barrister your boyfriend has hired costs. I can afford to wait you out if I want to. You want a house deposit? You'll have to work harder than that for it. Neil and I had to – it took us years to build up what you're hoping to ruin. At the very least, these photos are enough to create doubt over the paternity of your baby. They're certainly enough to insist on a DNA test.' I smiled sweetly at her. 'Don't you just love social media? You might have covered your tracks, but your boyfriend couldn't resist showing the world that he had you. And, as you've already pointed out, why wouldn't he? You are, after all, worth showing off.'

I could see the thoughts zipping through her brain.

'Neil would have told me if he'd had the snip,' she said, trying for a tone of confidence.

'Would he? He told me that you'd both decided children weren't an option – not for him, because he'd already been there and done that; and not for you, because you said there was no way you were letting some baby ruin your figure. There'd be no need for him to tell you after that. Besides, from what I can understand, there was a lot that he didn't tell you.'

'Why did he think the baby could be his then – if he knew it couldn't be?'

Despite her brief look of triumph I didn't miss a beat. 'Neil's never been great with biology.' I shrugged. 'It wouldn't occur to him that you'd be unfaithful, so he no doubt assumed the surgeon had stuffed up in some way.'

She tapped her fingers on the tabletop as she processed what I'd said. 'Did he have a vasectomy?' she asked.

I hesitated only briefly before answering, 'No. Not while he was married to me. He didn't need to – despite trying for a third child we never were able to fall pregnant again.'

She looked away from me, her eyes darting around the room. She pulled her phone out of her bag and flicked the screen on, before just as quickly turning it off again and putting it back into her bag.

'What are you going to do?' she asked. 'About the

photos, I mean.'

'I don't know who the father of your baby is, but I'm willing to take the gamble that it isn't Neil's. Somehow I don't think you'd be prepared to take the same risk.'

I let my words sink in for a few seconds, and had the satisfaction of seeing worry slide across her face.

'What am I going to do?' I went on. 'What Neil would have done – he was always much nicer than me. He loved you enough to bring you into our family – although listening to you now I have to wonder why. Neil never intended to walk away from this baby, so nor will I. He was retiring so he wouldn't have had an income to pay you maintenance. Instead he was prepared to offer you a lump sum settlement, and if you wanted him to be involved in your child's life, that was up to you. We could get on with our lives, and you could get on with yours. I'm prepared to do the same. My solicitor's sending through the offer this afternoon and I'd advise you to accept it, Vanessa. It's a generous offer, more generous than I think you deserve. Let's just finish this and move on.'

'And if I don't?'

'Regardless of how Neil would feel about it, I won't hesitate to use these photos. I'll make sure the court hears about everyone you've slept with. I'll get your colleagues on the stand, I'll get your boyfriend on the stand – you might need to think about a new solicitor if that's the case – and I'll insist on a DNA test. With these photos, I think the court will grant it. Then I'll drag the whole thing out for as long as it takes. Don't think that I won't. You might say you're doing this to protect your child – well, I'm protecting mine too, and I've had a lot more years of practice at that than you have.'

'I see.' She bent down to pick up her handbag and straightened, her hand supporting her back.

I couldn't resist asking the question. 'Did you ever love him?'

She lowered her eyes to the floor, then nodded, a slight movement. 'Yes – at least I did until I met Brandon. Neil was an easy man to love. You should have hung on to him when you had the chance. He would never have looked at me otherwise.'

She turned and left without waiting for my response. Still, I whispered it to the space where she'd been.

'I know. But I didn't.'

Last week, those words would have filled me with guilt and regret. Today, there was only acceptance of the past and a hope for what might be in my future.

Thirty-Two

With my hands on my hips, I stood back from the Christmas table and looked at it critically. Perfect. We'd set it simply, with linen placemats and napkins, sage green plates, and plenty of mismatching wine glasses. On each plate was a Christmas cracker that Ash had made and filled herself.

Nathan and Reece had attached fairy lights all the way around the deck. As an extra touch, they'd hung a tree branch over the table and strung round frosted-glass baubles from it. Ash had filled jam jars with seeded eucalyptus, silvery eucalyptus pods and delicate paper white flowers. In between I'd placed more glasses containing tea-light candles, and bowls filled with apple sauce, cranberry jelly, Marie Rose sauce, and the piccalilli I'd made during my cooking and baking blitz back in the early spring.

In the kitchen, the turkey and pork were cooked and carved and being kept warm. The roasted vegetables were in the oven, and the ham and prawns were on platters in the fridge ready to be served. For dessert I'd prepared a trifle, a pavlova tangy with lemon curd, and the lemony French-style baked cheesecake I'd tried at Jess's cafe. Max had come through on her promise to send me the recipe. I'd serve it with fresh raspberries and a raspberry coulis.

I'd decided to set the food out on the kitchen bench like a buffet. Those who'd already had Christmas lunch could pick at the ham and prawns or salads, and those who wanted something more substantial could make repeat visits.

Ash had spent Christmas morning and lunch with Reece's family, so she and Reece could have the evening with us. Nathan and I had gone out for brunch with Lachie and Mike, then come home to finish preparing the food. They'd join us soon – as would Dave and Maureen, Leanne and Simon, Libby and Russell, and Mari and Ross.

Ash came up and hugged me with one arm. 'It all looks so beautiful, Mum. I can't believe this is the last Christmas we'll be spending in this house.' Her voice caught on the words and she wiped a tear from her eye.

'Me neither.'

The house was going on the market at the end of January, when potential buyers would be back from their summer holidays, so we were all determined to make this last Christmas here one we'd all remember.

'I wish Dad was here,' Ash said.

'I know, darling. So do I.'

If I closed my eyes and tried really hard I could still see Neil in the kitchen, carving the Christmas pork with a silly paper hat on his head. As much as I still missed him, his image was fading and each day I had to try harder to bring it into focus.

Ash was pensive for a few seconds, remembering Christmases past, and then her face curled into a teasing grin. 'Have you heard from your Kiwi man today?'

'His name is Tom and he's not my man.'

'That's not what Nathan says.'

'Whatever Nathan has told you is an exaggeration. He's a lovely man and I think he'll be a good friend when I move over. It's way too early to contemplate anything else.'

I felt my cheeks grow warm as I spoke. Tom and I might have agreed we'd take it slowly, but we talked on the phone at least once each day and my pulse raced every time I heard his voice. I couldn't wait to see him again.

Vanessa had accepted the settlement, so I was free to move forward. The first thing I did was to phone the real estate agent in Arrowtown – followed quickly by an ecstatic call to Tom when my offer was accepted. I'd booked a flight to Queenstown in mid-January to spend some time with Tom before I got caught up in the pressure of getting this house ready to show each weekend. The cottage in Arrowtown wasn't due to settle until the end of February, so hopefully both the house and the Wollstonecraft apartment would have sold by then. If not, I'd already spoken to the bank about organising some short-term finance.

'You deserve to be happy, Mum,' Ash said. 'If not with Tom, then someone else. And if the way Nathan reacted when I teased him about that Jess girl is any indication, I think you could be seeing more of him than you'd expect to over there.'

'You could be right.' I watched Nathan and Reece open beers and toast each other. 'Are you sure you're okay with me doing this, darling?'

'Absolutely. We'll be fine. It's your turn now.' She smiled again. 'But you didn't answer my question before. Have you heard from Tom today?'

'He phoned this morning.' I felt my lips curve into a smile at the memory of the warmth of his voice. 'His kids are all going to be in Wellington so he was spending the morning with them. They'll go to his ex-wife and her husband and family for the rest of the day.'

'He's not welcome there?'

'He was invited, but I don't think he's comfortable going. He said he's moved on and they have their own lives now.'

'You know, we did well still including Dad for those years after he left. Even if it did mean we had to put up with the horrid Vanessa.' She pulled a face. 'I still can't believe I ever liked her. Do you think the baby really is Dad's?'

'I have no idea, and I don't think we'll ever know. Now, enough talk. The boys have the right idea – let's have a drink before we're inundated. There's some champagne in the fridge.'

'You stay here and admire your table a little more while I get the bottle,' she said.

The doorbell sounded. Nathan and Reece looked up but made no indication of moving from their position on the deck.

Ash popped her head back out. 'Don't worry, guys, I'll get that, shall I? You stay there.' She was soon back with the bottle of champagne and a wide grin. 'Umm, Mum, it's a delivery for you.'

I turned around to see Tom. He was smiling that crinkle-eyed smile of his, but there was some wariness in his eyes, as if he wasn't sure of his welcome. My tummy flipped at the sight of him and I hesitated only briefly before walking into his embrace.

'I hope you don't mind,' he said. 'It was such a last-minute thing. Yesterday I thought of the one person – other than my kids, of course – who I'd like to spend Christmas with and it was you.'

I stepped out of his arms and looked up at him. 'I'm glad you did. But how did you know?'

'Where to come? I texted Nathan and he told me. He also said that he thought it would be okay. Is it okay?'

I looked across at Nathan who raised his beer in

our direction.

'It's absolutely okay,' I said. 'Now, let me get you a drink and introduce you to my family.'

Hours later, when the food had been demolished and the leftovers packaged up for later, I sat back in my chair, sipped at my wine and watched my family and friends. Tom was leaning on the railing of the deck, red wine in hand, talking to Nathan and Russell.

Mari pulled her chair closer to mine. 'Your Kiwi seems nice.'

'He's not my Kiwi.'

'Maybe not yet, but I suspect he will be when you're ready for him to be.'

Tom looked up and our eyes met, sending a rush of sensation through my veins.

'Maybe,' I said. 'How will I know when I'm ready?'

'Are you talking about a sign or something?'

'Yes, I suppose that is what I'm talking about.'

She smiled and patted my leg. 'You'll know.'

Libby and Russell left soon after, followed by Leanne and Simon with Dave and Maureen.

As I saw them out, Maureen took me to one side. 'I know you still miss him, Kate, but don't let missing him stop you from finding happiness with someone else.' She tilted her head to let me know she was talking about Tom. 'I like him and I think he'll be good for you. I think Neil would have liked him too.'

My throat closed up and the back of my eyes burned. 'It's too soon.'

'Is it? Neil was gone for four years. I know he was still in your life, but during that time he lived his too. Now it's time for you to live yours.' She pulled me close. 'Dave and I will miss you.'

'What's that you're saying, Mo?' Dave stepped forward to kiss me goodbye.

'I was just saying how we're going to miss Kate when she leaves.'

Dave smiled and patted his stomach. 'I think my doctor will be glad to see the back of you. I might eat a bit healthier. But yes, we'll miss you.'

Back inside, the others had turned the carols down and moved their chairs closer to the table. More wine had been poured, and Tom, Lachie and Mike were having a good-natured argument about Australian music and whether or not Crowded House could be claimed by the Kiwis or belonged to Australia.

'Crowded House is Neil Finn, so of course it's one of ours,' said Tom. 'You can have Russell Crowe, but we're keeping Crowded House, Sam Neill and the pavlova.'

'How can you say that Crowded House is Kiwi?' asked Mike. 'The band was formed in Melbourne and had just one Kiwi in the original line-up – Neil Finn. The other two members were Aussies.'

'Come on,' said Tom, 'you get Midnight Oil. Let us

have Crowded House.'

'Are you an Oils fan?' I asked.

'Absolutely.'

'Did you ever see them play?'

'Just the once. It was here in Sydney, the Goat Island concert for Double J – or was it Triple J by then? Not that it matters, it was for their tenth birthday celebrations.'

'Were you still living in Australia then?' He'd told me he'd done his law degree in Sydney.

'Yes, it would have been my last year of uni. But that gig – oh man, it was memorable. I can still see that moment the fireboat sprayed water everywhere.' He smiled at the memory. 'I won the tickets – I think that was the only way you got in. I got talking to this guy in the crowd who said that as good as *Red Sails in the Sunset* was as an album, he thought we'd still be listening to songs from the *10 to 1* album for many years more. And he was right – "Power and the Passion" still holds up as a classic.'

I felt a tingle up my spine, as though the words he was saying were coming from someone else.

'Just how great were those political songs from the eighties?' he went on. 'You really felt part of the cause, you know? Remember how that Goanna song helped with raising awareness for the Gordon–Franklin protests? You just don't get that these days. I remember there was a rumour going around campus just before the Hiroshima Day march one year. It was my final year, so it must have been in '85. Anyway, people were saying the Oils were going to be playing at the Quay after the march. It was probably something someone said to get a bigger crowd behind the cause, but back in those days it could have been true.'

Mari's smile was wider than I'd seen it in years. She leaned across and whispered in my ear, 'I think somehow that's your sign.'

I stood and walked to the edge of the deck and leaned against the railing to look up at the stars. 'Thank you,' I whispered.

Tom joined me and I moved closer to him, resting my head against his arm.

He put his arm around me and kissed the top of my head. 'Everything alright?'

'Yes.' I turned to him and lifted my face to his. 'It really is.'

Acknoweldgements

Writing acknowledgements is both difficult and rewarding – difficult in that I know I'll never remember to thank everyone who needs to be thanked; and rewarding because this is my opportunity to publicly appreciate those who helped me tell Kate's story.

First and foremost, thank you to my brilliant editor, Nicola O'Shea. I can't express just how much I value having you on my team. You take my story and polish it until it shines.

Thanks also to Keith Stevenson at ebookedit for file conversions; and to Christa Moffitt from Christabella Designs for this gorgeous cover.

To Pieta – thank you for being my beta reader again. I'm sure my early drafts don't deserve the level of praise you give them, but I love it anyway!

An extra special thanks for this book has to go to one of my besties – Heather. Not only have you introduced me to your beautiful country, but you've been my tramping partner on both the Routeburn and Milford Tracks. Thank you for waiting for me to get down off that flipping mountain, for holding me together when I thought Mackinnon Pass had broken me, and for all the wines and laughs before and since. You know how I said I was never ever (I might even have added a couple more 'never evers') going to do another long-distance hike again? We need to talk.

I couldn't do what I do without the support of my husband and daughter. Thanks for suffering through the recipe testing and random disjointed sentences as I attempt to transfer the words from my head to the page; and thanks also to Adventure Spaniel for sitting by my feet as I do so.

Finally, thanks to Midnight Oil, Goanna and Redgum – for the music.

~

If you enjoyed *Happy Ever After* I'd love it if you left a review on Amazon or Goodreads. If you'd like to stay up to date with my next happy ending, you can sign up for my newsletter here: http://eepurl.com/cjeF5f

You can also drop by and see me – virtually speaking, of course – at any of these places:

My website: https://joannetracey.com
Facebook: https://facebook.com/joannetraceywriter
Twitter: @jotracey_
Instagram: https://www.instagram.com/jotracey/

About the Author

Joanne Tracey would like to say that she's a thirty-something, perky- pony-tailed marathon runner. Sadly, it wouldn't be true. What is true is that she's sometimes a corporate warrior, sometimes a domestic diva, sometimes a star-gazer, and absolutely always a believer in happy endings. Jo's novels are inspired by her travels and when she isn't writing words, she's procrastibaking, planning her next adventure or taking way too many photos of sunrises for Instagram.

Also by Joanne Tracey:
Baby, It's You
Big Girls Don't Cry
Wish You Were Here